ROYAL
GAME OF LOVE

Edward looked only at her. He slipped the snood from her hair, let the bright strands flow through his fingers. His voice was thick.

"Have you missed me, my Elizabeth?"

She couldn't speak, but her joyous smile and the thudding of her heart when he held her to him must have been answer enough. His laugh was confident, victorious. He kissed her mouth, his tongue seeking hers, and slid a hand inside her bodice, hurting the soft flesh.

She just managed to whisper, "No, no," and twisted away.

The worn cloth tore at the movement.

He pushed it farther down her shoulders, breathed, "Ah! I knew you'd be perfection," as he stared at the rounded bosom, the pliant waist. He lifted her, carried her to a wooden bench, and stroked her calf, her thigh.

A pulse beat in her throat. Color rushed to her face. He was the king, and he desired her. His royalty was as intoxicating as his youth and powerful body and passionate need of her. She could always relent, and pretend he forced her. No. She drew a quivering breath to still her own rising excitement. He was too used to having his lusty appetites appeased and then forgetting them. He had broken off his march to be with her. If his thirst for her were slaked, would he return again?

Also by Anne Powers:

SECRET SPLENDOR
RIDE EAST, RIDE WEST
THE THOUSAND FIRES
RACHEL
THE GALLANT YEARS
THE ONLY SIN

Queen's Ransom

Anne Powers

LEISURE BOOKS   NEW YORK CITY

Although the main characters in this book were real people, and the events herein depicted did take place, in some instances both the people and the events were fictionally intensified to add to the drama of the story.

A LEISURE BOOK

Published by

Dorchester Publishing Co., Inc.
6 East 39th Street
New York, NY 10016

Printed in the United States of America

To
three of my favorite people:
Wendy, Kimberly and Ryan.

Author's Note

A few phrases from a distant day and land crept into this story. Many readers will prefer to fill in their meanings from the context, but for those who feel a need to be sure, a short glossary is provided at the end of the book.

EDINBURGH

BERWICK-ON-TWEED

HEXHAM

Irish Sea

North Sea

SHERIFF HUTTON

YORK

KINGSTON-UPON-HULL

TOWTON
WAKEFIELD

ENGLAND

LUDLOW

BOSWORTH FIELD

LEICESTER

NORTHAMPTON
GRAFTON REGIS
STONY STRATFORD

LITTLE MALVERN
TEWKESBURY
GLOUCESTER
BERKELEY

ST. ALBANS
BARNET
LONDON

PEMBROKE
CASTLE

BRISTOL

BEAULIEU ABBEY

THE SOLENT

M.C. Donohue English Channel

PART I
Marguerite D'Anjou

CHAPTER 1

I sent for him that night. I'm not sorry now, I wasn't then, either. Though if my indiscretion—indiscretion? my driving need—were discovered, I knew what names would whirl about me like autumn leaves in a wind from the north. Unfaithful wife, whore, adultress. And a child would smugly and spitefully be proclaimed a bastard. A shattering victory for *Them*.

What persuaded me to that first hour with a lover? I had no thought of it when I woke happily on my birthday. I was twenty-two, and my husband Henry was planning a banquet in my honor. He had given me a new gown of green silk, the hem edged with fur. I thought of how fortunate I was as my ladies brushed my hair over my shoulders—hair that fell like a bright cloud before it was subdued by a circlet of pearls.

Kings aren't always affectionate toward their wives, but Henry loved me, even if he— He was kind and generous to all he cared for. A regal quality, only he couldn't afford his lavish spending, not when the Yorkists, the other side, year by year built up their reserves of land and money. His ministers warned Henry—futilely because he could believe ill of no one—that they were a threat and growing dangerously strong.

I shook my head at the unpleasant re-collection. This was my special day. I would allow nothing to disturb me. The court was at Windsor, and peers were driving in from their estates to greet me. The clatter of hoofs in the courtyard announced late arrivals, and I could hear doors opening and the sound of the guests hurrying to the great hall to be there when Henry and I entered.

We smiled an acknowledgement of their bows as we crossed the floor to the dais. The pale March sun, sifting through the oriel windows, gleamed on jewelled gowns and doublets with long dagged sleeves and on gold plates and Venetian glass goblets. I wondered briefly what Henry had pledged to redeem the dishes pawned to the goldsmiths' guild, then forgot the concern in my hunger which was sharpened by the sight of servants carrying great platters of meat and fish and manchets of bread.

Steam rose from the whiteherring and the roast swan, and the spicy odors of pepper, ginger and saffron drifted through the room. While I waited for Henry to cut into the flaky pastry of a pork coffyn with the delicate scent of pine cones in the sauce, I glanced up idly.

My resolve that today would be serene was

a charred ruin in the flame of my anger when I saw our guests' watching eyes. I didn't know which courtiers I hated most. Those who leered at my body to see if at last it was swelling with longawaited fruitfulness, or those who didn't even look at my waist, complacently sure that, after seven barren years of marriage, I would never have a child. While the Yorkists, the enemy, spawned every year.

My hand shook as I crumbled a honeyed manchet. I wanted to scream at the knowing faces and hypocritical mouths drawn back against greedy teeth. Unbearable that they should smirk at me, Marguerite of Anjou, because I had failed in my one duty to England. But perhaps, perhaps tonight Henry would be different.

I turned to him, smiling warmly. I looked well after an early ride in the park, I knew I did. Not that my vivid color mattered, he seemed to think me beautiful any time, declaring in a wild overstatement that I was the loveliest princess in Europe. His fingers touched my sleeve lightly. "Very becoming, my dear." My heart lightened at what I thought was a new ardor in his voice. Until he added, "You're a radiant child as always."

I suppose I murmured something through suddenly dry lips. Unbelievably his fond compliment had pleased me once. Surely he no longer saw me as a child? Though I wasn't, I admitted in despair, a woman either. Still he was only nine years older, a lusty age for most men. I mustn't give up hope too easily. I unpinned the brooch at my throat that held the frilled chemisette and pushed the fine linen into my bodice so he could see the first swelling of

17

my breasts.

But he leaned forward, not noticing, to nod to a deacon at the end of the hall. A moment later from behind a carved screen came a high clear chanting that drowned out the clatter of dishes and the hum of talk. Henry said, "An entertainment for you, my dear. As you know, I won't have the young exposed to the evils of court life, but an hour with us can do no harm, and I was sure you'd want to hear the choir boys from my new school at Eton."

I murmured, "A—a delightful surprise," though briefly the courtiers and I were one. Their faces appeared rapt with pleasure but they wished, as I did, that the musicians were playing gay lilting tunes that would give a promise of dancing later when benches and trestle tables were cleared away.

Henry was beaming as he listened intently, his shoulders slightly hunched under his dark blue gown, too sober, but at least it wasn't the monk's robe he favored. "They're like angels, aren't they, my dear? Their voices soar to heaven in their young purity."

I nodded, swallowing a strangled laugh or a shriek of fury. I wasn't sure which. Purity! I despised the word. They had told me, his ministers who had come to Lorraine to arrange our marriage, that Henry was pious and devoted to the church. So was I. Wasn't everyone? Even criminals have respect, flying to sanctuary to escape the law. I went to mass most days except when I was with Mother galloping across France to escape the troops pursuing us, but how intensely we prayed then!

So I understood what they meant, I was sure I understood. Religion was talking to God, wasn't it? asking help, thanking Him, or sometimes in a cathedral enjoying the quiet and the great columns reaching to the sky, and the light streaming through the jeweled reds, blues and greens of the windows.

How could I have imagined that devotion was a dour—not dour, Henry's temper was too sweet—that it might be a solemn denial of life? Must music be only for the church, and occasional gaiety borne with resignation because a king should appear loyal at all times?

Must the hope of giving life be confessed to a priest and atoned for in the cold dawn? Though it was no more than a hope; a feeble attempt. And not even that on holy days, the Lenten season or days of favorite saints. We needed sons. England needed an heir. Henry agreed. But to bed with a woman, wife or not, was sinful. His tutors had preached that since his babyhood.

It wasn't Henry's fault he had been taught by fanatics. I should not blame him for his austere chastity, but I did. It was unforgivable. It was inhuman never to feel the blood hammering within one in a mindless passion that demands fulfillment, never to know the heady rapture of the parched body when desire is slaked and never to know the sweetness of release.

What did I understand of that? Nothing beyond the magic of the troubadours' songs of Provence which had wakened vague urgencies within me. Were they inherited from the hot-blooded men and women I had sprung from? Or was it only normal to feel this discontent that flamed into resentment as the months and years passed and the Yorkists leered at me in triumph? But I was only twenty-two. There was still time.

"My dear," I glanced up eagerly as Henry's attention returned to me, though the boys were still chanting, "since it's your birthday, I wondered about some diversion for our guests. Would cards be amusing? I know you French have had them for years, but they're quite recent in England and the court I fear is overly fond of new sensations."

I thanked him, pleased that any pastime was planned. He spoiled the moment briefly by an immediate doubt. "Or should we have such games? It's St. Catherine's day and playing cards might show her disrespect." I didn't ask which St. Catherine he meant. Sometimes I thought he invented saints; he had so many on his lips. Then he added, "Forsooth! She wasn't a martyr or a missionary, and this is your day. Perhaps one can be too severe about small matters."

I coughed to cover a hysterical laugh at his admission that one might be too strict and stumbled to my feet as he rose. There was a clatter of benches as the guests stood up hurriedly. I hadn't realized the first course was over and dishes cleared away for the next one.

Below us sleeves fluttered like windblown pennants as everyone made the sign of the cross with Henry and listened dutifully to the prayer he intoned after each course. It was an eccentricity I'd become accustomed to, but I would never become accustomed to the next ritual. A steward brought a pastry with five hollows filled with a preserve of cherries, and Henry touched each glistening red mound reverently, saying as always, he hoped I would share his custom of showing devotion to the wounds of Christ.

I couldn't bring myself to touch the monstrous object and stared at the white marguerites on my gold plate until we sat down and were deftly served venison, breast of duck and a sauce with chopped hard-boiled eggs. I looked beyond the heaped dish at the guests who were growing noisier as their goblets were filled and refilled with malmsey or hippocras.

A young man coughed, put his *couverchef* to his mouth in a careless gesture that suggested he hadn't meant to draw attention. An elaborate pretense, for he stood out—even in that glittering crowd—in his scarlet doublet with a heavy chain reaching from shoulder to shoulder and gemmed sleeves pushed back to avoid the stewed figs on his dish.

He didn't need finery to be noticed. His narrow face wasn't handsome, but it had the intense eagerness of a greyhound, a thoroughbred, an expression of readiness to hurl himself into any cause, any adventure. Yet his smile had a quirk of humor to balance the intensity. Edmund Beaufort, second son of the Duke of Somerset—a Lancastrian and a distant cousin of Henry's.

He was younger than I but not too young for love, I heard. I could believe that from his sensual mouth and the way his eyes brushed over me. His gaze reminded me of my low neckline and I hastily repinned the chemisette. He grinned as if he understood exactly why I'd pushed down the linen frill, and that my gesture had been futile.

His amusement recalled the second time we'd met, or was it the third? We danced the carol, and in the hot confusion of swinging bodies and the lilting music, he whirled me laughingly, then drew me close, his thigh pressing against mine. I laughed too, my eyes shining. Not, of course, because of the warmth of his body briefly touching mine, but with pleasure at his lightheartedness.

He came to court often after that. We were never alone, but he let me know with carefully chosen words, which anyone might hear, that he loved me. And under his cool restraint I glimpsed a hunger, a controlled passion. I never let him forget, however, that I was Henry's wife; since he might have heard the malicious tales the Yorkists spread, that this lord or that one, including Edmund's father, was far too devoted to me. As if I, a princess, would seduce a married man. Because the Yorkists had no principles, they believed I had none.

I thought now—confusedly, breathlessly— Edmund isn't married, a childless king is vulnerable, and the Beauforts are of the same royal line as my husband. My cheeks were hot at the horrifying thoughts that slid so easily into my mind. My eyes went to Henry. Never, never would such a sinful idea even touch him. He was too good for this world, too good for me who wanted excitement and laughter, and he cared deeply for me. I mustn't hurt him. Then abruptly, unreasonably, I whispered to myself, *Why shouldn't you be hurt, Henry?* The years of our marriage with its nightly uncertainties had strained my nerves beyond bearing.

Did I really think that? I couldn't have. Why, he was telling the Chamberlain of the Palace now about the entertainment he planned for his dearly beloved queen. The officer beamed, masking his surprised relief. An idle afternoon was difficult when guests stayed only to demand more wine and mead and ale. Tempers became inflamed as tongues loosened and the two court factions stabbed each other with words since they couldn't draw weapons in the king's presence.

But before the chamberlain could answer Henry's question, there was a commotion at the door. A swarthy man, followed by a dozen guards, strode to the dais. Perspiration streaked his exhausted face in spite of the chill spring day as he knelt and scarcely waited permission to speak before he gasped, "Trouble, Your Highness. Your cousin—" He stopped for breath but there was no need to say the name. Trouble meant the forty-one-year-old Richard, Duke of York, whose one desire—he said—was to reform the country's law. What he actually craved, though he disclaimed this in hollow phrases, was to be the acknowledged heir to the crown.

He was heir presumptive, but the intangible power that surrounds the first prince of the blood wasn't enough for Henry's pushing, ambitious cousin. He was avid for the title of heir apparent, and the least perceptive could see he dreamed of how short a step it might be from heir apparent to ruler.

Anyone could see the duke's heated ambition except Henry who believed York was only a subject with a tiresome temper. He said calmly now to the messenger, "I have many cousins. Do you mean His Grace of York? Has he a new petition, or do you bring a report on disturbances in France or Scotland or Ireland?" He smiled slightly. "No need to spend yourself for that and possibly founder a good horse. There are always disturbances with those countries."

My fingers clenched on the arm of my chair as Henry went on and on maddeningly. The rustle of silk and satin, the clatter of plates being pushed aside made him finally aware of our guests' impatience to hear the message, and he nodded to the man.

"I'm not from the Duke of York, sire. He's—he's encamped south of London at Blackheath with an—an army. I was sent by the Duke of Somerset. He's holding the city and Tower against a possible attack and begs you to join him."

Benches scraped as half the men came to their feet. I wondered which of those who remained seated exchanging alert glances were Lancastrians deliberating how best to support the king, and which men were smiling inwardly that York was again in arms.

The first time was two years ago, I thought, as I waited for Henry to answer the messenger. York wasn't present then, staying discreetly at his post in Dublin, but few doubted the story that Jack Cade's rebellion was in fact directed by York. Immediately when Cade was defeated and killed, York went to England and aided the Royal Council in punishing the rebels to conceal the fact he was the greatest rebel of all.

The second time he came with his troops and actually confronted Henry with a dozen demands, aping Cade's empty mouthings to win over the citizens while he hid his true aim. But again, he didn't draw enough support so he had to renew his oath of fealty and disband his men. I hoped shakily that the affair now would be settled as swiftly. For all my distrust of this blustering soldier, I shrank from violence. I had seen too much of it in the endless provincial warfare my parents carried on.

I glanced at Henry, hoping to be reassured. He was rubbing his underlip with his thumb and appeared puzzled rather than upset. I willed him to speak, but he sat frowning thoughtfully. The long silence was suddenly too much for Edmund. He elbowed past his neighbors, strode to the dais and knelt briefly.

"We are ready to ride to London, sire, while we send to our estates for our retainers to join us there. We can be in the city by midnight."

Henry smiled gently. "Forsooth, my lord, you are too headlong. There's no need to be hasty."

Edmund's eyes glinted. "When there's an enemy to be faced? Only a traitor would march on London with an army."

"No, no, York is loyal. He gave me his oath last year. He's just trying to draw attention to whatever grievances he thinks he has." There was a stir, half-suppressed angry laughs. "York and I will discuss any differences peaceably."

One of the ministers near Henry said skeptically, "Perhaps, sire, but he has quite a number of complaints. His soldiers in Ireland are seldom paid, and he bears much of the expenses of his position as lord lieutenant."

"As I said. He comes only to right an injustice. The exchequer must give York the money due him."

"The treasury is practically empty. The duke has already received tallies of assignment but with no surety as to when they'll be redeemed."

Henry was displeased. "By St. John, that is not an honest way to treat a brave commander. New taxes or custom duties should be levied. It's quite simple."

The minister didn't appear impressed by the solution. "More levies, sire? Last year's crops were poor, and trade is falling off. But we'll discuss the money problem in Council later. York's next demand will be that you imprison your chief minister."

Henry straightened, said firmly, "I will never desert Somerset; York will be made to understand that. In return we could ask Parliament to proclaim him our heir. His resentment at being ignored is another point which," he smiled slightly, "you didn't mention."

The minister shrugged. "No, because all know that is his chief grievance though he scarcely hints at it. But would such a move be wise, sire? If—when you have a natural heir, it may be difficult to reclaim the title from York."

I felt sick—sick and cold, as Henry said only, "We'll see," and agreed the lords could summon their retainers but no one would ride to the city until tomorrow. Then I thought with sudden hope that Henry knows as I do that the unrest and instability that tempted the brawling duke to commit treason had one cause. We must have a son, or the Yorkists would trample over us in their arrogant reaching for the crown even while Henry of Lancaster was on the throne. That is why Henry delays leaving. The minister made him realize his first duty was to his dynasty, and tonight he'll embrace me as a man should.

My radiant smile for him became a travesty as he said, "I shall retire to the chapel, my dear, to pray for guidance and forgiveness for my sins. I have many to repent. While we didn't play cards, I had given my approval for an idle game which may be of the devil."

So. He would be on his knees for hours and not profane St. Catherine's day further by lying in his wife's bed. Atonement for what only he could believe were faults was more important than the threatening news that York was in arms. Edmund's impatient voice cut across my depressing thoughts. "Sire, give me leave to ride to London now. My father will expect some word of your plans."

Henry, always upset when affairs interfered with his routine, said testily, "Naturally I'll send Somerset a message. You will accompany me in the morning."

Color flamed in Edmund's face as he choked back a retort. His eyes went to me as if I could persuade the king to attend to worldly business. Then I forgot Henry. Edmund was a bachelor of the royal Lancastrian line, and I had my own duty. My throat muscles were tight. I hoped desperately that I sounded poised, and mercifully my words came out lightly. "You're right, Henry, that the men should rest before they march." I looked at Edmund. "The young are impatient, but maybe you'll find some diversion tonight to relieve the boredom of waiting."

I couldn't say more, nor dare to if I could. I prayed that Edmund understood me and, please God, that no one else did. Our glances met briefly. His brows went up in disbelief, then his eyes widened in eager acceptance. His expression then became blank almost instantly. Unlike me, he was used to such secret byplay and said casually, "I shall seek a distraction, madam. Hawking perhaps. My falcon is well known for searching out and capturing the highest prey. I doubt it would hesitate to plunge into an eagle's nest."

Henry saved me from the impossible task of answering. "A fine healthy sport. I wish all our young men engaged more in such innocent pleasures and less in—well, less in indulging earthy appetites." He rose. "I trust our courtiers will spend some time in prayer. We need the help of divine providence."

I murmured, "Yes, sire, we all do," and thought—especially a queen whose husband neglects what is due his wife and his country.

CHAPTER 2

He came as the bells pealed for *compline*. The clangor filled the air so I couldn't hear Edmund's words from the anteroom as he spoke in his clear incisive voice. He must be taken aback at meeting a lady-in-waiting, expecting I would be alone and there would be no need to invent an excuse for his presence.

I tried, God knew, to get rid of my attendants. I realized privacy was difficult, but never had I know such frustration as this evening. My ladies were kind, charming, solicitous. I hated them. I pretended I was exhausted from the day's excitement. Excitement! A dull banquet, an endless afternoon embroidering altar cloths, yet they nodded sympathetically.

Lady Dacres sent for a lute. I think it was Lady Dacres. What does it matter? While someone played, the women rethreaded their needles with gold and scarlet and sang a French song

thinking the selection would please me.
Nothing would please me except to have them
at the far end of the castle. Or the other side of
the world.

I said finally the music was delightful, but
they had my permission to leave. One of my
headaches was coming on. I never complained
of headaches, yet they exclaimed how coura-
geously I bore this constant affliction. I must lie
down and they would sit with me. I looked
briefly at the carpet so they wouldn't glimpse
my flashing eyes, then smiled bravely. "When
I'm in pain, I prefer being alone. Besides you'll
want to bid good-bye to husbands or brothers or
sons."

I had to repeat twice that I was better alone
before they put their stitching aside, helped me
undress, and at last I was in the wide bed and
they were leaving. Now I could think of Edmund; but they weren't going, not all of them.
Unbelievingly I heard a girl say, "I will stay. We
cannot, at least I can't, abandon a poor sick
woman. It wouldn't be right."

The high prim voice was Elizabeth Woodville's, my youngest lady. She was beautiful
with silver-gilt hair that contrasted brilliantly
with her dark eyes. Plump like many girls, but
in a year or so she'd undoubtedly be slim and
willowy and catch the eyes of any man near her.
God help him. She was a bitch. So demure, so
proper, so righteous and so greedy. Sweetly
insistent on doing any task her companions
disliked and then letting them know she
wouldn't refuse a small gift.

Perhaps the thought of the expected
present made my ladies hesitate, or she might
have made them ashamed. But she wouldn't let

them spoil her gesture, and what Elizabeth wanted she somehow managed to obtain. She said, "It's no hardship for me. My father and brothers and my husband, Sir John Grey, are loyal Lancastrians, but they weren't invited like your families." She added quickly, "It's quite natural. We don't have great titles, and even Windsor hasn't space for all the king's faithful followers."

The others drifted away while I thought I would have sent the royal carriages for them, father, mother, brothers, sisters—Elizabeth's mother, like York's wife, Proud Cis Neville, must have dropped a cub every year—if that would have persuaded the girl to leave.

Now Edmund was here. I was about to offer my body for the sake of the country yet I, the queen, was a prisoner of this creature. I had my ancestors' Angevin temper and tore at the sheet to control my fury while I whispered a prayer through clenched teeth for God to rid me of her. Had she boasted her family was Lancastrian? York himself could do me no more harm.

The bells faded into silence and I could hear Edmund saying he had vital news and her honeyed answer that I musn't be disturbed. She came to the doorway, overskirt and petticoat a pale yellow in the dim light, to explain in hushed tones she was refusing entry to a visitor.

Edmund was just behind her, his eyes gleaming at the sight of me with my hair streaming across the pillow. At that moment God answered my plea. I said weakly, "His lordship can give his message to Lady Dacres. And on his way he'll take you to your room, my dear. You're far too young for a night's vigil, and you must have an escort through the palace. So many pipes of wine were drunk for my birthday that the most disciplined soldiers could get out of hand."

She argued again about her duty. I smiled sweetly, just holding myself from spitting at her, until she was finally convinced. He returned quickly. Now after the lengthy effort to see him alone, I had sudden doubts. Was this assignation right? I wasn't harming a wife who would expect Edmund's loyalty. Nor Henry, either, who must in his daily prayers be pleading to heaven for a son. But Mother fiercely disapproved of love outside the marital chamber. Still she hadn't lived continently with a husband for seven years, nor did she have to bear York's boasting of his sons nor know the humiliation of being a barren queen.

My litany of excuses faltered at the sight of Edmund's flushed face and luminous eyes. I held the blankets tightly against my throat, waiting to pull them over my head. This was madness. He should go. At once. He didn't hear my whisper. He unbuttoned his doublet, tossed it to the floor, unbuckled his belt and tore off his tight hose. His underlinen was cast carelessly beside his outer garments.

I was shocked. I had never seen a naked man. Henry always snuffed out the candles before stripping off his clothes. But Edmund, outrageously without shame, was laughing. He was a young animal eager to enjoy the delights of love. But this wasn't love. I couldn't think further as he pulled back the blankets to gaze at me. My shift of heavy linen might as well have been transparent under his ardent eyes.

He was beside me, his lean length warm against my body, his hands impatiently dragging at the hem of my shift. My strangled, "No, please no," stopped his aggressive plundering though his husky voice was surprised. "We must make the most of our time. We don't know how long we'll have."

"We've had too much already." My tears spilled over. I dabbed at them angrily. "This is wrong. The fault's mine. I'm—I'm sorry."

He sat up. I thought he intended to leave. Instead his fingers touched my face, smoothed out the anxious lines on my brow. "I'm too hasty, I've always been." He tried to catch back the last words but I found them comforting. He had no doubts, no troubling conscience forbidding him to lie with a woman. He said tenderly, "You aren't like the others, jaded and looking only for a new sensation. You are bright and fresh, my darling. Do you know how I've hungered for you? But how could you, so untaught in the ways of men?"

I started to say stiffly I had a father and brothers. His irrepressible laughter stopped me. "I should have said untaught in the ways of love. I wasn't speaking of family affection." He smoothed my shift until it covered my knees and drew a little away, but he made no move to go.

I wasn't sure if I were glad or sorry. Before I could resolve the question, I felt his touch on my throat, on my breasts, sliding down to my thighs, but he carefully avoided further intimacy. My stomach muscles knotted as I realized unbelievably I wanted to turn to him, to answer his urgent seeking. That was dreadful, unforgivable. I hadn't summoned him that I might savor the heady taste of love. Lust rather, I thought with self-revulsion. I had summoned him as Elizabeth Woodville would have, for my own needs.

I was a sinner. But hadn't Henry sinned against me? Against life? My head twisted back and forth against the pillow. Edmund lifted a handful of hair. "When you move so, your hair is like autumn leaves streaming in the wind. Or like liquid fire cascading down a mountain to bury itself in snowy foothills." He laughed again. "I want to speak like a poet, but my thoughts aren't on ballads. What are a thousand lines compared to your bright hair rippling over snow-white breasts?" He added practically, "Or so I imagine them to be."

He was talking nonsense, giving me a minute to forget my uneasiness. I could still tell him to go. There were others at court who would welcome his company. But when I mentioned another woman he said cheerfully, "Oh no. We Beauforts prefer a royal mistress. And you, Marguerite, my Marguerite, would be royal if you were born in a peasant's hut." His voice thickened. "You are proud and frightened and, my own, infinitely desirable. And you will return my desire."

His arms were strong around my traitorous body. His lips hard on my mouth as his seeking tongue touched mine. I tried, I think I tried, to draw away, but he held me too firmly and then I was returning his kisses, shyly at first and finally with abandon. He jerked at the neckline of my shift. The heavy cloth tore under his impatient fingers.

I moved instinctively and futilely to cover myself with my hands. His glowing eyes swept over my body, dwelt lingeringly on my shrinking flesh. What would Mother—under his burning gaze and the sweet endearments hoarsely whispered the shame of my nakedness vanished.

I could feel the hard muscle of his arms. A sword arm to protect us against traitors. His young maleness was a shield I needed. And his broken phrases and roughly demanding hands were a blazing sign he needed me. Contentment edged with excitement flowed through me. I felt a brief sadness for Henry that his senses would never be stirred by such warmth, by the longing of a man and a woman to reach across their aloneness to each other.

And yet, yet I wasn't ready. Edmund had been patient in spite of his youth, which would expect his passion to be fulfilled now, at once. He'd wooed me slowly, considerately, as if aware of my inexperience. But how could he know—I hardly understood myself—what the years had done to me? Nights waiting for a husband's footsteps, and then Henry's embarrassment and fumbling attempts to do his duty.

Those hours had left me empty, defeated. So now, when I should be arrogantly triumphant that a man wanted me at an enormous risk, the enchanted oneness disappeared, and I felt only pain when he entered my body. I made a ghastly pretense at joy when he cried out with pleasure. But after the first heady minute he wasn't deceived.

His face darkened as if I'd betrayed him. Then he saw my stricken expression. Perhaps he became aware of the blood flowing from between my thighs onto the sheet. He brushed my cheek gently with his lips. "My darling, I didn't know—how could one? I've never taken a virgin before." His natural gaiety bubbled up.

"What's a marriage contract? You've become a wife, my wife. And next time or the next you'll learn the delights of love."

I said, "Yes," not really hearing him, too distraught at the betraying blood. Edmund had guessed that Henry was impotent, but he hadn't realized no other man had bedded me.

He touched my shoulder lightly when I didn't go on. "You're too silent. Unless of course you don't speak because you're reliving our too-short time together."

I nodded, at a loss again in any byplay of gallantry. "I'm—I'm concerned you might be seen leaving my room."

"I won't be. The sentries are guarding their posts with even less efficiency than usual. I wonder the king puts up with—but his mind's on other matters." He grinned. "While he prays for heaven's blessings, he's made me blessedly fortunate."

I hadn't shared his sensuous pleasure. I felt bruised, not unhappy but not happy either, and I was tempted to answer tartly. I swallowed my irritation. Partly, perhaps mostly, because I was unwilling to dull his pleasure. And partly out of cold calculation. It was unlikely I had conceived in my first intimacy. There would have to be other meetings. I said smiling, "Henry's devotions give you, us, security. The few nights he has an attendant in the chapel, the man falls asleep. So when the ladies see the—the sheet, they'll believe he was with me."

At the last words I caught my breath. They had waited years for the sign of my lost virginity and would be delighted, but they would know his gentle hesitant hands had never torn my shift. I would change to a fresh garment, but where could I hide this one? Then I thought wryly that Edmund was probably adept at disposing of a lady's unwanted linen. My request amused him, perhaps added a piquancy to the evening. He folded the shift under his doublet when he dressed. "My men are camping in the park where, luckily, they insist on luxuries like a fire. The odor of charred cloth isn't pleasant, but they'll understand I'm protecting some fair unknown."

A spurt of laughter rose in my throat, but I said coolly, "You're highly practical for an ardent lover."

"A useful trait I'm told." He threw out a hand impatiently. "Enough of that. When do we meet again, my love?"

I drew in my breath tiredly. Tonight's scene with my ladies couldn't be repeated often. "You'll be in London, and Henry may wish me to stay here while York is a threat."

"Ha! You'll do what you want and the king will agree. As to York," he spoke with youthful contempt, "a man planning to be a successful rebel needs more than bluster and a small army to have a chance against my father's—and the king's—troops." He turned to leave. "Next week, my darling. I can't wait longer." His eyes caressed me and then he was gone.

I stared after him, but I wasn't looking at the closed door. I was staring into the past; a handful of years ago, those days when I had Edmund's arrogant confidence in the future. Golden hours, stretching out from the morning the great English lord rode into Lorraine to my father's threadbare castle and said the King of England saw my portrait and wished to marry me. Two months before my fifteenth birthday.

From the minstrel's gallery I could see the legate, the Earl of Suffolk, a man in his early forties, and Father, who was smoothing his tunic over his paunch as he frowned thoughtfully. "An honorable proposal, still I need time. My daughter is a beautiful child with accomplishments to befit a queen, but she's young for marriage."

Suffolk agreed courteously with Father's description but disclaimed my age was a problem. The king was only twenty-three and would be gentle and understanding, and he was offering me a splendid position.

Father smiled blandly. "Ah, but Queen of England isn't that much greater a title than Princess of France." I clapped my hands to my mouth to suppress a giggle. I couldn't believe Henry of England really wanted me. I was a king's daughter, but King Rene held the title in name only. Yet he was airily sure a marriage would bring as much honor to Henry as to me. He went on, "If you'll make a few concessions in territory—" He paused as the earl's men grunted indignantly then explained pathetically that one of his possessions was Anjou, and that province and Maine on its border were overrun by the English. Could he be expected to hand over his daughter without some small return?

The earl looked grim. For a century England had fought to claim France as its own. The year before I was born, Jeanne d'Arc thrust the English out of the heart of the country, and burning her at the stake hadn't recovered their losses. Now they were asked to give up more land. Father retorted that everyone knew the English had lost steadily of late and needed peace more than France did, and he could persuade the French ministers to sign a two-year truce. If, that is, he could bear to part with me.

There was talk then that I had no dowry, but, having reluctantly agreed to hand over the provinces, the earl brushed aside the lack and soon the marriage contract was signed. The days rushed together. The French king and his queen, my aunt, arrived for the proxy wedding and for the festivities that filled every hour.

There were feasts in the castle and fires in every square where oxen and boar and sheep turned on spits so all could share in the gaiety. The air was heavy with odors of roasting meat and spices mixed with the less pleasant smell of unwashed bodies crowded around the flames with greasy hands outstretched for slices of pork, mutton and crisply curling strips of skin dripping with fat. There were tournaments, too, with pennants streaming above knights in brilliant surcoats and glittering steel. The world ran mad with blazing color and light, and I was giddy with it all, caught up in a troubadour's romance, a damozel loved by a king.

The earl's wife, Countess Alice, swept me into her care on the long ride across France to the coast. The excitement of meeting my bridegroom soon blunted my homesickness. I was happy, perhaps too happy because the countess was forever reminding me to be grave and dignified. But I forgot her, everyone, the last days of the voyage. The wind screamed out of the north, and the ship pitched in the choppy seas. I was sick and had to be carried ashore when we sailed up the Solent and brought in a litter to a convent that was heavenly—cool and quiet and clean.

I recovered quickly, helped by daily letters

from Henry saying he was eager to see me but was delayed by financial problems. I was impatient. Why would the king of a great country worry over money? But the countess was pleased at the wait. She sent to London for seamstresses as I must have a proper wardrobe. "What could be finer than my wedding gown? And my blue traveling dress and the green one for evening are of velvet from Lyons."

The ladies looked everywhere except at me, their expressions actually pitying. It was true the gold tassels on the wedding gown were tarnished, and the velvets were—yes—a little frayed. The countess explained anxiously that I had been too ill to be consulted and girls usually enjoyed pretty clothes.

I laughed and said I would love new dresses, but I did need advice. I knew nothing of the English style nor French, either. They were all relieved and chattered amiably about the latest fashions and how they looked forward to having a queen. It was half a century since one had given vitality to court life. Henry's mother had been in France with her husband, the Fifth Henry, the warrior king, and after he died she retired to a remote English manor. And before that the Fourth Henry wasn't well for years, and in any case not a man to encourage frivolous entertainment.

Now after two generations of neglect, the palaces and castles were being refurbished: Westminster, Eltham, the Tower, Greenwich, Shene, though the work wasn't completed. Carpenters and artisans had refused to pick up their tools until they were paid for the previous month's labor. I was horrified that subjects would defy their king. Surely no French or Burgundian ruler would tolerate their conduct. However, I was in England and must get used to these odd ways.

I resolved to love my subjects and to win their love. When the celebrations were over, I would send my French attendants home. I had heard that some queens surround themselves with their own people, but my friends and advisers would be English. I was lonely at the thought of dismissing my countrymen, but my homesickness was washed away by another message. Henry would be here in three days.

When he arrived at his Southwick Palace, ten miles away, he announced that the wedding would be tomorrow. People lined the road cheering me as I rode to Lichfield Abbey, and their shouts followed me into the church, which was packed with lords and ladies, merchants and their wives—anyone who could edge in.

Guards made an aisle for me to the altar where Henry stood, a blazing figure in gold and white. The sunlight through the stained windows made patterns of color on his velvet cape and tunic. I was only half aware of that. He was tall and thin, with brown curling hair, and his dark eyes and bony face were grave and remote. Then he smiled, a boyish welcoming smile, as he put out his hand to me. I trembled a little and clung to his supporting arm. My strong and gentle knight.

I was told there were showers that day, and that the skies were overcast when our glittering cavalcade rode to London. But it wasn't true, because I remembered the sun pouring down on rolling wooden hills, on flowering hedges and on wide fields where farmers were working. They ran to the road when they heard us approach with cheerful cries of good will for us.

I wanted to embrace them and the peaceful countryside delicately brushed with the tender green of spring, and the villages with their lime-washed cottages and thatched roofs and early blooming flowers. This land knew nothing of armies trampling down crops, plundering homes, raping the women. Then, with one lust scarcely slaked—fired with the blood lust to kill again—to destroy. There was no memory here of smoke wind-whipped above charred houses, burning fields and slaughtered men.

At the dark memories I leaned out of the carriage to look at Henry, who was a splendid rider. He had never seen the horrors of a ravaged country, yet he hoped the two-year treaty with France would lead to permanent peace, in spite of a faction who objected to our marriage because even a short truce was too long. I was told of other bickering at court, but I scarcely listened. Henry would handle the problems superbly while I would try to surround him with gaiety, and there would be witty talk of everything except politics and the disputes in the Council.

My plans for the future slipped away when Henry rode up to say there was a nearby abbey where we would stay the night. My cheeks warmed, and I twisted a sapphire ring back and forth until it made a red line on my finger. We were given the abbot's rooms, and servants covered the bare walls with tapestries and draped the bed with a satin coverlet that gleamed in the light from the flames on the hearth.

I grew shyer as the night came on, then was shocked into numbness when lords as well as ladies crowded into the chamber, making laughing jests that mercifully I only half understood. I was almost ready to cry as they trooped noisily out, but I should have known Henry would be kind. He said, "Don't be afraid, my dear wife. You're still a child and need time." He kissed me lightly on the mouth. "Sleep, my darling."

My eyes closed at his soothing words. I was being selfish, I shouldn't accept his sacrifice, but I stilled my conscience by thinking tomorrow would be different.

I was shy the next night too, but we were bedded more quietly, and I was willing to do my duty. I felt—not eager—but filled with an expectant wonder at the mystery awaiting me. But that night and the next he again only kissed me and turned over. He seemed—was it possible—embarrassed. I realized with a shock that the act might be new to him also. He was pious, but I had known devout young men who thought it only a venial sin, if sin at all, to couple with any willing maid.

His inexperience gave me courage to reach out to him. He patted my hand and said something indistinctly about waiting until we were in London. Had he vowed to delay marital pleasures in gratitude for some favor from Providence? He must have. The only other answer was that I repelled him, and he was too charmingly fond for me to believe that.

I was delighted when we neared the city. The mayor and aldermen in scarlet robes rode out to escort us across the Bridge. We were greeted by men in blue gowns with red hoods from the different guilds, and at every corner there was a tableau on justice or mercy, or a play from a Bible story. The sounds of cheering and trumpets, and the sight of laughing faces of men and women toasting me in the wine that splashed in the fountains, became a happy blur by the time we reached Westminster Palace.

On the walls of my rooms exquisite tapestries stirred in the warm May breeze. Henry smiled at my pleasure in my apartments, and when I admired a Venetian mirror framed in gold, said—with a lover's flattery—that no mirror could reflect my beauty. I kissed him spontaneously, my lips parting under the pressure.

He drew back a little. I sighed. I had forgotten the countess's rules and showed my feelings in front of my ladies and the king's gentlemen. I thought sulkily that Henry had been king since babyhood, how could I learn in a few weeks to act always with regal reserve? And was it really wrong to be affectionate to a new husband? Why, I had seen Englishwomen kiss visitors who were practially strangers to them.

Then I saw Henry wasn't annoyed. He said with regret, "My dear, I must leave you on your first day in our home. The Council meets at the Tower and I'll sleep there. My chief minister and good cousin Cardinal Beaufort has a fever, and without him as a restraint, the members will wrangle half the night on any issue that comes up."

I gaped stupidly. I thought his vow of abstinence must be paid by now since we were in London. He added cheerfully, "At least all agree on one point. Sunday you will be crowned. I wish the coronation to be at once to show the world how I value you."

I was dazzled by his kindness and choked back my disappointment that he couldn't spare an hour for me. The countess shook her head when he left. "I hoped—but there, a king can't always follow his preferences, and it's true the Council members are at each other's throats when the cardinal's absent."

One of the ladies laughed. "Or perhaps they'll be united since they'll be free to attack the cardinal for the profits he makes from his stews in Southwark. Well, I'm sure the Cardinal's Hat is safer for the guests than any other brothel in. . . ." She swallowed, made a resigned gesture. "Your Grace will hear this and worse from his opponents, but I notice the ministers don't object when the cardinal helps pay the king's debts."

I must have looked surprised that Henry really had financial problems because the countess said, "We shouldn't bother a bride about such matters. Good heavens, do you realize how little time we have before the coronation?"

I was surprised again. I expected I would simply walk up the nave of the Abbey to be anointed and crowned. Instead the hours tumbled over each other as I was drilled in my role, stood for the dressmakers to fit a new gown with the train to be carried by four noblewomen, and tried to memorize the names of the barons of the Cinque Ports who would hold a canopy above me while I went barefoot on the scarlet carpet to the altar.

I was exhausted, but I wanted Henry to be proud of me, when he watched from the gallery, as I moved slowly through the hushed Abbey to be blessed with the holy oil and feel the weight of the crown on my bowed head. And he *was* proud, Henry said at the banquet later in Westminster Hall, almost sinfully proud.

I thought nothing of his choice of words, but Cardinal Beaufort who had recovered from his illness, shot a glance at the king. The cardinal was a round smiling man in a red robe, and he sparkled with jewels. "If that is a sin, I'll have to absolve the whole company here." He waved a smooth white hand at the tables below the dais, the noisy laughing guests in their brilliant costumes, and the perspiring servants edging their way among the diners with platters of food.

He added, "Not forgetting to pardon myself. But I'd say blessedly proud, sire. Who wasn't delighted when our princess from a faraway land knelt to become our queen? The white shoulders and whiter breasts uncovered for the anointing, and the hair floating out as the crown was placed on the fair brow."

Henry winced, but naturally he was trying to conceal his own pleasure at the extravagant flattery; though he said the disrobing must be acceptable since it was sanctioned by custom too old to change. I realized then that he was simply concerned that I had found the ceremony an ordeal.

He had been too young at his own crowning to remember it, so couldn't know I was far too exalted by the sacred rites to think beyond them. I smiled reassuringly, and felt my color rise at the thought of later. He had been wise as well as good to wait until I no longer felt a stranger. If only out of gratitude, I would be eager to satisfy his passionate needs. But I felt more than gratitude, and in the intimacy of marriage, affection would become love.

He didn't visit me that night, or the next or the next. Perhaps he thought me too tired from the hours watching the jousting and the uproar of the boisterous spectators. How could he think me fatigued? It was all a joy as I sat under the silk canopy and watched the lords stride from their pavilions to mount and gallop down the lists in a thunder of hoofs. And no injuries marred the day as Henry insisted on blunted weapons; so it was maneuvering of war horses and skillful blows exchanged.

Then on an evening when the tournaments had ended, he came to my room with the cardinal, who invited us to be his guests at his home in Waltham Forest. A state apartment would be prepared for us and the promise of privacy. A young couple should have some time alone. Henry nodded and I was smilingly agreeable.

I didn't hear the cardinal's answer—a graceful phrase at the honor we did him—because I was stunned to see that when he turned to leave, Henry rose and was halfway to the door before the cardinal stopped him. "Sire, it is not for you to see a subject out. You mustn't waste time on me that you could spend with this delightful child." He smiled benevolently and left in a flurry of red robes.

I shook off the brief shock. Surely Henry hadn't needed prompting to visit his wife? No, because he pulled a bench close to my chair and talked animatedly of the schools he was founding at Eton and Cambridge to educate poor boys for the priesthood. I was so relieved that I had been mistaken that I fell in with his enthusiasm and asked if I could match his

King's College at Cambridge with a Queen's College.

He was pleased but became doubtful when I went on. "Women who have no money also need to learn useful skills. I was tutored at home though I was better in foreign languages than casting up accounts." I laughed. "Perhaps because it seemed useless to copy lists and lists of debts. As they'd never be repaid, why labor over the sums?"

He bit his lip. "You're charitable, my dear, but would the women you speak of profit by a foreign language? In fact, when ships from other countries arrive, the less the women know of a different tongue, the better off their souls are."

I swallowed a giggle and said I had just been chattering about my own education. I had a more practical idea. Mother planned when they won back their territory to teach poor women to weave silk so they wouldn't have to sell their.... So they could make an honest living.

Henry said, "Excellent!" and asked so many questions that I protested I just remembered it when he mentioned schools. Besides, I put up my hand to cover a yawn, I was sleepy. Wasn't he?

Now I had to believe the cardinal brought us together. Henry's smile was sweet, but his jaw muscles tightened as if in distaste. He could persuade himself, and me, that those first loveless nights were to reassure a young bride, but not the cardinal, who had probably lectured him that we should have sons to defend our country and daughters to make alliances with France, Castile, Burgundy.

Still, with the tensions of the festivities over, I hoped he would find unexpected joy in my body. He snuffed the candles, tugged off his hose in the dark and climbed into the high bed. He murmured something pleasant, but I felt his shrinking. His fingers groped inexpertly, and his breathing was uneven as he moved against me. There was an intimate fumbling, his thigh touching mine, and a choked sound of pain or of pleasure before he drew away.

He whispered, "I didn't hurt you, did I, my love?" I managed a strangled no. Did he think we had mated? Had he never seen couples in drafty corners or animals in the fields? I prayed he believed he was successful. If he knew how disastrously he failed, he might not come to me again.

I had no worries about that while we were at the cardinal's magnificent house. The cardinal wasn't a man to accept excuses even from a king. But at Eltham or Windsor or Westminster, we were seldom together except for a morning ride or an afternoon's hawking. I reassured myself we were young, we had years before us. But the leaders who had objected to our marriage since it meant a two-year truce, spread rumors that the cardinal and Suffolk had duped the king's trusting spirit, giving away provinces and all for a wife who was barren.

Cardinal Beaufort merely smiled at the attacks, but his massive calm was ruffled when the growing storm brought down Suffolk, my first English friend, who was tried for his so-called crime of selling our English interests to the French. But even the trial faded into the background when I discovered that the cardinal's health was failing. I couldn't think of life at court without him. He was dead within months. And Suffolk, exiled because of his unproved treason, was captured in the Channel and beheaded by brigands.

I searched for words to comfort his distraught widow. Overnight she had aged ten years. She paced my room, dry-eyed, saying over and over, "A traitor! They claim William was a traitor!"

I said softly, "But the king made your husband a duke; he doesn't believe the charge. And there was no evidence of treason, Alice dear, so the property wasn't confiscated. You and your son weren't robbed of your lands."

"Lands! Oh, if my grandfather were alive, he'd forget his pretty little tales and use his pen to shrivel the envious lords who murdered my husband."

For a moment I thought that grief had muddled her wits, then I recalled she was Alice Chaucer and had spoken once or twice of a grandfather, a custom's officer and poet who had written, what was it—*Canterbury Tales*. So her mind wasn't wandering. But I said she must have a long rest in one of her manors away from the reminders of these last months.

My apartments seemed empty when she left for the north, and the court was empty without the cardinal, with his suavely benevolent manner that disarmed his opponents and kept some peace in the Royal Council. He was replaced as chief minister, if anyone could replace him, by another Beaufort, the Duke of Somerset—a quick-tempered, domineering man —but equally loyal.

We hardly noticed there were other

changes. Richard Plantagenet, Duke of York, became the leader of the faction who opposed the king and Council on relations with France, domestic policies, and trade. He had been a successful commander overseas before the truce and was well-liked now in Ireland, so his sense of his own importance must have grown year by year. But we didn't realize how overbearing he was and thought his angry criticisms were motivated only by what he considered was good for the country. How could we have been so blind to his ambitious nature? And Henry, still blind, believed that a few words, a show of reason, would persuade York to forget his hunger for royal power.

My ladies explained at least twice before I understood that York claimed the throne through his descent from the third son, while Henry was descended from the fourth son of Edward III. But the issue of legitimacy was revived half a century too late. Henry's grandfather had the people's support and wore the crown by right of conquest, and few dared question the rule of Henry's father, the hero king of Agincourt. But now because my husband—like wise men everywhere—desired peace, York could hint at his true aim and chance plunging the country into civil war.

When we had an heir—I slid out of bed, groped for a fresh chemise in the wardrobe. Tonight, though Henry would never know, he had been served again by a Beaufort. Madness—but worth any risk to hold a man child in my arms and save the House of Lancaster.

Yet the memory of my first days with Henry made me want to cry. He should father my child. I tightened my lips to stop their trembling. What good were tears? Impatient with my moods, I pulled up the heavy blankets against the wind that tore at the loose panes of the window and crept coldly over my face. I was doing what I must, yet I was frightened at the shattering decision I had made. I needed someone with me, not an importunate lover, but Henry, who was quiet and gentle and undemanding.

The door creaked and I sat up alarmed. Unbelievably, Henry was there, peering to see if I were asleep. I held out my hands. "I thought—I thought you were in the chapel."

"I was, my dear, and will go back, but I worried that you're overly upset about York."

"Dear Heaven, yes!" I should be relieved that it could be proved he had come tonight, but I was too pleased to see him to care about trifles. "York's dangerous. How can you think a discussion will persuade him to return home?"

Henry said simply, "Because he's my subject, child."

I felt the familiar irritation at the endearment, yet stronger than the annoyance I felt a sudden faith in his calm belief in the authority of kingship. I thought confidently, York will agree to disband his army. I did not ask myself, *But for how long?*

CHAPTER 3

In the morning I watched Henry ride out from Windsor, with trumpets blasting and hoofs chattering down the tree-lined road. Men's confident voices echoed back until the last pennant, disappeared in the distance, and I felt carelessly certain that York would obey his anointed king. Only an hour later I thought with dismay—how much does a man threatening London respect royal authority? Perhaps an attack is already planned. Surely I would hear? Or would I? I *must* know what was happening.

The next day I followed Henry, not heeding my ladies, who were fearful of a detachment of Yorkists. Any danger was better than this isolation. But our journey was quiet, broken only by hearty cheers as we passed clusters of houses in the countryside drowsy under the early spring sun. No wild-eyed support here for a rebel, and, in the city, the streets were crowded with sedate merchants, ladies strolling from silkshop to goldsmiths, apprentices shouting their wares of hot pies, sausages, cakes and sprats. Our outriders brought news garnered from idlers. Londoners were men of business, and so far, York's army across the river was only good for gossip over a mug of ale or worried comments about sanitation. Too often there was plague in the wake of an army.

But Somerset, in spite of the calm, was taking no chances. On Tower Hill horsemen were gathered under his standard of the Golden Portcullis, and at the Tower itself there was scarcely room for my carriage to drive through the Lion and Byward Gates. I slipped out quickly and hurried up to the White Tower where more knights and foot soldiers were being formed into companies.

Guards dipped their pikes as I ran toward the great hall. At the door my stunned attention went past the group of councillors to Henry, who was being armed by his squire of the body. I had expected Somerset to be in command, not the last prince of Lancaster. My teeth clenched so I wouldn't cry out—though I was proud, too. Under Henry's gentleness was the iron will of his warrior ancestors.

Still a warrior's blood didn't sing through him. His face was tense as he nerved himself to fight as a king should, if York insisted on battle. Talk flew back and forth among the ministers— Somerset's voice the loudest—debating tactics, those complicated military procedures which I would never understand.

I moved forward as the squire buckled the

cuirass at Henry's shoulders, fastened the gorget about his neck, the pauldrons over the upper arms, and greaves and sabatons to protect legs and feet. A velvet surcoat, with Henry's standard of a white antelope on a blue field, was slipped over his head, and the sword-belt tightened about his hips, while another squire sheathed the shining blade and with the clank of steel, lifted gauntlets and helmet from the table.

As the Council—still arguing—started to leave, Henry caught sight of me. His startled expression changed to anxiety. "I thought you were at—had you any trouble on the road, my dear?"

He smiled with relief when I shook my head, still I stammered what I had resolved not to say, "You—you shouldn't be in the field. Your life is too valuable to your country, to—to me."

He was pleased but waved away my concern. "Battle plans! Forsooth, our troops are merely a show of strength to convince York we should meet peaceably."

I was only half-reassured, but his faith was justified. The indifference of the citizens might have given York second thoughts as much as the sight of the royal army. Henry invited me to be with him the next day in his royal pavilion at Blackheath. The sun sifted through the broad stripes of Lancastrian blue and white, and made a gold triangle on the floor where the light struck through the open flap.

The silk tent was hot and airless, but all thoughts of any discomfort slipped away when York strode in. He was short and stocky with powerful shoulders and a blunt-featured face.

He nodded in what was presumably a bow, and I forced a smile as Henry said, "Cousin, we must not be enemies. If you have some complaints—"

"Complaints!" He leaned forward, fists on the carved table. "I've a score. Last year your Council promised to look into my demands for reform if I'd disband my army. When I agreed, what did they do? Christ! Your ministers swilled down ale and leaped into the nearest harlot's bed, probably laughing so hard they couldn't manage an erection."

Henry paled. "Such—such language is unfit for anyone's ears. It is intolerable before your queen."

York's eyes scraped contemptuously from my face to the jewelled edge of my bodice. I remembered the report that his wife, Proud Cis, said *she* didn't dress like a woman of the street, making a spendthrift of her husband by adorning her body with diamonds and pearls. She dressed modestly, spent her hours caring for their children and household, and she read only religious books, and did not waste her days in wanton idleness.

I was amused. Her rigid ways wouldn't attract even Henry who wanted my clothes to be gay and flashing. Besides, I was sure one saint was enough for any family. I smiled involuntarily, became abruptly aware again of York. Now, under his venomous gaze, I wasn't amused at Cis's self-glorification. His eyes had reached my waist and his lips were drawn back in a complacent grimace. He had fathered enough whelps to recognize there was no sign of pregnancy.

I stiffened but my smile didn't waver, and

he turned to continue talking with Henry—if one could call York's shouted demands and Henry's occasional mild reply a conversation. The tirade ended with an order to dismiss Somerset as chief minister, a position that should be held only by a prince of the blood.

Henry smiled faintly. "The stress of the last weeks has made you forgetful. Somerset *is* a prince of the blood, cousin to us both."

York swept on. "And tried for his acts of treason."

"An unfounded accusation, by St. John. He," there was a pause to emphasize the pronoun, "would never take up arms to march against my capital." I was amazed at Henry's coolness, though the effort it cost him showed in the nervous movement of his hands and in the twitching of a muscle under his eye.

York, taken aback, growled less confidently, "There'd be no need for arms, sire, if the promised reform had been carried out. But," his assertiveness returned, "they won't be until Somerset's imprisoned."

Henry said quietly, "You are correct, Cousin, the law would need reform if I took your words seriously. You condemn a man whose crime, it appears, is shutting the gates of London against you."

York exploded, "Christ! If I'd come alone, I'd be in the Tower instead of that criminal you pigheadedly—obstinately defend." He slapped a roll of parchment on the table. "Here's a list of his misdeeds. Read them!"

Somerset was our friend. I blazed. "Surely an accused man has the right to hear his offenses," and nodded at a sentry near the inner chamber. A moment later Somerset entered.

The resemblance between him and York proclaimed their kinship. Both were stocky, with ruddy faces and dark hair, though Somerset's was thinning and York's was heavy and cut squarely across the brows. Both colored ominously as Henry read the charges of corruption, treason and—this with less certainty—hadn't Somerset profited by the king's generosity? That was a mistake. It was well known the wealthy Beauforts loaned the king money with no hope of repayment.

They turned on each other with threats and counterthreats in the uncontrolled Plantagenet rage that again marked their relationship. York broke off when Henry bowed his head, his lips moving in prayer. York snorted, "No wonder the country goes to pieces when it's ruled by a monk and an inter—" My eyes flashed. "And by a woman."

Henry smiled slightly. "If my wife and I rule, how can you say my lord of Somerset misgoverns?" His tone chilled. "Your accusations would be serious if true, but I'm afraid you are too credulous and listen to idle detractors."

Somerset grinned sourly. "Credulous! York spins his own lies." At the word lies, York's hand flew to his sword, but he only gripped the hilt. "Why not draw in the royal presence?" Somerset added, "You broke a greater law when you rebelled. I'd have you in irons."

Henry said, "My cousin didn't use his weapons. But he was illegally armed. While we look into his grievances, he'll be detained in his London house."

York was briefly speechless, then he shouted, "House arrest? For demanding justice? By the bones of Christ, do you think I'll sit quietly in Baynard Castle while my enemies try to stir up the people against me?" His lips drew back. "They won't succeed. The people love me and," he spaced out the next words that were aimed at my heart, "they love my young sons. Don't try me too far or you'll tempt me to signal my men to . . ."

Somerset chuckled. "I wouldn't give that signal, Your Grace. No, I really wouldn't. Your officers are with my commanders under close guard until you send them home." The hurt from York's taunt lessened a little at the knowledge there wouldn't even be a skirmish, though I wondered how long he would be a prisoner. He was popular, God knew why, and so, I unhappily admitted, were his young sons. And he was second in power only to the king.

I hadn't seen Edmund, but he was here with the royal troops. How could we meet? My frantic thoughts darted from one impossible scheme to another, but I must have a few hours. Virgin Mary, so little to ask. My poorest subject wouldn't have to beg for such a trifling gift. I caught my breath, briefly shocked that I should entertain such wickedness for a moment. I was irritated at my weak will. We had been too close to bloodshed for me to indulge in girlish indecision. Our one hope for peace was an heir.

Edmund's mention of hawking slid into my mind and Henry's approval of the sport. A falconing party would please the court, and would have a little space of time. I wouldn't be missed at once. When the beaters drove pheasants and quail into the air, the hawkers would scatter and if I were thought of at all, each group would believe I was with other riders.

A week later on a cool morning when the

sun was beginning to burn away the mist, we rode out of the city towards Waltham Forest. The name recalled Cardinal Beaufort, and my spirits lifted at the certainly that he would give his blessing to the ruse that would save us from civil war.

When I asked Edmund, his husky laugh was comforting. He had found a hut in a corpse of birches, and he was there when I came, splendid in green and silver. He held me a little away from him, his hands on my shoulders. His glowing eyes went from the heron feather in my blue velvet cap, to my tightly laced riding dress, down to my gold-embroidered slippers and traveled slowly back as if he were memorizing each detail of me. He said regretfully, "This isn't a place I'd choose but," he grinned engagingly, "surely no one will search for us in a woodcutter's hovel."

I stepped back, and glanced around the room. The walls were of rough logs with chinks of light where the mud had loosened and fallen onto the dirt floor. A bench and table stood near a blackened hole that served for a hearth, but the bed opposite was covered with a tapestry that caught the sun sifting through the cracks. The moment was solemn. My reputation, Edmund's life, were being staked. Still I couldn't restrain a giggle. "How did you explain carrying *that* to a hawking?"

His lips twitched. "No need. I brought it last night. Would I let you lie on an unwashed blanket? Though for what the woodcutter was paid, he could carpet the room in fresh linen."

He went on about the precautions he had taken. I wasn't really listening, but when his voice stopped I said quickly, "You overlooked one problem. What will you say when you return with less game than any beginner?" I didn't really care, I was talking of anything to cover my uneasiness. Having made myself a—a harlot once, I should move into Edmund's arms, not away from him.

Edmund watched me, with a slight smile. He said softly, caressingly, "Don't look like that, a bird beating its wings against the bars of its cage. If you wish to leave—" He didn't finish but pulled me against him and kissed me lightly before he threw my cap aside and unpinned my mesh snood so that my hair tumbled over my shoulders. His fingers worked clumsily at the brooch on my bodice. I hesitated, then unclasped it myself.

His hands slid over my bare shoulders and beneath the thick cloth to my breasts. He was breathing heavily. In the sweetness of being desired I swayed toward him. His heart beat jerkily. Or was it my own thudding against my ribs? He lifted me possessively and carried me to the bed. The tapestry was coarse on my skin when he helped me unfasten my robe.

He dropped his jerkin and hose beside my skirt, which was a pool of blue on the earthen floor. But I wasn't thinking of the finery. He touched me gently, murmuring nonsense words that oddly quieted me more than any heated argument that this was right, was necessary. He stroked my thighs, then moved slowly to more intimate caresses.

My breath came in small gasps, hastily swallowed. Words and thoughts left me. I reached for him. My nails cut into his hard shoulders. His low laugh was triumphant as he held me to him for a moment—or an hour. I was lightheaded. I wasn't myself. I was more myself than I had ever been, all my senses wakening, riveted on one object. I saw only Edmund's lean body, heard only his harsh breathing, tasted the slight saltiness of his tongue, smelled his man-odor and felt only his firm flesh.

This time there was no pain when we came together. There was the shock of closeness, of being one, of clinging to each other as if to hold life now, this moment, forever. The fever rose, engulfed us and was spent. I was limp, drained of emotion, yet my senses still had that curious clarity.

Edmund smiled lazily, opened his mouth to speak, then snapped it shut. I stared, then I also heard the sound of hoofs. Edmund put his hand over mine. I should be fearful at the very thought of discovery, but I felt only the pro-tective warmth of his presence.

He leaped up, pulled on his clothes and buckled his swordbelt. My brows rose in sur-prise at his expression. His eyes were alight with excitement and his lips drawn back in a silent laugh as if he welcomed the chance of facing an intruder. His exhilaration changed to resignation as the hoofbeats faded into the dis-tance.

We weren't missed that day nor the second time the court went hawking, but there were comments that Edmund wasn't the falconer he had been. These comments would lead in-evitably to laughing questions as to what sport he was indulging in. Was he hawking for more delightful game than feathered prey? Someone with careless malice might look for the answer.

I had glimpsed his love of danger, and I refused when he wanted to risk another meeting. He was angry at my insistence at waiting for a safer opportunity, arrogantly ignoring the fact we walked on the edge of a precipice. When I mentioned my fears for him, he retorted savagely that he would rather be in the Tower if he had to see me always at my husband's side, while he himself was denied the least intimacy. He also insisted that I knew nothing of love if I were content to withhold myself until we had a measure of security.

We could seldom talk without being overheard, so I was spared much of his furious pleading, or I might rashly have given in. My caution wasn't only for him, but for the son I prayed for, to hold our own against the enemy.

Their power was more evident every day as they stirred up the people with wild rumors that York was ill-treated. The Council felt it would be wise to release the duke if he would repeat his oath of allegiance. York didn't object. "Why should he?" I asked Henry. "He made or broke an oath with equal ease."

Henry said gravely, "This time it will be different. We will have a reconciliation in St. Paul's. You and York will lead the nobles to the altar where I'll accept his pledge of loyalty and the promise of the peers to keep the peace. Who'd dare break a solemn vow given in the sight of God?"

I didn't laugh at his confidence in a church ceremony, but even the least cynical turned his head to hide a smile when the procession walked down the nave to swear fealty to the king, and when Somerset and York, glowering, embraced briefly in a sign of eternal friendship.

Still, the duke might have learned that even so mild a king as Henry could be pushed too far, and the tension in the city eased when he left for his castle in Ludlow. But the clash had tired Henry, and we moved to Greenwich where I planned constant distractions. Pageants and balls followed one upon other. Mummers came from London with their latest offerings, and on sunny days we had riding, tennis, bowling on the lawn and dinners served on the wooded bank above the river.

Though Henry was ascetic, he spoke often of how dull the days were when there wasn't a queen to plan festivities. I was pleased that he had a reflected happiness from the court's enjoyment. I had too, except for Edmund's absence. I missed him, his engaging smile, the swift glance no one else could interpret. He gave the lame excuse that he must see to something or another on one of his father's manors, but we both knew his real reason for staying away. He was furious that I insisted on caution. In a brief encounter he asked why should he torment himself with the sight of me, aloof and untouchable; he even suggested I was tired of him, and was taking another lover or lovers.

My anger matched, perhaps overmatched his. I wanted to scream at him—*Do you think I am a whore, willing to sleep with any man?* Or storm at him that we belonged together and never would anyone take his place.

He finally came three weeks later. He was sulky and out of sorts because he couldn't stay away. He watched me as jealously as any Yorkist spy, but his sullenness vanished when I told him casually that I had found a place for us. We were on our way to chapel. I hoped the light in his eyes wouldn't give us away.

After the service the coutiers drifted out

while I waited for Henry. Most rulers would have commanded their attendants' presence, but Henry was too considerate to make demands. I felt a rush of affection for him that seeped away as the minutes passed. How long would he pray to atone for bedding with me last night?

For an insane moment I didn't care if he knew about Edmund. Nor if the world knew. Let it judge us. But judge Henry, too, and York, who had driven me to sin and deceit. Sanity returned. I drew a shuddering breath at what disclosure would mean. I must guard against such outbursts even to myself. I must not admit either, that while my first secret meeting with Edmund made me feel shabby and dishonest, now my pulses hammered at the thought of being with him.

I gazed past Henry to the triptych above the altar and sent a prayer winging to the Virgin holding a baby in her arms.

She had her child and would understand my needs.

She did understand, surely, because in the next months I was with Edmund once a week, sometimes twice, in the glorietta. It was not the large one at the curve of the river, but a small forgotten summer house built in a wooden hollow. God knows why the site was chosen. Still its inconvenience and dampness assured us of privacy, and, now that we were in the country, I could insist on walking alone in the grounds.

Those stolen afternoons I was swept into unthinking, uncaring emotion, responding to Edmund in drowsy pleasure. He was impetuous, not to be denied when his tender caresses became fiercely ardent, almost angry in their urgency. I hazily recalled Mother's warnings not to follow the example of my ancestors. She couldn't believe that my temptation had little to do with my hotblooded heritage, that the desire for my lover was heightened by my desperate need. She would retort sternly that it was God's will I was barren. I could not, would not, agree that God willed Henry to be a eunuch. Even if He had I could not believe that I should forget my duty to the dynasty and live like a nun.

Then, unbelievably, Henry changed. Did my experience create an aura about me, reminding him I was a woman and not a child? His usual affection became more tender, and one evening, instead of his grave enjoyment of a festivity, he smilingly waved away a young lord who was to partner me in the rondeau and led me out to the final gay dance. Then, with a gallant gesture, he escorted me from the hall, and pleased laughter sounded from all the courtiers. Except Edmund.

I waited breathlessly as Henry snuffed the candles at the bedside, undressed and turned to me eagerly. He faltered as he tried to embrace me, but this time he knew he failed and whispered that the next night we would be man and wife. My astonishment was lost in hope. Perhaps at last—at last my dreams would be fulfilled. My heart jerked as I became aware of what Edmund had realized instantly. If one's husband were potent, only a wanton—a whore —would take a lover.

And Henry was potent, yet I couldn't be sure if his thrust within me was too feeble to carry the seed of life. Three weeks later I was dizzy with joy, but my period was only late. Was the fault mine? Couldn't I conceive? I was in despair when we moved to Shene for Christmas. Unlike Greenwich, the palace was coldly unwelcoming. Possibly I thought that because my conscience was insistent that I give up Edmund.

I did give him up, but I was wicked; aching for my lover even when Henry was with me and I gave him that pleasure I once longed to do. The sight of Edmund was unbearable, and I begged him to leave, but he smiled coolly and said he was needed at court. I tried to dismiss whatever meaning was behind his odd smile and discovered that again his understanding was ahead of mine.

After Henry performed his marital duty, he grew more ascetic and prayed longer hours for forgiveness. I noticed too that he was growing quite thin from his fasting and sleepless nights, so I persuaded him to ride every morning even though snow powdered the countryside. He ate better after the exercise, and the wind brought some color to his pale face, but I saw finally what Edmund must have seen—that Henry's first delight in me was tinged with deepening remorse.

I turned on him one evening, storming that his remorse and acts of penance for being a true husband were more a transgression against God and me than a visit to the Southwark stews. I expected horror at such blasphemy, but he may as well not have heard me because he said, gently happy, that he pleaded to heaven for strength to restrain his gross indulgence of the flesh, and he had been answered. He had taken a vow of chastity and would no longer come to my bed. He had been weak to allow us to be occasions of sin for each other.

I said stunned, "But an heir, the country's unsettled as long as I am—am barren."

He shrank from me. Didn't I see a child would be proof of his sinfulness? My voice rose as I raged, repeating what his ministers had said a score, a hundred times, that only an heir would quiet Yorkist ambitions. York, eight years older than Henry, might decide not to wait until he would inherit the crown peacefully.

Henry, convinced that each man's first duty was to save his own soul, explained kindly that his ministers were so zealous that they saw dangers where there were none. He shrugged at mention of York's army. York was—well, high-spirited and his invasion was in the past. I was torn between fury and tears until I thought of Edmund. Yes, he was needed at court.

His love-making burned away the humiliation of being repulsed by my husband. And the miracle happened. I was pregnant; I would bear a Lancastrian heir. The signs came so soon I think Henry was the father. I waited until past the dangerous third month to tell Henry, partly because I couldn't endure the Yorkists' laughter if I miscarried, and partly in the hope that by then Henry wouldn't see the child as a sign of his weak flesh, but as a gift from heaven.

I dreamed of the bright future while the days slipped into golden spring. The birds sang through the lovely hours, and the green countryside was misted with buds bursting into flower. When finally I was sure I wouldn't lose the baby, I would tell Henry the dynasty was secure—tonight!

Secure? Dear and loving God, secure?

Henry's barber, a gossip, shattered my hopes. While he shaved the king, he went on as always about the latest court news, a voyage, an expected betrothal and finally—so my pregnancy wasn't a secret—of the celebration planned when the prince or princess was born. Henry looked at him, not speaking, a circumstance not noted by the garrulous servant until Henry, still speechless, fell forward from his chair.

He lay mute and helpless in spite of the physicians' potions, syrups, laxatives, bathings and head shaving. He did not respond to the noblemen who shook him, dragged him around the room, pushed and pulled him. I was too numbed from the disaster to do more than sit at his bedside and warm his cold hands with mine. I don't recall if I saw Edmund, but his father, the Duke of Somerset, arrived and said briskly we must move the king to Windsor where his condition could be concealed while he carried on the government as chief minister.

I nodded, too wrapped up in my ceaseless self-questioning to answer. Had the too-abrupt mention of my condition brought on Henry's state? Or had the barber merely precipitated him into an illness that was hereditary? His grandfather, the King of France, had been stricken like this, but no taint showed in his other French relatives. I revived a little at the thought that his grandfather's sickness had ended. So Henry might soon be well again.

I clung to that fiercely, it was all I had until the baby was born; screaming, healthy and a boy. Bells rang and bonfires were lit across the country to celebrate the birth of Edward Plantagenet. Edmund must have half-believed he was the father, but fortunately in the excitement no one noticed his harried expression when I was in labor nor his gaiety later.

I knew that no one noticed, because within days the Yorkists spread stories of the child's parentage, pointing to almost every man at court except Edmund. There were even whispers about Suffolk, murdered years ago. The very malice of the stories and the deluge of possible sires finally brought disbelieving laughter from all except the bitterest enemies.

They would be silenced when Henry acknowledged Edward his heir. I was desperate when Henry was unresponsive both to me and the child on my daily visits. On Christmas day he rallied slightly. His poor thin face was all smiles as if he had forgotten what the birth had first meant to him, and he held the baby lovingly, blessing him in the name of the Holy Trinity. Someone said spitefully that the king hadn't mentioned the Father and the Son, but only the Holy Spirit, leaving it clear that this birth was as miraculous as Christ's birth that very day.

I ignored the petty meannesses because the next day Henry relapsed into his stupor. How long could we keep his feebleness hidden? Somerset said flatly that before York discovered the situation, I should be regent. I agreed numbly. I wasn't a leader, I knew nothing of politics, but anything was better than having York seize power.

We should have known. When news seeped out, York came with his followers like a blast of bombards to Windsor. He howled with amusement at my being regent and persuaded or bribed the lords to refuse to accept me. Still they hesitated to give in to his demand to be named Protector, when the elderly Cardinal Archbishop of Canterbury spoke against the move.

Now the duke showed his true nature. The archbishop was bullied and harassed, his servants set upon, when he repeated firmly that the Royal Council should govern until the king was well. Courage wasn't enough, and the archbishop died. A heart attack was named the cause and the Archbishop was given a splendid funeral, though the pomp blinded few to the fact his death was brought on by the Yorkists' brutality.

Immediately a bill was rushed through, proclaiming York Protector, and on its heels a warrant for Somerset's arrest. I was in tears, but Somerset had the sour smile he kept for the Yorkists and said he wouldn't be in the Tower long. So I gave up my useless defense of him, and I accepted their offer of a thousand pounds yearly to me and the earldom of Chester for little Edward.

They thought I was unimportant, a woman easily bought off, when I also agreed to their order to retire to Greenwich to care for my child and sick husband. York chuckled, pleased that I knew a woman's place was in seclusion when she had no husband to protect her. Meaning, I suppose, that Proud Cis was in a more fortunate position, on her way to London to be queen in all but name.

I forced myself to smile as if grateful for the bribes, but my eyes were downcast, lest even the dull York be aware of my rage, or of my determination to nurse Henry back to health. The smile became real as I thought that the duke and his cubs shouldn't unpack their gear too quickly. They might be leaving London in as much haste as they had arrived.

CHAPTER 4

Only my determination to cure Henry saw me through those next weeks and months. I hadn't the vitality to think of York, much less hate him. I thought of him briefly when our position was thrust on us—the London apothecaries were slow to send medicines, our household staff was far too small—then forgot him again. My one thought was my husband, and I seldom left him. He rested better when I was there, and swallowed the thin soups and creamed sauces if I spooned them into his mouth.

I was rewarded. A flicker of life showed in his eyes one evening. I exchanged tense glances with my ladies. He relapsed into his coma, but each day he was more aware of us and could finally walk a few steps and go out to the gardens, then blooming in a wildly beautiful mass of color.

When he mounted a gelding for a short canter I, like him, saw the world around us again. I saw Edmund. I remembered vaguely that he always seemed within call, but my memory was a blur of endless hours. Now he was smiling as we rode behind Henry above the sparkling Thames.

"We'll be in London soon, my love. But we can seldom even talk there. I'm not so eager to return as I expected." His smile disappeared.

I laughed. "Nothing could keep you one unnecessary minute in exile."

"To be with you," his voice thickened, "a year, a decade wouldn't be too long."

I was amused at the thought of this restless young man living quietly in the country. If I needed him, he might tame his precipitate spirit, but that wasn't his meaning now. I answered what he was really asking before I spurred to catch up to Henry.

"Later. My ladies grow sleepy after dinner since they can rest easily now."

In the glorietta, his breath came quickly, shallowly. His hands touched my breasts, my hips, my thighs, gently at first then the pressure increased, his fingers digging into my flesh. His body was damp, his dark hair plastered over his forehead.

"It's been so long, my love, too long."

I started to protest that a meeting was unthinkable while Henry was ill, but he interrupted hoarsely, "Forget him, forget everything," and pulled me toward him.

I did forget, but briefly. A man loses himself in sensual pleasure, but when passion is spent a woman's thoughts dart from worry to worry. Little Edward was rosy this morning.

Was his color too high? A fever? And would Henry be overexcited in the whirl of packing to move to the city? If he were given his royal rights, hundreds of servitors would see that he was isolated from the upheaval.

I drew in my breath shakily as my stifled rage flamed. Edmund asked lazily what was the matter and grinned when I spat, "York." It wasn't, he said, the gentle tone expected from a lady who had just been embraced by her lover. Then he brought me upright on the couch as he added casually, "A pity your husband didn't share that anger and handle it like a man. Why didn't York die quietly when he was under house arrest?"

I gasped, "That would be murder!"

"Let's say a sensible precaution. There isn't enough room in the world for Yorkist and Lancastrian. Don't look horrified, my love. You have too much spirit as well as," he laughed, "passion and ordinary temper to put up forever with a rebel's arrogance."

I said that I would never be drawn into their savagery, but I remembered his words when Henry and I entered London and passed York marching out of the city. The duke reined in his charger to glower at me and the child in my arms. Then his tight mouth relaxed, and calculation replaced the baffled fury in his face.

His expression was so easily read he could have shouted his thoughts: an echo of my own fears. If Henry were ill again, the next Protectorate might last longer—until my son was eighteen. By then people would be used to York's rule and the true heir could be edged quietly aside. If, that is, the boy lived to reach his majority. I held my child more closely. The warmth of his small body pressed through my robe to my heart. Never would York harm my son, even if—

I couldn't finish the dreadful threat that sprang to my mind and turned quickly away. The crowds in Cheapside were cheering, overjoyed to see their king well. A kind and saintly man—who wouldn't love him? They shouted for Somerset, too, when he met us, surprisingly cheerful after his stay in the Tower. He shrugged away my concern—a wealthy prisoner could buy his comforts—and showed more interest in the young prince. He said Edward was more than a match for York's swaggering brats.

I agreed proudly. Every month, every week, I saw new promise in Edward. And I was happy that Henry was a loving father. While he had been aghast that the birth was proof of sin, he could never condemn the living child. The court doted on Edward too, but I wouldn't let him be spoiled. His destiny was too high for him to be ruined while still in the nursery. When he was two he could sit a horse—if his favorite groom held him. I refused to notice his tears the first time in the saddle. My eyes were also damp, but he must learn courage, and he must become a soldier ready to defend himself against any enemy.

Out of the west and the north came a faint rumbling as if confirming Edward's destiny. Troops were being raised for the border, we were told, and I prayed the report was true. I quickly stifled my anxiety. Henry was in excellent health, and Edward was accepted by the country as heir apparent. What could York hope to gain by causing trouble?

I was half-smiling at my instinctive fears when Somerset stormed into the great hall at Westminster. Henry was giving Edward comfits, and the boy greedily stuffed the dried fruit and nuts into his mouth while I wondered if that were proper food for the child. This trifling concern was brushed aside at the chief minister's first words. The army York was gathering was not because of border raids. For once the northern lords were at peace with Scotland. The forces were getting ready to march south, not north.

Henry said, impossible, his cousin York was loyal. The flat statement sparked Somerset's temper. He raged that the king's blindness endangered the realm. The royal warrant to recruit must be issued. Immediately.

Henry frowned, "By St. John, you cannot believe York is in arms against us after his oath!" He wiped Edward's lips with a napkin dipped in rose water. "It's the Scottish problem as usual."

Somerset snorted. "Then why is York howling to his troops that you must be protected from your evil advisers?" He added at Henry's puzzled expression, "He means me. And your wife. Your whole council for that matter, but he'll settle for ridding you of our influence."

Henry smiled. "You've been misinformed. No one would speak so wickedly about you and my beloved Marguerite."

Somerset gaped, then flung out furiously, "Jesus Christ! Even you must know that while York pretends his one wish is to remove your so-called evil advisers—well, no pretense about that—he does! But his real motive is to seize the throne he has coveted for years."

Henry shook his head, unable to accept anything that upset his saintly vision of peace. I wished fiercely I, too, could close my ears to Somerset's warning, return to the serenity of an hour ago. I had come into the hall laughing like any fond mother at some antic of Edward's. There was no laughter in me now. Since Henry wouldn't face the threat, someone must. Should I? But what could a woman do. I thought desperately—nothing. Nothing except hope that Somerset is wrong. But if he isn't wrong?

I stood up painfully, stammered out before Henry could forbid recruiting, speaking as if it were an ordinary thing for a queen to give a military order. "You have our permission to raise an army, my lord. The king will sign any papers later."

Somerset grinned and was gone before Henry could say that there was no reason for haste. I groped for my chair, sank into it, stunned at what I had done. Still Henry would have taken Somerset's advice in a day or two, and he did sign the document, though reluctantly, worried that his cousin would be offended by his lack of trust.

Soon he had to credit the report that York was indeed marching toward London. And this time the duke had an ally among the nobles, Proud Cis's nephew, the powerful Earl of Warwick, and Warwick's father who had both been staunch Lancastrians. Ahead of the troops came an endless stream of demands that Henry arrest Somerset, dismiss his Council and return the government to law and order. I screamed at Henry that York was the real menace to stability. I couldn't abide their arrogant certainty that they had only to snarl and Henry would concede anything.

But he didn't concede and rode out with our army to St. Albans. When the next Yorkist herald brought the same insolent message, Henry said, "Rather than give up my lord of Somerset or any lord with me, I will this day stand to live or die."

The hoofs of the herald's horse sent up clouds of dust as he galloped back down the narrow road. It spite of the dryness of the lane, the fields stretching out from the town were gold and green from the early shoots of grain and the hedges starry with opening buds. This quiet countryside wouldn't explode into war. York would see our forest of bright banners, the foot soldiers and cavalry and men-at-arms and retire again.

But Somerset wasn't chancing that York would be reasonable. When I went into the royal pavilion, he was showing Henry a rough sketch of a battle plan, though I was more aware of the two young men standing beside him: Somerset's older sons. They were much alike with their lean bodies, straight dark hair and narrow alert faces, but Edmund had a special brilliance. I smiled at them impartially while I thought, York is forever bragging of his sons. Does he forget Somerset also has a strong line to carry on and protect our cause?

I turned as Henry said that, though he was sure there would be no fighting, he wouldn't risk my being in danger. I should go to Greenwich. The staff agreed so loudly I had no chance to protest if I'd wanted to. I was quite willing to leave because Edward was at the palace.

I started to say, "Yes, Your Grace," when I

was interrupted by Somerset still studying his sketch. "I'll command the right wing, sire, since you'll insist on the center—"

Henry said quietly, "No. If there is a battle, I shall be in the Abbey praying for a just victory."

I stared at him, as did the other men who looked equally shocked. We all remembered that at Blackheath he had been in command, and that a short while ago he had said firmly that this day he would stand to live or die.

I said faintly, "As you know, my lord king has been ill, his physicians won't allow him to overexert himself."

I slipped out of the tent, knowing these hard-faced men believed sickness was a lame excuse. They didn't realize, as I did, that Henry would leave his prayers to be the first in the field if it were necessary.

At Greenwich I pushed my uneasiness aside as I waited to hear that York had merely growled, taken another oath and withdrawn. I wasn't prepared—holy Virgin—how could I have been—for the messengers who began to arrive at dawn. My ladies tried to soften the reports as they flooded in.

I could only gasp. "No, no, no, these men are York's agents. They're lying. They must be."

But I couldn't disbelieve my attendants' kindly distress. Nor the fact that if the men were from York, it was final proof that the armies had clashed and our troops had been defeated.

Somerset was slain. I put my hand to my damp forehead, then dropped it limply. He had been right. This was war, not the empty gesture of a blusterer. Henry, who was wounded slightly by an arrow in the neck, was brought to London by the victors and sent contemptuously to live in the Bishop's palace. The Beaufort sons, like many of the Lancastrian officers, fled to their estates. Neither the older one, now Duke of Somerset, nor Edmund, gambled on York's mercy, fortunately, because the captured lords were beheaded or exiled as enemies of the state.

I said dully, "Enemies for supporting their king? And York is a friend? But I suppose he has pledged allegiance again."

Their hurried assurances that York had sworn fealty broke off at my bleak expression. No doubt York, residing at Westminster, referred to Henry as king a hundred times a day, but my husband was still his cousin's prisoner. And alone. I was ordered to remain at Greenwich. I was in a stupor; going through the routine of washing, dressing, eating, answering the letters which became fewer each week.

I understood why. The writers were with us in their hearts, but messages could be intercepted and twisted into a charge of treason. I could offer no protection. I couldn't even protect myself from York's and Warwick's slanders, which they spread through the country. I was French, so an enemy, and the cause of our being routed in France, when the war had flared up again, leaving only Calais to the English.

I repressed a hysterical laugh that they found me to be so powerful when I wasn't even allowed to see Henry. However, the diatribes weren't for people who could think for themselves but for those who needed a scapegoat. In their screaming obscenities, they smeared me as a harlot as well as a traitor. I would never forgive York nor Warwick, who once was our supporter. In my rage, I hardly noticed a lesser betrayal. My chamberlain, the dour Sir John Wenlock, left. He had been a Lancastrian as long as Warwick. Now he thundered against us in Parliament as Warwick's spokesman.

I shrugged off his betrayal, but I dreamed of the day when Henry would somehow put the Yorkists down. Even my dreams failed me. A month later Henry had a relapse, and York, callously brutal, led him before the House of Lords to show that the king was unfit to rule, and was himself again named Protector.

In his arrogance, he made one mistake. Contemptuously, he sent Henry to join me, with a command that we retire further from court. I was distraught at Henry's appearance. His thinness had become emaciation; his beard was untrimmed, and his monk's robe was stained and worn. So! York thought so little of me that he believed that I was helpless to react against this cruelty toward his anointed king. He thought so little of me, I heard, that he waved away the advice of his followers and of Proud Cis to put me in a nunnery. I smiled bleakly. A few weeks ago, a month perhaps, and an abbess and a few stones might have held me. Not now.

I put aside my bitterness to nurse Henry while we moved in cumbersome wagons to a country house. The manor was small, but on a sunny slope above the river, and in our care, Henry grew stronger. My spirits rose, too, because York became overconfident. Merchants and tradesmen had been promised so much that they weren't aware at first that York spent more time adding to his own swollen properties than to improving trade. As the months passed, they grumbled that York's wonderful new world was somehow not much different from the world they had always known.

Disenchanted citizens would welcome Henry's return to power. Soon, I begged silently, let the king recover soon. When he did, we would have more than the support of an unorganized populace which could shift at every wind. I remembered the day that I had told Somerset to recruit. Could I—I must—take over authority again. I sent for all nearby Lancastrians. Henry watched anxiously as I strode back and forth in the cramped hall, asking, begging, promising awards for lists of men and weapons we could depend on. These meetings weren't good for him. He wanted to talk wistfully about Eton and of our colleges at Cambridge and my silk women, unable to see that our need was for an army, or that I was no longer his child bride.

I had to turn away so I wouldn't hurl words at him that I learned from my father's troopers. His gentle pathos restrained me from storming at him that if he were more of a man, York wouldn't have rebelled and I could be the sweet young princess he yearned for. Young! I was in my twenties, but I felt much older.

During these times the sight of my son riding a docile mare, or scowling fiercely as he notched the arrow on his bow, revived me. He had only me to uphold his rights and to save the Lancastrian cause.

Before long I found I wasn't alone. Edmund slipped past the guards one night. He hoped for an hour of love, but I said there was time for nothing now but finding ways to raise troops.

He laughed, kissing my mouth too hard for me to ask him what the Beauforts could promise.

He moved back. "I've thought day and night of the sweetness of your lips, your generous loving, the delight we have in each other. And you talk of war supplies." He smiled engagingly. "Don't say we'll be interrupted. I waited at the window while your last lady yawned and drooped until you sent her to bed."

Further protests died unspoken. I went to him wordlessly and felt his arms warm and comforting about me. He said I looked frail and exhausted from trying to do a man's work. My eyes flashed.

"I'm not trying, I'm doing it." I waved to my desk, overflowing with lists. "The names of our supporters, and there'll be more."

He conceded the point laughingly but repeated it was too much for any woman, even a Marguerite of Anjou. He was right. I was deadly tired, but realizing he would share the burdens made me hopeful, and I knew again the need for love. Perhaps, too, there would be a second child to put against York's brood.

Edmund was rough at first, too demanding, but he leashed his eagerness when he became aware that my body couldn't respond so swiftly to the change from loneliness to the warm security of having a companion, a lover, beside me. His patience calmed my ragged nerves, and my senses came slowly to life and responded as eagerly as he to the need for satisfaction.

Later his fingers lingered on my shoulder and slid to the hollow of my throat, but he was alert and ready now to talk of men and munitions. The Beauforts were recruiting, and the Tudors would rouse most of Wales. The

Tudors were unwaveringly loyal, as the younger sons were Henry's half-brothers. His mother had married or lived with Owen Tudor, a Welsh groom of the bedchamber, and Henry had bestowed honors on the boys when they had come briefly to court.

I said, "The Tudors will support the king, but they've no love for your house. Will they listen to you?"

Edmund said carelessly, "If I speak for the king, yes. Besides it's Father they disliked. The king asked him to consent to a betrothal between my cousin Margaret and a Tudor boy. Father pointed out tactlessly that Margaret was a Beaufort and a wealthy heiress. Who were the Tudors? Nobodies. But they wed, of course, and the bride's dowry softened resentment. They'll be with us."

My spirits rose at the encouragement, and a month later they soared. Henry recovered, and we returned triumphantly to Westminster. I vowed there wouldn't be a third protectorate, but Henry suggested a move almost as dangerous. York should be chief minister. I begged, I wept, I raged. Council and Parliament agreed with me that York should be sent away, but York naturally shouted that I alone influenced the king against him.

I wished with a new savagery that I had such power. Our finances were desperate, yet Henry gave the duke the gold and silver mines in Devon and Cornwall. My one consolation was that Henry's generosity drove a wedge between the people and York. When York piously complained that taxes were high because the king presented too many revenues to his wife and friends, the accusation brought laughter and jibes. Was it proper for York to accept crown lands since he wasn't a friend?

The Council used the wave of unpopularity to persuade the king that the duke should retire, and York left sulkily. Still I was uneasy—with good reason. York had tasted royal powers too long, and soon rumors spread he was recruiting again. Henry discounted the stories as malicious gossip, but eventually he had to believe and the Council insisted he call up our troops. York had his recently acquired mines to pay his men, but we had little money to entice citizens to enlist. Even with the lords who had promised to back us during our exile, there weren't enough, not nearly enough.

Henry, forgetting those militant meetings, was horrified when I suggested that I help. War wasn't woman's work.

I swallowed a bitter retort and said coaxingly, "I thought only to travel with my—our—son to his earldom in Chester. He isn't six yet. Won't the women weep at the sight of the prince and urge their men to take up arms against any enemy who would disinherit a child?"

He hesitated. True, Edward was appealing and the traveling wouldn't be too hard, but he couldn't believe York meant any harm to the boy. He finally consented, perhaps to quiet me, but we must stop often to rest, we must bring our own cooks and scullions and beds, we must—I stopped listening. What I must do was think like a man. I would ride lightly with a mounted company and chance the hospitality of country inns or sleep in the fields—no hardship that warm dry August.

I knew the Beauforts were rounding up foot

soldiers and cavalry, but I sent no message of what I was doing. Even Edmund was convinced that a woman should wait while men marched to battle, and wouldn't be pleased to hear that I was rousing Chester and giving out Edward's silver medallions of the Swan, a reminder that had been the emblem of Edward the Third, a true king. This would remind them that York was an upstart kinsman raising arms against Henry, another true king.

Thousands came forward, prodded by wives and sweethearts, but this still wasn't enough. A Lord Audeley, heavy and middle aged, arrived one day and said he would speak to the lords who were secretly with us. At my answer that I would accompany him, his grizzled face broke into a smile. He didn't scorn a woman's aid, and we pushed ourselves mile after dusty mile from manor house to castle.

It was almost impossible to sleep at night after entreaties virtually torn from my heart, and almost equally impossible to stay awake the next day—as we rode through a blur of green fields and late summer flowers. I remembered hazily my first days in England when I hadn't known—oh god—those serene days when I had known nothing.

Even those days of cajoling and pleading seemed serene looking back after Blore Heath. Audeley's forces joined Henry there. Altogether we had eleven thousand men. The Yorkists would be crushed in an hour—two hours. But Audeley was killed, and we were drivn from the field. Edmund and I looked at each other, refusing to believe we were defeated.

He galloped north, and I rode hundreds of miles, and in three weeks we had another army drawn up near Ludlow. This time Warwick, the deserter, was himself deserted. His great captain, Andrew Trollope, had been promised that there would be no fight with the king. When Trollope learned the truth, he came to us with his eight hundred crimson-coated veterans. The expected battle was scarcely more than a skirmish, and all the Yorkist leaders fled. York fled to his post in Dublin, while his boasted-of sons went to Flanders and Warwick sailed to Calais.

Now I could reward our faithful friends and have again a lighthearted household where a frivolous queen would rule. Proud Cis, I suppose, thought of herself as a queen, but she knew nothing of the demands of royalty. When a struggle has been won, one should give pleasure. Cis, coldly ambitious, welcomed only useful courtiers by her rigid schedule while once we returned to Westminster, the foreign ambassadors were writing their rulers that our court was brilliant, a diplomatic victory for us.

Enthusiasm was apparent as ambassadors followed us from Westminster to Shene or Greenwich or Windsor for the feasting and dancing and tournaments, the glitter of new gowns and doublets and the hunting and laughter. Henry was placidly pleased at the return to normal life, believing we were again in the early days of our marriage. But I had changed. I buried a girl's romantic dreams and put aside a woman's softness to rally men to the Leopard, while he dreamed and prayed away the hours, heedless of his dynasty.

Perhaps he remained the same because of his absolute belief in his own royalty. At any time when his rights were questioned, he answered unvaryingly, "My grandfather was king, my father was king, and I've worn the crown since I was a baby. By St. John, every man knows that."

His quiet finality made warnings of treason useless so I had to find occasional hours to consult with the Beauforts and with Captain Trollope on the news from overseas. We were joined by a young lord, John Clifford, who had recently come to court. Edmund was foolishly jealous. He should have seen that Clifford was no gallant with the ladies, but on fire for revenge on the Yorkists for killing his father in battle.

His scarcely banked fury kept us alert when we might have become careless because of heartening reports from our scouts that the Yorkist leader were still scattered and that in Flanders two of the York's sons were making the most of their respite from Proud Cis's domination. Edward, the oldest, spent night after night on a successful prowl for women. And the third, George, was becoming a drunkard, encouraged by the Flemish lords who were amused to see a boy downing cup after cup of wine.

Henry shook his head in sorrow over the young sinners, but others laughed. Edmund said, "York's a good soldier. Not as great as he thinks, still good enough. But if he's depending on his boys, well, they appear to have less military spirit than our—our young prince."

I caught my breath, certain that he had been about to say "our son," but after a moment he went on smoothly, "Why not have a special entertainment since it appears these last months of peace will continue?"

My ladies looked up with interest. They were refashioning their headdresses, sewing in new jewels or stitching a pale gauze veil to a gemmed band. But before they could speak, Clifford spat, "Can you talk of peace while those Yorkist murderers live? We should be hunting them down like animals."

His voice was chilling. He was like a killer hawk restrained by jesses and leash while its prey escaped. The goshawk, which unlike the falcon, slays not for food but out of a primitive need for bloody death. His mood was dissipated by my ladies' eager chatter about a festivity. They heard only Edmund's words, however. They didn't see how his narrowed eyes gleamed as they met mine, nor interpreted the tight smile that meant he had been denied too long.

My hand went to my throat to conceal the heavy beating of my heart under my wide sleeve. Rashness now could be disastrous. And yet, and yet, I thought unhappily, I, too, needed to love and be loved—to have a brief release from the anxieties that haunted me.

Edmund, turning to the king, said, "Next week is the queen's birthday, sire. A fitting occasion to honor her despite Lord Clifford's understandable objections to peaceful pursuits. At our London house."

Henry nodded, pleased as always at any special attention to me. At the banquet he was gravely appreciative of the choristers who sang continually through the dinner. Edmund must have searched all over London for the finest boys, and their young voices brought everyone's applause. My husband's solemn enjoyment didn't extend to the mazers of Spanish wine and the twenty courses of fish, beef, venison and pork, with geese and fruit and sweet meats. Still he smiled benignly at the feasting and at me later when the musicians played and the Milanese ambassador led us in the *padovana*, the latest dance from Italy, and I whirled and curtseyed through the measures.

I glimpsed Edmund across the hall and wondered if I had misread his expression. He must know how surrounded we would be tonight. I hadn't misjudged him. When we stopped for a breath, the new Duke of Somerset mentioned the house had to be redecorated after the Yorkists' occupation. Edmund seized on the remark, urging his brother to show the guests a Flemish tapestry in one room, a French *escritoire* in another, the freshly painted rooms below.

Willing or unwilling, the guests politely murmured their interest and followed the duke. In the melee Edmund caught my arm and swept me up a staircase to a small room. The bolt screeched as he latched the door, and he swung about to face me. I tried to say no, not here, not now, but my face was pressed against his tunic, and when he released me I didn't want to speak. I knew I was where I belonged.

Yet uneasiness was like a scarlet thread through the golden fabric of these minutes together. Anyone might try the door, and the bolt would raise questions and brows. The thread was fragile and almost snapped as his desire rose to blind passion. I forgot a threatening world and a husband unable to shield himself or his family from its violence. I forgot my fear of discovery. The room was dim and the cold March wind searched out the corners, yet it glowed with warmth and joy.

The brilliance faded and I was over-whelmed with the dangers of so mad a love. Edmund didn't share my change of mood. He held me as if he would never let me go, saying roughly that his thirst was scarcely slaked. We needed time to talk freely, to kiss, to be together with no watching eyes. Time for more than a brief meeting of our bodies. We needed a life-time.

My lips opened, then closed. There was no answer. I could only smooth out my undertunic and button the sleeves of my surcoat with un-steady fingers and hope the Virgin heard my silent frenzied prayer to guard us from a chance encounter before we joined the courtiers. I should ask forgiveness, too, but that was only granted if one repented.

Edmund's head was bent as he helped adjust my coif and veil. His face was tender though his half-smile held a bitter resignation. I wanted to fling myself into his arms again, say the words he willed me to speak, that I would risk everything—son, husband, throne—to be with him always. I said nothing of course. Neither of us was that far into madness to believe it was possible.

I sent a grateful thank you to the Virgin when we weren't seen leaving that room where happiness gave me strength for the future. All the guests seemed to enjoy the evening, especially our sail up the Thames to West-minster. We were huddled in furs against the icy wind, and the streaming torches lighted laughing faces along with the blue jackets of yeomen rowers. Henry's standard of a white antelope whipped about in the gusts, and the gray waves pounded against our barges.

I should have forgotten the laughter and remembered the ominous water through which the oarsmen rowed valiantly to keep a steady course. Three months later at Coventry on a soft summer day, when a breeze scarcely stirred the roses and bleeding-hearts in the garden where I was walking with Lord Clifford and my ladies, a messenger rode past us, flogging his lathered horse.

His mount staggered and fell, but the man ran into the castle. Clifford, quicker than I, was on his heels. There was no need to hurry. Within minutes the report reached to the town walls and beyond. The Earl of Warwick joined by York's oldest son, had exploded out of Calais and was marching on London.

With sickening certainty I knew that the city wouldn't shut its gates against the rebels. Londoners, fearful for their trade, took neither side, and Warwick was adept in handling them. He would pay for supplies, allow no looting and say plausibly that his intentions were peaceful. He would then add inevitably that he was loyal to Henry and wished only to rid the king of his evil advisers. I wondered dully if anyone would laugh at the repetition of the tired theme.

They had the advantage of surprise, but we had that of distance. Henry, of late, preferred meeting with the Council at Conventry instead of Westminster. Because of Trollope and Clifford and Edmund, we were well armed with serpentines, bombards and hundreds of pounds of gunpowder, as well as having expert French gunners to fire the cannon. In these last months Captain Trollope had tutored me in warfare and urged me to persuade Henry to go into debt to strengthen our artillery in the hope that our bristling defense would discourage the Yorkists.

I wondered if anything would check their insane greed. Edmund, when I went into the great hall, grinned at my anxious expression. His eyes were alight and his body was a coiled spring ready for action.

He said carelessly, "If Warwick risks meeting us, we're prepared. The troops are already moving toward Northampton. There's a natural site—you won't understand, but our position will be impregnable, the captains entrenched behind deep ditches and palisades and the rear protected by the river." He frowned as if worried he would be cheated of a battle.

I laughed, heartened by his confidence in our strength which surely, would make the Yorkists pause. I should have known better, since I wasn't surprised when Warwick's heralds arrived with the arrogant demand that the Royal Council be dismissed. More insolently, the king was given only until two hours after noon to agree. I waited proudly for Henry to retort again than rather give up one minister, he would stand this day to live or die. But Henry sent the heralds away with no answer at all, saying to me that perhaps the Yorkists had been ill-used. He would retire to the Friary to ask for guidance.

I whispered *no, no, no,* and minute by minute watched the sun reach its zenith and slide toward the west. The crash of guns brought me out of my shocked state. With a dozen men-at-arms I rode out and drew up at a rise above the field. I could not wait quietly behind walls. I had to know, I had to see our triumph.

The noise was incredible. Sound and sight became one so that the shattering pounding of the bombards, the screams of wounded men, the blaring trumpets and high whine of bow strings blended with the dull gleam of the cannon, the knights' glittering armor and the leather coats of the foot soldiers.

When I could sort out details, I saw that our guns were cutting swathes in the Yorkist lines. My escort cheered as gunner after gunner put glowing matches to touch holes. The iron balls plowed through the enemy while the archers sent flights of arrows that struck down soldiers and captains.

The Yorkists advance, flung back by the deadly serpentines, re-formed raggedly. I thought that the battle would be over soon, too soon for Edmund, when I realized the sky was darkening. A heavy cloud hid the sun, and lightning streaked jaggedly through the breathless air, followed by a roll of thunder that sounded as if new cannon were brought into play. A spatter of rain changed into a downpour.

Anguished words hammered at me. This can't happen. Our strength is in our firing power; our field guns will be useless. Two bombards were already abandoned while the Yorkists plodded across the mired earth toward the first ditch. When I saw the loyal Lord Grey de Ruthvyn bring his veterans forward, I almost cried out in relief.

Though I myself witnessed what came next, I could scarcely believe it. His men threw down their weapons and reached out to help the enemy climb up the embankment where they then fell upon our own soldiers who were thrown into confusion by the incredible betrayal. Some were killed where they stood, others fled from the butchers who even stabbed the wounded crawling from the bloody field.

I glimpsed the Golden Portcullis in the right wing before it disappeared. I hoped Edmund and his brother could draw off their men in some formation as I swung my horse about, vaguely surprised to notice my riding gown was plastered wetly to my skin. I had no real attention for anything except to reach the Friary before Warwick.

I spurred ahead of my escort across fields and muddy lanes to dismount and plunge into the hall. Henry, in his monk's robe, looked up from a desk in mild astonishment. I didn't want to upset him—upset? dear God!—so I said quietly we must leave at once to rally the remnants of our army. Henry shook his head. Too much blood had been shed. He would have no more on his conscience.

I blurted that the next blood would be ours, but he said mildly, that no one would touch the royal family. I shouted that he could wait to be Warwick's prisoner, but never would I allow my son or myself to fall into enemy hands. He begged me to stay with him, but I ran up the curved staircase to Edward. While someone fetched his cloak that was oiled against the steady rain, I flung jewels and dresses into chests. I would meet our troops looking like a queen, not a beggarwoman.

In the courtyard I smiled grimly when only four men volunteered to accompany my son and

me, but a handful was better than a company
led by such as the traitor de Ruthvyn. We struck
west for Wales in a nightmare journey, sleeping
by day and riding through the night. Then in a
glade palely lit by moonlight, we were
ambushed by men almost as ruthless as the
enemy behind us.

I was chilled at sight of the robbers' scarred
faces with matted beards and eyes like dull
pebbles, and I held Edward tightly to me. They
stripped us of our baggage. I waited for the
chance to escape. It came when the jewels
spilled out. The glittering splash of color
brought stunned silence soon followed by wild
shouts, as the brigands clawed for the gleaming
stones. Daggers were out as they turned against
each other, and in a breath, we mounted and
slid back into the night—west again toward the
Severn and across the river into Wales.

In the tumble of mountains, the fog was
thick above the steep wooded slopes, thinning
into a mist in the deep glens. Here we could ford
streams by day, and we met a traveler with
enough English to tell us that Jasper Tudor was
at Pembroke Castle. I didn't know whether to
laugh or cry or just kneel in gratitude, when I
saw the battlemented castle rise before us on a
sunny afternoon, with the standard of the Red
Dragon on the highest tower.

Jasper, Earl of Pembroke, was in the fore-
court, his eyes warily hostile under thick
brows. He was a rugged, bearded man at home
in this wild country. His stained tunic hung
awry on his heavy body, but his powerful
shoulders and air of command hadn't changed
since I met this half-brother of Henry's at
Westminster. Then he was cleanshaven and

fashionably clothed, And I, too was richly dressed in silks and furs.

I started to give my name, expecting a contemptuous denial, but his bellow of welcome cut me short. I thought my trace of a French accent gave me away, but he said that he would have known me anywhere—a lovely lady with the proud bearing of a queen. I wondered if he meant proud or haughty, as my enemies called me.

I dismissed the question. What difference did it make? He said that we must have rest and food, and I was swept away by two maids before I could ask news of our army. One girl cleaned and mended my muddied gown, while the other brushed my tangled hair. I couldn't wash away all the marks of the last weeks, but my appearance was rewarded with a lascivious grin when I joined Jasper in the hall.

I had to wait until he chewed through what looked like a haunch of venison, gulped down three cups of mead, and soaked up the meat juices on his wooden plate with half a loaf of bread. Impatience allowed me only to sip at red wine and nibble at a meat pastry, as I glanced restlessly about the great room where his horde of retainers scuffled over tankards of ale, their noise mingling with the barks of hunting dogs begging for scraps.

I was relieved when Jasper finally pushed his trencher aside and started to talk. He spoke with the quick decisiveness of a soldier—and it was a soldier we needed—touching only the salient points. Warwick paraded Henry through the London streets as proof he was still king, but few were deceived by the show. The Yorkists were too obviously in command, attainting Lancastrian lords and scooping up their property.

Anger laced my spurt of sympathy for Henry. He was safe, but what of the Beauforts—all the leaders—what of them? Jasper grinned derisively. "How Warwick and York's son would love to capture them, but hundreds of Lancastrians are on the Continent, and the Beauforts are sitting securely in their strongest manors ready to signal the exiles when we're ready. They lost one battle. They expect to win the next one."

I could have hugged him at those words, but I said only, "Then you're in touch with each other?"

"Aye, but 'tis slow work, my lass, we must have patience and more patience. Never strike until you can strike to the hilt."

Easily said, I thought, I could have given the same advice myself. I wondered if I would go mad waiting in this far corner of the world for a plan to evolve by men who would determine my son's future. My thoughts were interrupted by a small boy coming toward us with his nurse.

Jasper held out his arms but the child—he must have been about three—didn't leap into them as my son would have. He only kissed the outstretched hand, but Jasper beamed. "My nephew Henry Tudor. He may have a great future, a very great future."

I agreed politely, though I saw nothing in this puny boy with his mousy brown hair and close-set eyes to confirm such a prophecy. Jasper leaned forward. "Your son and my nephew are the last hopes of the Lancastrian line." He evidently saw my bewilderment. "His mother is Margaret Beaufort, a cousin to the Duke of Somerset."

I recalled now that she had been a ward of the present duke's father who had been reluctant to let her marry into a family of nobodies, but I still didn't understand. Jasper looked surprised. "His mother—lassie—a Beaufort, descended from John of Gaunt. Poor woman—her husband died before Henry was born so I persuaded her to let him live with me. He is too valuable to risk having the Yorkists take him and then declare later that he 'died' from some childhood ailment."

I stared at the boy. A Lancastrian hope? I said carefully, "The Beauforts were made legitimate, but they are barred from the succession." I knew many believed the family had a distant claim to the throne.

He nodded unconcernedly. "What one Parliament decrees, another can change. Also," his eyes gleamed, "we Tudors descend from the old British kings so my nephew is royal on both sides."

I was astonished that Jasper thought this fanciful tale could possibly appeal to the English lords. He mistook my surprise and said anxiously, "I haven't forgotten your son is the heir, but Prince Edward is only seven, isn't he? With no brothers or sisters he is vulnerable, because that rebel York has daughters and a quiverful of boys nearing manhood."

This reasoning made his wild dream sound slightly more sensible, but my son had the bearing of royalty; this unattractive child could be any peasant's offspring.

About two months later—I'd lost count of

the days—events erased all thoughts of the Lancastrian hope. When I drew up near the stables after a ride, I saw Jasper shouting at a terrified messenger, his big hands crushing a document as if it were an enemy's neck.

The messenger muttered something and Jasper roared, "Go, go, damn you, out of my sight!" He swung about, saw me and attempted a smile. "I've good news, lassie. The Welsh chieftains will soon be ready to march and in England plans are going forward to destroy those rebel bastards." But his tone said it wasn't good news, that it was no news at all.

My heart beat so hard I had trouble gasping, "Something is—what is wrong?"

He hesitated, then his words spilled out. York had delayed in Dublin until he was certain of Warwick's victory at Northampton, then rode into London as if he had been the conqueror. I thought that Warwick should be annoyed, but why should it infuriate Jasper? He explained that York didn't stop at this effrontery, but went on to the throne and in Parliament, repeated his endless claim to the crown.

Jasper stayed my scream of outrage. No, the duke's followers hadn't applauded his shocking gesture. They muttered angrily, and even Warwick was appalled. York, stony-faced over his defeat, forced the king out of the royal apartments, moving in himself. Surely a degrading situation for Henry, but there must be more to explain Jasper's rage.

He told me then. The Yorkist lords suggested a compromise. Henry would remain king; York named heir apparent.

I shook my head. "Impossible! Henry would never disown Edward in favor of a traitor. Besides he'd know the child's life wouldn't be safe. What did he say?"

"King Henry agreed."

I stared speechlessly at Jasper. Henry's final weakness gave Richard Plantagenet, the Duke of York, a complete victory without drawing a sword. Why didn't Henry's distaste for bloodshed extend to his family? He must know that York wouldn't rest while the rightful heir lived.

Jasper said thickly, "Christ! The end of the Lancastrians, of my nephews hopes. We're betrayed by our own king."

His temper mounted, but mine cooled to icy clarity. "I want a ship. Tomorrow. Ready to sail to Scotland."

Jasper gaped. "A lassie out there in an autumn storm? No, you and your son will stay at Pembroke through the winter. Tis as snug a refuge as you'll find at the Scottish court."

My voice was clear and cold. "I'm not seeking asylum. We need men and supplies. Send word to the Lancastrian leaders to be in Yorkshire the end of next month. With or without Scottish aid, I'll meet them at Kingston-on-Hull."

He stared at me as if I had lost my reason. "I—I just told you, the Lancastrians are finished, lassie. You see," he spoke with careful patience of one addressing someone witless or very ill, "now our king's with the Yorkists, we have no one to be a figurehead, much less lead an army."

My eyes flashed. "No leader? The troops

will rally to the prince, their future king, under the royal standards of the Leopard and the arms of Anjou."

CHAPTER 5

Kingston-on-Hull. A gray day in a town with the waters on the Hull River plunging east toward the North Sea. I was in the town square, waiting for my officers to ride in from their camp in the fields. The December wind cut through my heavy cloak and tore at loose strands of hair under my hood, but I didn't notice the chill when I heard approaching hoofs.

Edmund was in the lead and leaped from his saddle when he saw me. I looked long at him, at his brother and Lord Clifford and half a dozen more lords in their half-armor and brilliant cloaks and high boots. They appeared splendid and young and dangerous. Impossible to believe that these men had ever been defeated or could ever be.

Edmund lifted me onto his great chestnut charger and walked ahead as I directed him to the mayor's house where I was lodged. I laughed down at him from my perch and smiled at Captain Trollope, Warwick's former officer who had refused to fight his anointed king. He didn't return my smile, because he was anxious to talk to me before we decided on our final strategy. I said, "We'll soon be indoors and the whole staff will want to hear your plans."

He shook his iron-gray head. "Not they. Will a duke or baron admit that a mere captain has better ideas than theirs?"

We turned into a narrow street where the gabled houses leaned toward each other and I replied, "They'll listen. They know without you we'd have lost at Ludlow."

"But then I was an unexpected ally—" He broke off as his horse reared when a pig streaked almost under the hoofs. Above us a housewife dumped a basin of slops that just missed Edmund's shoulder, and a flock of honking geese waddled unheedingly through the gutter in the middle of the road.

Trollope said severely, "Pigs and geese aren't supposed to roam. They should be driven into the fields with the other livestock. And look at that!" He waved to a shedlike construction build against the wall of a house. "Absolutely forbidden, a latrine jutting over a street."

He might have gone on, but we were at the house now and the mayor was welcoming us, his face beaming. When I arrived two days ago he said this was still a Lancastrian town and offered shelter to me and my small escort. Far too small as the mayor launched into a speech. I had chosen the wrong time to ask Scotland for help. Their king had died, the court was in mourning, and the council of regency wasn't interested in petitions.

Mary of Guelders, the widowed queen, appeared understanding, but she was tired of somber etiquette after a royal death and used my visit as an excuse for entertainment and excursions. I had already met with her, and she was sympathetic over my losses and generously provided me with a proper wardrobe. I was grateful. I was also frustrated, irritated, and finally angry that when I mentioned the Yorkists, she changed the subject to a new fashion or the latest gossip. At last she said wearily that she could do nothing, and the council would open the exchequer on one condition, that I turn over Berwick Castle and nearby fortresses to them.

This was an impossible demand, so I rode to Kingston with only a few score Lancastrians who fled to Scotland after the Northampton disaster. Still the lords had brought their own levies, and the northern shires were sending volunteers every day.

I realized the mayor had finished his welcoming speech and I thanked him and followed him to a state room. We paid our respects and he left us to our meeting. Chairs scraped across the wooden floor and pewter clattered as servants poured wine and withdrew. Instantly half a dozen voices rose until Edmund's brother Somerset ordered one to speak at a time. It took more than a single command to quiet them, and even then there were mutters of "March on London."

I had studied reports sent to me in Edinburgh and was puzzled. "But isn't York taking up winter headquarters in the north at Castle Sendal? If we move on London, he could cut us off from our loyal counties."

Edmund smiled indulgently. "This is man's work, my—Your Grace. The military tradition is to hold the main city and then put down rebellious risings."

Trollope snorted, "Tradition! A lame excuse for making errors. Fight today's battles, not yesterday's. York's the spearhead. He must be defeated. Afterwards—"

Percy from Northumberland interrupted him as if he hadn't spoken. "When we have London, we'll strike against York and then crush York's son who's in the Welsh Marches."

Lord Clifford, an elbow on the table and chin on his hand, glanced disparagingly around the table. "There's one trifling flaw. While we move south, what will York and his son do? Play chess? Or join their forces to attack us from the rear? We won't take the city in a day. Warwick's in command."

Trollope nodded vigorously. "And he has the old—the king to show off if any sympathizers would open the gates to us."

Edmund shrugged. "A risk, but if we had both London and King Henry, the country would be ours. We might bribe the people."

A tempting thought to have the capital in our hands, but Edmund was too headlong. I said bitterly, "The citizens are already bribed. By that traitor and falsifier Warwick. He wins our subjects by feeding half the populace. He can afford to be lavish. His wife is a wealthy heiress, he has stolen Lancastrian lands and has the receipts from a dozen royal offices. What can we offer?"

Edmund said kindly, "We aren't poverty-stricken, and once inside we can redeem our promises twice over."

Clifford lost his easy air. "Jesus! We waste time dreaming of London. Trollope's right. First destroy York," he ignored indignant grunts, "before, as Her Grace mentioned, our loyal shires are cut off and the traitor's son reinforces him."

It took an hour to persuade the staff, reluctant to accept military suggestions from a woman and a base-born captain. Clifford was a lord and thus they gave in at last. Two days later we were on the road. The cold was bitter. Trees were rimmed with snow, brooks were silent under their cover of ice, and the wind out of the north was relentless, tearing at loose garments, and freezing the rutted lanes.

I could have wept for some of the men, their thin coats ragged and strips of cloth knotted around their feet. But the companies slogged on, mile after mile. Prickers ran along the lines prodding the laggards, but Clifford was worth a score of them. His Dragons, all veterans, were in the advance under his standard of the Red-winged Wyvern, a two-legged dragon with a serpent's tail. He moved among the other companies, cheering them on. Frost-bitten feet? They would soon have fine boots from the Yorkist dead. Rusted swords? They would be exchanged for weapons the rebels had drawn from the Tower armoury. A reward for avenging their dead—his voice flared—and fighting for their country and their queen.

When they heard my name they shouted for me, their breaths steaming in the icy air, and for the prince with his Swan on his sleeve and surcoat. I was in black except for the silver plume of my chaperon. I wore the black as mourning for all of us dispossessed by the enemy, the silver as a symbol of victory. I wished I had armor like Jeanne d'Arc, but the lords would grumble; Clifford probably, and certainly Edmund.

Though Edmund was lighthearted about our destination, once the decision was made to move first against York he encouraged the men with talk of lusty women eager for true men instead of cowardly rebels. Or he scoffed at hardships. Was a bit of snow, half-cooked black bread, or rising before dawn too difficult? Did they hear a whimper from a gently bred woman or a young boy?

We needed Clifford and Edmund who aroused the men's grim country humor and their obstinate determination to finish what they had begun. When we saw Sendal Castle high above Wakefield village, the other lords said tersely that we would go into winter quarters in Pontefract. It was impossible to attack that stronghold successfully, and a siege in this weather would be impractical, even if York's son wasn't expected with an army. No one campaigned this time of year.

I could barely restrain myself from reminding them that nothing was impossible if it weren't for their pigheaded insistence on following what everyone else did. The castle did appear impregnable, a mass of stone two or three hundred feet above the plain and protected by the winding Calder River. Yet, there must be a way, there had to be. I looked at Clifford who was talking earnestly to Captain Trollope and Edmund.

Clifford, head jutting forward, was again the goshawk, the killer falcon. "York has four thousand men. They'll need provisions. My Dragons will cut down the foraging parties but," his voice was just above a whisper, "I want York himself."

Edmund laughed. "Patience isn't a virtue I value. We're here. Let's attack."

Clifford said harshly, "No, a waste of men. We'll meet York in the field." Against an outcry that York wouldn't risk open battle when delay would bring him reinforcements, Clifford grinned derisively. "Trollope suggests we send Her Highness's herald to demand the castle's surrender. A blusterer like York won't huddle behind walls when he's challenged by a woman."

Remembering my staff's attitude, I thought this just might draw York out. Some men repeated that no one fought in winter, but others appeared half-convinced.

I said crisply, "What can we lose? Give your instructions to my herald, Lord Clifford."

The next morning the herald was received in the castle while the Dragons swooped down on the foragers, killing them and burning the wagons. At noon the herald returned. The coup had worked. York who had been dining, stood up knocking over his chair in his fury.

"That French bitch! If she had double her troops, we'd still give her a trouncing."

His advisers begged him to wait for his son, but he roared that he would be dishonored to sit like a bird in a cage fearful of a vixen and her bastard pup. By the time the herald left, the Yorkists were arming.

My staff galloped off to form their

companies while I thought frantically, *Hurry, hurry*! No one expected so immediate a response, and Clifford was forward alone on the Calder plain. The trumpets sounded at last, and the army moved ponderously down the sunken lanes. The wind, screaming through the tree-tops, scattered broken branches across the way and buffeted the soldiers who were singing wild northern songs.

I rode beside them, trying not to resent that I was only a figurehead, an animate standard. But I could command a mounted troop to surge ahead to Clifford with his two hundred Dragons. I followed them, ignoring the shouts to stay in the rear. Snow was falling again, and I could just make out Clifford as our troop left their horses and ran forward to join him. The Dragons were falling back toward the river, recklessly tempting the Yorkists farther and farther from the castle.

I pressed my hand against my cold lips as I saw thousands of the enemy hurling themselves toward the pitifully few Dragons. But our troops had reached Clifford now, and the Lancastrian advance thundered past me onto the field and Edmund's company poured through the tree-lined lane. He swerved to remind me that I promised to stay out of danger because without me, there'd be no one to carry on our cause. I nodded, though I was bitter that I could send men into battle and do no more than watch them die. The argument wouldn't have moved him, and he was gone before I could speak.

Already it was growing dark, and I could see only swirling masses of men clashing, breaking apart, re-forming. Feathered arrows cut through the air, pikes and halberds leaped with their deadly work, and the snowy field was strewn with the wounded and dying, their blood scarlet against the whiteness.

In the first rush the Yorkists thrust Clifford and our advance back, but now slowly, deliberately, our army pushed massively across the open space. The Yorkists held until trumpets blared again and our reserve, concealed behind a hill, swept across the frozen ground to strike with shattering force. The enemy broke. In less than half an hour the battle was over. The yells of victory were demonic in this sweetly heady moment of revenge for our past defeats.

I rode forward, dazed at the swift triumph. Some yeomen ran up with torches that sizzled as snowflakes fell on the flames. Edmund was there laughing.

I asked, "York?"

"Killed, so was Salisbury." He jerked his head toward a circle of men fastening some objects onto two pikes. I stared, then tried to look away but couldn't as the poles were lifted and carried to me. On the first was the head of Warwick's father, Earl of Salisbury, and from the second pole York's face sneered down at me. A paper crown was on his head.

Someone jeered, "Wanted to be a king, eh? Well, York's got his crown."

I hated York and his ruthless ambition, but I sickened at this vengeance on a dead man. The soldiers watched me, waiting for praise. They thought this would please me. The deed couldn't be undone. I said hoarsely, "We will retire to his city of York and will put the heads above the gates to warn others of the price of treason."

The men danced about their ghastly prizes,

but even they stopped when Clifford strode across the bloodstained snow. His set, grinning face seemed as much a death's head as what he held high by long brown hair. The dreadful thing was once a boy.

I choked, "No, dear God, no."

Clifford's voice was flint. "York's second son. He snivelled for mercy when I caught him on the bridge. I said his father killed mine, now I would kill him." He flung the head at my feet. "So die all the queen's enemies."

A boy—who begged for his life. Unforgivable. But I couldn't say this crime tarnished our standard, not to Clifford who'd brought us today's victory. Not to a goshawk who knew only beak and claws and death to the prey.

But Edmund—Edmund just shrugged at my shocked expression and said carelessly, "Another head for the gate."

That night he came to me. My lips parted in disbelief. I couldn't forget that boy who was little more than a child, nor the sight and sounds of the wounded. How could he brush aside that terrible half-hour? Then from his tone, his clipped words, I realized he hadn't brushed it aside. He was reliving every minute in gloating triumph.

He was amused at my shrinking. "Marguerite! Marguerite! Did you march across England to see a bloodless tournament?"

I laughed shakily and found I, too, could taste the savage delight in the defeat of an implacable enemy. Yet our time together gave me little pleasure. His exultation made him too urgent, too demanding. The odor of death was all about me, and it wasn't love but lust that made his body a driven force, possessing me

114

without tenderness. The experience, loveless and exhausting, left me feeling alone in a world of too many men.

I longed for my ladies, forgetting how often their solicitude infuriated me, wanting now their chatter and happy pursuit of small pleasures. In York I would have a dozen young women to attend me between staff meetings, which I was sure would be stormy. The lords appeared to think that now we would go into winter quarters, but I agreed with Captain Trollope that a delay would be fatal. I could count on Clifford's support only. I thought drily that Edmund could be easily persuaded to plunge on so long as the advice didn't come from me.

We swung down the road to York past snow-covered fields, the edged wind tinged with the smell of the conifers lining the icy lanes. The city was ready to welcome us when we reached the Mickle Bar, the Great Gate. Above it I saw the Yorkist heads and glanced hastily back to the shivering groups of mayor and aldermen, mummers and musicians.

Mercifully their speeches and entertainment were brief and I was taken to my lodging at the Abbot's House near Bootham Bar. Pine cones on the leaping flames on the hearth deadened the stench from outside where tanners and whittawyers scalded hides for their leather work, and butchers tossed offal into the gutters. At that moment I wanted to sink down in the quiet and warmth and stay here for weeks, for months, a wish my staff would gladly urge me to indulge.

However, we could not stop now, and as it turned out we had no choice. Twenty days after we arrived in York, we were asked politely but determinedly to leave. An understandable request, since our camp sprawled on the fields around the town walls. The regulars could be kept in some sort of order but not the hundreds of volunteers who arrived daily; undisciplined men in ragged sheepskin jackets with ancient weapons perched jauntily on their shoulders. At night the brawling kept the citizens awake, and cleanliness seemed unheard of. When I visited the grounds—without my women whose fantasies dwelt romantically on knights rescuing their queen—garbage was piled beside the tents, there was an acrid odor of unwashed bodies and clothes, and any ditch was used as a latrine.

The mayor and council worried about plague and there were also complaints of hens and sheep being stolen. I agreed quickly that we would go. The lords agreed to go only to Pontefract, heedless of my pleas to reach London before York's son. They smiled indulgently as usual, complimented me extravagantly, called me their Captain Margaret, but they wouldn't risk another unorthodox battle. Instead, they would send the recruits home to rendezvous again in early April.

They had no answer to my question whether discharged men would return months from now. Clifford was the exception. He said coldly that only a fool would throw away our advantage. These thousands of loyal followers were heady over our victory at Wakefield, but who could be certain of their morale in the spring?

The lords were won over. Now we faced our perpetual problem of how to feed an army grown to such an enormous size. Clifford looked at me, knowing there was only one reply. I glanced from him to Trollope. Their unyielding faces demanded I say the words. I wet my lips with my tongue. "The army will—will live off the land."

Angry protests broke out. A horde let loose on the countryside? Plundering would lose us more support than we would gain by any battle. We would be hated throughout the realm. Then Edmund said surprisingly, "I like this no better than Mar—than Her Grace or any of you. But what else?"

The troops cheered the decision, anticipating the looting. I was sickened, but later I would repay any ill-used subjects from the royal treasury. We could delay the marauding because the city of York, probably out of gratitude for our prompt departure, gave us supplies. We were heartened too by a report from Jasper Tudor. His Welshmen were moving to cut off York's son from London.

A young man arrived about this time with his cavalry. I didn't recognize him, but his name, Sir John Grey of Groby, was familiar, and I remembered he was married to my lady-in-waiting, Elizabeth Woodville. Memory of her came sharp and clear: the evening I frantically arranged my first meeting with Edmund. Not that long ago in years, but a century in experience. I smiled at my old irritation and asked of her. He said eagerly she was more beautiful every year, and they had a second son. I repressed a jealous twinge at nature's prodigality to other women. Still a dozen children couldn't replace Edward, my charming, appealingly belligerent, small son.

I watched him proudly when we rode through the first towns where the women especially applauded him as he sat regally erect on his gray jennet. They shouted for me too and stared at my standard of gold silk with the White Swan and red roses and at my herald decked in the arms of England and Anjou.

However, there were no cheers when the army flowed south, raiding outbuildings and looting homes. The village streets were deserted, men and women huddling behind barred doors. The officers tried to enforce order, and food was to be bought with receipts to be paid from the treasury, but the sergeants either couldn't control their men or joined them in the pillaging.

I didn't fully anticipate the horror of troops plundering my own subjects, breaking into taverns, becoming animals in their drunkenness. I ordered longer marches each day in order to reach London quickly so that we could buy provisions and put an end to this terror. The men accepted the command cheerfully, but they had to eat and no farmhouse or village was safe. Word came that the Yorkists were spreading stories that made the truth of our dreadful advance sound commonplace. I wondered who would believe such tales and knew that half the country would.

The next report was more crushing. York's oldest son had defeated Jasper's Welsh at Mortimer's Cross, though Jasper himself managed to escape the slaughter of officers. I let out a breath of relief for Jasper Tudor and urged haste while I sent scouts ahead for news of Warwick's plans. They returned with word that the earl would draw up his army at St. Albans across the road to London.

I leaned over the map Trollope unrolled briskly, hardly hearing the mutters of dismay. St. Albans had been our first battle and first defeat six years ago, and Warwick had carried that day as he had Northampton last year. Clifford was coldly derisive of their alarm and looked at Trollope, waiting for him to speak. Clifford was the deadly hawk, but he didn't pretend to be a stragegist.

I said slowly, "So Warwick is certain we'll take the Great North Road. Should we?"

Trollope was contemptuous. "That's according to the manual like Warwick's defense, but why do what the enemy expects?"

A few lords frowned at the blunt dismissal of the great Warwick's tactics, a reflection on them. Noblemen fought chivalrously, like gentlemen. Trollope snorted, "Why not, if your wish is to die like gentlemen? Mine is to destroy the Yorkist army."

He drew a line on the map with a dirty fingernail along the Great North Road almost to St. Albans, then a deeper groove east where we could swing about to strike against the earl's right wing and roll it back into the center. Clifford's bleak approval stopped protests, and nine miles from St. Alban's we turned to follow the old Roman Watling Street and almost met with disaster.

A company of two hundred Yorkists were camped in the district. If one slipped way to report our new position, we would lose all the advantage of surprise. Before I had completed the thought, Clifford was in his saddle, his

Dragons spurring after him. No Yorkist would live to carry vital news to Warwick.

The horses' hoofs muffled with straw, our advance moved forward at sundown, and through the night our vast army rolled on to the Hadley-Barnet plateau. At dawn our trumpets blared as our companies struck against the foot soldiers. Warwick sent out to delay us while he re-formed his center. His troops, extending five miles from St. Albans to beyond Barnard's Heath, were in wild disorder, due as much to his changed command as to our furious attack. Culverins and falconets were dragged up the slope, but the iron balls fell short of our lines.

Trollope, far ahead with Clifford, went down. He pulled himself up and plunged on limping. He must have stepped on a *caltrop* with its sharp daggers projecting from the steel ball. Clifford fell back briefly as cord nets with upright nails and steel-barbed lattices broke his rush, then he flung himself toward their center, the Dragons' weapons glittering arcs slicing into the massed enemy. Behind him a bombard thudded into our ranks and Sir John Grey, poor Elizabeth Woodville's husband, fell, but our army went on in wave after shouting wave of desperate men hungry for victory.

In the distance the Beaufort's Golden Portcullis moved from right to left to right again. I wondered at the erratic changes until I saw Warwick on his black charger riding from foot column to gunners to archers, drawing in his lines to strengthen his front. I thought, *Edmund Edmund, my darling, be careful*! and didn't even smile at the voiceless warning to a loved one seeking to cut down our most dangerous enemy.

Warwick, unresting, whipped up his men to mount an attack. The Golden Portcullis was driven back into a division of Lancastrians retreating under the sudden onslaught. The Yorkists yelled triumphantly, but our division held where it stood, then charged savagely forward. Warwick, his voice thunder, tried to replace the gaps in his broken ranks. At that moment an officer deserted the earl and sent his soldiers surging against his former comrades.

The Yorkists melted away at the treachery, or rather a reversal to the true king. Warwick was a dark figure against the dull February sky as he made a last vain attempt to stop the flight, then he, too, galloped toward London. I felt a bitter satisfaction. His insults that I was a whore with a bastard son wouldn't ease the disgrace of being defeated by troops marching under a woman's standard.

But he still had—Unbelievably Henry had been brought like a corded package into the field. He was sitting under an oak tree laughing softly. He said affectionately, "My dear Marguerite! By St. John, I have missed you, my love. A sad time but now it is over."

I choked, unable to find words. Did he feel no anger toward the men who had forced him to sign away his son's rights, and branded him a usurper? I said at last, "It will be over, my dear lord, when your enemies pay for their treason."

His thin face was distressed. "No more blood spilled, my little Marguerite. They'll be reasonable. Why look you," he glanced at two men I hadn't noticed, "Warwick has such care of me he had these gentlemen to guard me."

His trusting smile scraped my raw nerves,

but I didn't tell him they were there to slip a dagger in his back if he tried to escape. I gazed at him in fury, recognizing them. Turncoats both.

I said flatly, "They will be judged. By one who must learn how to rule," and sent for Prince Edward. I added as Henry babbled of mercy, "They'll have Yorkist mercy." I turned to Edward who ran up in gold half-armor. "My son, how should these men be punished?"

His small laughing face became grave and he smoothed his unruly chestnut curls as he asked what they had done. "They broke their oaths and rebelled against their lawful king."

There wasn't much of Henry in his reply. His childish voice was firm. "Let them have their heads taken off!"

For a breath I thought that no, enough harm has been done, we can afford to forgive if only as a gesture to the people ravaged by my army. My nerves had been stretched too tightly for too long, and I craved an end to savagery. But my woman's weakness disappeared at the sight of tears on Henry's lashes. I nodded to three soldiers to carry out the prince's command.

One of the prisoners said harshly, "I've fought overseas for my country and am now condemned by a child. May God strike down those who taught him."

I held myself stiffly, unyielding, as he strode away. I must not be ruled by my over-wrought state. I had over twenty thousand Lancastrians at the gates of London begging for the order to attack, yet I hesitated. The eyes in those starved, weathered faces were avid, gloating, as the men spoke of the gold and women they would plunder.

No quarter was given on the battlefield, but neither York nor Lancaster seized and looted a city. My staff was uncertain too. Clifford's instinct to kill didn't include defenseless citizens, and the other lords feared the country would turn against us if our army were loosed on the capital. Yet how else would Henry be acknowledged king again? Tomorrow I would give the word.

The next day the London Council promised supplies and money if I would withdraw. I suggested a compromise, that the royal family be allowed in the city with only a small escort. The Council asked a guarantee that the city wouldn't be sacked, and I wrote in Edward's name that he, the heir of this realm, would never destroy London which was his father's and his own greatest treasure.

While I waited a reply, I inspected the troops, proudly aware of the loyal hearts in this enormous camp. There was no answer. It was Edmund who told me the Council had broken off negotiations.

I spat, "Since they won't discuss terms, the burden of suffering is on them. We will attack at dawn."

He smiled faintly, aware of the reluctance under my anger. "We've been here a week. You must decide soon." I hoped he knew what should be done, but the impossible morass we were in cooled even his usual precipitation. I knew that he would be the first on the walls if I hurled the army against my own capital.

By the next day it was too late. The walls

which had been half-manned were crowded now with jeering soldiers. I knew that Warwick was raising fresh levies in the south; at least a month's work. But he had accomplished it in days, and joined with the forces of York's son. It was they who entered the traitorous town which closed its gates against the true king.

The fatal news stunned me. I agreed tonelessly when my staff said we must withdraw. Most of the north was Lancastrian. We would face the rebels there. The army broke camp and trudged back along the Great North Road, still hungry, with no riches to show for smashing the enemy at Wakefield and St. Albans. Our sole gain was that we had the king, so the Yorkists couldn't parade him to mask their illegal government.

The men were sullen. There were no cheers to warm the wind out of the east when I rode among them, no rough jesting with my son, and when Henry appeared, the silence was deathly. Yet they went on, indifferent to hostile villages or a sleet storm or a fresh fall of snow. It was March but the bone-chilling cold gave no promise of spring, and the long winter had drained supplies, so that there was little to show for raids on smokehouses or sheepfolds or hencoops.

Spirits lightened a little as we went farther north. Here townspeople didn't hide behind bolted doors. Some gave bread and hard cheese from their meager stores, and occasionally a tavern keeper offered a barrel of ale. These were pitiful donations but the friendliness brought smiles to hardened faces.

I tried to smile too, but my senses were still deadened with shock. Like the soldiers, I pushed on, knowing I must but not knowing to what end. There was nothing to say between Henry and me, and even Edmund could coax no response with a pleasant recollection or an amusing story. His words out of a dead past could not touch the dead present.

Suddenly, I was jolted back to life. A scout galloped into camp on a frosty night brilliant with stars in the dark arch of the sky. Warwick had waited almost two weeks before he had set off in pursuit. I listened indifferently. We already knew we were well ahead of his army though no one could say why the earl delayed.

Now I was told. I stared unbelievingly. "You said he—you said York's son—"

"Aye, Your Grace. It took—took time to bribe or bully the citizens, but the earl had Edward of York proclaimed Edward the Fourth, King of England." The scout added painstakingly, "By a mob in Smithfield."

"That cannot be. The king is here."

"Y—es, Your Grace, b-but—" He looked too frightened to say more if there were more to say. I sent for my staff. They were relieved to see the color flaming in my face, my eyes snapping.

"My lords, you said we'd make a stand here in Lancastrian country. Where? The traitor's son must be destroyed."

From their lack of surprise they must have heard the news which swept like fire through dry leaves. They decided on a site, probably selected by Captain Trollope, because it was Clifford who answered crisply. It was near the village of Towton where the Cock River and the hills made a natural defense. A two-day march. We must move quickly. The Yorkists were making up time lost in that little charade at Smithfield.

My stricken army came to life as quickly as I had. I was Captain Margaret again, and they barked out soldiers' songs as we faced into the cutting wind. Our supply wagons and few bombards jolted down the rutted road much too slowly. *Everything was too slow*, I thought in an agony that almost made me wish my senses hadn't wakened to this intense awareness.

The Yorkists were closing up when we reached Towton late Friday, the twenty-seventh. Our lines covered the town of York to the north to keep the enemy from the safety of its walls. To the south was an elevated plateau cut into two by a depression. If the snow flurries became heavier, firing the guns would be uncertain, but we had superior numbers and the hills protected our flanks.

The staff approved our position. A massed frontal assault would smash the enemy.

Trollope said, "Jesus!" His adam's apple was prominent as he forced back stronger epithets. He went on tactlessly. "Only idiots would wedge the army into a pocket. Keep the wings free to maneuver."

I nodded as my eyes went over the rough terrain. If our men were a solid mass, the Yorkists could sweep down from left or right and drive our companies into each other. As always, Edmund smiled indulgently when I spoke of military affairs.

"My dear—madam, the enemy will be equally hemmed in. It will be sword to sword, and our greater weight will crush them. That's always been—"

I snapped, "We defeated Warwick because

he couldn't fight an army that does the unexpected. You must see the wings should be
placed so they can thrust and retreat and thrust
again, giving us the offensive.''

They were all smiling now, saying the tricks
and stratagems of women were delightful in the
boudoir but that ladies, quite properly, knew
nothing of the battlefield. I shot a glance at
Clifford. He started to say he had no quarrel
with tactics which had won Wakefield and St.
Albans, stopped as an armed man panted up the
stony slope to gasp that a Yorkist advance
company had driven us from the ford we held at
Ferrybridge.

"So?" Clifford's lips pulled back in a deadly
grin as he sent his squire for his Dragons. In a
moment he was gone. They thundered down the
slope, flowed through a copse of bare trees
below and were lost in the gathering dusk. I
turned away. Useless now to appeal to the lords
who insanely preferred risking a glorious
defeat than accepting the unknightly schemes
of a woman and a mere captain.

Tomorrow Clifford could ram our plans
down those obstinate throats, but as the hours
passed, he didn't return. I was uneasy. His way
was to strike swiftly, unerringly and swoop
back to his aerie. At midnight I heard hoofbeats
and ran out from my shabby pavilion across the
frozen earth to where less than a score of horsemen sat motionless in their saddles. The moonlight spilled over the arrogant standard of the
Redwinged Wyvern. "Where—where are the
rest? Where—is Lord Clifford?"

They only stared, except for an old man
whose wrinkled cheeks were wet. He said
haltingly that the Dragons cut down every man

at the ford but then, more Yorkists crossed the river with a body of archers. Clifford died with an arrow in his throat.

I couldn't speak. Not Clifford, not my faithful hawk, the flashing avenger of the Lancastrians. I stumbled away and later I lay sleepless on my pallet. My scattered thoughts weren't only for Clifford, but for my army too, my faithful veterans. Would the lords listen to Trollope and to me?

The answer next morning was still no. The word was said courteously, pleasantly, solicitously. Their solicitude flowed over into a demand that I go with my husband and son to the Abbot's Manor in York. I gaped. Not be here where all my hopes might flower into victory or be trodden into defeat? I had never sent out an order once a battle was joined, but they didn't trust me since I opposed their plans.

They explained soothingly that my staff were all experienced soldiers and added polite words of regret for Clifford's death. A pity he dashed away with only his Dragons, not waiting for advice. But then, coldly, they added, he was more apt to give advice than to take it even if it was but repeating a woman's counsel. They just stopped themselves short of reminding me, I was sure, of my fatal hesitation after St. Albans.

Edmund said kindly, "Madam, you aren't only a wife and," his eyes narrowed slightly, "a mother, you are our standard. We must know you and your family are safe."

He said more, they all said more, until I agreed to be caged while the day, my life, was decided for me. My son, though too young to understand, was enough of a soldier to resent being sent from camp. Henry promised to pray for victory but forbade an assault tomorrow. Palm Sunday mustn't be profaned with the spilling of blood. He fortunately didn't see the men were already moving forward into position, and I could scarcely bear to look before we left for York.

Our lodgings were comfortable, but what were warmth and ease when less than a dozen miles away my veterans faced Warwick and the usurper, York's son? I knew it was too early for the messages that Edmund, with a lover's wish to please, had promised to send. I turned tautly when our door opened, but at the entrance was only a woman with a tureen of soup and manchets of white bread.

I sipped the hot liquid, put my spoon down. The maid clucked worriedly, but when she plunged a burning stick into a pitcher of malmsey, I found I could drink a little of the mulled wine. She fairly beamed when at last, a scout arrived with a youthful appetite for soup and bread and wine. He talked while he ate, his young voice confident.

As was decided yesterday, the Lancastrians were on the narrow plateau between Saxton and Towton, the frontage thirty feet deep, with the right wing above the Cock River and hills protecting the left. The Yorkists across the depression in the same formation could never survive our attack. I remembered despairingly our lost opportunity to strike at their flanks and rear. Then with determined hope, I thought that since both sides followed traditional tactics, our greater force would carry the day.

The scout left swaggering a little in his certainty of victory. Edmund had sent him before the battle joined, knowing I would be avid for news. It would be hours before I could expect anything definite. I stared out the window while the slow minutes dropped into eternity. The snow was falling more heavily, plastering the steep gabled roofs and shrouding the narrow streets. The wind rattled the casements, scooped out mounds of white to fling the heavy snow into high drifts. I beat my hand on the arm of a chair. How could they tell friend from foe when standards would be covered by the treacherous clinging flakes?

Abruptly my hand stilled. The wind was swinging from the east to the southeast. No, I couldn't believe the mindless elements would so cruelly come to the Yorkists' aid. But I had to believe it as snow was blown against the window on my right, and the next messenger, breathing hard from his struggle through the drifts, agreed reluctantly that the wind added to our difficulties. The shafts of our archers fell short while the enemy arrows streaked through the swirling flakes to find their marks among our massed soldiers.

I waited paralyzed until he added that our billmen were infuriated by the deadly unseen missiles. They plunged into the depression and up the far slope, their blades cutting through the Yorkist ranks, and our center followed them. The enemy, caught off balance by the unexpected move, had fallen back.

I breathed again. But what had happened since? What was happening now? As he pulled on his gauntlets, he could only give me Edmund's lighthearted assurance that the day was going well. I managed a bleak smile and asked if he could find his way back through the storm. He nodded carelessly while I wondered if another scout could reach me before the early dusk make riding impossible.

A leathery-faced man came, saying cheerfully the Lancastrian attack made victory certain. Then his correct mask slipped and words tumbled out. He was a veteran but never had he seen a battle like today's. The Yorkists, recovered from our assault, charged. In the wildly whirling snow the massed fronts broke into pockets of attack and defense, no one knowing who stood or fell beside him. Invisible trumpets screamed into the white vastness, and men-at-arms clashed savagely, some slipping in the snow to die under the thrust of a sword point or the blade of a battleaxe. The soldiers were butchers—worse. Butchers killed swine cleanly, without ferocity.

The flakes swiftly hid the scarlet splotches from wounded men being trampled by steel-encased feet of knights or boots of the infantry. Our men crawled over the piles of dead and injured to attack and attack again. Both sides floundered through freezing rivulets of blood and hurled themselves over the mounds of the fallen to sheathe sword or lance into the flesh of those who still stood. No one cried for quarter. None would have been given.

The snow pounding into the faces of our men blinded them, but the murderous struggle went on. Raging, the Lancastrians re-formed again. The Yorkists wavered. and then from a woods Captain Trollope swooped down on the enemy flank. Trollope, my captain, had defied the lords and their wedged formation, waiting until he could fling his veterans like cannon against their reserves.

I could have wept and prayed and laughed,

but the horrors the scout had seen held me from giving way to hysterics. He had no more to say, not knowing if our army had taken advantage of Trollope's onslaught to roll up the enemy's center. He was swaying with exhaustion but he wanted to return. I wouldn't let him. In the fading light even a fresh man might get lost in the blizzard that was blanketing landmarks and roads.

I thought practically that I should sleep, there would be no more news tonight. My pulsing blood and thudding heart kept me pacing, though I knew Edmund couldn't send another messenger. None was necessary. Men came by the score, by the hundred, sobs tearing through clenched teeth. A few stopped in their flight to stammer that Edmund was attempting an orderly retreat but instructed me to ride north immediately to Scotland. Edmund would meet me there.

I ordered horses to be saddled, my husband and son awakened, but I wouldn't move until I heard what happened after Trollope's brilliant strike. I was told quickly. York's son rounded up their scattered reserves to strengthen the center which was giving way under the iron blows of my ragged army, but the Yorkists moved slowly, too battered by our relentless hammering, our companies refusing to let the icy wind and blinding snow drive them from the field.

The victory was almost in the bony fingers of my faithful veterans. Then trumpets sounded from behind the enemy ranks. A late-arriving ally, the Duke of Norfolk, pounded forward to launch an attack on our left wing. And as

Trollope predicted, we were thrust back into the raging confusion of our center.

There was no panic, not yet. The armies fought hand to hand, stumbling over bodies, sliding in the scarlet channels lacing the snow. Exhausted, wounded, our men struggled to stop a division fresh to the field. They were rolled back to the river. In that narrow corridor there was no space to escape along the banks of the swollen Cock.

Captain Trollope and hundreds were slaughtered where they stood. Others plunged into the black water with its skimming of ice and were dragged to the bottom by their armor. There were so many dead that the corpses made a bridge for their comrades. And for the pursuing Yorkists as the terrible killing went on into the night.

I said, "Lord Beaufort's brother—Somerset? Was he killed?" There was no answer at first, then reluctantly someone muttered that the duke talked of surrendering to the so-called king, Edward IV. I thought dully, *Why not?* For years Somerset spent himself vainly for our cause. The thousands who still hold out will be hunted down like wild animals. Those who escape will be exiles like Edmund . . . Edmund, my love.

Yet Edmund accepted the risk, carelessly, jauntily. What of widows and orphans caught in the net? I remembered Elizabeth Woodville fleetingly. Her husband had died gallantly for us. Surely she and her sons would be spared. Sir John had been only a country gentleman, his holdings too unimportant for even the greedy Yorkists. Still everyone would suffer.

My eyes were dry. What use were tears after today's red ruin? I walked out to the courtyard, had to be helped into the saddle, unable to control the shudders that racked me. I was leaving England. So few years since I'd come, radiantly happy, to be England's queen.

I was still queen, I was Marguerite d'Anjou. And there were still loyal Lancastrians. The usurper would be swept aside, and once again London would welcome its rightful king and his young heir.

PART II
Elizabeth Woodville

CHAPTER 6

Elizabeth Woodville hummed softly as she glanced around the kitchen. At the hearth a boy turned a lamb on the spit, and at the long table a woman was shaping bread, while another scraped coals from the oven in readiness to bake the round loaves. The click of knife against wood sounded from across the stone-flagged room where the elderly steward notched a stick as he counted the flagons of wine to be stored.

Bradgate Manor was finally returning to the pleasant routine of last spring. Through the window she could see cherry and apple trees in their transient bloom of pink and white, and beyond stretched the fields, a haze of gold under the warm sun. The harvest would be good this year, the scars of battle covered and one day forgotten.

If only John— Her blue eyes misted with

tears. Three months since he fell at St. Albans. The whole winter had been dreadful with John away on the queen's campaigns, and she was inexperienced in running the estate. But then, at least, she could hope for his return. From outside she heard her two sons shouting at some game, and she smiled involuntarily. She must be grateful for them, not sadden them with her own grief.

Other sounds drifted in, booted feet in the lane and men's voices. She crossed the flags to the outer door, thinking with dismay that they were travelers. Life with Sir John had made her aware of a landowners' duties. She saw worriedly there were almost a dozen men and the roasting lamb shrank in size. Would there be enough meat? Perhaps with the bread—

Her housewifely concern was interrupted by the steward who darted past her to shut and bolt the heavy door. "Get your sons!" He hooked the window shutters and ran to the hall.

She shuttered, "But—but you can't bar the house against travelers. We—we should welcome them."

He flung over his shoulder, "Welcome *them?* They're Yorkists, devils, who would murder any Lancastrian who refuses to give his property to the king. The king!" He spat, wiped his mouth on his sleeve. "But we can hold out against their filthy tricks."

She hurried after him to call her sons. It was too late. The men were at the hall door, gouging the wood with their daggers as they pushed their way in. A ginger-haired man who appeared to be the leader snarled, "Stop, you imbeciles. We don't want the king's property damaged, not when we can walk in."

Her eyes went to the deep cuts in the panelled oak, and stayed there fascinated. This was John's home, hers. These marauders, how could she have believed them innocent travelers? The steward, gray hair streaming, rushed at the invaders with his notched stick. The leader struck him contemptuously. He stumbled an fell. She heard his bones creak as he pulled himself up to throw himself again at the men, and stared in horror while a soldier casually drove a sword into the steward's chest.

She was on her knees, cradling the bloody body. Ginger-hair said roughly, "Come on! He's dead. Now, lady, time for you to move. This is the king's house. Out! Take your family and get outta here by evening."

She wanted to be like the steward and spit at the very name of the Yorkist usurper. Would she have the courage if she had no children? She didn't know. She stood up, aimlessly stroking the red stain on her bodice as she nodded, saying she would change and gather their clothes.

Ginger-haired grinned. "Sure, sure, but no keepsakes, nothing valuable."

She turned on him. "All that I value are my sons." Still her gaze lingered on the French taspestry on the east wall, a cherry table set with silver plates, as she moved to the staircase. Three maids huddling in the shadows whispered timidly that they would pack a chest for her and fled. She put a hand dazedly to her temple. She would go to her parents in Grafton Regis. After the defeat at Towton, her father put aside his Lancastrian sympathies and made peace with the man calling himself Edward IV. She would be safe there, and they would welcome her.

She had so many brothers and sisters however, that three more dependents would be a burden. In some bright future she would repay them, but now she had nothing. Tears spilled down her cheeks.

Ginger-Hair broke off a shout for ale to say awkwardly, "Ah, stay 'til morning, lady. The king ain't in that much hurry."

Her temper flared. "We'll leave within the hour. We mustn't interfere with your business. Robbing the poor for the royal exchequer."

His shoulders moved uncomfortably. "Ain't my fault, lady, it's just—just my duty." His gaze followed hers to the door marred with dagger cuts. "My boys get too excited, lady, but—"

She was halfway up the steps, not hearing what else he had to say, complacently aware she'd made him ashamed. A small victory that faded instantly. It counted for nothing against being dispossessed of home and livelihood.

Two days later her mother, Jacquetta, put her arms warmly around Elizabeth while she suppressed her anger at a husband who would die for a lost cause and cast his family on the world.

"We're happy to see you, my poor child." She stepped back to look at her daughter's perfect oval face, the deep blue eyes and fall of hair reaching almost to the knees. "With your beauty, you won't be here long. We'll find—no, your future husband will find *you* and be enchanted."

Elizabeth smiled forlornly. "A widow in her twenties with two sons and no dowry? The best I can expect is an aging invalid who needs constant nursing."

"Tush! I hadn't half your beauty and no great dowry either, but I became a duchess." She was the wife of Henry VI's uncle, the Duke of Bedford, and after his death married a plain knight, Sir Richard Woodville.

"But you were the Count of St. Pol's daughter."

Jacquetta said sharply, "Remember that, that I came from a great house. The court has ignored me since the dear duke died and I wed again, this time for love." She smiled at mention of her husband, then sighed. "He's brilliant, but who cares for the qualities of a man who is land poor? Now you—you must love your bride-groom naturally, but choose one with a fortune."

Elizabeth shook her head tiredly. "Choose? I'm no longer a fresh young girl." She wasn't ready for her mother's brisk planning within minutes of entering her home.

"Hmm, true but your beauty has matured, and you have an elegance that more than offsets a few years. Still, time enough for that. I'll send for the family. You came so unexpectedly that they haven't heard the news, and your father and Anthony will be here tonight."

Elizabeth was pleased, Anthony was her favorite brother. His gaiety made her sparkle, and while she didn't understand his deep interest in books, it gave a final polish to his natural air of sophistication. Further thought of him was driven from her mind by the noisy arrival of her brothers and sisters. Their delight at seeing her enveloped her sons, who soon lost their fright at being evicted and talked as loudly as any in the room. She wondered if the welcome would remain as warm when they realized she would

141

be living here, a constant drain on the household.

She discovered gratefully that they accepted her changed situation casually as the fortunes of war. She slipped back into her girlhood routine, spinning and weaving, laughing with her sisters as they turned hems on gowns and mended tears in tunics and hose. Still there were desperate moments when the laughter was strained. Would they all go on forever busy over the small daily tasks as one year passed and the next, with no dowry for the girls and the boys without means to support a wife? Her older brothers didn't have Anthony's charm, which had won him Lord Scale's daughter. And her sons were tutored by a village priest instead of having a proper education.

Too many nights she lay awake questioning restlessly if soon she would be content to accept an aging invalid husband. She winced, but marriage would give her a place of her own, a position in life. If anyone offered— She threw back the blanket, then drew it up as a sister on either side of her mumbled drowsily. In spite of the crowded bed, she felt alone. She wished. . . . She closed her eyes, willing herself to go to sleep. Well-brought-up young women didn't entertain such thoughts.

Her mother had no such restraint. Jacquetta, who was inspecting kitchen supplies, was on her way to the milk house. She stopped on the sandy path to look at Elizabeth kneeling beside the herb garden.

"You aren't sleeping well, your eyes are heavy." She nodded with satisfaction. "So? You miss having a man."

Elizabeth carefully placed sprigs of parsley

in a basket. "There are men enough about, with Father and my brothers and their friends in and out all day. The wind wakes me."

"You wouldn't hear it if there was a man in bed with you. I've been worried. I thought you might be content to live alone. Some widows never want a man near them again. But I see you aren't like that. Good! You hunger for a man's embrace. That is as it should be."

Elizabeth said bitterly, "Good? To yearn for what you can't have?"

"Ah, but it means you're a natural woman with human needs. Men will sense that unfulfilled desire and be drawn to it. Only," Jacquetta's voice sharpened, "you have an astonishing beauty, but never forget that is all you do have. Don't accept a man to quiet his passion . . . or yours. Except in marriage."

"I haven't been tempted, madam, though suitors would be here quickly enough were I the owner of three farms."

Jacquetta smiled knowingly. "You don't value yourself highly enough, but be patient. Things will improve. Everyone's poorer since the wars with the armies stealing food and slaughtering our animals." She then remembered that her husband had recently sworn fealty to the Yorkist king. "Though of course, Queen Marguerite's troops were the worst, barbarians pillaging the countryside!"

Elizabeth shrugged. "Less civilized than the present king's marauders who drove me from my home?"

Jacquetta waved away the past. "The future will be brighter. But you've been careless of late. Stay out of the sun in midday, and I'll order more of the apothecary's special lotion for you. I wish we could buy good Castile soap, but imports are too expensive these days. Still Bristol soap—it's gray but it isn't harsh like the black liquid soap."

She went on, but Elizabeth, sitting back on her heels, didn't listen to the patter of house-wifely details. Her mother's words stirred up her restlenessness again. She considered her perfectly proportioned face and slim figure. She had no sense of vanity. Her beauty had always been taken for granted so she didn't think of it as something to be used. Was her mother right that she would attract a man of consequence? But who, in a country village?

A memory of a lively court and a brilliant queen made her sigh. Life had been exciting then. The queen had been kind to her, though there was one evening she had been annoyed. Elizabeth wasn't sure why, but whatever the reason she had been forgiven, and she loved reveling in the entertainments and mingling with glittering courtiers and foreign am-bassadors who, she realized suddenly, had been flatteringly attentive.

Soon, too soon, she left court for her duties as Sir John's wife. She had become used to the placid daily rounds except for an occasional sharp wish that John were less content on his estate and would take her to London. She re-proached herself for wanting him to change. Their years together had been pleasant, and she was Lady Grey, a personage.

She half-whispered. "If I could return to those days, I'd give—give anything." She wouldn't admit even to herself that John's image was fading—that the future her mother was so confident of held hope, elusive but shimmering.

But that hope, like her memory of John, paled as summer drifted into fall and winter. Fires blazed on the hearths, and winds searched out crannies and rattled windows, and she was glad enough to have her sisters share the cold bed. Now in the chill nights she brooded over an unexpected proposal from one of her father's visitors. The suitor was in his sixties and could afford to take a dowerless woman. He needed a mother for his ten children, the offspring of two marriages and said kindly he didn't object to her sons accompanying her.

But he had scarcely glanced at her, giving her less attention than a master groom he might hire. Her first reaction was a contemptuous refusal. She swallowed her anger, thanked him for the honor, but a young woman must have time before making such an important decision.

He did look at her then, and her anger turned to hate as he said brusquely, "You're not that young. Can't have a wife too near the age of my oldest daughters."

For all her resentment his remark stayed with her, fraying her self-confidence. In a few years she mightn't receive even such an offer as this. Her father evidently thought so, too, because he explained carefully that the man had a substantial estate and an income of a hundred pounds a year. The words came out with difficulty, apologetically.

Jacquetta snorted, "Now, Richard, don't start blaming yourself because our daughter isn't handsomely dowered so she can choose between this suitor and that one. We have something better. Elizabeth is our treasure, not a brood mare and housekeeper for a common fellow who can't appreciate her. When he presses you for an answer, tell him—tell him anything but put him off. As Elizabeth said, one must have time."

The suitor grumbled and said ungraciously that he expected a reply soon and stumped to his carriage, leaving Elizabeth divided between relief at his absence and fear she might follow him one day. She thought an angry *No* one hour and a *perhaps* the next when she wondered uneasily if Jacquetta's confidence was also wavering. Two months since the proposal. *She couldn't hesitate much longer,* she thought, as she walked into the village to the apothecary's shop.

The low-ceilinged room was crowded, but she ignored the swirl of talk while she stared blindly at the rows of spices. She looked up at the owner's voice and asked for fennel seed and pepper. He weighted them and reached for a jar of lotion, a smile on his wizened face.

"Why a young lady like you, blooming like a flower wants this, I don't know, but your mother asked for it."

She nodded her thanks, wondering herself why she went through the morning and nightly ritual. For all her suitor cared, her skin could be leather.

The apothecary cut through the unhappy reflection. "Exciting news, eh? Nobody can do nothing but talk about it." She looked at him blankly. He gaped. "You ain't heard with all this clacking around you? Why the king's coming to hunt in Whittlebury Forest. Next week. We'll all be out to see him. A grand young man they say, with a jolly laugh and a kiss for pretty ladies like you." He swallowed. "I forgot. You're a—"

She said firmly, "My husband was a Lancastrian, but my parents are loyal Yorkists." For their sake, she repressed the retort that to her this Edward of York, hardly more than twenty, was a traitor, a usurper and a robber, and strode home indignantly. Let the villagers shout for him, she wouldn't so much as look at him.

Her mother listened to the outburst. Yes, she quite understood Elizabeth's feelings. Henry VI was a good man, a saint, the country loved him, but the country needed a strong ruler. For all his piety no one could say Henry was that. And the Yorkists had a valid claim.

Elizabeth shook her head stubbornly, but Jacquetta's gaze was withdrawn. "If this Edward were evil, your father wouldn't have sworn allegiance to him. We must live with things as they are, and the way things are—well, if you want your manor returned, who can give it to you except the one who took it?"

"I? Beg him—him—" she choked.

"The king has a weakness for women, and you outshine anyone." Jacquetta added temptingly, "Think what it would mean to be independent. To be able to write your boorish suitor to look elsewhere for a wife to trample on."

Elizabeth's nostrils flared at her sudden intake of breath. "Yes! And he'll remember my letter." She sobered. "You really believe it would be right?"

Jacquetta said briskly, "Who could fault you for asking a robber to disgorge his spoils?

But first you must meet him, and not in a screaming crowd where you might be elbowed aside." She paused thoughtfully. "Ah! Richard will find out where the king—and remember he *is* the king—plans to hunt. I understand he often rides alone. You'll be with your sons in the woods; he'll meet you unexpectedly and see a fair widow, two pathetic orphans clinging to her hands. Though I do wish, Elizabeth, your oldest boy were less robust. It would look more natural if you were clinging to him. Well, well, keep him in the background."

Elizabeth half-smiled, became serious again. "What about a gown, madam? My best one, the blue, is faded."

"Hmm, a pity. You shouldn't appear too prosperous, but you are a Woodville. You must be decently dressed. Not that he's likely to note your clothes, but we don't want you too much of a contrast to the fashionable women at court."

Elizabeth lips parted at the last word. If the usurper, the king, found her attractive he might invite her to Westminster. Her eyes gleamed. To be again where there were festivities and sophisticated conversation, which wasn't limited to how well the hens laid and whether a cow were going dry. And gentlemen of rank there might think highly of a Lady Gray with property and offer—

She realized her mother was speaking. Jacquetta said drily, "You're dreaming, child, this isn't the time. Now. Your dark gray has excellent lines, revealing yet properly modest. Too modest. We'll cut the neckline lower."

"A neighbor's wife who was in London said now bodices are buttoned to the throat."

"So? Will the king think of fashion when he

has a glimpse of white shoulders and the first curve of breasts? Only a glimpse of course, no need to be obvious. You could tuck in a transparent gauze for the king to see it's no whiter than the flesh beneath. And gold embroidery at your wrists will add elegance. We can take it from the altar cloth in the chapel.''

Elizabeth looked shocked. Jacquetta laughed, said it might carry heaven's blessing, and Elizabeth laughed with her. Then she bit her lip. Her mother could shrug at the latest style, but what if the king saw her as a dowdy country gentlewoman and rode past with no more than a bored glance? Still she had no choice, the dark gray must do.

Ten days later Sir Richard heard the beaters would sleep that night in the fields close to their home. As the king hunted early, Elizabeth was roused while it was still dark. She staggered out of bed, eyes heavy with sleep, resentful of having to waylay the usurper, the king, and more resentful of her mother's brisk cheerfulness at breakfast.

Elizabeth eyed her mug of ale and the loaf of dark bread with distaste. Why trouble? The king wouldn't rein in his horse for her. If indeed she were lucky enough to be near him. Her irritation deepened as the boys came in, grumbling. Their yesterday's enthusiasm for a picnic was evaporating in the chill dawn air. What had they to complain of when they had nothing to do for hours except play?

She scowled at them and at her mother who was wrapping two roasted chickens in napkins to place in a basket with dried figs and white bread and a flask of wine.

Jacquetta said, "Our best moselle. When

you meet the—er—young man, he may be thirsty."

"I'll probably return frozen, fortunate if I've seen a rabbit."

"Perhaps today." Jacquetta glanced warningly toward the boys who hadn't been told why a cold March day was chosen for a pleasure jaunt. But they were interested only in the basket and the younger, Rich, cut a strip of crisp skin, licked his fingers as his older brother Tom hesitated, then broke off a wing. Jacquetta automatically shook her head at them and went on to her daughter. "What if it's two days, three? A small price."

Elizabeth wondered bitterly through the slow hours if the price were so small when there was no certainty of seeing the king. She pulled her heavy cloak more closely around her as she walked back and forth in the grove to keep warm, stopping only to placate the boys who had tired of sailing roughly whittled boats down an icy stream. They cheered up when she said they could eat but were puzzled at her order that one hen must be saved in case—in case a traveler came by. They shrugged resignedly and tore at the chicken bones with their teeth and gulped down their ale. The day crawled agonizingly until the early dusk when she agreed with set mouth they could go home.

Jacquetta, placing rush lights on the table for their supper of dried herring and bread and spiced beef, glanced at Elizabeth derisively.

"He didn't come? That's fortunate and you looking as if you had the misery. When you return tomorrow," her frown quelled the boys' protests, "be a little merry. A sour face holds no charm."

Elizabeth was about to say—another day? Never!—She didn't speak, realizing in that instant that today's frustation heightened her determination. Nothing could keep her away from the hope of having her estate returned and perhaps an invitation to court. So again a tin tub was carried to her room, a fire laid and she sponged herself shiveringly in aromatic water.

Few travelers straggled past the next morning or afternoon. It was the fourth day before he came, and miraculously just as she was opening the basket. She signalled the boys, who hurried to the edge of the copse. This tall splendidly dressed young rider with the red-gold Plantagenet hair must be Edward. She sank to her knees overwhelmed, even while she noted with relief he was unattended.

"Sire! Your Highness." She couldn't go on.

He swung to the ground, eyes twinkling as he raised her to her feet. "By God, a wood nymph! Such as you kneel to no man, king or not." He kissed her lightly on the mouth.

She regained her composure and said demurely, "Alas, sire, I'm only a poor widow trying to give a little pleasure to my fatherless sons. We were about to—to dine when I heard you and wondered who would be on this deserted road."

His eyes flickered toward the boys and returned to her face, slid to her breast as she let her cloak fall open. "I'll believe you're mortal, but never the mother of those husky children, a delicate creature like you." He looked up then. "A widow, you said? You must have a dozen, a score of wealthy suitors begging to marry you."

She smiled bravely. "No, sire. There are few men prosperous enough to burden them-

selves with a penniless woman and two boys."
She wondered how soon he would tire of the
meaningless conversation and spring into his
saddle as swiftly as he'd dismounted. "I—I
thought—but maybe I'm too bold—" She gazed
at him timidly.

"You too bold? Is there some favor you
wish? Ask and it's yours."

She hesitated, deciding to delay her request
for her property. "You don't realize what an
honor you'd bestow if—if you'd share our poor
meal, sire. It's not grand, but my mother's cook
is well trained, and the boys would boast forever that they dined with the King of England."

His laugh rang out. "You honor *me* with the
invitation." He tethered his horse and followed
her to the tree stump where she had placed the
basket. He ate as heartily as Tom and Rich and
drank deeply of the moselle and entertained
them all with lively stories of the years he was
in exile when he'd have envied the man who
could sit down to a feast like this.

He turned to Elizabeth. "Give my compliments to your wine steward on his taste and to
your mother on her cook's abilities." He
frowned. "But why do you live in your parents
home? Did your husband make no provision for
you?"

She blessed the instinct that had warned
her to wait and faltered. "He—he did, sire,
but—No, it's an unhappy story. I can't offend
you by the telling when you've been so kind."

She shook her head when he said he must
hear, that so charming a lady could never
offend him, but was finally persuaded to explain Sir John Grey was considered a traitor
and his property was—oh, quite rightly—con-

fiscated. She pushed aside the memory of that day, lest anger spill out. She had, she smiled bravely again, known the widow of a Lancastrian knight could expect nothing else than the attainder of his estates.

Edward's eyes flashed. "That is not right! Wars should not touch women and children." She restrained a cynical comment that he couldn't possibly believe only men in the field suffered, when armies swept across the country, and instead gazed at him admiringly. He leaned toward her, forgetting for a moment to speak, then said he would mention the case to his chancellor and she would have the deed to her own home in a week. The name was Sir John Grey? What was hers?

"Elizabeth Woodville, sire, and my father and brother have pledged you their loyalty."

He nodded, then grinned. "I must return or my escort will be beating the woods for me, but I must see you again. Tomorrow? And without—" He jerked his head at the boys.

"You flatter me, sire." She dimpled. "I'll come alone, but let me bring another basket to share."

Jacquetta received the news of the king's grant placidly, but she straightened alertly at his interest in meeting again. "Ah, I said you are our treasure. Who knows what will come of this?" She added sternly. "Remember he's—well a womanizer. Charms a lady, plunders her body and forgets her. Don't let the game be too easy to bring down. A king's mistress has a place in the world, but a few lusty nights with a country gentlewoman will hardly raise her to that position."

"Madam! You cautioned me to guard my

virtue."

Jacquetta said impatiently, "Don't pretend to be shocked. A king is different, though still a man."

Elizabeth thought, *Yes, especially this king.* Even without the aura of royalty, he had a magnetism that would draw any woman. She must never forget he was spoiled by too-quick conquests or she might let herself be as quickly used and as quickly discarded. And she was five years older than he.

Her brows came together. She had to make him aware that she found him attractive, almost irresistible, yet remain enveloped in chaste widowhood. He might be so shaken by a refusal he would ask her to court, certain to win her there.

She kept firmly to her resolution. He was eager, importunate, expectant, finally disbelieving. Why agree to meet him if she allowed only an arm about her shoulders, a light kiss?

She whispered as she pleated and unpleated a fold in her wool skirt. "I'm sorry, sire, I shouldn't have come, I knew that." She raised her startlingly blue eyes. "I tried to stay away. I couldn't."

He laughed genially. "Well then?"

"I—I won't be so weak again. But I had to see my king one last time." His face hardened. She smiled tremulously. "You cannot guess how I would delight to give you pleasure, but I—I cannot play the wanton. Please, please say you understand and that I haven't displeased Your Grace."

His good humor returned. "I don't understand, but I can't be displeased by a beautiful woman." His callused hand touched her cheek, was warmly rough against her throat but strayed no farther. "That soft flesh cannot conceal a heart of ice."

She had a mad impulse to throw her arms about his powerful young body, her lips parted enticingly for the pressure of his wide sensual mouth.

She swallowed, then said primly, "Not by nature, sire. But I must deny even a king. A man is admired for feats of love that are condemned in a woman." She turned away. "I brought pheasant and mead. Will you share them before you return to the hunt?"

His eyes sparkled at the last word though his voice was rueful. "Where my hunting has a chance of success? But I don't give up easily. We'll have your pleasant feast if you'll promise this isn't our final meeting."

"Whatever you—you command, sire." Her cloak slipped from her shoulders. She made a distressed sound but didn't object when he wrapped it around her slowly, tying the ribbons so awkwardly that his fingers lingered on her breast.

They met every day for a week. Elizabeth refusing any intimacies but with obvious reluctance and he showing more patience, though she saw the growing determination in his smiling watchful eyes. One morning when she was happily wrapping a haunch of roast venison—he had killed the stag himself he boasted with boyish enthusiasm—a royal messenger arrived. He gave her a letter, said the king had left for London at dawn, and galloped off.

The parchment dropped from her hand. She stooped painfully to pick it up, but her fingers were too nerveless to break the seal. He was gone. She sat heavily on a bench, her face stricken. He had tired of her, of her prim rejections.

Jacquetta, crossing the hall, stopped abruptly. Elizabeth held out the letter, said stiffly, "He—the king—rode off this morning."

No more private meetings, never again the sight of him, red-gold head flung back, nor the sweetness of a light kiss demurely returned.

Only when Jacquetta asked impatiently what the message said could she force herself to break the seal. Her voice was breathless. "He says—he says he's coming back soon, the very moment he's free. He hurried away to consult with the Council because of Lancastrian uprisings and—but this can't be true."

"I've learned to believe that anything can happen."

"You may be right, madam. This is about the Duke of Somerset. I could hardly believe it when I heard that he deserted the queen, the former queen, and pledged loyalty to King Edward. The king returned his estates and they became great friends—you know that. Yet now," she stared at the scrawled writing, "Somerset is leading a force of rebels at Hexham. What chance has he? He must know he will be executed. Why is he so rash?"

Jacquetta said drily, "A Beaufort doesn't need a reason for any madness. I suppose he suddenly remembered that Angevin woman who calls herself queen, a lover's pledge perhaps. It's said she shared her bed with half the lords on her staff."

"That's a Yorkist—I mean it's only a rumor."

It had been years since she had thought of Somerset, but now she recalled that he had been among the courtiers who had paid her lavish compliments and danced with her. That dark young head on the block—She shook herself. He was bringing his death on himself.

"I suppose his younger brother—Edmund I think the name is—will be the next duke, at least the title will be his."

Jacquetta snapped, "What does it matter? The Beauforts are only trouble to a true Yorkist. To rebel now, now when the king was showing such interest in you." She lowered her rising voice. "Still being parted from you may—will make him keener than ever to renew the chase."

Elizabeth stirred uneasily at the forced confidence in her mother's tone. Her heart had soared so high at the king's promise to return, that in her certainty of seeing him soon, she actually let her thoughts drift to the irrelevant reason for his absence. How long before he came? Would his ardor have cooled?

She watched for the carrier wagons bringing correspondence, gifts and supplies from friends or tradesmen in London. But the driver seldom stopped at Grafton Regis and then only with a packet from her brother Anthony or a length of wool her mother had ordered. The only other message was from her suitor who wanted a housekeeper. If she didn't answer soon, he would withdraw his offer. A widow in Maidstone would be deeply grateful for a proposal which Lady Grey was treating with a lightness he found distasteful.

She laughed shortly as she tossed the letter aside. She had forgotten him so completely in

the heady glow of the king's affection that she
hadn't written him the scornful refusal she had
planned. She forgot him again instantly as she
frenziedly went over and over the same
questions. When would Edward return? *Would*
he return? At meals she pushed aside her food
uneaten, at night she tossed so restlessly that
her sisters grumbled bitterly. She didn't hear
them, going through her daily routine heavily,
sights and sounds a blur to her.

This went on until one day she heard a rider
gallop into the courtyard. She knew only one
person who rode at that breakneck speed,
slithering abruptly to a halt, his mount rearing
dangerously. It couldn't be the king. But she
was on her feet, running down the hall and
through the heavy door. He strode toward her,
and she was in his arms. His voice was scarcely
audible as he kissed her hair, her lips.

"As beautiful, more beautiful, than ever."

She tried to pull back in sudden dismay at
her appearance. Her hair was caught carelessly
in a snood, and there was lint on her shabby
dress.

"Please! I must change—I must—"

Servants and stable boys in the yard were
staring open-mouthed. He said firmly, "You
must show me a place where we can be alone,
my dear love."

Had he really said "love?" He repeated it
again, tenderly. Mechanically, like a toy doll,
she led the way to the walled garden near the
orchard. Espaliered peach trees were heavy
green webs against a sunny wall, the leaves
stirring in the capricious wind, and beyond
were rows of peas and string beans, their early
shoots pale against the brown earth.

Edward looked only at her. He slipped the snood from her hair, let the bright strands flow through his fingers. His voice was thick.

"I shouldn't be here. My army is on the way to Hexham, and I'm playing truant. My staff thinks I'm with some—God knows what they think. If they saw you, they would understand I couldn't bear to be a few miles away and not come to you. Have you missed me, my Elizabeth?"

She couldn't speak, but her joyous smile and the thudding of her heart when he held her to him must have been answer enough. His laugh was confident, victorious. He kissed her mouth, his tongue seeking hers, and slid a hand inside her bodice, hurting the soft flesh as he cradled her breast.

She just managed to whisper, "No, no," and twisted away.

The worn cloth tore at the movement.

He pushed it farther down her shoulders, breathed, "Ah! I knew you'd be perfection," as he stared at the rounded bosom, the plaint waist. He lifted her, carried her to a wooden bench, and stroked her calf, her thigh.

A pulse beat in her throat. Color rushed to her face. He was the king, and he desired her. His royalty was as intoxicating as his youth and powerful body and passionate need of her. She could always relent, and pretend he forced her. No. She drew a quivering breath to still her own rising excitement. He was too used to having his lusty appetites appeased and then forgetting them. He had broken off his march to be with her. If his thirst for her were slaked, would he return again?

She made herself say coolly, "Sire, you

show that I've found favor with you. All my life I'll remember that you called me your dear love. I know it's only a pretty term for any woman who pleases you, yet I will never forget it." She drew away from him, pulling together the ragged edges of her bodice. She almost smiled at his bewildered astonishment when he must have believed her a willing victim to his charm. He must never guess how willing.

He caught her by the shoulders, shouted, "But you are my dear love! I've said that to no one else."

He probably thought he spoke the truth. She did not. "Then I'm grateful I've been so honored. I would I dared say to you—still it's proper for a subject to love her king, isn't it?"

"I don't want a subject's love. I want—" His angry voice softened to pleading and she finished the sentence for him.

"A mistress, sire. But I—you must give me time. I know I'm not good enough to be your wife. But—but I've always thought myself too good to be a wanton."

A bird chirped in the sudden quiet. A frog leaped across the path in front of them. The fragrance of early primroses weighted the air. He broke the silence, his furious words tumbling together.

"Who says—who dares say—that you, the most beautiful woman in England aren't good enough to be my wife? Think you I want to lie with a foreign princess like that Angevin bitch? England has its own roses and you are the fairest of all."

She was frozen, unable to answer. She couldn't have heard what she thought she had heard. Was he asking her to be—Even in his hotblooded arrogance he wouldn't be so rash. A king marry a commoner? She must not be dazzled by the impetuous proposal of a lovesick young man. But to be a queen—He hadn't meant that. She lifted her eyes to his.

He was smiling, in control of himself. "You think I spoke heedlessly to seduce you? You are my dear love. When will you marry me?"

"Your Grace, I—I'd give my life for such happiness—"

He grinned. "Like most women, you exaggerate. I wouldn't look forward to embracing a dead bride. Name the day. Though, until these uprisings are put down and I'm accepted as the true king, the wedding must be secret."

Wedding. He was serious. She to be queen of England? She stuttered, "How—however, when—whenever you wish."

"Tonight! I'm not a patient man." He waved away her stilted protests at the difficulties. "This evening, this evening, my sweet, you will know what love is."

He was gone. She stared at the empty garden, wondering if this last half-hour had been real. Her mother, too, was unbelieving, but only briefly. She became practical almost immediately. No need to tell the family. Sir Richard might think it a misalliance and persuade the king to delay, and the girls were too young. Though they would be moved out of the bedroom. Elizabeth had a fever and must sleep alone. Jacquetta's lips turned down sardonically. Not quite a lie, was it? She'd send for the village priest, call two servants as witnesses and it would be done. The Duchess of Bedford would be mother to the queen.

The hours dragged, yet passed too swiftly.

So much to be done and no time at all. Frilled lace from a faded surcoat to be sewn on a pale blue brocade, food and wine to to set out. The king would be hungry when he rode back from camp. Sheets to be laundered. She thought nervously she would never be ready, and what if Sir Richard asked about all the bustle?

Jacquetta smiled placidly. Sir Richard noticed nothing so long as meals were on the table and he was surrounded by a cheerful family. And her sisters hadn't questioned sharing a room with the younger children. Elizabeth's bright eyes and flushed cheeks did look feverish. Her father, though yawning after a day inspecting the outlying farms, dawdled over a game of dominoes with his older grandson until Elizabeth said firmly it was time for Tom to go upstairs. The others followed in a leisurely manner that set her teeth on edge.

Now Elizabeth couldn't hide her uneasiness. The priest arrived, an elderly man who showed no surprise at the odd hour for a wedding. But where was the bridegroom? He said aloud the painful question which had been an anxious thread through their hurried preparations. The king might have changed his mind. His horse could have stumbled and thrown him, or—

He was there. He had come quietly through the open door and was half across the hall before Elizabeth saw him, tall and broad and golden. Her eyes misted as she ran to him so that the gold of hair and tunic and scrolled boots were a gleaming streak in the flickering light.

He caught her to him, gulped down a goblet of wine but shook his head at the delicacies spread on the table. Jacquetta nodded under-standingly. He came to marry not to feast. The food would be brought to his chamber. He would have more appetite later. She summoned a middle-aged couple from the kitchen. They stood open-mouthed through the brief cere-mony, put an *X* beside their names and backed timidly from the room.

Elizabeth didn't see them. She was aware of nothing except this man beside her, the king, her husband. And the terrifying question which made a mockery of her earlier worries. Would he who had slept with doxies and duchesses be disappointed tonight? She had no knowledge of men except for John—quiet, undemanding, easily satisfied.

Edward smiled lazily as she lay beside him, unable to stop herself from stammering out her fears. He was filmed with perspiration, his eyes glowing, but he stroked her gently, murmuring incoherently. Or perhaps the blood drumming in her ears deafened her so she heard only sweetheart, perfection, marble flesh aquiver with life. Then his mouth was greedily on hers, tongue probing, hands lost in her fall of hair.

Her fingers dug into his shoulders, cut into the taut skin. She moaned, arched against him, her body melting against his damp chest and thighs. His triumphant laugh was unsteady as he swung over her and took her with an almost frightening ferocity. She clung to him, wel-coming his weight and strength, crying out softly in so sharp a pleasure it was shot with anguish.

He sank back at last. "My love, my dearest," then with surprise, "my wife!"

Her fears flooded back. "Do—do you regret

it, sire?"

His eyes slid caressingly from her bright unbound hair to the ivory-tinted shoulders and breasts and thighs. "Sorry you are mine and that no one else will know the delights of your body? Regret you have bewitched me? I will show you soon how much I rue the day I chanced on you in the woods."

The night was a whirl of emotion. He plunged into her eagerly but more gently the second time, and she responded with an abandon born of confidence. She laughed when he leaped from the bed to wolf down plover's eggs and roast beef and comfits, then sat beside her insisting she share everything with him. She watched him fascinated as he drank goblet after goblet of malmsey, yet he was awake before the first light crept through the window.

"I must leave, my love. How I wish I could flaunt you to the world as my wife now, today. But soon, my dearest, you will be crowned, Elizabeth, Queen of England." He chuckled. "Poor Warwick won't approve. He thinks to find me a French princess. Well, that will keep him busy drawing up tiresome contracts while I—mistress, beloved, wife, I must have a stirrup cup before riding into battle."

She was in his arms, drowsily content at his exuberant lovemaking that demanded nothing of her except she be there. She shivered in the chill air when he left, pulled a blanket over her shoulders, too sleepy to feel the full impact of the words she whispered over and over, "Not a king's mistress but Queen of England."

CHAPTER 7

Elizabeth's bright smile didn't waver as she nodded graciously to the peers of the realm who came forward, grave and deferential, to meet their new queen. But she was sure gravity and deference vanished when they returned to their places. She absently smoothed her blue satin robe and adjusted the long sleeves stiff with pearls, that matched the diadem encircling her tall headdress.

Edward, his big body too large for his chair of state, was comfortingly close to her in the chapel of Reading Abbey. She remembered his amused remark that Warwick wouldn't approve of the marriage. A wild understatement. The earl was seething. He had come back triumphantly from France with a contract betrothal to Bona of Savoy and a promise of an enormous dowry from the French king. For weeks Edward had pretended to consider Bona, then offhandedly announced the shattering news. He was already married. He gave Warwick the task of summoning the lords to meet his wife at Reading on Michaelmas Day.

Warwick was masking his outrage this afternoon, but a far less suspicious person than Elizabeth could see how tightly his real feelings were leashed. She was suspicious of all the courtiers, sensing their desire to tear her down from her high position. Edward was unaware of any tension, but she overheard whispers. If the king were so blinded by passion for an older woman, a commoner, how would he act in state affairs? Henry VI, being hunted in the north after the last futile uprising, had his faults, but he understood that England's ruler took no one less than a princess to wife. And Marguerite, headstrong as she was, created a court all Europe admired. What could one expect from an Elizabeth Woodville?

She paled with anger at the malice, but no one infuriated her as much as Edward's second brother, George, Duke of Clarence. She glanced at him lounging near the king. He had the Plantagenet good looks, but they were spoiled by his petulant mouth, the lips not meeting over his projecting teeth which gave him a perpetual—and false—smile. Though stll in his teens, his ruddy face made him appear never quite sober. Nor did she like having his costume outshine even the king's, a velvet tunic with gold tags and knots, slashed sleeves to reveal white lawn beneath, fingers covered with rings.

She had been told that women found him charming. Her hand clenched. Charming? He stared at her arrogantly last night and said in an audible aside to the king's youngest brother,

Richard, "Edward is mad or she put a spell on him. Why else would he marry *her*?"

"Our new queen needs no magic beyond her beauty." Richard spoke coolly as if pronouncing a considered judgment.

He was slight and wiry, his plain black velvet tunic not quite concealing a deformity hat raised his left shoulder higher than his right. She warmed to him and would have been more grateful except that he was only an unimportant twelve-year-old.

She needed powerful friends. If not among the old notibility, then who? She had her family, intelligent and handsome, the kind of people Edward enjoyed around him. He reached across to stroke her hand.

"I thought it might take time for them to love you, but look at them!" He jerked his head toward the throng below the dais. "You've conquered their hearts as you did mine. Every man here, even Warwick, is jealous he can't have my place in your bed tonight."

She was incredulous he could be so blind, to not feel the chill contempt in the air nor read the fury under the earl's mask of courtesy. Richard Neville, Earl of Warwick, was far too strong for a subject. That would be changed when she persuaded Edward to advance her family, giving her a faction to support her against the envious and the arrogant. She smiled.

Edward's eyes lighted. "You look as if you're having pleasant thoughts. Tell me."

She was startled, recovered quickly. "Need you ask, sire? It was you who—who spoke of—of pleasure later."

He grinned delightedly. "Ah, you find me a

satisfactory lover, sweetheart?" He stood up. "Let's end this audience. We'll sup in the abbot's chamber. Without, needless to say, the abbot."

He swept her through the crowded chapel, flashing a broad smile, and the peers responded to his high good humor and careless confidence. Perhaps he was right and in time they would accept her. But the day had depressed her too much to believe that, and it took all Edward's coaxing to make her dip her spoon into the thick soup and taste the spiced roast pork and truffles.

It took more coaxing before she would say why she was upset. He laughed. The women were jealous of her beauty, and the men annoyed because, if he intended to marry an Englishwoman, why not one of their dull sisters or daughters? He frowned slightly over Clarence's words, then said tolerantly the boy often talked wildly, but he had a loyal heart. The three brothers had been through too much together to hold grudges. And Richard had answered cleverly, hadn't he?

He was eager to have her meet his mother. Duchess Cicely, too. Elizabeth would like her, he teased. They both had the same high principles, disapproving of love unblessed by the church. Elizabeth bit her lip worriedly. She hadn't given a thought to his mother, but she knew of Proud Cis and wondered what the duchess would say of this impulsive marriage?

Edward's voice interrupted the uneasy reflection. "—since we're decently married even in madam mother's view, let us enjoy the benefits, dear love." He unfastened her robe, and would have let drop to the floor but she caught it to her, stroking the shining satin and ermine hem.

"Be careful! I've never had, never seen, such a beautiful gown."

But he tossed it aside to the table which held his all-night supply of bread and half-gallon of wine, promising she would have a hundred, a thousand robes if she wished. His eyes were on her bare arms as he unbuttoned the tunic of blue and gold, tearing off the last buttons when they didn't give way quickly.

She smiled ruefully at the damage, but her lips parted when he bent to kiss her and then carried her to the abbot's narrow bed. His words ran together in a fever of impatience. She thought exultantly let people sneer, here she was the queen. She would be crowned in Westminster Abbey and have jewelled gowns and ornaments richer than any woman's in the kingdom.

She sighed pleasurably. He evidently thought the sigh an invitation and took her fiercely, violently, releasing her at last with reluctance.

She murmured, "My dear lord," and smiled drowsily, her long hair silver-gilt in the glow of the tapers, when he said, "No man has ever had such a wife as you. What can I give you to show my gratitude?"

She shook her head. She was well content and needed nothing. She would wait as she had at their first meeting to ask for favors and didn't speak of her family until they were on the way to Shene to spend Christmas. Her voice was wistful and he said exuberantly, "Now I know how to please you, sweetheart. You're lonely for your family. They must all come to court, and the queen's father shall have grants and custom fees to support his position properly."

She thanked him happily, but she was almost too overwhelmed by his generosity at Christmas to speak at all. Estates worth four thousand marks a year as well as the palaces of Greenwich and Shene and five hundred pounds for their upkeep. She could only stutter and try to ignore Clarence.

This time Edward was also angry and rated the young duke for his slurred remarks that the gifts would have been bountiful bestowed on a princess, but for a Lady Grey they were madly extravagant. When his anger cooled, however, Edward said the drunken ranting should be forgotten—Clarence was a good-hearted lad. She nodded pleasantly and didn't say furiously that she would forget only when she could see that quality for herself.

The noisy gaiety of the household was hushed briefly when Proud Cis wrote she'd be at the palace for Twelfth Night. There was a dampening of spirits, then voices rose again and the musicians played more loudly than ever. Elizabeth, revelling in the merriment of the small court—the hostile peers were away for the Yule season—determined every moment would be enjoyed until her mother-in-law appeared.

Snow drifted down and gusts of wind whipped across the fields, but she remembered Queen Marguerite's entertainments and there were hunting and hawking parties and dancing and music and feasting. She was rewarded by Edward's open admiration and compliments from the courtiers which held a hint of relief.

She thanked them, putting firmly aside the uncomfortable reflection that at Marguerite's festivities, no guests would have shown surprise at the former queen's *ability to provide* a brilliant fortnight.

Duchess Cicely's coach drove up the next morning. She entered as if she were mistress, throwing commands to footmen and maids about her baggage, nodding graciously to the lords and ladies in the hall to greet her, holding out her hand for Clarence and Richard to kiss, and managing in the whirl to ignore Elizabeth. She gave her hand to Edward, too, but he grinned, kissed her on both cheeks and swung her around to meet his beloved wife, the queen.

The duchess's eyes, alert and dark in the lined face, slid over Elizabeth from the tendrils of hair escaping the headdress to the gold velvet shoes and back again. An aristocrat patronizing a commoner. But even in her rising anger, Elizabeth realized it was more than that. This was a woman cheated of the throne because her husband, York, had refused to believe he could be defeated by a woman with superior forces and a subtlety he would never understand. Cicely would probably never forgive Elizabeth for being queen when *she* should be wearing the crown.

Elizabeth choked back her irritation. "We are honored at your visit, Your Grace."

"I wished to see my son's wife." Then like Clarence she didn't trouble to lower her voice. "I had hoped the reports were wrong, Edward, and that you married a girl of your own age, a virgin, to carry on our line."

He threw back his head in laughter. "But, madam mother, haven't I done better? A virgin might be barren. Elizabeth has two sons, and as you know I've fathered a child or two—proof we'll have children to smash forever the claims of Marguerite's boy in France who pretends that he is heir to the realm. Come, you're tired. Rest an hour and we'll dine together, a happy family after all our misadventures."

She said stiffly, "I will retire but not to rest. I brought my chaplain with me, George, Richard, you'll attend service with me. No use, I can see, to ask you to join us. Edward."

"Well, there's a time to laugh and a time to weep, a time to—I forget the rest of the Bible verses you had us learn except there a passage about a time to rejoice? And what else can I do with my beautiful Elizabeth?

Her eyes scraped over Elizabeth again. "I'll pray you have healthy sons, and that she won't give you only girls."

"Equally welcome," he said smiling. "As you're well aware that I dote on them."

She turned away. Elizabeth, trembling with indignation, stared after the erect figure as Richard obediently followed with Clarence, whose mouth was sullen. Edward was amused.

"Mother has an unfortunate way of saying things, but it means nothing. You'll learn to love her as I do."

She didn't trust herself to answer. Did he expect her to smile sweetly at every hateful remark his family made?

She forgot them when she made her triumphant entry into London beside Edward, who was to open a new session of Parliament. He said resignedly he supposed he'd have to go, but as Warwick handled all his other affairs why not this too? She thought again that Warwick was too powerful, but that also slid from her mind at sight of the mayor and aldermen waiting to escort her through the streets, where crowds waved pennants and cheered hoarsely. She remembered attending Marguerite through such mobs, but Marguerite was in France, and Proud Cis no doubt sulking in Baynard's Castle above the Thames, while she, Elizabeth Woodville, was being acclaimed throughout the city.

Even that triumph paled beside the splendor of her coronation. She rode in her gold and white litter to the Abbey where the king helped her alight to stand on the red cloth leading into the church, and above her was a canopy carried by the barons of the Cinque Ports. Ahead was the sergeant-at-arms and the heralds in their brilliant tabards, the Archbishop of Canterbury walking behind a great gold cross with priests and bishops and abbots, and around her were the peers in strict order.

Her head was proudly high until Edward said he would be watching from behind a latticed screen and stepped back. She felt utterly alone, longing for him to be near though she knew that was impossible because he was crowned four years ago. For a terrifying breath she was sure they were here, all of them, to destroy her, their cheers changing to a paean of hate for a woman abandoned by husband and friends.

A sibilant whisper brought her out of her paralysis, and she moved gracefully forward, happiness surging through her again. Jewels on arms and breasts and fingers flashing in the May sun were no more dazzling than her smile and unbound silver-gilt hair. Now she felt she was borne forward by the good will of the clamorous throng who cheered for the king who had the wit to give them an English queen.

The light through the stained glass windows sifted warmly on silks and satins and velvets and ermine, as she walked down the nave to the altar. She knelt to be blessed, anointed and crowned, her voice clear as she promised to serve king and country.

Clarions and trumpets blared when she crossed to Westminster Hall for the coronation feast. Inside, the minstrels' playing echoed back from the high hammerbeam roof, almost drowning the voices and clatter of dishes where the hall was filled with laughter, jostling guests. Today the peers at the high table seemed friendly, entertaining her with stories of exploits at sea or amusing gossip as if they accepted her now she was truly the queen. A fact no one must forget.

She glanced at the ladies kneeling at her feet while she ate the first course. Her eyes gleamed. Princess Margaret, the king's own sister, knelt like the others. Jacquette too, her face lined with weariness, but Elizabeth was sure her mother wouldn't rise even if begged to. She was as determined as her daughter that the world should know Elizabeth took precedence over every woman in the kingdom.

A month later Elizabeth was dazzlingly certain her position would be more important because she was carrying an heir. Edward's delight made her forget her swelling figure and growing awkwardness, and the court astrologer predicted that the birth would be easy and the child would be a boy. But he was right only in that the birth was easy—not a difficult guess with this her third childbearing. The midwife told him disdainfully that the heir was a girl.

Edward, however, was all smiles when he held the baby with clumsy tenderness. There would be plenty of time for sons, and he wouldn't exchange this beautiful daughter for half a dozen boys. He promptly named her Elizabeth, little Bessie. The queen smiled too then, reassured at his pleasure.

Duchess Cicely didn't smile. She rustled into the room in her black gown and white wimple to point out that no matter what the king said he was deeply disappointed. Next time Elizabeth must have a son. *She* had given York four boys. The second—she touched her *couver-chef* to her eyes—was murdered by that evil Frenchwoman who called herself queen, but there were three strong sons left.

One too many, Elizabeth thought bitterly as Cicely left. Clarence. The young duke had been heard to mutter that he was better fitted for the throne than Edward, who had besottedly married a commoner and was forcing her greedy family down the throats of the old nobility. Elizabeth smiled with grim satisfaction. One of her sisters had married the Earl of Arundel's heir, and another the heir to the earldom of Pembroke, which was given the Herbert family after Jasper Tudor's attainder.

Soon she was pregnant again, and forgot Clarence. When her son was born, the whole country would rejoice and she could laugh at the long faces of those who opposed her. But there was no laughter when Mistress Cobbe held out the child, another girl. Edward scoffed at Elizabeth's depression. He was delighted to have a second daughter as healthy and lovely as the first. How did she like the name Mary?

Elizabeth nodded dully, nodded again when he repeated there was plenty of time for sons. She tried not to think of Clarence's pleased grin or the courtiers' whispers that if Edward had listened to Warwick and married Bona of Savoy, matters would be different. Bona might also have had only daughters, but at least the children would be royal on both sides and make better marriage alliances for the country.

Bona would also have brought money to a realm recovering from war, instead of spending so much on herself and family that Edward had to demand what he called benefices, and others called blackmail. Edward had a list of lords and merchants and gentry who had, even briefly, favored the Lancastrian cause. Among these some paid willingly enough since it was well known, they would add with a leer, that wives urged their husbands to give generously to this handsome king with his easy good humor.

Far more important, if Bona were queen there would be no disturbing reports from across the Channel that France was encouraging Marguerite and that dreadful boy of hers with promises of men and money. Everyone had believed the Lancastrian cause was finished after Somerset was beheaded and Henry VI was finally captured and sent to the Tower. But now the Spider Louis, King of France, was showing that he didn't like his generous dowry of Bona flung back in his teeth. Nor did he care for a peaceful England with leisure to dream of regaining lost provinces in Europe. Would there be an invasion? Because Edward had been, was still, infatuated with a commoner?

Elizabeth resolved stormily to ignore the malicious attacks, until Edward's friend, the

Earl of Desmond, went too far. Edward told her casually that he had asked the earl's opinion of his marriage. Desmond hesitated, then blurted out that perhaps a foreign princess would have been better policy than—than a Grey mare. Edward roared at the story and—incredibly— expected her to share his amusement, saying no offense was meant. Desmond had been honest as friends should be.

She tried to smother her fury but the unforgivable words burned into her. When Edward was away for a fortnight, she wrote out a warrant for Desmond's execution. Her pen paused then drove on to add the names of his two sons. She stamped the document with Edward's seal and sent it to the lord lieutenant of Ireland. When the king returned, the deadly Plantagenet temper flared out. His friend! She had murdered his friend! He hadn't believed her frightened excuse that Desmond was in a Lancastrian conspiracy and flung at her as he left, "Were the two young boys also traitors?"

He went to another woman. She was resentful at first. *His* enemies were sent to the block. After Hexham the executions had included even the old king's attendants, men not in the battle. So why not Desmond who had insulted her so deeply? But she did wish that she hadn't added the sons' names.

Her resentment changed to anxiety, then finally to desperation. He must come back—she had too many gloating enemies at court. When he did return—had he tired of his paramour?— she was charming, helpless, appealingly dependent. He seemed to accept her explanation that she tried to protect him from a turncoat who pretended to be a friend. He was

177

as loving again as in the days he had courted her, so she could now show the sneering courtiers that she was the queen.

She was coldly aloof to Warwick, and even made Clarence hesitate over his choice of words and, unlike the king, she didn't rise from her chair of state when the ambassadors from France and Burgundy presented themselves. Let them, too, recognize her rank. She allowed her ladies to dance when the feasting was over, but they knelt when she spoke to them—even Jacquetta.

In the queen's rooms, however, Jacquetta took the lead. She applauded Elizabeth's regal attitude, but the icy manner wasn't enough. Warwick, who despised the Woodvilles, must learn respect for the queen's family.

Elizabeth bit her lip angrily. "You know he's far too powerful to touch. He never forgets he made Edward king, and he doesn't let Edward forget. No subject should be so strong that he's more the ruler than his king."

"Exactly." Jacquetta reached for a sweetmeat, nibbled the honeyed confection thoughtfully. "But a captain storms the walls before he can attack the castle. Let's see now. One Neville kinsman is treasurer of England though he's not a tenth as capable as your father. Why not speak to your husband? It isn't much to ask that the queen's father—well, you'll know what to say."

Elizabeth nodded, eyes sparkling. Jacquetta went on dreamily. "Warwick's nephew is betrothed to the Duke of Exeter's daughter. Now, your son Tom is Marquess of Dorset. Isn't he as good a match as any Neville?" Jacquetta paused to select another sweetmeat. "I hear the Duchess of Exeter is fond of money. A few thousand pounds, would break the engagement, enrich Tom and teach Warwick it isn't wise to despise us."

Elizabeth laughed, pulled off her headdress and unpinned her hair. It fell around her like a cloak, silvery gold.

Jacquetta said, "Lovely. The king can deny you nothing. There's your sister Kate too. The Duke of Buckingham needs a wife." She smiled ironically. "He thinks himself important, boasting he is a Plantagenet, and is looking for a bride worthy of him. Well, who is more worthy than the queen's sister?"

"Excellent, madam. I'll speak to the king some morning when he's going over his accounts. He's determined to cut down household expenses so he'll be interested in seeing us prosper."

Jacquetta's brows rose. "Won't a favor be more readily granted at night? A man is—well, amenable if he fears his wife will withhold her love."

Elizabeth said decisively, "The king must realize I love him for himself, not for what he can give me. When an enemy hints that I married for greed, Edward will remember that I ask for nothing; at the moment he's most anxious to please me. Besides," she added demurely, "he's even more generous the next day since he's again been assured I care only for him."

Jacquetta chuckled, but Elizabeth's smile was mechanical as she dismissed her mother. She wanted to be alone. Neither Jacquetta nor her ladies must guess her self-confidence was more pretense than real. Edward hadn't been with her for four nights. Was he with the merchants as he claimed, discussing ways to increase trade so England would be prosperous again? He was exporting wool himself. Between that and the benefices, he said laughing, the Crown would be independent. No need to call Parliament to beg for money.

Or was he with some merchant's pretty little wife? Was his renewed love fading? She dared not believe that. She thought more cheerfully, *He'll come tonight*. The mayor and merchants won't gather in the Guildhall on Sunday. Even if—if he's had some doxie, he doesn't want me to suspect. He cares for me that much.

Her ladies combed her hair until the strands floated out, a shining web in the candlelight, and touched her mouth with cochineal. She stared into the mirror. She looked well, she thought, then saw in the reflection that two of her ladies were exchanging glances above her head. So they wondered if the king would again be absent. She stood up to slip on a blue satin robe and nodded as one asked hurriedly if she wished for music.

She said stiffly, "And cards."

If—when—Edward came the scene would be lively and inviting, not a drab chamber where a reproachful wife waited. They played for farthings and pennies, and as the cards were snapped on the table, voices rose excitedly when one or another gathered in a small pile of coppers. Elizabeth's quick anger faded at the sprightly air the lutist played, and she found herself smiling, when heavily ringed hands reached eagerly for winnings which would scarcely buy a plain hood.

They rose hastily as a guard swung open the door and Edward strode in. "No, no, back to your game, a charming sight."

Elizabeth said gaily. "Perhaps you'll bring me luck in this round, sire. I've lost every hand."

She signalled the lutist to pour the king a cup of wine, shook her head in mock displeasure as she lost again though it was difficult even to pretend displeasure when her heart was singing a brighter tune than the lutist strummed.

The king chatted easily as cards were put away and the ladies fluttered around him until he made it clear soon that their presence was unnecessary. He smiled at Elizabeth across the rim of the goblet.

"I've missed you, sweetheart, all those days and evenings talking, talking, talking to sober men who haven't a thought beyond their purses. Well, well, the profit's worth it I suppose, but I grew weary for the sight of you."

She sighed happily, caught her breath at the intensity of his kiss as he put the wine down and held her against him. "I missed you too, dear sire, though I remind myself you have a thousand duties that give you little time for a wife."

He said extravagantly, "I'd think it too little if I could spend every hour of the day and night with you."

Her laugh was light. "I fear you'd be bored, sire." And so, unbelievably the thought crashed down on her as he carried her to the bed, and so would I.

She doubted now if he had been whoring. He was taking as much lusty pleasure as ever

when he helped her disrobe, pausing to kiss her
white throat, her breasts, as the gown slipped
from her. She forced herself to relax, to smile at
him, in swift denial of the truth that she
couldn't respond to him, that she wanted to
draw away from his hot possessive hands.
Impossible when she had wished so fiercely
that he would come. Then she realized with
chill clarity that she felt triumphant, not loving.
His presence answered the exchanged glances
of her ladies, reassured her she was still his
beloved queen.

She murmured, "My dear one, the hours
are long without you, but when you're here you
give me such delight the lonely days are forgotten. I would I could please you as well."

He said hoarsely, "You do, my love, a
thousand times more than you can guess. You
grow more beautiful—" He broke off to take
her feverishly, hungrily, sank back at last like a
parched man intoxicated with thirst-quenching
wine.

He slept and she gazed at him with faint
almost maternal amusement. He noticed no
lack of response, no difference from other
nights when she'd gone gladly to his arms. But
he was blind to so many things. He saw himself
as he was a few years ago when exile and the
discipline of leading armies had kept him lean,
hard-muscled, temperate. He wasn't a sot like
Clarence, but he indulged himself at the table
with huge servings of meat and pastries washed
down by cup after cup of wine.

Nor did he realize how every month Warwick held the government more tightly in his
hands, dictating to the Council, making his own
plans for another French marriage, this time an

alliance for Edward's young sister Margaret to a French prince. That might, Elizabeth admitted, restrain the Spider King from aiding the Lancastrians, but a powerful Warwick was a greater immediate danger to the Woodvilles.

Her eyes closed. She thought drowsily, *Tomorrow*. She stayed in bed late the next morning. She wanted to look rested, at her loveliest. Someone might have suggested the king had done quite enough for her family, but she had promised herself that she would repay them for welcoming her when she lost her home. What did the hostile ministers, anxious enough to receive favors themselves, know of poverty? Of the monotonous days, the tiresome chores at Grafton, the mended clothes. They only grumbled when her brother Anthony was given new estates and, more, the friendship of the king who admired both Anthony's scholarship and his skill in tournaments.

She was glad she was dressed elegantly when she saw that the king was attended by his two brothers. Not that they cared, in fact they would prefer to see her in sackcloth, especially Clarence—in spite of his own cloak and tunic of green velvet and his flashing jewels. But she felt at ease, knowing she looked her best.

The king and Clarence, shouting at each other, didn't notice her, but Richard bowed to her. She nodded carelessly, then eyed him more closely. A slight wiry boy, dressed in his usual unadorned black tunic and hose, left shoulder high, she paid little attention to him whenever he returned reluctantly from his beloved Yorkshire. To her, he was still the quiet and reserved youth she met over three years ago at Reading, of little importance, though he'd been given the ridiculous title of Admiral of England.

Today he appeared mature, older than his fifteen years, and she was vaguely uneasy at his expression as he gazed at her. His was a cool reserve, which admitted her to the family out of loyalty to Edward, but never warmed to her. She thought impatiently, *He's a mere youngster*, and turned at Edward's roar.

"Quiet! Not even a brother speaks to the king as you have." He glanced up, smiled grimly as he saw Elizabeth. "Clarence takes me to be the same fool he is. The answer is no and again no."

Clarence sneered, "You married a commoner of no family yet deny my right to wed Warwick's older daughter, a girl whose lineage makes her a fit bride for a prince."

"You're a sot who can't see that Warwick's pushing this Isabel at you to gain even more power for himself. People believe he's the real ruler, but I've grown tired of his tutelage. Tell him that when you give him my answer on this marriage."

Elizabeth breathed in relief. So Edward wasn't completely blind to the earl's domination.

Clarence's lips drew back maliciously. "The answer would be different if your favorite brother asked. Tell him, Richard, how fond you are of the little Anne you saw so often when you were in Warwick's household and of the earl's suggestion of a betrothal. The earl's two daughters to the king's two brothers. You didn't say no."

Richard said with cool precision, "I didn't say no, nor did I say yes. I told him I'd never consider taking a wife without the king's consent."

Clarence's red face darkened to purple while Edward beamed. "You live up to your motto, 'Loyaultie Binds me.' I've another command our great earl won't like. He's to break off negotiations on a French prince for our sister Margaret. She'll marry the Duke of Burgundy, an alliance much more profitable for the country."

Clarence spat out, "Does Duke Charles agree? I hear things, such as that he wants to marry that French whore, Marguerite of Anjou, though she's penniless. *He* doesn't have to beg your permission."

Edward's shoulders lifted. "Ah, but she has a husband, and Henry will remain in good health in the Tower," his light blue eyes hardened, "as long as that bastard of hers is alive." His usual good humor returned. "Charles isn't patient, he'll accept our offer." He waved his brothers out and turned to Elizabeth. "Did you want anything, sweetheart?"

Her smile was brilliant. "Like your faithful Richard, my answer could be yes or no, depending on your will." He was always pleased when his youngest brother was commended. "Yes, if you think my idea has merit, but a hundred times no if you believe I shouldn't make such a request."

He pulled her onto his lap, one hand pressing against her bodice. "What would you have, my love, you who give so much and ask for so little?"

She said hesitantly how she admired his

masterful handling of Warwick's interference in royal affairs, but didn't other Nevilles like the treasurer interfere too? She paused, went on still hesitantly to say her father wasn't only capable but as treasurer he wouldn't be stiff-necked like—well, like others—and dally over orders from his king.

There was a dreadful moment of silence before he laughed uproariously. "Excellent, sweetheart. Have you more bright ideas in that lovely little head?"

She had meant to delay speaking of her son Tom and Exeter's daughter, but the moment was right. The only problem, she explained timidly, 'was money to persuade the girl's mother to ask for the church's dispensation to annul the betrothal to Warwick's nephew.

"My dear wife, I marvel at your wisdom. Give the old bitch whatever she wants, the privy purse will pay for it. A small price to buy me what I need, a faction devoted to me."

Her teeth bit into her lower lip. She was bitterly aware why he was so willing to advance her family. With the Woodvilles completely dependent on him, he would have his own party to balance the arrogant lords. But he did love her.

She said mischievously, "There's Buckingham too, sire, and my sister Kate—"

He agreed delightedly before she could finish. "Since this is the morning for weddings, shall I tell you your brother John asked permission for his? To the Duchess of Norfolk." He chucked. "At a kindly guess she's eighty, but her wealth will smooth away wrinkles, replace lost teeth and clothe again bones with fair flesh for a twenty-year-old bridegroom. I consented."

She was half amused, half shocked at her younger brother. Laughter won out. With her relatives so highly placed, no need to worry about the future of her still-unmarried sisters, promotion for her brother in the navy or the youngest who was entering holy orders.

Edward said complacently, "Poor Warwick, his schemes for his daughters rejected, while Woodvilles marry where they will." He kissed her resoundingly. "He won't like it nor will Clarence, but let them sulk. It'll do no harm."

No harm, she thought uneasily, if Edward angered only Clarence, but Warwick? The earl answered her unspoken question by storming out of London with Clarence to sail to his captaincy in Calais, a stronghold where he was wildly acclaimed whenever he appeared. Edward frowned but forgot them when Elizabeth said she was pregnant and was sure she was carrying a boy.

Her certainty made her less impatient than usual with Bessie and Mary when she visited the nursery and they toddled to her, stroked her gay gowns, showed her their toys. It wasn't their fault they were female, yet she couldn't suppress her resentment. She was aware of Mistress Cobbe's silent disapproval, but when her son was born she would experience a maternal love that would enfold all her children.

She was numb with disappointment at the birth, unable to rouse herself at Edward's cheerful statement that the baby was beautiful and next time they'd have a boy. Did she object to naming the child Cicely after his mother? Elizabeth said heavily, "What you will," and closed her eyes.

Three girls. She was indifferent to everything, even news from Calais that Clarence had
married Isabel. Edward was furious. Treason to
go against the king's express wish. Clarence
thought himself heir to the throne, did he?
Above royal displeasure. He and the earl would
be arrested and thrown in the Tower. She
thought dully that she had always known Warwick was too powerful and too popular, and
while Edward was still raging word came of
risings in the north.

The anticipation of battle made the king's
eyes gleam as he rode out to put down the
rebels. Whether against Warwick's supporters
or Lancastrians who'd leaped to their weapons
at the rift among the Yorkists, it was all the
same. He wrote Elizabeth with careless confidence that he would soon scatter the malcontents and the affair would be over before
she could miss him.

Her spirits lifted a little. Perhaps she was
too pessimistic. No. Warwick and Clarence
landed on the coast and three days later
marched through London, proclaiming their
loyalty to the king. Their only intent was to save
him from his evil advisers. The crowds cheered.
Elizabeth's nostrils flared at the insolence, an
echo from the days of Marguerite. Except now
the "evil advisers" meant the Woodvilles.

No longer numb, she prayed desperately
for victory and went over each new letter
eagerly, a skirmish won, an ambush easily dis-
persed, levies ready to meet Warwick. She
broke the seal of the next dispatch almost
casually, read it, read it again, her lips forming
each syllable. The words made no sense.

Unthinkingly, she handed the document to her mother. Jacquetta's scream echoed through the room, rebounded from the walls until the thin body fell in a motionless heap on the floor. The ladies stumbled over each other in their haste to fetch rose water, perfume, a burning twig for the acrid smell to revive the stricken woman.

Elizabeth stared paralyzed, remembering now every fateful word. Edward was a prisoner and his captors had her father—Earl Rivers, she thought with a pitiful pride—and her brother John beheaded at Chepstow without trial, the old nobility exercising a bloody revenge on the king's new favorites. How would Jacquetta live without her Richard? How would she herself manage? But at least Edward was alive, courteously called a guest, in Warwick's castle in Middleham. Warwick was king.

But only for a brief time. She heard later he was defeated, not by an army, but by Edward's unvarying good humor. The king said chattily he always enjoyed his visits to Middleham as a boy and was indeed pleased to rest from his usual round of duties. He had leisure now to realize that Warwick's struggle to make him king hadn't been properly appreciated. He would amend his ways.

One obstacle unhappily prevented him from taking full pleasure in the earl's hospitality. The uprisings were spreading. It was true his young brother Richard had some-how rounded up troops, but the men stubbornly refused to march unless the king led them. A note of apology crept into Edward's voice as he pointed out that if the rebels weren't stopped, Neville lands would be overrun.

Warwick, unable to fight both rebels and the royal army, released him grudgingly. But when Edward sent from the field for reinforcements, neither the earl nor Clarence obeyed the command. They sailed again for Calais but arrived too late. Edward had sent an order for the city to close the harbor.

The king, laughing, said he needed no help from renegades and crushed the last flickers of rebellion. Then, not laughing, face merciless and light blue eyes hard, the captured enemy was executed on a scale that made even his officers demur. Leaders were expected to be beheaded but not the lesser soldiers. Why feed the hatred of the defeated? Edward looked bleakly at the speakers, and hangmen and headsmen went on quickly and efficiently to dispatch the prisoners.

Edward turned south, clattering through towns and villages, waving at the shouting citizens, and on to London, where the crowds which had cheered Warwick now yelled for him. He shrugged when Elizabeth's anger spilled over against the fickle citizens. They loved the earl and naturally believed in his loyalty until he refused to aid the king against the rebels.

Elizabeth said bitterly, "His loyalty to you. They don't care that he showed none to their queen.

"Sweetheart, you take these matters too seriously. Londoners dote on a spectacle, and Warwick's men with the Bear and Ragged Staff catch the eye."

Her anger rose. He couldn't or wouldn't understand how she and her family had been insulted by Warwick's "evil advisers." Or, she caught her breath, did Edward think she was more at fault than the earl as even her mother had said last week? Jacquetta had said stonily she was returning to Grafton Regis to mourn her dead husband, and then unbelievably turned on Elizabeth. It was madness to have made such great marriages for her sisters and brothers. Warwick had been pushed too far. Had Elizabeth been less ambitious, the old nobility would never had been so vengeful.

Elizabeth gasped, "It was you, madam, who urged me—"

Jacquetta said lifelessly that she had been misunderstood. Now with the queen's permission she would retire to the country.

Elizabeth, choking with frustration, was restrained by her mother's grief from answering that she was right to aid her family, that Edward himself had wished it. But did he regret his generosity now? By driving Warwick to treason, could he believe the price was too high? She must know.

She said softly, "You're right, sire, I'm a woman and take things too much to heart. Though who would not, with John and Father brutally executed? Still it's proof how the peers hate us, so perhaps you'd have my brother Anthony go into retirement as my mother has?"

He exploded. "Do you think I'd cast a friend aside? No! Those arrogant men will see how highly I value my wife and her kinsmen." He grinned. "I have it! Imagine Warwick's face when he hears I'm appointing Anthony to be Lieutenant of Calais and Captain of the King's Armada."

She faltered, "Sire!" and was unable to say more, too astounded at the powerful position and too dizzy with triumph that the port and navy the earl considered his should be given a hated Woodville. When Calais was closed to him, Warwick had gone to the French court, and he probably expected his old positions would soon be his again.

Edward smiled at her open-mouthed astonishment. "My love, my love, you can't know how I've missed you." He swept her into his arms and she melted against him, sweetly pliant.

Two months later her peace was shattered. She ran to Edward, frightened tears on her long lashes. He said soothingly that she was easily upset because she was pregnant again; women were always emotional at such times. The reports she heard meant nothing except that the French king delighted in keeping England in a ferment. The Spider made promises and forgot them.

"But he won't have to promise supplies, at least very little, if he can persuade the queen—persuade Marguerite—and Warwick to bury their enmity and become allies."

He laughed. "My love, even the Spider will find that task too difficult. Warwick might forgive Marguerite, but will she forgive him the stories of bastardy? No."

Her voice was a whisper. "For her son's rights, she may."

He said carelessly, "Remember they'll need my brother's backing. Clarence would never really turn against me. The invasion a few months ago wasn't to oust me, he was just in a choleric humor."

"You have faith in Clarence? He'd gladly

see you dead tomorrow for the crown on his own head the day after."

He said flatly, "No one can believe he'd rebel so that Marguerite could give that crown to her husband or son. You are overanxious because of the coming child or never would you think so meanly of my brother."

His tone warned her that she had gone too far, and he had been generous with Anthony. "Forgive me, sire, I know your three brothers are devoted to each other, but it's true a mother has strange fears. Warwick might put Clarence under house arrest," *or get him drunk, which would be equally effective,* she thought furiously, "and go ahead with his own plans. What if there *is* an invasion?"

He laughed. "I'll suppose the impossible if it'll comfort you. You'd simply retire to Westminster Abbey for sanctuary until the traitors were defeated."

She smiled brilliantly, warmed that he thought instantly of sure protection. She wouldn't be upset further, it might be harmful for the baby which would surely, surely be a boy. Her eyes went appraisingly to gold candlesticks, the tapestries on the walls. They could be packed with her gowns and jewels. If she had to leave, she wouldn't be like Marguerite and escape almost empty-handed.

She was disturbing herself again. The Lancastrians were finished. The queen, Marguerite rather—why should she think of her as the queen tonight?—would never forgive Warwick the vicious stories of whoring, pillage and murder that had destroyed her reputation as a wife and a queen.

PART III
Marguerite D'Anjou

CHAPTER 8

I jerked out a thistle, absently sucked at a
thorn in my finger while with the other hand
I smoothed the soil around the green fronds of
carrots and the sturdier beet leaves. The June
sun was warm on my shoulder, and the breeze
rippling through our vegetable garden tugged
lightly at my hair.

A horn blared in the distance. I wondered
indifferently who would bother to announce his
coming at the ruined castle gates, but I stood up
and brushed the clinging earth from my skirt.
With so few of us at St. Mihiel le Bar, no one
could be idle, though my three ladies were horrified when I stated that since we all ate, we
must all work. They wanted me to spend my
days embroidering delicate silks with my
badge, ignoring the fact we had neither silk nor
the thread to create white marguerites with
golden hearts.

Or, they agreed reluctantly, weaving was acceptable, but not a gardener's duties. Besides I ate so little. I laughed and said my son made up for that, but at their retort that then he should care for the vegetables, I shook my head. He had his studying to prepare him for kingship, constant practice with sword, mace and spear to be ready to wrest that kingship from the Yorkists, and his work in the kitchens.

Our chef, so enormous he had difficulty walking from cutting table to hearth, was always amiable except when a woman invaded his domain. No female was allowed there so Edward was pressed into service after a hunt. Unlike most cooks, ours couldn't bear to disjoint animals, though he happily sliced stag flesh into thin strips to be cooked in a soup with egg yolks and sugar for a venison frumenty, or pulped fresh beef or pork to be strained into a pot with eggs and spices. When he had fresh beef or pork. But he paled at sight of a dead rabbit or deer.

Edward, gay and laughing, was quite willing to wield axe or knife on the day's kill, in spite of my ladies who scolded that it was highly unsuitable. But they didn't have the memories Edward and I shared after our flight from Scotland, with three of my ladies and half a score of gentlemen, to this castle of my father's. The few servants had been unsupervised for years and the place was in disrepair, but, I said practically, we had a roof and four walls until Edward reached manhood and returned to England as heir and Prince of Wales. The work seemed endless, but all were willing to do the meanest duties, shocked only that Edward and I shared the menial tasks. I smiled a little grimly. Remembering the weeks we had been hunted and the gales in the North Seas, I found tending a garden a small chore.

Hoofs clattered in the yard now, and I moved to a bench under a rose bower where in the summer I received occasional visitors. The flowers, sweetly fragrant in the warm air, were a mass of pink blossoms, and the forested slopes beyond the broken walls ranged from the silver-green of poplar to the deeper greens of oak and pines. I pushed back the frayed lace at my wrists. No use to change, I thought wryly, my other dresses were little better. Brocade and ermine would be more fitting, but I was Marguerite. I need make no concession to appear royal. If I were in rags, I would still be princess of Anjou and queen of England.

I looked up as steps approached, stiffened warily when the gardener's son, acting as page, escorted a herald with the three gold lilies of France glittering on his tabard. What could King Louis want of me? My pleas for aid had been answered with empty promises, their sole purpose to annoy the Yorkist usurper in London, Louis failing me as he failed all who trusted him. The herald was kneeling. I nodded for him to rise.

He handed me a document with scarlet ribbons and seal, and said he could explain what was in the letter and answer any questions. He spoke hesitantly. Dear God, well he should have. I heard him out in silence. When the last word was said he waited, his face expectant as if he thought to see tears of joy or hear broken phrases of gratitude.

I should have had him thrown from the tower. To bring me, me such a message. I am a

Christian, but I do not forgive my enemies. In the quite I heard our huntsmen returning. Someone must have told them of the newcomer because within minutes Edward hurried toward me—tall and strong and regal—through he wasn't quite seventeen. Edmund, lean and lithe as always, followed, wiping his damp forehead with his sleeve. Both were in high spirits—the hunt must have been successful—and they were openly curious when they saw the herald's fleur-de-lis.

Edmund said cheerfully, "So distinguished a messenger, he must have important news." His voice was ironic. News from the French court meant talk and more talk and nothing fulfilled.

The herald stuttered, "Y—yes. Her H—Highness is so astonished at my w—wonderful tidings, she's quite unable to speak, Your Grace."

At "Your Grace" I thought mechanically that I should call Edmund "Somerset." The ducal title was his, though the property was attainted after the executions at Hexham at Warwick's command. I looked at the herald, choking back my fury.

"I am well able to speak. Your tidings weren't worth your journey." I turned to Edmund, to Somerset. "Cousin Louis informs me the Earl of Warwick and York's son Clarence have deserted the so-called king of England and are in Paris."

His engaging smile lighted his narrow face. "At least the news is good. I'm more than content to hear the Yorkists are falling out."

"I too, but Louis has lost his reason. He has the arrogance to suggest we come to terms with

Warwick. Warwick! The earl needs our royal standard to rally supporters to fight his battles, the battles of a man who imprisoned the rightful king, beheaded your father and brother." I flung the unopened parchment at the herald's feet. "The answer is no."

He gaped. "Madam, Your—Your Highness, our great king respects you, he does not insist on the alliance. He only orders—re-requests—your presence at Tours to meet with him and the earl who could restore your husband."

I said bleakly, "For how long? Warwick is a man without honor. He turned against his true king, gave the crown to York's son who, I suppose now, wishes to rule for himself so the turncoat seeks another puppet. I gave you my answer."

But we went to Tours. Within the walls the narrow streets were raucous after St. Mihiel. Apprentices and pedlars brawled their wares of pewter pots, snails, eels, roasted chestnuts, hot sausages. From the cook-shops, jutting into the cramped road came the warm smells of baked bread and spiced beef, always ready for passer-bys who hadn't time to eat at an inn. Another day the odors from the steaming food would have made me hungry, but I was too much on edge.

Louis, not accepting my refusal, had sent a larger delegation, and Edmund—Somerset—persuaded me this might be the opportunity we needed, since the courts of Castile, Aragon, Portugal and Austria sent sympathetic answers but little more to my dispatches. I said finally, icily, that I would listen to Warwick but I promised nothing, agreeing to that much because I wasn't sure what was best for my son.

And there was Henry, shut away in the Tower. I
pitied him as I would pity anyone I knew long
ago but who no longer mattered. Except that he
must be proclaimed king again, and Edward his
heir.

Perhaps my strongest reason for agreeing
was to please Somerset. I owed the duke more
than I could ever repay. The usurper, delighted
to have one Beaufort briefly seduced from the
Lancastrian cause, would welcome Edmund
and restore his estates. But Edmund only
laughed when I mentioned what he was sac-
rificing and said it was enough we were
together. I knew his unswerving loyalty. I knew
also that his words were a gallant lie. An exile's
life was against his precipitate nature.

He was speaking cheerfuly now of the
squares and houses as we trotted past, waved at
the Loire flowing below us, a rippling silver
with a hint of blue. I would have a gown of that
exact color, his first gift to me, when we
returned to England. I smiled absently at his
optimism, but my thoughts were on Warwick,
who turned against the Yorkists because the
usurper's wife advanced her family over the
mighty Nevilles.

I remembered Elizabeth Woodville's determination to have her own way, and her striking
beauty, once she'd grown out of her girlhood
plumpness. I wasn't surprised tht the so-called
king was besotted with her. Somerset said,
inelegantly, that beneath the demure manner
was a bitch too calculating ever to be in heat
except when it was profitable. He preferred a
woman with warmth and passion. When I
laughed he stumbled through a tangled explanation that he didn't mean I wasn't

beautiful. I was more—vital and radiant. I laughed again. Radiant didn't necessary mean lovely, and Elizabeth was dazzling.

I forgot her as we reached Plessis les Tours, the king's residence. His favorite chateau, Louis said, when he greeted us in the hall. He was smiling his thin smile as if to distract me from the half-closed crafty eyes, the pointed face, jutting head and stooping shoulders thrusting forward to overwhelm me. He kissed me, his lips as cold as my skin in spite of the summer sun tracing patterns of light and shadow on the floor.

He insisted we refresh ourselves, and I nibbled at fresh bread and strawberries while we waited for Warwick. Louis, however, acted as if we were there only to see him and chatted amiably about the town and the prosperous silk trade he established. I remembered my silk women and said eagerly how they had been trained in a useful skill, stopped abruptly as he nodded. He knew about them, he knew about everything. Except whether I would ally myself with the earl.

I sat back, letting the Spider and Somerset carry the conversation. Louis said at last, "You wish to meet my guests, cousin?"

I shrugged. "It was your desire, not mine, sire. I had no thought of dealing with traitors."

His smiled was forced as he jerked his head at a page to summon the two men. I just glanced at Clarence—thick-waisted, red, indecisive face, sullen mouth, a nobody—and let my eyes rest briefly on Warwick. My fingers closed over the chair arm so tightly that the carved fleur-de-lis cut into my palms as I struggled for self-possession. The sight of him, so little changed from the day he'd gone over to the Yorkists and defeated Henry at the first St. Albans, brought the betraying blood to my cheeks.

I swallowed the wild rage that made my heart pound. And held back too the elation that pulsed through me. I hated him. I could have seen him dead at my feet and been glad. Yet this black-browed man with the high cheekbones and tanned skin had an aura of force, of leashed power. If anyone could storm England in behalf of the true king, this was the man.

At a gesture from Louis he knelt, pleading that he had been misled, and he begged to be allowed to return to his first duty. I stared at him haughtily, not speaking. Not speaking because I could not. I was too shaken with conflicting emotions, one moment fury at his treachery that had made exiles of faithful Lancastrians, the next a soaring hope that my own son would be restored.

My chill silence disconcerted even Louis who said persuasively that the earl repented his great fault which had been a tragic error, that he would support me loyally. And what strength he could bring our cause! The vast Neville family and their levies, his followers in the southeast to unite with the Lancastrians in the west and north. And there were recruits from Calais. Sir John Wenlock had closed the port to Warwick because his officers had made him obey the usurper's orders, but Wenlock and his men would join the earl.

I said with distaste, "Sir John has always been Warwick's man. He was my chamberlain until the earl deserted us."

Warwick's voice was clipped. "I was opposed like many another Englishman to the

Council's mismanagement. After the Chief minister was killed, we treated King Henry with every honor."

I held back a retort. It was undignified to argue with a suppliant at one's feet. But Somerset said crisply, "The king was a prisoner in the Bishop's palace until he was believed so hopelessly ill it was safe to send him to his wife, the queen, who was denied entry to her own capital. Few would care to be so honored."

Warwick sprang up. "And how were York and his son treated at Wakefield?"

Somerset's smile was tight. "As traitors should be."

Louis said softly, persuasively, that it was all in the past. Errors, grave errors on both sides, though the fault lay more heavily on the earl. A warning note must have reminded Warwick that he was the beggar and he knelt again, smoothing out his scowl with an obvious effort.

I had him stay on his knees for three hours until even the infinitely patient Louis appeared ready to concede that Warwick's humiliating appeal was useless. Then I said graciously, "Rise, my lord. Now. What are your plans for invasion?"

Instantly he forgot our enmity and answered with swift competence. "I'll sail in a month, five weeks at the most, land in Devonshire while my supporters ignite a rising in the north to draw the king—the usurper—there. Jasper Tudor—you know him?"

"He was my host at his Welsh castle when you—when I had to escape the Yorkists. Go on."

"Tudor will march to Wales to rouse the patriots, and I'll take the London road."

"The Londoners love the Yorkist traitors."

The earl smiled faintly. "They're also devoted to me. And the merchants want peace to trade. The gates will be open. With you beside your husband, the Lancastrians—"

I stopped him. "Your plans are well thought out. But before my son and I sail, I must be assured of success. When Henry's on the throne again, we will join you."

It was apparent to a two-year-old that I still didn't trust him completely. Before he might flare out, Louis said, "Warwick is risking his life for you, cousin, and will swear his allegiance on the true cross in the cathedral. I will be his surety."

"Such guarantees are excellent." I eyed Louis sardonically. "We have the same blood, I but ape your ways. Have confidence in no one before it's proved beyond doubt."

He chuckled drily; he wasn't used to laughter, and added, "There's another small matter. This is a bold venture with Edward of York solidly on the throne. Without a close tie between you to show the earl is invading in your name, the Lancastrians won't rise." I waited tensely. "The earl suggests your son marry his younger daughter."

Before I could scream "Never!" Clarence started forward and spoke for the first time—growled rather. "You promised that when I married Isabel and after my brother was overthrown, I'd inherit."

I stared at him in amazed contempt, but Louis cut in suavely. "You'll still be heir. If Prince Edward and Anne Neville have no issue. Your Grace is next in line."

Clarence shook himself dazedly as if that single outburst had used up all his resources of intelligence. I turned stonily to Warwick, "You ask too much," and swept out of the room.

I was defeated, not by Louis or Warwick but by my own son. He had met Anne, an exquisite child. He must have her. It was useless to point out he knew so few girls of good family he could compare her to no other.

He said tenderly, "If I'd met a thousand, ten thousand, she'd still be incomparable. But come, see for yourself and then if you can, refuse me."

Reluctantly I let him bring her to me. She was a helpless little thing, but charming. She was also daughter of a turncoat. Edward only laughed at that. I weakened, gave way finally because they were so openly in love. But so heartbreakingly young. At their wedding they looked like happy children on the threshold of an enchanted country, not a Prince and Princess of Wales, attainted and landless.

Warwick, grimly satisfied with the alliance, didn't protest my resolve that he must prepare the way. I felt a wry admiration for him. He never wasted time bemoaning the birth of two girls instead of sons. With his usual competence he used them to ally himself to a prince and a duke.

I found soon I, too, had reason to be pleased. Somerset, precipitate and on fire for action, cut through Clarence's futile attempts to handle the thousand details of recruiting ships and men and became the earl's chief support and was insistent on landing with the first company. He was a Beaufort; I had expected that. My great fear was that my son, so like him and trained for this venture, would demand permission to be in the van too.

A month before, nothing would have held him back. I thought to plead that if he were killed our cause was lost. While all England loved Henry, who had drawn a sword to defend him from his captors? But I didn't have to beg. He agreed that he was needed to gather reinforcements so we could land with a strong party even before I finished speaking.

I saw why immediately. His eyes had gone beyond me to Anne Neville at the oriel window. She was leaning forward, her blue-gray eyes wide and her young face strained in a mute appeal for him not to leave her, not so soon. I choked back a thankful laugh and left them alone, refusing to indulge a flicker of envy because my husband hadn't once looked at me in the same way.

The weeks, the months, whipped by. Warwick was welcomed when he landed, and recruits joined him daily as he marched triumphantly to London where, as he predicted, the citizens cheered him wildly. The usurper, overconfident and unprepared, fled to Burgundy. Our time had come. I hoped for more fighting men, but Lancastrians in England wrote that I wouldn't lack adherents. Many who hadn't followed Warwick would rally to the royal standard.

Louis gave us ships and money, and I had experts examine our equipment. Hand-gonnes and bombards must be the best, competent sailors hired, the Swan badge sewed on tunics, ships caulked, heavy structures built on deck to secure the cannon. I grew frantic as the days passed too swiftly, though it was my own insistence on quality which delayed our departure. That, and the winter storms that lashed the Channel into towering white-crested waves when we reached Harfleur. I waited, then gave the order to embark. There were mutterings which grew louder when, after the wind drove us back to port, I again announced we would sail, and again we were forced to make for the harbor.

At our third failure, some whispered of black magic: We must find and burn the witches or warlocks who cast a spell over our enterprise. Others said the gales were a warning from God to stay on shore. Edward, too busy comforting his seasick bride, scarcely heard the discontent. I ignored the superstitious nonsense and said we would leave when the ships were repaired.

The captains clawed their way out into the raging seas. We were drenched when any of us struggled onto the deck for air, an act which infuriated our captain, who bellowed we would be swept overboard. From his expression I doubted if he would be displeased if he could so easily get rid of the women. I didn't object to his manner. He was making slow headway against the shrieking wind. I asked no more of him.

It was almost three weeks before we landed at Weymouth, battered, ill, our ship listing heavily from the bombards which had broken loose from their fastenings. But we were in England, and one by one the other ships limped into harbor. Anne, her mother and her sister, Isabel, and our attendants were welcomed at Cerne Abbey, but unlike them, I didn't wait to bathe or change my dripping gown. Dispatches must go instantly to Warwick and friends told of our arrival.

Supporters streamed in and cheered at

sight of Edward, a stalwart prince, another warrior king. I thanked them and went on to inspect the cannon being brought ashore and to see that both men and horses were fed and sheltered. But only half my mind was on equipment and troops. No word had come from London. Would Warwick—no, he'd never turn against his daughter who'd one day be queen. I was too impatient. A report would arrive tomorrow, the next day. Edward and Anne, happily planning their bright future, were unaware of my restless pacing, my constant gazing at the road twisting to the north.

I was in the courtyard when I saw a small band approaching, the Golden Portcullis glittering above the men's heads. I ran forward and Somerset put his horse to the gallop, flung himself from his saddle when he reached me. His breath was rasping, and he looked sick with exhaustion.

"I'm overjoyed to see you, but there's no need for such haste as this, my lord."

He rubbed his bloodshot eyes, and said raggedly, "There is need—" and stopped.

One of the men said hoarsely, "It was the mist, Your Highness, the cursed mist." The others repeated the words as if too dazed to say more.

I didn't understand, but my heart was a hammer against my ribs. When they spoke, it was in spurts. Henry was in the Tower again and York's son Edward had regained the throne. He returned from Burgundy with his brother Richard. At first, towns closed the gates against them. People wanted no more ruinous fighting. The city of York, his last hope, also refused entry until Edward swore he was loyal to Henry, and his lies convinced the mayor that he came only for his inheritance of the duchy of York.

With the city as a base, he rallied a few supporters and started south, but openly now under his own banner of the Three Sunnes. Volunteers began to flock to him.

I gasped, "But—Warwick—what was—"

Somerset said thickly, "He didn't desert our cause. He tried to block the Yorkists at Coventry, but somehow they slipped around him. That wouldn't have been fatal except Clarence sent word that his seven thousand men were on their way so Warwick waited to make victory certain." He laughed harshly. "Clarence was on his way, but to his brother Edward, and his men tore off the Swan badge to show the White Rose beneath. His next message was for Warwick to abandon Lancaster."

I shook my head hopelessly. Somerset said more strongly, "Warwick refused. He would fight until he was killed or he conquered. The Earl of Oxford and I joined him near Barnet and deployed our forces across Hadley Green. That night our cannon pounded the Yorkists, and in the morning Oxford drove their left wing back through the town. I—we all—thought the battle was as good as over. Warwick was smiling as he threw his men against their wavering center."

I could imagine that terrible smile, lips drawn back against his teeth, watchful eyes under black brows savage with triumph.

Somerset went on dully, "Then the mist, God! it swirled around us as if it came from a witch's cauldron. One hardly knew who was next to one with that damnable fog a gray hell around us. Only an occasional glimpse of a badge kept us from slaughtering our own comrades, and even that—Christ! The devil brewed that mist for the Yorkists."

He swallowed, said more calmly, "Sometimes it thinned, and we saw the Yorkists scattering before us. But then, then Oxford's men pursued the left wing too far and were plundering the village. Oxford returned with whatever Lancastrians he could round up and found us—I was told later—from the sounds of the fighting. Later! Jesus, we knew it all later. His troops rushed to join us, but in that hellish twilight their badges of the Radiant Star were like Edward's Three Sunnes. My archers turned on them. And even when, God's blood, the fog lifted and Oxford was recognized, yells of 'treason,' 'another Clarence' went insanely from man to man. Between the enemy and us, he was forced from the field."

The dreadful words echoed through me. It was Towton again, I thought despairingly. Towton and the blinding snow. Northampton and the slashing rain. Now Barnet and the treacherous mist. From what inferno could the usurper conjure up weather to fight his battles? I wet my dry lips.

"You—were you wounded?"

"A slight cut when Edward's young brother Richard attacked. He's no Clarence. His first battle, but he's a born soldier. He struck again and again and again. Warwick shouted to stand fast and the day was ours. But how many could hear him? My own ranks faltered."

He paused as if reliving the moment. "We had to retreat. We begged Warwick to withdraw too. He had only his honor guard from Calais, nine hundred men sworn to die for him. We

pleaded they would be massacred, he should
save them, himself, to fight again when your
army arrived, madam. He refused. In the end he
was beaten to the ground and his visor torn
open for some bastard to drive in his sword.
The battle was over, but there was mass
murder. And Edward, once Warwick's friend,
had the body stripped to lie naked at St. Paul's
so all would know the great earl was dead."

I held myself upright to hear everything,
now I slumped to the stones. I was carried to
my bed and revived. Too soon. I wanted to
return to the merciful darkness, but the noise
around me didn't give me that respite. I tried to
check tears of outrage at fate and asked
desolately what was happening.

They said I was not to worry, they were
packing to move to Beaulieu Abbey for
sanctuary until we could make plans. I didn't
understand, why not stay at Cerne? And learned
Beaulieu had special sanctuary privileges not
given to every church. What did sanctuary
matter? We would return to France and wait
for a day that we would be assured of success.

At Beaulieu, in the abbot's room above the
gatehouse, I repeated my resolve to Somerset,
to Edward, to the men who swarmed to us out
of loyalty, or from bitter fury at the killing of
father, brother, son, long after Barnet was won.
Vengeance! I said I wouldn't risk my son's life; I
would wait until he was older.

Somerset, eyes gleaming, retorted the
situation wasn't as bad as I thought. We would
march through the south where volunteers
would pour in, join Jasper Tudor and his Welsh
across the Severn and push north to Lancashire
to make a stand in the Lancastrian west

country.

He wouldn't listen, none of the young nobles would, to my protests that we needed leaders. My son had never been in battle. At that, Edward tossed his green velvet cloak onto a bench—everyone was splendidly and defiantly dressed in the French clothes bought for our entry into London—and took my hands laughingly.

"How much experience had you, madam, before you defeated the Yorkists? And you a woman." He added hastily, "So you naturally weren't trained for warfare."

Somerset said, "As to the prince's safety, we have the very captain for the bodyguard of the Swan. And hour ago Sir John Wenlock rode in. He escaped, God knows how, after Warwick was killed, and made his way here."

My son didn't look overly pleased, rightly suspecting Wenlock would be a nursemaid rather than his own captain, but he was too eager to push on to object. His frown disappeared suddenly. "You said, my lord of Somerset, that Barnet was Richard's first battle and he did well though he's only two or three years older than I. Why wouldn't I equal him? Madam, we can't return to France, we're too close to victory."

He thought himself a man, he looked it in his passionate certainty of success, but he wasn't eighteen and we needed tried officers like my old staff, Edmund's brother and Captain Trollope and Lord Clifford and all the leaders who were slain or beheaded. I said since we had waited years, we could wait a little longer.

Somerset said startled, "Madam, you didn't

hear the news? While she was in Westminster sanctuary, Elizabeth Woodville at last bore a son. If our prince leaves now, England may look to the Yorkist boy as the heir."

I crossed to the narrow window above the gardens where I could see the monks working in the fields. Somerset, all of them, were wrong. I sensed disaster in the golden spring air which should have been alive with hope, but who would accept that as a reason to withdraw?

I said, "Without Warwick—"

Somerset's voice was buoyant. "The enemy also lost men and guns. Our army's fresh. Our artillery, as you well know, is in excellent condition."

They battered at me with their arguments, their confidence. The lords of Exeter and Devon had sent in lists of array they would raise for us, and other peers would join, once assured of our purpose. I turned to sit on a hard chair fashioned like a choir stall, loosened my veil that caught in the carved back, smoothed the wide sleeves of my robe, the nervous gestures giving me a moment to think, to decide.

Perhaps I was too exhausted by the sea voyage, by Warwick's defeat, to see clearly. There had been bleaker times when I hadn't hesitated. Was I trying to be too safe when there was no safety? A storm at sea or the usurper's fleet could be as dangerous as a battle.

I still sensed disaster but I said, "Very well, my lords, we will march in three days."

They swept out of the room, laughing and cheering as if going to a tourney, clattered down the stairs, shouting orders as they burst through the great oak door below. The clamor grew louder as wagons were brought in, supplies loaded and bombards lashed to heavy carts. Now, with the decision made, I was in as much haste as anyone, sending scouts for word of the usurper's movements, planning our route, overseeing provisions.

We left in a gray dawn. The bucklers and steel-tipped lances of the men-at-arms gleamed in the faint light. The heralds' brilliant tabards repeated the standards of the Swan, the Golden Portcullis, Henry's White Antelope, the Fleurs-de-Lis of Anjou. Following the pikemen and the volunteers with broadswords, scythes or bill-hooks were French crossbowmen and English archers with their long bows.

After them our great traveling carriage swung onto the road. Anne leaned out to wave at my son. I was uneasy at her presence. She was far too young for such a bridal journey as this, but she refused to wait in sanctuary with her mother, the Countess of Warwick, and she didn't complain when the whirlicote tilted sharply as the wheels bumped over ruts. Dust from the companies ahead dried our mouths and throats, and behind us the oxen-drawn provision wagons surrounded by boys and camp women pounded up more dust.

Prickers moved constantly along the columns, rounding up stragglers and tightening ranks when new recruits couldn't keep up with the deceptively easy stride of the veterans. I wished fiercely we had only veterans, my straining nerves demanding we hurry, hurry. I was only vaguely aware that we rode through a world blooming with spring, beeches and oaks and pines a vivid green across the low hills, or how on either side wild roses and clumps of gorse were dun-brown from the dirt churned up by mounted men and foot soldiers or that the streams were undrinkable from horse droppings and refuse.

I sat forward tensely, my taut muscles aching. Our sprawling army was moving too slowly. At Bath I wanted to swing directly north, but I was dissuaded. Bristol was Lancastrian and we must have food. The city was generous with provisions and a company with three bombards. I was grateful, yet the need for meat and guns clashed with my frantic urgency to cross the Severn and join Jasper Tudor before the usurper cut us off.

The usurper, where was he? We were ten miles from Bristol when we heard he was poised northeast of us and nearer the river crossing than we were. Scouts said the best stand was on an open plain close to Chipping Sodbury. Wenlock nodded, but Somerset and I doubted if we could take up a strategic position in time, and we were intent on linking up with the Welsh before facing the enemy.

Gloucester, we must reach the bridge at Gloucester. I knew too well the staff's attitude on what they called a woman's tricks, but I said, "Our one chance is to have the Yorkists think we're drawn up on the plain. We'll send a small force, and while they attack, the bulk of our army will continue north."

Wenlock grunted his disapproval. "A company won't hold the enemy long and, madam, their orders are to take no prisoners."

Dear God, did he think I didn't know? That it wasn't agony to me to send men into a mortal trap? I said grimly, "The delay will give us a few hours."

Wenlock fought in the savage French wars

and must realize better than any of us this was war to the hilt, but his stubborn opposition didn't change.

I glanced at Somerset. His smile was tight. "I agree. With you, I mean. I hate to sacrifice even one man, but the feint would swing their army away from the river as well as waste their time in battle maneuvers."

We reached Berkeley Castle, my herald shouting to the guard above the barbican gate that the queen asked to enter her castle, when three begrimed horsemen rode up. They were the only survivors of Sodbury, but the strategem had succeeded. We were a dozen miles ahead of the Yorkists. If we could press on now. . . . The half-formed thought faded at sight of the men, exhausted after a merciless march of twenty-five miles since morning.

They were sprawled on the ground, on their faces a single question, *Would the gates open for us?* The clank of chains brought them upright to watch the drawbridge being lowered across the dark moat. They surged forward yelling until I said sharply that we wouldn't storm across like a mob but as soldiers, and some sort of lines were formed by the sergeants.

The constable who was in charge gave me his room to change my dusty black costume for a green velvet robe and a highconed headdress. I entered the great hall with Edward and Anne, both in cloth of silver, and we were cheered by soldiers and servants who were hastily setting up trestles. The table on the dais was spread with linen; gold plates and a candelabra were brought out, and pitchers of wine and ale. The men who couldn't crowd in were in the courtyard around spits and haunches of venison and beef turning above blazing fires.

For one moment the bright tunics of my officers and the cheerful shouts of the men, of necessity still unwashed, gave the illusion we were a victorious army returning home. The brief dream was shattered by a spate of talk on how soon we would meet the usurper who bought his kingship with perjury, imprisoned the true king and destroyed the country's peace, and I was again tense with the need to hurry, hurry.

The moon rose at midnight. An hour later I gave the orders to march. Grumbling, cursing, the troops staggered along the wagon lane toward Gloucester. The prickers waked men who crawled under bushes to sleep, but they could do nothing about the scores who slipped away into the night. But the desertions didn't cut into the main forces, who plodded on through the wretched hours, dogged, sullen, relieving their feelings with muttered obscenities. They sank into mud from recent rains, dragged at weary horses pulling the bombards, or with shoulders against the carts held the transports from turning over when the road pitched steeply to one side.

At dawn they fell out for their meager breakfasts of black bread and a few swallows of ale. Somerset said cheerfully that they would eat well in Gloucester, but many fell asleep, crusts clenched in their hands, too tired to finish the sparse food. They didn't stir when standards were raised again and trumpets blared. I fought down panic. My stained and muddied troops, their breastplates dulled with dust from the horsemen in the van, were more like refugees fleeing a doomed city than an army.

Sir John Wenlock, a superb captain in a crisis, whipped out orders that brought the men to their feet and into line. The road narrowed, and a ditch on our right was a constant danger to the lumbering wagons. Half-a-dozen bombards crashed down the slope. The horses were cut loose, but the cannon had to be left glinting among the weeds.

We went on, sergeants swearing at the men to keep in formation, wagoners prodding the oxen with steel goads. Only two miles to Gloucester . . . one. Then the city was before us, the encircling walls promising food, rest, protection. I could not look long enough at the gray towers or the stone bridge across the swift current of the Severn, my eyes blinking to hold back tears. Men-at-arms glittered above the west gate, archers lined the walls, and polished cannon gleamed in the embrasures.

My herald rode forward. The May sun was brilliant on his royal tabard and on the standards of England and Anjou. His voice rang out asking passage across the river for the queen. There was silence and he shouted again. Still no answer. Then a knight in authority appeared, a Dun Buck's head on his tabard proclaiming him a Beauchamp, kinsman to the murdered Warwick. He turned to speak to someone beside him, and I waited for the ironbarred gates to open.

Instead an arrow was a black splinter in the air, striking the ground at the herald's feet. There was some mistake. A barbarian wouldn't shoot at an unarmed herald. A second arrow made a furrow in the earth beside the first one.

A roar went up from my army. The bridge was there. We had only to march across the stone span to be in Wales.

Somerset galloped to me, his horse rearing as he dragged on the reins. "We'll storm the walls and hang that gutless traitor from the highest tower." I stopped him as he swung away. Even if we had siege weapons, a thousand battering rams and scaling ladders and moving turrets would be useless. The usurper was in pursuit. We had no time.

Before I could choke out the words, Edward and the young lords came up, grinning with enthusiasm. They would follow Somerset over the walls and burn the treacherous city. But Wenlock spoke aloud my thoughts that we would be caught between Yorkist city and Yorkist army. He added, coldly precise, "There's a ford at Tewkesbury where we can ferry the cannon. It's only eight, nine miles."

Hysteria swelled in my throat. Eight, nine miles for men who'd marched through half the night and all morning? Who were lean with hunger, savage with frustration or numb from despair? My son must have seen I was unstrung because he broke off his wild threats of Beauchamp's fate and said, with an attempt at lightness, that he would tell his gentlemen and lances to prepare to move on as he had a short distance to cover before meeting with Tudor. He tried to smile, then gave it up.

Wenlock frowned as the prince turned away. I said dully, "He knows his escort is under your command, Sir John, but what harm to let him think they're his? We aren't in the field."

"No. There, the company takes orders only

from me."

I wondered how he could be affronted at such a moment, then forgot him in my pride that my son accepted this bitter disappointment so well. He was a boy less than three weeks ago when we heard of Warwick's defeat. In that little time he had become a man. And I must be Captain Margaret again.

We went from company to company, urging the men to form ranks quickly. Tewkesbury and the ford were near. Incredibly, they picked up muddied weapons, tightened boots or re-tied rags about their feet and, stumbling, falling against each other, they dragged themselves north. Flies had been irritating from the first day, but now they came in stinging swarms. Still not far, not too far to Wales. The cry was half a curse, half a prayer.

Not far! A hundred yards was too far for hollow-eyed men who had almost forgotten why they were here. A few miles was half around the world. But a vision of the ford gave the strength to put down one foot and then the other. And an occasional glimpse of the green-gray Severn tumbling between its banks was a reminder that soon we'd be across and find food and rest and friends.

Shouts and a clash of steel sounded from the rear. Somerset, unresting as he rode back and forth along the rutted track, called out that a troop from Gloucester was attacking, and he was sending spearmen and archers to drive them off. The skirmish was short, but some provision wagons were taken and two more cannon driven off the road.

When he returned, we knew without words we wouldn't cross tonight. We were moving too slowly, the Yorkists were closing in and might reach us when only half our army was on the far side of the river. We looked at each other, not daring to speak. If the men guessed we must take our stand at Tewkesbury, perhaps they would scatter in a frenzy of desperation, plunge into the swirling Severn or throw themselves on the mercy of an enemy who knew no mercy.

But once we drew up in a sound defensive position, I knew my troopers—they'd fight for the rightful king, their prince, their queen. They were so fiercely loyal, I could weep at their scant reward. The usurper's supporters were bought with property stolen from faithful Lancastrian adherents. If—when the battle went against them, the Yorkist whelps would be deserted.

At sight of the Cathedral Abbey of Tewkesbury glowing in the rays of the western sun, the companies were awed into silence, then ran toward the town, shouting, laughing, their exhaustion forgotten. They had trusted their captains, now they were as good as in Wales. Where was the ford? They seemed unaware of the broken ground and the brambles concealing dikes and muddy ditches, picking themselves up when they fell, hardly losing a stride as they hurtled forward.

Again Wenlock showed his skill as a captain. And his chill lack of understanding that men driven so hard would not be easily stopped by the division, he flung across the bank with naked swords to bar the way. I mounted a white mare stiffly, muscles aching from the hours in the jolting carriage, and rode up to the horde of raging men, ready to break past the line of steel.

The warm breeze stirred through my hair

as I pushed back my hood. "Soldiers of the king, if any would desert, no one will hold you. My lords and I stay here. The cannon can't be ferried tonight, and I will not let it fall into the hands of murderers to use against us." As my words were repeated by the sergeants, faces were still sullen, but the terrible anger at being balked was slowly fading.

Somerset cantered up and heads swung toward him, the captain-general of the Lancastrians. He called out with cheerful confidence, "Our battle plans are made. The left wing will block the Yorkists coming from Cheltenham, the center under your prince, and Sir John will hold the way to Tewkesbury, and on the right I'll cut off any traitors from Gloucester. You remember Gloucester?"

A low growl answered him, proving his wit in focusing their hatred to dull their fears. Then someone yelled that we couldn't defend ourselves in this terrible corner. Somerset grinned. "The terrain is our security, friend. The Yorkists will have to batter their way through hedges and across dikes, and in the rear we're protected by the Swilgate Brook and the Avon and Severn rivers."

A few cheered when he added that together we would stand here, many only stared out of hollow eyes, but they came back raggedly, shoulders hunched, feet dragging, to dig earthworks and make camp on a ridge above a broad meadow. I ordered the provision wagons to be emptied and the oxen slaughtered. Tonight the men must eat. Tomorrow we'd feast on Yorkists' supplies or we—tomorrow we'd feast on Yorkists' supplies. The bread was hard and the meat stringy, but the men were heartened by the food before they dropped to the ground in a stupor of sleep.

I woke before the trumpets blared at dawn. Anne and our attendants shivered at the ringing notes that blasted through the sweetness of the early spring morning. I was scarcely aware of them as I threw back the tent flap. Somerset, a few feet away turned swiftly.

"The escort is ready, Mar—madam, to take you across the Severn. To Little Malvern Priory."

I was scarcely aware of him either. My eyes were on the archers stumbling through weeds and bushes that hid treacherous ditches, on the gunners positioning bombards and lighting slowburning matches, on the pikemen trailing the heavy hafts of their weapons and on the men-at-arms in freshly polished steel. And there, there on a hillock in the center, just visible in the dawn mist, my son sat proudly on his gray, surrounded by his gentlemen and three hundred picked lancers under Wenlock's command.

I said, "Sir John's an experienced officer, but I hoped that you—"

Somerset shook his head decisively. "The prince is too valuable to our cause and to you, my—madam. Our right is forward and will be attacked first. The risk is a little less where he is."

He smiled wryly, knowing I realized there was no safety on a battlefield. The thought must have recalled the escort to him, and he signalled a dozen men-at-arms to come forward.

Foolishly, like any woman, I wanted to cry out, *Don't be too rash, Edmund, you also are valuable to our cause and to me, to me.* The escort was too near.

I said tartly, "I shall not go to the priory. My ladies may if they wish, but one guard will do. Send the others to the lines where they're needed."

He protested irritably at first and then furiously. I said I'd withdraw to the rear, but I would not leave the field as I had at Towton, waiting for news through endless hours of terror. My son and husband had been my concern then, now Edward was here.

The mist was lifting and we could see the first lines of Yorkists. Minutes later the thunder of their bombards sounded and chainshot thudded into the earth ahead of our ranks. Somerset said, "Christ!" and was gone. The gunners' aim was short, but the next shots struck our earthworks. Howls of pain were drowned by the screaming curses of sergeants to return the fire. Our cannon roared and the balls arched with mortal accuracy to smash into the enemy.

Hands tugged at my sleeves. I looked blankly around at my ladies who were trying to pull me away. I shook them off as more guns pounded, aimed at Somerset's right wing. Our iron balls answered, but he had lost too many bombards on our march and when the Yorkists surged forward in a massive formation, we cut few swatches in their advance. Then both sides held their fire as thousands of Yorkists, under the usurper's Three Sunnes, stormed toward Somerset.

A whimper reminded me of my attendants. Anne Neville stood a little apart, a frightened child pretending to be brave. I mentioned the priory briskly, and relief brought color back to their faces until they discovered I was staying. I said impatiently I'd be on horseback and could escape to the Cathedral Abbey if necessary. Their one care was my son's wife, their future queen. I motioned the guard to escort them quickly.

They slipped from my mind as the Yorkist wave flowed down the slope into the broken land between our forces. Their arrows streaked through the air, our right again bearing the brunt of the attack. My heart slammed against my ribs and then didn't beat at all. Somerset's archers weren't returning the deadly hail. Dear God, they *must* shoot. The Yorkists were at the edge of the meadow with its tumble of ridges and scrub brush, their broadswords and axes and pikes at the ready to roll back our wing against the center. And still no movement from Somerset.

They were almost at the hedges screening the wing. Abruptly Somerset's trumpets shrilled. A cloud of arrows, deadly at this close range, struck the enemy. And Somerset, sword flashing, Golden Portcullis high, his men-at-arms following, was a steel torrent thrusting back the faltering ranks of what had seemed an invincible charge. Yorkist trumpets sounded the retreat, and yells of triumph echoed around me.

The hoarse shouts were heady, but were they too soon? For paralyzed minutes, hours, it was impossible to see the right wing's maneuvers through the trampled thickets. The front lines seemed thinner, as if only a detachment was in pursuit of the enemy, but surely Somerset wouldn't hold back his main force.

I glanced to our center. The prince and the lancers were obviously eager for the command to attack, but Wenlock sat motionless in his saddle, head jutting forward as if he had eyes only for the enemy. I wondered what strategy had been planned as I followed his gaze to the far slope.

A Yorkist officer was galloping back and forth, striking foot soldiers with the flat of his sword in evident rage. Then I saw his standard, the Fanged Boar. Richard, youngest brother of the usurper. He was trying to re-form his men who'd crumpled under Somerset's blows. I caught my breath. In the disorder he left his flank unprotected.

Before I could do more than hope that Somerset realized the situation, trumpets on the right blared, blared again. Somerset had slipped the main body of his troops through the bracken close to the Yorkist line and now hurled them against Richard's exposed flank. The scene was a whirl of steel, men fighting hand to hand, the confusion so great one didn't know whether to cry out in relief or despair when men limped or crawled from the field. The screams of wounded men and horses, the shrilling of trumpets, the ringing of weapon against armor pounded on the ears.

Richard's half-formed ranks broke, were flung into the usurper's companies. Elation swelled my throat, then I stiffened tensely. The usurper swung his center around, the heavy reinforcements a wall of iron, to meet Somerset. I looked again toward Wenlock, froze in shock. I expected to see the center streaming down the slope, but he still sat motionless. Was this part of the strategy? Edward, in his helmet with the three ostrich feathers of the Prince of Wales, pushed his horse to Wenlock, gauntleted hands expressive of his urgent pleading. Other lancers rode up too, their gestures obviously backing my son's demands.

Wenlock only shook his head and lifted an arm to point at the few soldiers Somerset had left in the right wing when he'd made his sortie. An all-important defensive position, but no enemy was advancing against the post. I spurred my mare viciously. But before I crossed half the distance to Sir John to command that he send in the center no matter what tactics had been agreed on, Yorkist spearmen exploded from an ambush behind Somerset.

Hammered in front and rear, our men fell apart. They slid away through brush, leaped into dikes, ran toward the meadow where they were pinned to the earth by sword and pike. Somerset retreated step by step, the small force which hadn't deserted in close formation about him. As they fought their way back, our cannons roared and the pursuers halted. To regroup for another assault.

I reached Wenlock, but it was too late to do anything except watch Somerset gallop toward us, shouting commands to the captains of the archers, the pikemen, the men-at-arms, the gunners. He swung from his saddle, strode to Sir John, the deadly purpose in every movement silencing us. His breastplate was dented, blood streamed from his shoulder between gorget and pauldron, and his belt axe was scarlet. His accusing face didn't need the words he panted hoarsely.

"Traitor! You sat here while two thousand

men died. How much did York pay?"

Wenlock dismounted and said coldly, "My orders were to keep the prince safe. He has not been touched."

He reeled and fell under the blow of Edmund's gauntlet. "Safe? While you let his army be destroyed?" He tore off Sir John's helmet. There were cries. "Kill!" "Kill the traitor!" Somerset's axe flashed twice. He glanced at the slain man, then at Edward. "Send a platoon if you must, but the queen must go to the priory."

I thought with anguish that I couldn't leave my ragged faithful army, but I went. The howling Yorkists were massing for another attack, and Somerset was drawing in our companies for a tight defense. If I refused to leave, he would set aside too many men to make a protective ring of steel about me.

Three hours later I was in the prior's solar, staring blindly at the window that opened onto a sweetly-fragrant garden of marigold and daffodils surrounded by a clipped hedge of yew. I think my ladies were with me, I'm not sure. Anne was, her cold hand creeping into mine to share our dread for the prince.

No word from the field. Even known disaster was easier to bear than this terrifying silence, when a flicker of hope was quenched by remembered tears after Northampton, Towton, Barnet. I must not think of defeat. Somerset had been given time to draw up the army in battle order. God had granted him that, our cause was just, and we had suffered enough to placate the angriest deity. This moment the Yorkists were being broken as wave after wave crashed uselessly against our defense.

Hoofs flailed the stone yard outside, then

someone pounded at the door below. I was on my feet, a hand at my throat as I waited in agony. A man entered the room, face streaked with perspiration that made rivulets through the dirt on his skin. His clothes were torn, and he had lost a boot, but he had Edward's Swan on his sleeve. I tried to speak . . . couldn't.

He swallowed, swallowed again. "We lost, Your Highness. God, God, it was a shambles, murder. The Duke of Somerset and his officers had to fly to the Abbey for sanctuary."

More horses were galloping down the road, slithered to a stop, and heavy boots were loud on the stairs. I screamed above the noise, "What of the prince, of my son?"

"I do not know. His lancers were making for the Avon—"

A harsh voice spoke from the open door. "I can tell you of your son." I turned slowly. A big officer filled the door, four retainers looming behind him. He was smiling. Hope flared.

"He's in sanctuary too?"

The smile widened, showing a broken tooth. I thought him friendly, his expression plainly showing his pleasure in the message he brought. I wasn't sure now. The black brows meeting above his nose were faintly familiar, and the scar on his temple. Then I recognized him. It took all my endurance, every lesson in control I had learned, not to shriek out his name. His news would be evil.

I drew myself up, somehow managed to say politely, "Lord Stanley, aren't you? You have word of Prince Edward?"

Stanley, a Yorkist lackey, had once served us. Whatever price they paid, it was too high. A born renegade, a few pieces of gold would have bought him.

"Prince Edward?" He pretended surprise. "The only Prince Edward I know is a baby with his mother Queen Elizabeth Woodville at Windsor." He waited, gloating. I stared at him haughtily because I couldn't trust my voice to rephrase my question. He gave in ill-temperedly.

"Perhaps you speak of Edward the bastard? No, your son's not in sanctuary. Sanctuary! Our good King Edward had the traitors hauled out of church. They fought, preferring to die by the sword today than the headman's axe tomorrow, but they'll be given the rebel's death they earned."

He paused again, hoping to force me, Marguerite of Anjou, to plead with him to go on. I might have if I had been able to push the words past my throat clogged with horror at the thought of Somerset, proud and faithful and precipitate and loving, on the scaffold. A steel claw fastened around my heart, slashed into my ribs, and splinters of ice slowed my pulsing blood.

I closed my eyes, then opened them at the sound of a blow, to see a new horror. One of the retainers had stabbed my foot soldier. Scarlet seeped through the torn tunic and trickled to the floor. Stanley smiled.

"So die all traitors. As did your son."

I almost answered his smile, the remark was so absurd. He said Edward wasn't in sanctuary so my son had escaped. When the murdering Yorkists returned to their homes or to London or to the hell where they belonged, Edward would come to me and we would—

I clung to the bright hope even as another

retainer said, "Our King Edward don't like no one calling your son a prince. He hit the bastard, the king did, when that boy declared he was in England to claim his rightful inheritance. Him a prince! Well, he don't need a kingdom now. The officers cut him down, but the king, he's soft, said the bastard could be buried in the Abbey."

Edward would come to me and we would. . . . My hands closed tightly to hold the last shreds of my fantasy until I was strong enough to bear the truth.

Stanley frowned, looking annoyed that he hadn't spoken those words, each one a blow on my heart.

He said swiftly before he could again be cheated of his pleasure, "You're to come with me. A carriage is in the courtyard." Saliva slid from the corner of his mouth. "To the Tower. Her, too." He jerked his head at Anne who appeared as if—mercifully—she'd been bludgeoned into unconsciousness. "London, not the Tower for her. She is His Grace of Clarence's sister-in-law, she'll be all right, but they have a cell waiting for you." He wiped his wet lips with his sleeve.

Some small part of me that was still alive wondered he thought anything he said could possibly touch me now that I was almost accepting the death of my son. Incredibly my voice was steady when I spoke, and no useless tears pricked at my eyes. They would come when the ice within me melted.

"When you are ready, my lord—your men will need food before riding farther—you may escort your queen to the carriage."

He started to bow, stopped himself and

stamped out of the room. What did it matter where I went, royal apartments or cell? Edward dead. Tomorrow Edmund, the last Duke of Somerset. Had the usurper a twinge of guilt that he had bloodily violated sanctuary, though the Lancastrian had allowed his wife to stay peacefully in the church's protection for her son's birth? No. He would smile as Stanley smiled while he planned his next murder. Of Henry, my husband, true and lawful king.

PART IV
Elizabeth Woodville

CHAPTER 9

She must see the king. At once. A mist of
tears blurred her sight. She blinked them
back as her ladies fastened a sapphire necklace
about her throat, the jewels matching her blue
gown and intensifying the blue of her eyes,
while they murmured flatteringly, "Beautiful,
madam!" "Never so lovely!" Elizabeth
supposed she did look well as always when
three months pregnant, but their compliments
slid off her.

They probably thought she was upset over
Mistress Shore. As if that Shore creature were
important now. Or her own beauty, either. But
she must be calm. How could one? The tale
might be true. No, no, he wouldn't have done
that to her—not Edward. She whispered the
reassuring words over and over to herself as
she left her bedchamber and walked slowly

down the staircase to her husband's audience room.

It was empty, except for Lord Hastings who rose at her entrance and crossed negligently to block the closed door in the opposite wall. Another of Edward's devoted friends who despised the Woodvilles. She looked at him with hatred, knowing why he was on the threshold like a watch-dog. Dog was the right name for this portly, red-faced man with a paunch that his expensive tailor couldn't quite conceal. He believed he held a special position at court because he shared the king's exile and later shared his women with Edward, except for this last whore whom he had to surrender gracefully.

A girl's laugh sounded from the inner room. The sight of Hastings had prepared her for that; still she tensed with frustration that Edward wasn't alone. But she had to see him. She went past Hastings, ignoring his quickly arrested gesture to stop her.

Was it only last year that she had been wildly happy when Edward had taken his family from sanctuary down the Thames to Baynard's Castle? The sun was brilliant on the gray waves, and she was heady with the feel of freedom and with his pleasure in his heir, little Ned. Laughter erased the memory of the lonely winter months, the river fog that crept into the Abbey and the chill drafts that brought on constant colds. Helped her forget how the shivering little girls, restless and bored with the monotonous life, made her frantic with their whimpering to go home.

In her relief at their returning, she had been amused at Edward's wry expression when he noticed the roughly patched sanctuary wall which had been broken open to let in the carts of jewelry, plate, tapestries, inlaid tables; and in his admiring remark that she could always take care of herself. Now she thought angrily that she had been forced to take care of herself since he was so carelessly unprepared for Warwick's invasion. Nor had he shown any apologetic understanding of her suffering through those dreary days.

He only smiled at her, at his daughters, at Ned, at his unpleasant brothers, at the cheering crowds, at his mother. Though he hadn't listened to Proud Cis's sedate welcome that first night, refusing good-humoredly to give thanks in the chapel, so eager was he to bed with his wife. He turned to Elizabeth, who was pleased to see that he was lean and youthful again and his face had lost the puffiness of the self-indulgent years of his kingship. He was the young Edward once more, scarcely waiting to woo her before he took her vigorously, impatiently, quenching his need of her again and again. She glowed at his delight in her, at his generous new grants to her family. She hadn't lost her influence. Let the old nobility sneer.

They did soon enough. Her hand tightened furiously on the latch now. They hadn't bothered to hide their smirks when Edward's doting smiles on his family went beyond them to rest on a girl, pretty, but so common that one expected her to be polishing the iron fire dogs or scrubbing the kitchen stoves. He asked her name and Hastings knew, of course. Why wouldn't he?

"Mistress Jane Shore, sire. Husband's a goldsmith, a brute. I rescued her."

Edward had seemed to forget Jane until at the festivities for the Lord Mayor she came brazenly into the great hall on Hasting's arm and even glided and curtseyed through the rondeau. She moved awkwardly; the girl had no breeding or training, but Elizabeth noted that men's eyes followed the trollop, Edward's too. Elizabeth watched angrily, but later said to him coolly that Hastings' mistress was rather attractive, though he'd been unkind to bring her, as she must feel clumsy and out of place.

Edward's lips had twitched, and the girl returned often after that and didn't always go home with Hastings. Never before had Edward had a woman of the streets openly in the palace, and it was all Elizabeth could do to pretend blindness. Her compliant attitude brought him back as she expected it would, slightly shamefaced, but he didn't dismiss the strumpet. What did that matter now? She pushed on the latch, swung the door wide.

Edward stood in the garish afternoon light, one arm negligently around Jane's shoulders. The girl's brown hair was loose, and a mass of curls was untidily pushed back from the laughing face. Elizabeth knew only too well why it was so tangled, but the creature didn't shrink at her entrance, nor did Edward seem embarrassed.

"Ah, Elizabeth! Mistress Shore brings me all the amusing gossip. Did you hear about the French ambassador at the Cardinal's Hat—"

She didn't listen. She thought her presence would make the girl hurry away, realized the hope was futile. Edward's lips had stopped moving. She had to say something or he'd believe she'd come to spy on him.

"I—I was at the Tower yesterday, sire, and saw the qu— the Princess Marguerite. She looks wretched, and her room is so bare and cold."

Edward shrugged. "The war was expensive. When the French Spider pays her ransom, she'll be released."

Jane said warmly, "Is the poor princess still in prison? I thought," she rounded on Edward, "You'd sent her back to France. The poor, poor thing."

Another time Elizabeth would have frozen the girl with an icy stare. Now she thought tiredly, *What is it to you?* and said, "I wondered if the princess could have more comfortable quarters, sire? The dowager Duchess of Suffolk has offered to care for her while she's in England. The duchess was Marguerite's chief lady—or did you know?—when the princess came for her wedding." She spoke heavily. She was sorry for the former queen, but now everything except the one question she must ask Edward privately seemed too much trouble.

He was unconcerned. "My dear Elizabeth, don't waste pity on the enemy. Royalty can't afford to be soft." She supposed without interest he was remembering the opportune death of Henry VI in the Tower the very night Marguerite was imprisoned.

She was roused from her indifference by Jane's voice. Mistress Shore was said to ask favors for others but not for herself. There was no need. Her robe was velvet, and her fingers were heavy with rings; gaudery forbidden by law and unsuitable for one of her station. Jane, oblivious of such niceties, clapped those ringed hangs and said with unbelievable obtuseness, "My dear liege, do grant the queen's request."

Elizabeth went rigid at the insolence. "We can speak of this another time, sire. I must visit Ned who's having trouble teething." The reminder she was his wife in the eyes of the world and had given him an heir, as no mistress could, made her smile dazzling.

His voice was thick. "Do what you will about Marguerite, sweetheart. I don't feel kindly toward the bitch, but I can't deny a beautiful woman." His tone said, as you will not deny me tonight. She sighed with relief, started to turn away, paused as his glance went beyond her and he grunted, "Oh God, no!"

Edward's two brothers were entering the room. Clarence was ahead, a swaggering figure in peacock blue and with slippers that had points so long they were fastened to his calves with jeweled chains. She hated and feared the drunken smirk as he looked from her to Jane and back again and had only the small satisfaction that his fine clothes only emphasized his gross figure and the broken wood veins in his face, making him appear twice his twenty-three years.

The smirk changed to a scowl. He jerked a thumb at Richard, lean and wiry in his austere black. "I came to shee justice—" He broke off. "Thish is a family mtter. Get that whore out of here!"

His wide gesture could have indicated either Jane or herself, Elizabeth noted, her blood pulsing. She saw Edward was furious too, but as usual he was easily placated by a brother. A slurred apology and Jane walked gracefully out, half-smiling as Richard's polite bow didn't hide his distaste for her.

Elizabeth wished she could follow the girl,

but leaving would make her of no more account than Jane. She stayed grimly, bracing herself for another of the brothers' interminable quarrels. Edward said sharply, "Justice? Didn't I forgive your treason?"

"What else could you do? You needed my seven thoushand men at Barnet. So you alsho—also—" Clarence gulped, breathed deeply and went on more distinctly, "promised my wife would inherit her father's property."

Richard stepped forward, "Half. Isabel and Anne are joint heiresses of Warwick."

"Anne Neville's my ward." He glared at Richard. "You want to rob me by marrying that milk-faced child. I won't have it."

Edward said ironically, "Hardly a child. She was wife for some months to Marguerite's bastard. As you should remember. You must have attended the wedding with Warwick." He added impatiently, "I'm tired of this constant wrangling."

Richard said eagerly, "Then give your consent, sire. I love Anne and have since we were children together at Middleham."

Clarence guffawed. "But does she love you?" He stared at Richard's raised left shoulder.

"Yes, and will marry me with the King's permission."

Edward looked unhappily from one to the other. Elizbeth knew why he hesitated. He wanted to please the loyal brother, but he might renew the war with France and then must have the support of that drunken sot Clarence. She didn't care whether or not Richard ever married, but he was at least coldly polite to her. If ever the dreadful question stifling her were answered, as she hoped passionately, she would speak to him. Though why did he wait for the royal consent? Even Clarence hadn't been so weak and was pardoned for acting against the king's wishes.

Edward glanced at her, smiled faintly. "I married for love; Clarence too. Or should I say he chose his own wife? Why shouldn't Richard?"

The young man's stumbling words of gratitude were cut across by Clarence's bellow. "God's blood, it's for me to say who weds my ward—"

He was interrupted by Edward's roar. Did Clarence think himself greater than his king?

Clarence choked, then mumbled abruptly he was sorry and went out, steps slightly uneven. Elizabeth thought, *Perhaps now?* but Edward began to ask about Richard's administration in the north. She thought mechanically as she left that it was unfitting for a twenty-year-old to be Constable of England and Warden of the Marches when her own brother Anthony in his thirties was far more experienced—

She caught herself up. How could she think of such matters now? She went out to the gardens where the nurses brought their charges every afternoon. She was hardly aware of the profusion of yellow and pink and white flowers within severely clipped borders, and little more aware of the children except to note Ned was well today. He was toddling from bench to bush, his small face sober. He was a serious infant as if he knew one day he would have heavy responsibilities.

Bessie, more like their father, was playing

tag with her younger sisters, fair hair streaming out, laughing and shouting too loudly for a princess almost seven. She stumbled, caught her foot in her skirt, tearing the cloth, and laughed at that too. Another day Elizabeth would have shown disapproval, but she stopped only to ask Ned's nurse about his health, was reassured that all the children were recovered from the miserable winter in sanctuary, and went up to her audience chamber.

Her chamberlain bustled forward with a list of guests to be invited to a banquet. She had forgotten the festivities and agreed absently with his selection. She was equally inattentive to her Master of the Horse who wanted to purchase two jennets just arrived from Spain and told the bailiff from her Palace of Shene to return tomorrow. There were a dozen citizens, too, with God knew how many petitions. She couldn't meet them. Edward might arrive early to have supper with her.

He didn't join her at table, and she learned from discreet questions that he had ridden out, no one knew where. Except Hastings, she thought with anger first and then depression. She misread Edward's expression, the lustful look hadn't been for her. But it had. She sat up eagerly, then stared blankly as he stormed across the room, face dark. She almost wept that of all nights this was the one when he lost his usual good humor.

She said timidly, "My love, sire, have I—I offended you?" She breathed in relief when he shook his head.

"Not you, my sweet." He bent to kiss her. "Clarence, who else? You know he has sworn for months that Richard won't have Anne. Well, he's trying to keep his word, a point that seldom bothers him. I asked Richard about border raids but—" he grinned, "I should have known better. With my permission to marry, he could do nothing but babble about Anne so I said for the love of God go see her and then I might get some sensible answers."

She was puzzled. "What has that to do with Clarence?"

"He made the girl disappear, damn him. Perhaps today, perhaps a week ago. Richard sent me a frantic message and I went to Clarence's home. I didn't believe him when he said that Anne was gone, but her sister was so distraught I had to believe her. Ordinarily Richard is almost too restrained, but he was outroaring Clarence and ready to murder him."

Elizabeth thought, *Blessed Virgin, I wish he had!* She tried to repent the guilty wish, but the words only dropped deeper into her mind.

"Richard will be useless until he finds the girl, though Christ knows where he'll search for her. He thinks she has been hidden though Clarence swears she ran away." His smile flashed. "Well, if *you* disappeared, sweetheart, I wouldn't rest, either."

She was pleased but drew back as he jerked off his surcoat and tunic and slid in beside her. She had planned a dozen ways of how to put the impossible question, and could remember none. Her body was stiff and her lips cold under his ardent mouth. He asked carelessly if she were worried, became more concerned when she didn't answer, and finally coaxed her to confide in him.

She blurted, "Sire, am I your wife?" He stared, as unable to speak now as she had been.

She went on haltingly, "I—I heard—Anthony said once when Clarence was drinking, your brother hinted about a story of Bishop Stillington's. The bishop said you were—were precontracted to another woman. That would mean that we—we aren't married." Her voice was anguished. "Sire, is that true?"

Edward's expression was bewildered. He rubbed his jaw with his forefinger, said in embarrassment, "I might have made some extravagant promises—young men do—but what lady was my worthless brother talking about?" He ran a big hand through his hair. "Not Frances or Lucy or one of those Flemish girls, they wouldn't expect—" He broke off. "Oh, it must be the Talbot girl, what's her name? Eleanor. Eleanor Butler, rather. She came with some request about revenues, I think, from her late husband's estate. She was a widow, no innocent virgin. She knew any promise I gave was only to quiet her conscience. I didn't hear from her again after the baby died."

"You—you had a child by her?"

His brows rose in surprise. "You knew before we married that I've sired several children, possibly more than I realize." His arm slid around her shoulders. "Forget that Butler woman, sweet. She retired to a convent, to atone for her sins, I suppose. If she thought us legally bound, what sin had she committed?"

Elizabeth stuttered, "But—but Clarence—"

He stopped her protest with a swift kiss. "I'll speak to Clarence. As for Eleanor, if she believed herself my wife, her delicate conscience would never allow me to live in adultery."

She sighed happily, said she was sorry, she should have had faith, but she had to learn the truth and from him. Heady with relief after the slow agonized hours, she reached for him. His laugh rang out as he stroked her silken skin, and buried his face in the flow of gilt hair, muttering she was sweet, desirable, the loveliest woman in the kingdom, his bright jewel. His words set at rest a nagging doubt that had been lost in her greater fear. Was Edward, five years younger than she, tiring of her, thinking her too old, comparing her with Jane's youth?

She smiled. Let him have his mistress when there were moments like this between them. Perhaps the child she was carrying would be another boy, a support to his older brother. She, she alone, could give the king legitimate sons, not only in the eyes of the world as she thought desperately today, but in her own.

She whispered, "My love, my love," as he pressed down on her, leashing his eagerness, trying to take her gently. Her smile deepened. She said there was no need for such care yet, and he let his desire overwhelm his caution for the unborn baby.

He lay quietly beside her then. "You are my jewel, sweetheart, and I can talk to you as I can't to others. This French war—"

She shivered. "Must there be more battles? I could not bear it if you should be killed."

"I won't be. That isn't braggart's talk, sweet." He grinned. "I need money, but if I asked for a tax to fill my privy purse, there'd be howls across the country that I'm a spendthrift, that we live extravagantly. People forget I began my rule with an empty treasury. Still, borrowing had a pleasant side. I was so far in debt with the merchants that London had to support the Yorkists if they hoped ever to be paid."

She said loyally, "The Londoners love you."

"Perhaps, but they aren't anxious to give me more credit. So I'll levy a tax that our subjects will be eager—well, at least willing—to pay. What do they always want? War with France, the ancient enemy."

"But you said—said you'd be safe."

"One can declare war and then—not fight it. The Spider has enough trouble with Burgundy on one side, Brittany on another, and too-powerful nobles at home. After we invade, he and I can reach a very pleasant agreement without any blood spilling."

She gnawed at her lower lip worriedly. Wouldn't a make-believe war be dangerously unpopular? She remembered Marguerite's enemies, hostile before they saw her because her marriage meant truce with France. Then she relaxed, her head against Edward's naked chest. He knew how to handle malcontents. Her thoughts slid to the coming birth, which would make the succession doubly secure if the child were a boy.

It was a girl, born prematurely and too fragile to live. She wept, but the king was more devastated than she. She was puzzled. She would have understood if the infant had been a son, but they already had three daughters. His sorrow was dispelled soon when he rode through the shires to urge citizens to offer benevolences on top of the war tax for his glorious invasion to reconquer provinces that their ancestors had won.

He returned to Windsor triumphantly where the mood was gay. Richard had found his Anne, and they were to be married at once. How he had searched her out Richard didn't say, and Anne was too worn to be questioned. He hovered over her possessively. Elizabeth was surprised at his obvious delight in the girl. Anne was sweet-natured and soft-spoken, traits one wouldn't expect in the Earl of Warwick's daughter, but perhaps appealing to Richard, whose home in the north probably resembled a barracks.

Anne would be a restful wife to come home to after the constant fighting among the northern lords and the Scots. But her beauty would never draw him. She was palely pretty, her only outstanding features her heavy hair and wide gray eyes. Elizabeth wondered as she watched Richard wrap a fur cape around the frail shoulders if he would be as devoted if Anne weren't one of the wealthiest heiresses in the kingdom.

Well, he was happy and Edward, who was pleased for him, even had Jane Shore remain in London since Richard disapproved of a king's mistress being welcomed at court. An unusual attitude for a Plantagenet, but Richard, sickly as a child, had been dominated by his mother, Proud Cis. He overcame his physical weakness, Edward had said, by working interminable hours with sword and shield and lance, forcing himself to be as skilled a fighter as his brother so effortlessly was.

Elizabeth had agreed his persistence was admirable and didn't add she was tired of the king's pride in his prudish young brother who had so little to distinguish him. Though he wasn't always prudish. He had a daughter and son of unknown mother or mothers whom he was bringing up in his own household. But once married, she doubted if he would ever stray from his Anne.

She shrugged aside the dull bridal couple when musicians streamed into the hall, and to the strumming of lute and viol Edward led out Anne for a sedate measure. Elizabeth shook her head when Richard came up. She was being careful this time, sure she would have a son who mustn't repeat the tragedy of being born too early.

With the wedding and the whirl around Edward as he prepared for the invasion, the months slipped away. She retired to Shene, and when the midwife put the squawling red-faced baby in her arms, she felt a passionate gratitude. A second son. She scarcely hesitated when Edward suggested the baby be named after Richard, though her younger boy by John Grey was also a Richard.

She nodded, kissed the soft down on the small head and murmured, "Dickon, my little Dickon."

She wasn't so easily reconciled to the king's next words. Ned was to be sent to Ludlow Castle so the Welsh could know and love their Prince of Wales. She protested that Ned was scarcely three, she couldn't part with him. Edward was firm. "He will be a king, he must have his own household. Ludlow is beautiful, I spent years there until," he grimaced, "the Lancastrians defeated Father and we went into exile. Don't cry, love, there's no Lancastrian danger to fear for Ned and we'll see him often."

She refused to be comforted until he said,

"You haven't asked who's to accompany the prince. What do you think of an uncle as his guardian?"

She gasped horrified, "Clarence? *Clarence?*" She knew it wouldn't be Richard. He had hurried north with his bride who showed some vitality at being again in her old home of Middleham Castle and not too far from her sister Isabel who was occasionally at Warwick Castle, Clarence's part of the inheritance which the brothers still wrangled over.

Edward laughed at her tone, sobered immediately. "Would I trust our heir to a drunkard who would snatch the crown from me? His latest story is that he's rightful king since I'm a bastard, the son of some French archer." He shrugged. "No matter. Ned has other uncles. What of Anthony, Lord Rivers?"

Her glowing face answered him. Anthony would train Ned well and be a strong Woodville influence. She said worriedly, "I can bear the separation then, but he's still having trouble with his teeth and should have our best physician."

Edward agreed and galloped back to London. From the window Elizabeth could see his tall heavy form followed by his escort riding down the leafy path until they disappeared with a clatter of steel and leather. She was worried about him, too. Indulgence in wine and food were again thickening his figure, and he was working too hard. Not only for the invasion but for laws to suppress disorder, and to improve his own commercial ventures and the country's finances.

Elizabeth nodded at his patient explanations, but need he drive himself so hard that he

felt justified in any excesses? Even his robust
health could fail. With no serious contender for
the throne, he could go to Bath for the waters
with a physician to restrict his inordinate
wining and gluttonous dinners.

He smiled at her strictures and pointed out
that a rival could always be found. But if the
people had confidence in his efforts for them,
they wouldn't look to Clarence. Or to that dull
young man, Henry Tudor, who was in Brittany
with his uncle Jasper, claiming he was king of
England. Elizabeth sighed, then smiled at the
wriggling bundle in her arms before handing
the child to a wet nurse.

She saw little of Edward except for a short
visit to his huge encampment on the coast when
the army was embarking. The noise was incredible, the creaking of ships swaying in the
light breeze, the beating of drums, hounds
baying, the clatter of hoofs as horses with
gilded reins were led past to where vissiers
were swung around, stern into the shore, to
take aboard war stallions, baggage horses, then
sheep and squealing pigs. Later, provisions of
wheat, bacon, salted beef, oats, tallow for
candles, kettles and pans were carried to the
dock, and after that household gear, weapons
and armor.

Elizabeth said wonderingly, "I understand
now why the plans took so long but oh, my love,
it's so real."

This vast array of men boarding ships at the
quay or being rowed out to the cogs, couldn't
possibly be for a make-believe campaign. She
pretended to accept Edward's reassurances,
but her fears wakened her at night after he left.
Then a messenger arrived with a document, the

⸗a wax stamped with Edward's ring. She was afraid to open it even while her fingers tore at the gold and scarlet ribbons.

Her eyes skimmed over the page, then returned to the beginning to read the letter slowly, tasting each word. There had been no battle. Louis had seen that a fresh, well-provisioned army marching toward the Somme could undo his years of trying to unite his restless lords. He agreed quickly to meet with Edward at Picquigny near Amiens where a bridge was thrown across the Somme so the kings could step from opposite banks to walk to the center.

Edward was amused that the Spider had a barricade built in the middle, with slits to speak through yet too small for the thrust of dagger or sword. But the agreements that were reached! Only a madman would object to Louis's excessive precautions. The English were offered fifty thousand crowns for an immediate withdrawal, another fifty every year to Edward for permanent peace, gold for the English lords, a ransom for Marguerite and terms to improve trade between the two countries. As a final victory in the bloodless war, their daughter Bessie was to be betrothed to the Dauphin so she would one day be queen of France.

Elizabeth's smile was brilliant. Edward, the whole army, home soon, their oldest daughter the Dauphiness, and mountainous debts to goldsmiths, drapers, vintners, victuallers could begin to be paid. She wondered that Edward had a thought for two minor disappointments. Louis refused to persuade the Duke of Brittany to release Henry Tudor to English custody, and Richard would not touch a single French coin.

Richard didn't quite say that the treaty was dishonorable, but it was implicit in his scorn for Clarence, Hastings, all the lords who eagerly accepted bribes to keep weapons sheathed. Richard said angrily that the great army had been raised to regain lost provinces, now the troops were to sail home as if they were lowborn tradesmen who'd bargained successfully over the price of wool and mutton.

She shrugged Richard's tiresome attitude aside and plunged into preparations for Edward's return, ordering his favorite dishes of roast swan, wild boar, capons, breast of doves, and venison. There were grumblings, of course, by some hot-heads over the tame end of a glorious campaign—where were their taxes which had paid for it—but Edward laughingly ignored the discontent when he came back. Hunting, hawking, banqueting, dancing filled the days and nights until he came to her one evening, raging.

Elizabeth knew that Clarence's wife had died in childbirth? She stared. He went on before she could frame a question. His sister Margaret, Duchess of Burgundy, had a stepdaughter who was sole heiress to the vast Burgundian holdings, and Margaret wanted her favorite brother Clarence to marry the girl. Clarence was delighted at the suggestion though he, Edward the king, naturally forbade the alliance.

Clarence sneered at the command and had to be watched to make sure he didn't slip across the Channel. In the watching, disagreeable facts had come out. Clarence was again spreading his vicious stories of Edward's bastardy and telling his followers to be ready to take up arms.

Elizabeth whispered, "Does he talk too of our marriage?" At a reluctant nod she blazed, "Then fetch this Lady Eleanor from her convent to deny the vile lie."

"I wish I could, sweetheart; but I inquired some time ago. She's dead, so Clarence can speak freely." He added that among Clarence's misdemeanors was taking the royal law into his own hands by executing two servants and—

Her voice cut across his. "Misdemeanors! Clarence would have been proclaimed traitor long since if he weren't one of your precious brothers."

His mouth fell open that she dared interrupt him and with such words. "You forget yourself, madam. I am your king."

"And my husband. Shall I be silent while you endanger yourself, all of us, to shield an ingrate and rebel?" Her face was stony as he repeated his usual excuses of exile, that he had lost one brother as well as his father at Wakefield, that his mother would be heartbroken if Clarence were disgraced.

"Clarence would risk much to marry the heiress," her voice was flint, there was no security while Clarence lived, "and have the Burgundian army at his back."

As she hoped Edward's anger was renewed. "He'll be tried by his peers at Westminster."

She suppressed a satisfied smile. Even the faction who, like Clarence, despised the Woodvilles, couldn't overlook the evidence against a rebel who had been forgiven, and now, carelessly confident, was plotting high treason again.

The trial was brief and the sentence was death. Clarence was stunned when the men he thought were his friends spoke up weakly for him, if at all. He recovered quickly, saying he was content to wait in the Tower until his brother came to his senses and released him. The king would never sign the execution warrant.

Elizabeth wondered uneasily if he were right. Richard hurried from the north to champion the traitor though he could say nothing after Edward showed him a report that the Spider promised to support Clarence's revolt. Proud Cis was more difficult. Clarence was the victim of a Woodville conspiracy to tempt Edward to commit that primal sin of brother murdering brother. But she, too, was silence by the list of offenses.

Anthony, escorting Ned for a short court visit, sympathized with the king, who at one moment vowed that he would put his seal on the warrant, and the next pushed it out of sight. Still, Anthony said to Elizabeth, he had no regret over Clarence who had ordered the executions of their father and their brother John, so shortly wed to the aging Duchess of Norfolk.

At that she flamed anew against Clarence. If he were freed, he would destroy her and her children. Anthony smiled comfortingly. Clarence repeated the story of the pre-contract when he was drunk, but sober he realized that no one would believe she wasn't properly married.

He unwrapped the linen covering of a package he held and handed it to her. "One of the wonders of the world. Open it!"

She was surprised at his excitement, more surprised at the pages. "Why, it isn't written by scribes. Where—"

"From Will Caxton. He has set up a printing shop at the sign of the Red Pale at Westminster. He was governor of the Merchant Adventurers in the Low Countries—well, you wouldn't know of him, but he learned printing in Cologne." His eyes sparkled. "He asked me to write a philosophical tract. Think of it! I'll be the author of the first book to be printed in English." He tried unsuccessfully to hide his pride.

"That's wonderful, Anthony." But his triumph was overshadowed by Clarence in Bowyer's Tower, and then by the illness of their mother Jacquetta who had never been well since her husband's death, and, with the prospect of seeing her beloved Sir Richard, had no will to get better.

Elizabeth was in a stupor after the funeral. She thought of Jacquetta as always there, ready with shrewd and cynical advice. She was roused by her sister Kate who had married the un-willing Duke of Buckingham. Kate, dark and lively, said crisply that Elizabeth had grieved long enough, and she had news. Her husband sulked that he had been forced to wed beneath him, but he did listen to her at times. He stood up in Parliament to request that Edward carry out the sentence on Clarence and the lords backed his demand.

"Good! What of Bishop Stillington? He was arrested because he shares Clarence's guilt."

"Bishop—Oh, I'd forgotten him. How could I when he's the man who told that devilish lie about a pre-contract? But he's the kind of person one *does* forget. He'll probably be released since he is of the cloth, but he isn't dangerous. Who except Clarence would listen to his fantasy?"

Kate added hesitantly, "You know Edward is often with Jane Shore. Mother would say you should be a more cheerful companion to your husband. Why not talk to him? About Clarence, I mean. Jane's just a harmless little flirt who's now gazing at your son Tom. With reason. Edward's so heavy he can hardly ride a horse, and naturally Jane—"

Her giggle was so contagious Elizabeth smiled, then bit her lip thoughtfully. A quiet supper with the Milanese ambassador was planned tonight. She would follow Kate's advise and be lighthearted for Edward. But how could she prod him to sign the warrant? She couldn't mention Clarence's name, which had been a constraint between them, since she lashed out that he was protecting the duke out of family feeling.

The ambassador, however, touched on the subject obliquely, making it apparent his Italian mind couldn't comprehend a king who would allow a convicted traitor to live. Did he have so few enemies that one was of no consequence? Or so many that one more made little difference? Edward was wryly amused, but he swiftly changed the discussion to trade.

In her privy chamber later, he walked up and down, his blue and gold tunic straining across his thickened body. His expression was defensive as if he expected her to point up the ambassador's words, but she had grown wiser. She said softly she had been wrong when she accused him of too much brotherly affection. Why, if the culprit were Anthony, she would never be able to order his execution, never.

He said unthinkingly, "But if the safety of the realm depended on—"

She lowered her eyes. "Even then, I couldn't, sire."

"A woman of course. . . . But by God, I'm a man and a king. My country comes first. I shall sign the warrant tomorrow."

She had won. That easily. She smiled invitingly. "You are tired, my love, with so many burdens."

"I'm never weary when I'm with you, sweetheart." His arm around her shoulders was crushing as he drew her into the bedroom beyond. She sighed. Not too long ago, he would have carried her to the velvet-hung bed.

His appetite for love hadn't diminished as his body became more unwieldy, and tonight he was insatiable. But there was a darkness in his lust as if he tried to forget that he was about to send his brother into eternity. He confirmed the thought when he lay back at last and said in slurred tones, "He'll have a priest to shrive him, and there'll be no public execution. I'll let him choose his own manner of death." A shudder ran through him. She brought him wine and sat next to him until he slept.

She felt her own eyes wouldn't close until the warrant was carried out. Two days later the Constable of the Tower reported that George, Duke of Clarence, was dead, and his body to be laid beside his wife's in Tewkesbury Abbey. Immediately wild stories sprang up. He had been stabbed, poisoned, drowned in a butt of malmsey, had hanged himself. Elizabeth wondered if a public execution branding Clarence a traitor mightn't have been better than these rumors, which evoked sympathy for the duke.

Still, with the means uncertain, the court could go into decorous mourning since the death might have been accidental. Edward didn't speak of his brother until the next child, a boy, was born and he hesitantly suggested that the name should be George. And then, when the yearly plague crept out of London to find its deadly way to Windsor to claim the baby, he wept and stormed that everything to do with Clarence, even his name, carried a mortal sickness.

Elizabeth put aside her grief in a greater worry over Ned. The Scots were raiding over the borders, and Ned was to march north with the army to besiege the key stronghold of Berwick, now in Scots' hands. To all her pleas that the boy was too young, Edward said a future king must learn the arts of war, but, as Richard was in command, the battle would be short. And there wouldn't be a wretched waiting for news. He had created a courier system with stations thirty miles apart to bring swift reports.

Berwick was retaken, and the church bells of London were ringing out triumphantly when word came from Paris. The victory worried the Spider, and he was withdrawing the promise of betrothal between the Dauphin and Bessie to ally his heir to an Austrian princess.

Elizabeth said ruefully, "How shall we tell Bessie she won't be Queen of France? Her wardrobe's almost ready."

Edward's rage at the broken treaty subsided. "Perhaps it's just as well, sweetheart. Do we want our Bessie at the Spider's court? And she can wear her new gowns when Richard and Ned return to celebrate their success."

Her eyes lighted at the prospect of seeing

Ned soon. She said she doubted if he had much part in the success, but couldn't just the family sup together the first evening?

He agreed indulgently, and now she looked proudly around the table set up in her audience chamber. Anthony had trained Ned well. The boy had charming manners and could talk on subjects from tourneys to foreign policy. But he was still as solemn as when he was a baby, unlike Dickon who never was serious for a full hour in his life.

Her eyes went from her sons to Bessie in a velvet robe trimmed with miniver. The girl had been disappointed for a day over the contract, but then said that Paris was so far away she would seldom see her family. Why couldn't she marry an English lord and for love? Elizabeth had been grateful her daughter wasn't hurt by the humiliating rejection and was amused at the word *love* on the childish lips. But now she felt faintly disturbed.

Bessie turned her golden head to smile at Richard on her right, and there was nothing childlike in that smile. Or in her admiring expression as Richard, less grave than usual, talked to her animatedly. Well, why shouldn't an uncle and niece enjoy each other's company? He was thirteen years older, a much narrower age gap than between Bessie and Uncle Anthony, so she might think of Richard as young. He was handsome enough in spite of his raised shoulder, Elizabeth admitted grudgingly. His face, both intense and reserved, held a vitality when he spoke, his lean body was muscular, and he had, too, the attraction of a comparative stranger since he wasn't often at court.

Elizabeth glanced toward Edward, but his attention was divided between a brisk conversation with Anthony and washing down his baked trout with constantly refilled goblets of hippocras. He was right not to notice the unimportant by-play. Still she must remember that Bessie was rapidly outgrowing childhood and should be betrothed soon. The resolution strenghtened when Bessie danced later. As she curtseyed and exchanged light kisses, Richard always seemed to be opposite her.

A matter of chance, Elizabeth thought, but a pity Anne hadn't come with Richard. He said his wife's health was delicate and she was worried over their small son who had inherited her frailty. Well, fortunately he would leave in a few days. While he was usually with the king, he rode and hawked with Bessie a little too frequently, though no doubt only because he didn't make friends easily, and his niece's obvious enjoyment of his companionship broke through his stiff reserve.

Still she was relieved when he galloped away, the standard of the Boar whipping in the wind, and more pleased when she saw no change in Bessie's manner until the day Ned was to return to Ludlow. Bessie said sadly she thought brothers and sisters should never be parted. Elizabeth pulled the girl close to her in an unusual gesture of affection and said surely Ned wouldn't be away too long. He must be educated to be King of England as well as Prince of Wales. Bessie nodded and ran lightly off to the dovecote, anxious to see if the eggs of her pet barb were hatching.

Elizabeth smiled at the unnecessary worry over Richard. Bessie was far from grown-up.

Her thoughts were diverted to Lord Stanley as she waved at her son's cavalcade disappearing in the green distance. Her brows rose as Stanley approached. A big overbearing man, she avoided him when she could, an easy matter because as steward of the king's household, he was often away arranging for a royal progress or at his own estates.

His smile exposed a broken tooth which emphasized his unattractiveness. His voice boomed out. "I have a request, Your Grace." She thought indifferently he would always want a favor though this one was natural and unimportant. "I've married again and ask permission to bring my wife to court."

She agreed absently. Did she know his new wife? He said, "She has lived in retirement for years with her second husband, but you must have met her, Lady Margaret Beaufort."

Elizabeth was startled. She had believed, if she considered it at all, that the Lancastrian Beauforts were dead. Margaret? She frowned, then recalled a prim young girl at Queen Marguerite's court and later an equally prim young woman among the courtiers at her own. Margaret was Lady Stafford then, but before that? Memory came with a rush. Her first husband had been a Tudor, and her son Henry in Brittany was the Lancastrian pretender to the throne.

She said stiffly, "I will welcome Lady Stanley, but as Henry Tudor's mother, the king may not."

His broken tooth showed again. "His Grace has kindly consented to receive her. He doesn't hold her responsible for the antics of a son she hasn't seen for years, and as my wife she is, of course, a loyal Yorkist." He bowed and left.

Elizabeth gazed after him. Loyal? It was a word he didn't understand. At first she watched Lady Margaret sharply, but Margaret was pleasant, quiet, well-read and so unobtrusive she faded into the background through a rain-drenched fall and a bitterly cold winter.

Food was scarce and Edward scowled over the rising prices of meat, grain, oats, tallow, fuel, when he inspected his careful household expenses. The lords must have fewer attendants at court, and their allotment of candles and wood be strictly supervised. Elizabeth was amused at his earnestness, well aware he would soon hand the lists impatiently to his chamberlain and lean back in his chair to sleep. Then her amusement vanished. He was putting on far too much weight, yet he only laughed when his physicians warned he should exercise, ride at least an hour daily. Like many men, he felt his paunch meant superb health.

He was irritated when she echoed the master surgeon's advice. Not only about weight but about his sporadic bouts and his excesses with women to prove he was as young and energetic as he had ever been, not a man who would soon be forty-one and looked ten years older. So she forced herself not to show her concern when he insisted on going out on the river on an icy day in early April.

He returned saying the fishing had been excellent sport, but he couldn't conceal the shivers that ran through him. By morning his reddened eyes were puffy and he had a fever. He said in a day, two days, he'd be up again, but an onslaught of pain in his groin choked off his words. . . .

He was dying. The physicians went to Lord Hastings, not daring to tell Edward or Elizabeth, to say that if the king had any unfinished business, it must be settled soon. Hastings shook his head. How could he put the matter to Edward? It wasn't necessary. Edward knew. He whispered in anguish that Ned was only twelve, the country would again have a boy king, as during Henry's minority. But there must be none of the quarrels that divided the land then.

Hastings and the lords on one side of his bed must swear friendship with the Woodvilles, represented on the other side by Elizabeth's brother Edward and her son Tom Grey, Marquess of Dorset. They repeated the oaths of fealty given Ned when he was named Prince of Wales and added hurriedly he shouldn't give up, tomorrow—a physician packed hot cloths on his right side, and he smiled as the heat relieved the pain.

"Tomorrow is—is yours, but I'm—at peace. You will care for my family, and I—I've done what I hoped. The realm prospers, I've ended the civil wars—" His eyes closed as he slept briefly, then the lids opened and there was a glint of the light blue eyes. "I've lived as—as I wanted to, enjoying every hour. Can you or you or you say that?"

He slept again. They looked at each other in consternation. When . . . how should they inform the queen? Had it been kindness to deceive her as Edward insisted, pretending this was a passing illness? Tom Grey gulped and said he would fetch his mother.

Elizabeth hastily caught up a robe and returned with him. When she saw Edward from the doorway, she flung herself on her knees beside him. "No, oh God, no, Edward! Edward, my love." Her loose hair was a silver-gilt coverlet on the bed, and her tears on his hand roused him.

In a last flicker of vitality he gasped, "Sweetheart, you will be all right. Our heir—it's been sworn. Richard will—will protect—" He half sat up, fell back.

Someone led her to the bedchamber, gave her a draught to swallow. Her ladies hovered around her while she stared at the tapestry on the wall, not believing—Edward was not dead— yet knowing it was true. Ned must come home. At once. In her shock she was torn with fears. He wasn't safe so far away, she told Bessie, the Council and her ladies.

The members of the Council agreed soothingly that they would send for the heir, soon to be crowned Edward V. A pity he would be too late for the funeral. But when she stated that the royal archers must march northwest to meet him, while Anthony raised the Cheshire militia to escort Ned to London, there was an indrawing of breath.

Lord Hastings blurted, "Four thousand men to guard the prince, Your Grace! From whom?" He went on relentlessly as she stared at him, tears pricking her eyes. "Who is this enemy you imagine? Myself? Lord Stanley here? Or perhaps the late king's devoted brother Richard, Duke of Gloucester?"

The air was chill, hostile. The lords, who had never accepted her had no need now for the thin mask of deference worn for Edward's sake. She said helplessly, "He's so young, and there have been so many dreadful conflicts. I must know he's safe."

Stanley broke in his too-loud voice. "The last Lancastrian battle was more than a decade ago, madam. Let the people forget those days, not be reminded by an army swarming over the countryside. Half the Cheshire militia perhaps, but not the archers too."

Tom Grey fingered the gold chain at his neck and said negligently, "Why not? The new king is my half-brother. I will accompany the archers myself to show him proper respect."

Stanley snarled, "To honor him or the Woodvilles? The queen's son to meet the Prince of Wales who's in charge of the queen's brother! Whose companion is yet another young Gray!"

Elizabeth blazed, "I can trust my family, my lord—" She stopped, said more quietly, "In a time of grief, one needs those closest to one." It was useless. They would never understand that a widow's frantic worries might be baseless, but they couldn't be dismissed after the years behind her of ambushes and battles. These hard-faced men saw only a powerful Woodville faction.

She left the meeting tight-lipped, then her mouth softened. Ned would want her family to continue strong. He loved his uncle Anthony and his half-brothers, and he would listen to her advice. With him she wouldn't have to—a sense of relief tinged with guilt flowed through her—to concern herself with his moods, his desires, his drunken need for a mistress which had grown stronger since he signed Clarence's death warrant.

Now she must prepare for the coronation. Bessie's wan young face was puzzled as Elizabeth ordered bolts of gold tissue and brocade and velvet. King Edward had scarcely been buried in the chapel of St. George at Windsor, yet stewards and seamstresses and masters of revelry were constantly in attendance . . . as if for a wedding feast.

Elizabeth said, "My dear, Ned is a child. Would you have him sad when he's crowned? The country expects a brilliant coronation, and it's Ned's right. Do stand still while Lady Scrope holds the material. The pale yellow sarcenet with ermine will be perfect for you. Now! What of your sisters?"

She ignored Bessie's indifference. The girl didn't know how much the queen herself had lost. Elizabeth had forgotten that moment of mingled relief and guilt in the stark realization that Edward had been security. In the Council she struggled for her position as the heir's mother and was shrugged aside. At her flat statement that she should be regent until Ned was of age, they didn't bother to hide their smiles. Richard of Gloucester would be named Lord Protector in accordance with the late king's final words.

She said wildly that those weren't Edward's words. The king had muttered, "Richard will protect—" meaning Richard would protect her and the young princes and princesses. They disagreed suavely, led by Lord Hastings and Kate's tiresome husband, the Duke of Buckingham, who was so pompously aware of his trickle of Plantagenet blood. She eyed him grimly while she thought of ways to balance Richard's position. She would imitate Warwick and have her chamberlain provide food and wine lavishly for the people who lined the streets for the coronation, a popular gesture.

She was so deep in plans that she didn't listen at first to her ladies' chatter until she caught Hastings' and Buckingham's names repeated several times. She glanced up questioningly. A waiting woman laughed.

"The usual ploy for advancement, madam. Lord Hastings is flaunting his devotion to our new Lord Protector by sending couriers galloping madly north, God knows why. And the duke left three days ago with an escort of honor for Lord Richard." She returned to a study of a brown velvet ribbon on her silk kirtle.

Elizabeth shrugged. What did it matter how those disagreeable men pushed for position? But the next day, Lady Scrope, her chief lady-in-waiting, said tartly, "I understand that Hastings' letters persuaded the Protector to march south so quickly that he met our young king at Stony Stratford. Why the haste?" She answered her own question. "The Protector was never a friend to your brother, madam. I suppose he wants to show his authority by superseding Anthony, Lord Rivers, when the procession rides into London."

Elizabeth nodded absently. She was aware that Richard would try to keep her family in the background, but Ned would insist his uncle be treated with proper respect at court and at the coronation. For that she would lay aside her widow's white barb and robes. She wouldn't wear gold which might make her appear to outshine Ned, but perhaps a silver brocade— Her thoughts were interrupted by a foot soldier with matted hair and stained deerskin jacket who pushed past a page before the boy could announce him. Dangling threads on his sleeve showed where a badge had been ripped off.

He said hoarsely that he was one of Lord Rivers' men. The queen should know—he stared wildly around as if not sure how to give his message—the queen should know the Protector had met the cavalcade from Ludlow. At the assurance they had already heard that he gasped, "But that's not all, that's not all."

At his tone, a woman brushing Elizabeth's gilt hair, a seamstress hemming Bessie's robe, a lutist strumming a gay tune, all froze. The Protector had been friendly and invited Lord Rivers, Richard Grey and the chamberlain to his own quarters to dine. Then, with the dishes set out and wine poured, His Grace of Buckingham had stood up and—he stood up and said he had proof their guests were plotting to murder Richard. Armed men swarmed into the room to arrest the three on charges of treason.

Elizabeth wondered if the soldier were crazed from a wound. There was no more loyal subject than Anthony, but she signalled for him to go on as she thought, with a touch of nostalgia, how close Stony Stratford was to her childhood home at Grafton Regis.

He wiped his mouth with a callused hand, said proudly, "Our young prince, he showed he was a real king, he did. He asked for his companions, and the Protector," he spat on the floor not noticing the horrified exclamations at his manners, "the Protector said they were under guard. It was his duty to remove traitors from office. The prince was scared like any little boy, you could see that, but he spoke up, said they were his kinsmen and friends, and he would believe no charge against them unless proved."

He gulped for breath, "And then our prince, he told his trumpeter to signal his troops. But they, the cowards, they weren't there. The Protector promised pardon to all who returned quietly to their homes. Pardon for what? But they—they went. I slipped away to tell you." He bowed and was gone.

Elizabeth whispered, "If the story's true—but how can it be? The soldier was lying."

Lady Scrope rose decisively. "Your Grace, you may be right that the report is false. Nothing disloyal has ever been said of the Protector. Yet. But think of the temptation to rule England through your son without fear of closer advisers. We will go into sanctuary until we know Lord Richard's intentions."

Bessie whirled. "Ridiculous! My uncle's kind, he's—"

Her voice was lost in the swirl of activity as servants swept up bolts of material, unhooked the great tapestries, brought the queen's jewels. Lady Scrope said, "The Abbot can't support the household, as you know from last time, madam. We need money."

Elizabeth nodded and wrote out an order stamped with the great seal for the Tower treasury to be delivered to her. Lady Scrope smiled approvingly. "Since your brother Sir Edward is captain of the Channel fleet, he'll have to pay his sailors, fit out the ships. Shall I send some of the treasury to him?"

As Elizabeth agreed, Bessie cried out, "You sound as if we're at war! As if my—my uncle Richard were a Lancastrian invader like the Earl of Warwick."

"The earl," Lady Scrope said repressively,

"was also once devotedly loyal until he craved more power."

The flat statement sent a shiver through the room as it echoed memories of betrayals, and within hours they were clattering down Cheapside, up Ludgate to the Strand and along the Thames to the towering bulk of Westminster. Passers-by stared at the procession, then cheered, calling out to Bessie riding side-saddle and Dickon who stood in his stirrups to wave. Elizabeth was warmed by the hearty good will and by the thought their stay would be short, lasting only until Ned was crowned.

In the meantime, robes and gowns and doublets must be made ready. Ringed fingers skilled only in embroidery helped with the endless cutting and fine stitching. The chill rains changed to sunny May days which drifted into June. But the children couldn't run off their restlessness in the abbey's kitchen gardens, and they tired of their books and games of Spillikins and Hoodman's-blind. Why couldn't they join their brother Ned who was lodged at the royal apartments in the Tower while he waited his coronation? The women brushed the complaints aside, too busy to do more than occasionally regret the restrictions on their freedom, and lightheartedly sure this was only an interlude.

The mood changed to doubt as rumors crept into the refuge that Richard had brought his nephew, not into his care but into his power. Elizabeth said tautly that was impossible. Once Ned was on the throne all laws and warrants must carry his signature for all his lack of years. Uneasiness stirred within her, though, when she heard Richard was gaining almost regal power. He was now named Defender of the Realm as well as Lord Protector. She smoothed out the lines between the brows with her fingertips. She must be patient. Soon, soon, she'd be at court again and Richard would find the Woodvilles weren't to be easily thrust aside.

If there were a struggle for power, he would also discover that the beauty which had made her queen and was still famous throughout Europe would bring her strong support. She pushed aside the thought that men had never rallied around her as they had around Marguerite. Many hated Marguerite as a foreign princess, yet the Beauforts—three Dukes of Somerset—Lord Clifford and a dozen other lords had died for her cause. Why? Her first young radiance had turned to steel, but her followers had gone to death or exile for her. Who would risk their lives for her, Elizabeth? None. The women, of course, were jealous of her astonishing looks, the men envious of her family—though every member had earned his right to high honors.

The bitter words hammering at her, in spite of her attempt to dismiss them, were swept away by a message. From her enemy, Lord Hastings, the man who'd made certain Richard intercepted Ned and arrested her brother and her son, Rich Grey. She opened the letter with contempt, choked back a scream. The scrawled words leaped from the page. Whatever she heard, she should be of good heart. He would always be faithful to the children of the late king. If the Prince of Wales weren't crowned, his younger brother would be.

Ned not crowned? Had he angered the Protector? How else explain Dickon might take his place? Or was this the maundering of a drunken man trying to crawl into favor with her? Perhaps he wished to throw in his lot with her because he realized at last Richard was weak. Her lips turned down as she thought of the Protector, quiet, subservient, forever in King Edward's shadow, dull and austere, of no consequence.

That picture was still before her eyes when she was told that at a Council meeting Richard accused Hastings of joining a Woodville conspiracy against him and within the hour and without a trial Lord Hastings was beheaded. She swayed with shock. Was this the real Richard? Had she been wrong all these years and never seen the treachery behind his masked reserve?

"He's a monster," the words were torn out of her, "a devil."

Bessie, holding out a glass of wine, said softly, "Madam, I thought well of him. I don't know what to think now. But, but you never cared for Lord Hastings. Perhaps he was guilty. I mean of a plot, his own, nothing to do with the Woodvilles. Because Ned's to be crowned—the Abbot told me—in nine days."

Color returned to Elizabeth's face. "You are sure? Oh God, I don't know what to believe." She turned as booted feet thudded in the anteroom.

The door swung open, and some creature with Richard's badge of the Boar, a balding thickset man, faced her. Foot soldiers followed him in and then the Abbot, his thin face anxious. The thickset man spoke with more courtesy than she expected from his hard expression.

"Your Grace, the Lord Protector asks that Lord Edward's brother be allowed to come with us. The Prince of Wales is lonely and needs companionship."

She stared, gasped, "Give up another son? Never."

There was no courtesy now. "Then we will take him." He jerked his head at his men. They hesitated as Elizabeth screamed, "You cannot. We are in sanctuary."

He sneered, "He said you would claim that though His Grace knows well you're holding the prince hostage. A child can't commit a crime so what is sanctuary to him? None but criminals seek refuge in the Church."

Elizabeth appealed to the abbot. "Tell him, Father. Sanctuary is inviolate." A memory like a half-seen shadow darkened the moment—her husband, after Tewkesbury, pursuing the Lancastrians into the abbey. That was different. Tewksbury Abbey didn't have the special sanctuary privileges of Westminster.

The abbot said helplessly, "It is true Westminster is a refuge for sinners, madam. But it is also true your young son is not a sinner. Your Grace, he will be safe. I beg you—if he's taken by force, will not force to used again and again so that sanctuary will be meaningless?"

She stammered. "After—after the coronation, then—then come for him."

The leader growled, "Madam, as you must know, the Lord Protector regrets your flight and would welcome all of you into the royal household. But he insists the young prince be at court. All Christendom would be scandalized if he weren't at his brother's crowning."

276

Dickon had run out at the stir. He was laughing. "My brother asks for me? Madam mother, I must go. And it's so dull here." His fair hair glittered in a beam of light through the open window.

Kate, who joined Elizabeth three days ago said, "My dear, why do you hesitate? You know how the Protector has heaped honors on my husband. Buckingham is practically a king in the west. Do you think he'd let anything happen to Dickon? And is it right to deny Ned his brother's company?"

The abbot put in quickly, "The Lord Protector is honorable; your son will come to no harm. And if you will not give him up, Your Grace—armed men in this holy place—madam!"

Elizabeth's face was stony. "Then go with them, Dickon, and God go with you." She blinked back her tears, though she couldn't believe anyone would dare hurt the son of the beloved King Edward.

Four days later Kate came to her while her serving women were searching for a window where she might glimpse the coronation procession. Kate's voice was stricken. "Elizabeth, my dear sister—I can't tell you—I—"

Elizabeth smiled faintly. Kate, gay and lively, enjoyed being dramatic. "The coronation robes aren't finished for Ned? The lords of the Cinque Ports can't attend because of the French fleet? There are other peers to hold the canopy for the king."

Kate's cheeks were wet. "My darling, if that were all!" She looked desperately around but no one was near. "Oh God, I promised that my husband would see Dickon was safe." She added hastily, "Oh, he's all right, shooting his arrows in the Tower garden with Ned, but they shouldn't have time for games."

"They must have some amusement while they wait."

Kate pressed her hand hard against her lips. "And I told you only an idiot like Clarence would believe Bishop Stillington's story of a pre-contract with that Butler woman." She stopped, went on dully, "There will be no coronation for Ned. Richard has proclaimed you were never truly wed to King Edward so your sons are bastard. He has too much respect for the law to allow Ned to be anointed king. And—and—"

Elizabeth was beyond feeling. "And what? What could be worse than what you have already said?"

Kate's broken sentences were scarcely audible. "My own husband stood up in Parliament to declare that Richard is the legitimate heir. He—he will be crowned next week—Richard III. With—with such power he no longer masks his devil's face. Our brother Anthony and your son Rich were beheaded at Pontefract. For treason against Richard, a king who was not a king."

Not Anthony, so bright, so shining. Not Rich who had been with her in the forest the day they met the young King Edward, lustfully demanding she be his. Her fingers dug into her throat as she tried to deny Kate's story though she knew in all its horror that it was true.

She said at last bleakly, "Edward said Ned would be safe at Ludlow. The Lancastrians were finished. The Council refused to give Ned a strong escort, the wars were over. Dear

Christ, who needs an enemy when the Lord Protector is his uncle? But you said my sons are alive, that they're well?"

For how long? for how long? She understood bitterly now Marguerite of Anjou's passionate struggle to insure her son's future.

PART V
Marguerite D'Anjou

CHAPTER 10

I'm shaken by the beauty of the day. Am I so easily pleased because I'm not well? I don't remember that I delighted so in the countryside when I first fled to France after our defeat at Towton. But then my thoughts were on soldiers and supplies and ships. Later, there was despair. Now hope has returned.

The physician warns me sternly not to leave my bed. As if all his medicines could revive me as this scene does. On the slope below my cushioned seat the yew hedges scarcely stir in the breeze, but the massed flowers sway on their stems, rippling in waves of red and pink and white and translucent yellow. Overhead, birds wing like arrows against the intense blue of the sky; their thin gay trilling answered below by the absurd honking of geese being driven into their pens.

The priest came today to give me Extreme

Unction. The physician frowned. I wasn't old, I might recover from this wasting disease, and the finality of the sacrament might sap my will to live.

I smiled at him. "Will to live? The body is stronger than the will." He pretended to agree, a patient musn't be disturbed. He didn't understand. How could he? How even guess that I'm being given the last sacrament years too late, not a few days early? Because then, those years ago, my body refused to surrender to death.

Would I be as strong now if I were needed? My eyes half closed, hedges and flowers a blur of color under the hot sun. Yes, if I carried the only standard to rally men. I would sail again on the stormy voyage to England. And if the same disastrous mistake were made, I would be in the lead on the dreadful, shattering, slogging thrust to the Severn to join with Jasper Tudor. Be with my ragged troops, too many with rusty weapons, and with too few bombards, shuffling past treacherous Gloucester with its closed gates. Poor, undisciplined recruits struggling along rutted lanes, their first eager enthusiasm dulled by thirst and hunger and despair.

A cursing dissolute army which would rather be drunkenly bedded with a whore than on that terrible march. But they went on through the heat and the stench and the mud and the steel pricks of Yorkist ambushes. They plodded forward, my army of heroes, to Tewkesbury. To die.

I died with them that day. I could forgive the usurper Edward and his bought friends, *my* death. I will never forgive them with their faces and hearts of stone that they buried my son, they buried my lover, but they did not bury me.

"The Yorkists do not war against women."
Their iron tongues clanged with the lying words
which they called merciful because I wasn't beheaded while their barred doors clanged behind
me in the Tower. I don't remember the days or
the nights. I remember pacing the room. Ten
steps this way and back, twelve steps across
and back. I didn't need the single candle
flickering in the shadows. I knew the way,
following the path other prisoners had worn in
the paved floor.

The iron-bound door was unlocked one day,
and I was allowed to await my ransom with my
old friend, the Dowager Duchess of Suffolk. I
was grateful to be at Wallingford Castle instead
of in a cell. At least, I tried to be. I recalled how
the duchess had come with her husband for my
proxy wedding to the young and ardent king of
England. Later I wondered why Henry insisted
on marrying me; but oh God, those first bright
days, every hour drenched with sunlight.

I will not think of them, but of the duchess.
I believe I was comfortable with her, servants at
my call, hot broth, roast pheasant, oranges
from Spain, spices from the East, flasks of
wine, bowls of hippocras. She was as generous
and motherly as when I'd had to leave my own
mother. She was entertaining then with the wit
one would expect of the granddaughter of
Geoffrey Chaucer. I suppose she still was if I
could have heard her voice above the clamor in
my heart.

Suddenly she told me I was free, and I
returned to France. I had to sign away my
English possessions—since when had I had the
use of them—to the usurper, and any inheritance from my father to the Spider King. So?

What was land to me? If I had been a man, I would have married again, a Lancastrian, and had a second family. Then I wouldn't have given up an acre, a foot of territory. A second son would never make me forget my Edward, but I would have a reason to live. To taste the savage joy of revenge, to claim my own in triumph.

Are such thoughts wicked? Perhaps. But what do I care for the milk-and-water preachers who—bearing now injuries they should forgive —storm at others to accept the will of God? As if it were God's will, not man's, that the envious Duke of York and his Proud Cis snatched at the crown, when at last England could have rested from war. My marriage brought peace after a century of battles with France. I wasn't thanked for stopping the useless bloodshed. And when my husband and I needed support, I was slandered because we hired French gunners. I've heard no word against the usurper who employed Burgundian troops.

No matter. I have hope again. Through Jasper Tudor who escaped when the Yorkists hunted him after Tewkesbury. I've only a vague memory of his three-year-old nephew when I was given refuge in Pembroke Castle, but Jasper's words still ring in my ears.

"Henry Tudor, the hope of the Lancastrians." Then I had only a startled contempt at so high-sounding a title for an unattractive child. But Jasper was shiningly right. And loyally resolute.

Almost alone, he rebuilt our cause among secret partisans in Wales and the West. And in France we have supporters who are openly friendly, because the so-called Edward IV promises full pardon one day and seizes a lord's property the next for past crimes against the government, his usurper's government.

Jasper is under guard now in Brittany with his nephew who is still not attractive, I hear. Who wouldn't be too old for his years, a prisoner most of his life? But he will become kingly when he has his rightful position as the next Lancastrian Henry on the throne of England.

One Yorkist that I pray he'll treat kindly—though she married into the usurper's family—My son's wife, Anne Neville. A shy girl, scarcely more than a child, I didn't know her well. There was too little time and she had no understanding of invasions and battles, which were my constant concern. But I think she understood my son. A tender happiness glowed about them when they snatched a brief hour together.

So frighteningly young, the bride and bridegroom, in those months that should have been gaily festive. Instead of a royal progress through their own country, their wedding journey was a desperate push to outdistance the enemy. There was no light sweet music of viol and tabor and bells but the thunder of bombards spitting death. And rather than banquet following banquet, their last feast was a sharing of stringy roast oxen with exhausted, muddied, sullen soldiers. But through it all Anne gave my son love, so she has mine. Let Henry Tudor be generous with her when he is crowned.

I will not see that day. It is enough that I know it will come. I don't wish to linger on since I'm not needed for their victory. I have another hope. I will see my son again, Edward, Prince of

Wales, who should have soldiers gathering to his standard of Leopard and Lilies, not under the Tudor banner. . . .

I won't distress myself with such thoughts. I will be with my son. And with Edmund Beaufort, Duke of Somerset, gaily confident, precipitate, loving and gallant. And with Henry, who'll forgive my sin, committed for him, to give him an heir. And Andrew Trollope, Lord Clifford, so many dear to me.

The priest said I must repent. I should, I suppose, but I can think only that God created me a princess of France and queen of England with all the duties of my position. I didn't hedge or calculate which way was easy, which was safe. I poured out my strength for my husband and my son and my country.

Was I too fiercely proud? I don't know. I know only I'm dying as I lived. So I have one small offering to bring to God. To be Marguerite of Anjou one had to have courage.

PART VI
Anne Neville

CHAPTER 11

"Sleep, my little lady, I am here. You aren't frightened, no, no, you're just tired, my poppet, or we'd hear your laughter from the kitchens to the hall. Dream of tomorrow and leaving Middleham for the grand palaces in London, leaving as Duchess of Gloucester and when you return, why you'll be Queen Anne." The old nurse nodded happily as she loosened the stiff folds of her wimple where the linen cut into her wrinkled skin.

Anne Neville moved her head restlessly on the pillow. Her fair braided hair was coming undone, making a shining cobweb pattern against the white linen. Her thin fingers twisted a blanket fringe, smoothed it out, twisted it again.

"I've been up so many nights with my little boy that I'm too exhausted to feel as I should. But now that he's better I'll soon be as merry as you wish." Her brows drew together. "Only I don't understand. About Elizabeth Woodville, I mean, that her marriage wasn't a marriage."

She added hastily, so that Mistress Roxburgh wouldn't try to explain endlessly, "Everything happened so quickly, I was dazed. That's
why I seemed uneasy, but of course I'm not
really."

She musn't admit London was so noisy and
crowded she felt she'd be crushed by the mobs.
Nor that the city held memories she shrank
from, that she feared would be awakened.

Mistress Roxburgh resettled her heavy
body on the wooden stool. "Since you were a
wee child, you always liked having me chatter
to you at bedtime. I know you couldn't be afraid
with all the great gentlemen and ladies to
attend you. Think how glorious it'll be and you
walking up the Abbey so proud to be crowned
with your husband, King Richard. The cheers,
they'll deafen you, my lamb, and so much wine
it'll be flowing in the gutters, and roses strewn
on the streets for you."

Anne nodded vaguely. Dear heavens, why
didn't her old nurse leave or at least be silent?
But nothing short of paralysis or death would
stop the flow of words. Mistress Roxburgh
cleared her throat.

"It was just a whim you dreaded the
change, my little love. Such a fanciful thing you
always were. Why, you, one of the richest
heiresses in England, wanted to go into a convent instead of to France with your father—but
the Earl of Warwick would have none of that. A
great man, a good man he was until the day he
had you wed the Lancastrian bastard. And what
could you do but marry the son of that whore?
Your father hated Marguerite as all decent men
did, but he needed her and her dreadful son."

Anne half sat up. "Oh, but it wasn't like

that. The prince wasn't dreadful.''

"You're a saint, you'd think well of the fiend himself."

"But after I saw he prince, it was—was different. He wanted to marry me. We cared for each other." She shook her head. "It's so long ago, twelve years, I was fifteen. I can't quite remember his face. He was boyish and so sure of success when they—'when we invaded. I prayed so hard, only I didn't know what to pray for. I didn't want him hurt, but I'd known King Edward so long, I didn't want him hurt either. Nor my father. I think, I think I just prayed for everyone." She laughed shakily.

"You didn't—you couldn't—Lady Anne, on your soul you *didn't* pray for the she-wolf?"

Anne said with unusual firmness, "She was a woman and alone. My father had just—just been killed. She wanted to go home to wait as I would, as any woman would, but my husband and the Lancastrian lords wouldn't let her. They kept at her and at her so, the poor woman—"

"She was a witch out of hell. Oh, that I could have been with you then, my poor darling, and later when you lived with the Duke of Clarence and had to run away because he would have married you to some groom. And you in that horrible cook-shop—"

Anne stiffened, but she yawned convincingly. "I'm drowsy now, and you must rest too against the morning." She closed her eyes, certain that the nurse creeping softly out was congratulating herself on lulling her charge to sleep. If she could only sleep. Still she prevented Mistress Roxburgh from more reliving of the past, but how stop her tomorrow and the next day and the next?

But now she would forget the nurse's gloomy enjoyment of unpleasant details. There were pleasant memories too. She smiled faintly, thinking of her childhood here at Middleham before she'd been flung into a larger and terrifying world. Richard was in her father's household then to be trained as page and squire and knight. She'd thought him the cleverest boy in the world, much cleverer than his older brothers. But so serious. He knew more Latin and French at ten than those brothers of his ever would. Yet she'd felt sorry for him, forever practicing with war stallion and sword and lance when he wasn't at his studies.

His determination made him too intense, set him apart, so he could never match his brother King Edward's carelessly gay manner and hearty good fellowship that drew others. Edward became gross, a lecher, greedy, but always a certain charm clung to him so that men served him willingly. Richard, dear Richard, austerely aloof, commanded a dedicated devotion from a few friends and, blinded by his hero worship of his oldest brother, expected no more. But how, how after his unswerving loyalty to the king, could he announce to the world that Edward had lived in adultery for nineteen years?

Richard believed the story was true, of that she was sure. Was he also swayed by the fact that a minor would again be on the throne? And knowing his own competence, Richard might have felt—she didn't want to face the thought, but she was the Kingmaker's daughter and had a faint understanding—had he felt the searing flame of ambition? A Lord Protector was powerful, but for how long? When Edward's son ruled in his own name, the boy might listen only to the Woodvilles and strip the Protector of honors and revenues the late king had lavished on him.

This would mean a death blow to Richard's pride from a woman he held in cold contempt. Anne wondered at the hostility between the two, as she recalled the flawless beauty of Queen Elizabeth, who was now simply Lady Grey. She was also a mother deprived of her sons. But she, Anne, would put that right. If for some obscure political reason the young princes in the Tower couldn't live with Elizabeth, they would stay with her, be companions for the orphans of her sister Isabel and Clarence and for her own nine-year-old Eddie. Children were easy to love, not retiring into dark brooding silences like older people—like Richard, making them strangers.

She tossed restlessly while she vainly willed herself to sleep. It was almost dawn before she sank into unconsciousness to be roused an hour later by her waiting women. Eddie's excitement helped her forget her weariness. He waved to the men clattering along the line of carriages and wagons and said eagerly that next time he would be riding with the escort. And he was pleased with the changing landscape—"All mine some day, isn't that right, madam?"—as they went past villages and manor houses lying amid huge fields divided by grass balks to mark the holdings of lord or peasant.

Flowering hedgrows gave way to stretches of heath where sheep grazed, their clumsy shapes gray against green grass and yellow gorse. The carriages swayed along rutted lanes and Eddie, tired at last of his intent watching, put his head against her shoulder. She smiled and touched his thin cheek which would soon be round with health.

Mistress Roxburgh's voice cut through the welcome quiet. "You're thinking of being queen now, aren't you, my lamb, not of those terrible days when you were hiding?"

"Yes, yes, of course, no need to talk of them, please."

"Of course not, my angel. Why remember that you, gently reared and hardly more than a child, worked like a serf in that grimy inn? You didn't realize that servants carried pails and pails of hot water to your room each day and had to scrub linen and hang it out to dry. By night your poor hands were chapped and stiff with the cold, and then in the morning you had to stumble out of your pallet to scrub greasy floors or serve those boors with the stench of the barnyard on them."

Ann said breathlessly, "The landlord's wife was quite—quite kind to me though she thought I would be useless since I'd never worked in an inn and didn't talk like the others."

The overburdened wife *had* been kind enough and sympathetic over her story that she did only light tasks as a companion to an aunt who had died and left her nothing. "But let's not speak of it, that was years ago."

"Yes, yes, my lady, how much better to forget. I know why your heart is beating painfully now. Not thinking of the drudgery though I could see all your bones when you returned. It's the men, isn't it? Their dirty hands and sweating bodies and their lustful, bestial mouths crushing the lips of my sweet darling."

Anne wondered why, in her distress, she had ever confided a word to her old nurse. She said quickly, "Does the Abbot of St. Mary's know we lodge there tonight?"

But Mistress Roxburgh went on, heedless of the question. "They stank—their clothes, their breath, their unwashed bodies. Don't be upset, we won't speak of it anymore. I can't bear thinking of their filthy, seeking fingers thrusting beneath your ragged bodice to fondle your poor starved breasts. We won't talk of them, it's too painful to remember how your patched skirt tore when they fumbled at your thighs and you pressed against the wall, not even able to scream. You're so pale, poor child, but the duke saved you from those louts. Ah, it's right the lovely man is now our king. Doesn't that bring a smile to your pale face?"

Anne whispered, "Yes. He was kind, sending me to a convent where I would be secure. I recall nothing else of those months."

"My angel, how happy that makes me! I've always said, and I'll say it again, one must go on, not think of them days. But how else could you escape from His Grace of Clarence's wardship? Why sometimes, I believe he was as bad in his greed as them filthy clods lusting for your wasted body. Saliva dribbling down their beards while they ripped at their hose, letting you see their naked buttocks and their— their—" She shuddered. "But that gave you a chance to slide away and run to the goodwife."

Anne stared numbly out the window, not seeing the fields of grain or the rocky valley beyond with hogs rooting at the sparse grass and furze. The goodwife had protected her that time, but Anne shivered at the woman's specul-

ative expression. A girl too ladylike for most of
the customers, eh? But occasionally there were
gentlemen who came and saw how much more
attractive this innocent morsel was than the
harlots across the river at the Cardinal's Hat.
The woman said roughly, "Drink this!" and
filled a wooden bowl with thick soup simmering
on the hearth.

Anne forced the hot liquid down her throat,
savoring the chopped cabbage swimming in the
stock, in spite of knowing it wasn't kindness,
but profit, that urged unexpected food on her.
What gentleman would care to bed a bony
creature?

She said clearly, "Thank you, madam. I've
washed the mugs and plates so I can go to the
fish market for you if you're busy." She looked
down so the woman wouldn't guess her
urgency.

"Huh, they wouldn't know what you
wanted, you with your fine-lady voice." The
cross lines disappeared in a smile. "Still you
can point to the shellfish and salmon and the
sun'll give you some color. You're too peaked
for the fancy of—of some people."

She hurried through the crowded streets.
How could she get a message to Richard? She
was afraid of him, too. He might have become
her enemy as Clarence had, but desperation
gave her no choice. Perhaps he would remember their childhood friendship. Only she had no
way to write him. She had taken a handful of
silver when she ran away, but where did one
buy paper and ink? Unconsciously she looked
around for a servant, saw a scribe hunched
against a hitching post waiting for customers.

He grinned skeptically at her request. A

serving wench send a letter to the Duke of Gloucester, the Constable of England? The guards would die of laughter—after they threw him into a cell. Her eyes flashed at his insolence. Perhaps it was her manner—she as the Kingmaker's daughter—or her ability to read the words he wrote, or the purse of coins she prodigally handed him, but he went to Baynard's Castle. If the duke were absent, the letter should be given his mother, Proud Cis—the Dowager Duchess of York.

Richard came that afternoon in a whirl of velvet and silver and foot soldiers while the goodwife was rating her over the poor quality of the fish—all bought at the first asking price. Did this drudge think every cheating shopkeeper was to be paid as if he were supplying food fit for the king's table? Her hand was raised to strike the girl's face when the door was flung open and Richard said, "Anne!" in a voice she had never heard.

He said "Anne!" again when he strode into her audience chamber in the royal apartments at the Tower, kissed her and lifted his son into his arms.

Eddie squirmed loose, and said indignantly, "I'm not a baby, sire. When can I go riding? Madam, my mother, says I'm not strong enough yet, but I am. Look at me!" He stood straight, thin shoulders pushed back.

Richard glanced at Anne, saw her concern. "In a few days, after the coronation. It's the tradition to stay in the Tower until the crowning."

The boy appeared only half-resigned. "All right, but why weren't you here when we arrived this morning? We've been waiting hours for you."

"Hush! Your father has too many state affairs to be on the watch for us." She smiled apologetically at Richard. "I'm afraid—Eddie's sick so often—well, he's rather used to speaking too freely." She tucked in her yellow linen skirt and put her hand on the seat beside her. "Tell me the important news."

He laughed and sat down, his dark chestnut hair and black tunic contrasting with her fairness. "Including why I kept you waiting hours? Ah, Anne, I didn't want to, but there was a council meeting, the first since Hastings—since Hastings died."

He added at her puzzled expression, "He was Edward's Lord Chamberlain, but he wasn't fit to live. He corrupted my brother, wasted him as Jane Shore did. That strumpet will do public penance for her sins, but Hastings was a traitor. I had him—you'll hear this anyway—executed within the hour I heard of his treachery."

She gasped, "That—that's not like you, Richard. You're always so deliberate in your judgments and seldom ask the death penalty. He and Jane Shore must have been very wicked."

He said tightly, "They were evil creatures as many others are. Still, some I must pardon like Elizabeth, Lady Grey rather, if she ever comes out of sanctuary with her brood of daughters."

Anne smiled. "That's more what I'd expect of you." She slipped off her butterfly headdress, shook out her loosened hair. "Though I didn't know she was guilty of any wrongdoing."

"She lived in fornication with my brother for nineteen years. Is that a sign of a good woman? She must have known the truth, he doted on her, told her everything. Even if he didn't, she, too wasted my brother's health, squandered his money and stole the Tower treasury so we're almost bankrupt."

"I—I suppose the queen—Lady Grey— acted ill, but she was so lovely, so poised. If only I looked like her, how proud you'd be of me."

"Madam! You, my wife, compare yourself to a whore?" His stony voice softened. "I'm sorry, you're like a child with your heedless remarks. But you're sweet and gentle, too, and I'd change nothing about you."

She sighed. "If all women had such a kind husband, they'd be as happy as we are."

"I rejoice you and I are so well content in our marriage." He lifted her hand, traced the veins and tendons with a fingertip. "You're too thin, my dear. You must rest now. Our coronation will be tiring, and I can't have you fainting from fatigue."

She noticed his eyes lighted when he said "our coronation," and when he mentioned the tasks to be done that only a king could see to. She turned her face for his kiss as he stood up, while she thought some men wouldn't leave a wife so soon after being separated for almost two months, but his unswerving devotion to duty made him the ruler England needed.

As he went out, Mistress Roxburgh bustled into the room. "His Grace insists you sleep, my lamb. Most husbands would demand their own selfish pleasures, but the king thinks only of you."

Anne smiled faintly. "He thinks of other matters too. He must consult with my Lord of Buckingham and has a score of other affairs."

The nurse nodded with the gloomy enjoyment Anne dreaded, "Plots, my angel, to murder him and put King Edward's bastard son on the throne. Such a wicked world, but His Grace is strong. Traitors must die or we'll have anarchy. Anarchy! But come, my poppet, we will slip off your robe and you can dream of your great day. Them criminals won't be so bold after they see—"

Anne said quickly as her clothes were laid aside, "I'm sure you're right, but now you must make certain the seamstresses are working on my coronation gown." She added firmly when the nurse pulled out a stool to sit beside the bed, "At once, there's so little time."

She went limp as Mistress Roxburgh left reluctantly. She couldn't endure an eager prattling of treason and death, forcing her to picture the axe and blood spurting from a headless body which minutes before had been a man. A man alive and vital, gazing at the green earth and the cloud-streaked sky. Executions were necessary, Richard was always just, but she wouldn't have in her dreams a disturbing vision of scarlet pools on a scaffold and sun glinting on reddened steel. She would dwell instead on Westminster Abbey and Richard's crown.

They rode to the Abbey on a hot July day. The sun was brassy above the city that flamed with the colors of banners and pennants whipping above lordly cavalcades or hung from windows and balconies. The noise was shattering with travelers crowding into a city already so overflowing that many slept in the streets. Cheers echoed and re-echoed among the high gabled houses at the most magnificent coronation in memory. Anne stiffened herself

against the raucous sounds, the stench of
sweating bodies and garbage rotting in the
gutters. Yet she felt, too, an unexpected pulse of
excitement when her name was cried out and,
though more subdued, her father's too. London
loved the Earl of Warwick.

She was walking barefoot now on the red
carpet into the church, following the royal
musicians and heralds, lines of priests, abbots,
bishops, the peerage. Buckingham's blue velvet
glittering with gold embroidery outshone even
the king, whose train he held, a reminder to all
that he was the first lord because he demanded
that Parliament proclaim Richard the rightful
heir. She shivered a little. Was it wise to be a
kingmaker?

Her own train was carried by Lady Margaret Beaufort, an odd choice to have Henry
Tudor's mother so honored. Richard explained
that if Lady Margaret had ever had hopes, she
long ago gave up any nonsense about her son's
ridiculous claims. She was honored only as the
wife of Lord Stanley, one of Richard's most
powerful nobles. Anne nodded silently. Perhaps
she was foolish, she knew so little of courtiers,
but she wasn't quite convinced that Lady Margaret's cool reserved face and pious air held no
secret ambitions. While court life was strange
to her, betrayal upon betrayal was not.

Lady Margaret, everyone, slipped from her
mind when she walked with Richard to the high
altar where they were stripped to the waist to
be anointed before being robed in cloth of gold.
The sounds were golden too, the *Te Deum* and
the chanting of the high mass soaring through
the great abbey and later the full-throated blast
of trumpets and clarions when they crossed to

Westminster Hall.

They had a brief respite before the coronation banquet, but she found it difficult to sit erect through course after course and not to frown when a cloth of estate was swung over her head every time she lifted her spoon, or reached for a goblet of hippocras. She welcomed the diversion, when the king's champion clattered into the hall on a horse caparisoned in red and white silk to challenge any who would question Richard's right to the throne and the guests' answering shouts of loyalty.

She was retiring wearily when she realized she hadn't spoken to Richard about Queen Elizabeth's—Lady Grey's—young sons. Quite dreadful that they were still in the Tower, though maybe the decision was practical until after the crowning. She would mention her plan for them the first moment Richard wasn't busy. But the next week he was never at leisure. Still, he took time to send her a document granting her the Shene, the home the second Richard built for his Anne of Bohemia.

She was delighted with the manor and its gardens and orchards. Richard must come here with her, away from the relentless demands of ministers and petitioners and magistrates. She hurried to thank him for his gift when she returned to Westminster, brushing past three harassed secretaries. He waved the men out and smiled at her pleasure, but a visit to Shene must wait until after their royal progress through the Midlands and up to York, his favorite city.

She said eagerly the traveling would surely be good for Eddie, and they could leave him in the north to avoid the summer illnesses of the city. His smile fled as she added, "When you and I have to come back, he'll love having his cousins for companions even if they are a little older."

"His—cousins? He sees them often. Why should he be particularly pleased with their company now?"

Her hands flew out, the ballooning sleeves like gray birds. "Not Isabel's children. Your brother Edward's—Ned and Dickon." She stopped as his brown eyes widened, then narrowed.

He said neutrally, "They're well tended. And have you no thought of their mother? I doubt Lady Grey would like them so far away."

"Oh, she would, the climate's so much healthier. Besides she never sees them so—" She stopped again, puzzled at the tight lines on his lean face. "Isn't that your intention, to take the boys into our household?"

"No. It is not." He spaced out each word. "Because you're crowned, would you issue royal commands on what to do with this prison— this subject or that one? You forget that you, too, are my subject, and I do not like my authority questioned."

She stared. He had never spoken like that to her. "Richard, how absurd. When have I interfered?"

"Once is enough. Don't mention that whore's sons again." He relented slightly at her stunned expression. "These aren't ordinary boys. Wherever they live, they'll be a focal point for every malcontent, so they'll remain safely in the Tower until times are more settled. After that—we will see."

She ached to say, *Then I must visit them, they may be lonely and afraid.* One said that only to a husband, not to this dark brooding stranger. But even if she had spoken, her low voice would have been lost as Buckingham strode into the audience chamber in a swirl of gold velvet. He laughingly called out some jest which brought forth one of Richard's rare smiles and went past her, unnoticing.

She stepped back, struggling for air. She was short of breath, too often of late, and yesterday there was a trace of blood on her couverchef. The talk of the two men swept past her as she tried to hold back a convulsive cough. They were speaking of Buckingham's duties as Constable of England and Warden of the Welsh Marches. The positions weren't too great a reward, Richard had told her, for the duke's cousinly help in avoiding the perils of an illegitimate minor on the throne.

She supposed the high offices were deserved, but she wasn't interested, as her breathing eased. She turned to leave, but was held by a sudden tension in the air. Buckingham was lounging in one of the secretaries' chairs. He had the Plantagenet good looks from a great-great grandfather, and his heavy build dwarfed Richard's slight figure, but his face was weak while Richard's had a disciplined austerity. He was saying something about bringing up a small matter concerning the earldom of Hereford, which had reverted to the crown and that by rights he—

Richard's expression would have stopped any man. "You believe it should be yours? An unfortunate inheritance, wouldn't you say? It reminds one that an earlier Earl of Hereford was the Lancastrian usurper who murdered his anointed king and seized the throne. Or do you

request the earldom because you're in want,
because I haven't been liberal enough?"

The silence was heavy, frightening. Then
Buckingham managed a laugh. "You've been so
generous, I've no words to thank you, sire. I was
about to say that—that the earldom be given
your son. Or were you thinking of the revenues
for those so-called princes in the Tower?"

Richard said coldly, "Their needs are
supplied from my own purse. A pity my brother
coupled with a—" He broke off.

Buckingham's nervousness slipped away
and he was abruptly smilingly bland. "The
princes are pleasant young lads and quite harmless. Or are they? I suppose the snake in Eden
first seemed—"

Richard lifted his hand, stopping further
words. The ruby he always wore caught the
light and reflected redly on the parchments
before him. He didn't look toward Anne, but she
knew he hadn't forgotten she was there.
Richard never forgot anything, anybody.

"Eden? You've been studying your
scripture. And I've the man to help you in that
worthy pursuit. You know Bishop Morton—a
Lancastrian, then a Yorkist, now in the Tower
because he's Lancastrian again, one of Tudor's
spies. But I prefer not to hold him in London,
the commons howl when a clergyman is in
prison. So. I'd be grateful if you'd keep him
under house arrest. Your wife won't object, will
she?"

"Kate? She's like all the Woodvilles—so
busy dabbling in this or that she won't know we
have a guest in custody. But can't I be of greater
service than housing a treasonous bishop? As
Constable I can send a trusted servant

into—well, into any stronghold." He appeared intent on erasing the brief unpleasantness over the Hereford earldom.

Richard's knuckles were pressed against his mouth while his eyes went beyond the duke as though probing a dark shadow invisible to others. Then his gaze returned to Buckingham. "No. Oh, it'd be easy enough, tempting too, as even dispossessed figureheads can be dangerous. But not as dangerous—if I understand you right—as your mad scheme which you'd find as deadly as your scriptural snake." He glanced around. "Are you quite all right now, Anne? I'll send my physician to you. I want to see some color in those pretty cheeks, my dear."

She murmured something and stumbled out, hardly aware of the duke's startled intake of breath as he became aware of her presence, or of Richard's calm reassurance that she couldn't possibly have read anything into Buckingham's words. He could have added, she thought bewildered, that she understood nothing, especially about her husband when he was in a black mood.

But he was himself again, her Richard, when they rode north where highways and village streets were lined with cheering crowds. And the applause grew louder at each town as mayor and aldermen met him with a purse of gold and Richard, smiling, refused the gift.

"I do not want your money but your hearts." Never had King Edward turned back a shilling, a farthing, nor remitted half the year's taxes as Richard was doing.

Mistress Roxburgh didn't share Anne's pleasure in the loyal cries. She said darkly, "His

Grace would do better to take what he can get. Coins are more useful than all this screaming. Win people's hearts! Money, that'll buy anything."

Anne laughed at the old nurse's peasant thrift. Laughter came easily these days. Richard was happy, Eddie growing stronger, and she hadn't coughed for a week. Mistress Roxburgh, like many of her class, enjoyed dire forebodings, but even the nurse must be impressed by the city of York's welcome. The royal procession was met by town officials, crowds of well-wishers and a guard of honor.

There was one heart-stopping moment when Richard reined in his horse sharply at the gate and looked up to where his father's and brother's heads had been impaled on spikes. And another moment in Yorkminster when their son was invested as Prince of Wales and given the golden wand and wreath. Her first husband had also been Edward, Prince of Wales, before his death at the hands of the Yorkists. By order of Richard's brother.

She turned in her chair of state to gaze at Richard as if she had never seen him before. He smiled warmly, like any father delighting in his son's new rank. She sighed in memory of that other Edward, but it was long ago and she had known him only for a few months. Her smile answered Richard's as they watched the thin little boy walk from the altar, his steps careful so the wreath wouldn't slip.

But after the wearing ceremony, he had to spend days in bed. Richard said comfortingly he, too, had been sickly. Their son took after him and in a year or so would be in glowing health. She was reassured, especially when

Eddie insisted one morning he must see the city, and how soon could he have his own household in Ludlow now that he was Prince of Wales?

Richard didn't share her amusement when she repeated the boy's eager question, only nodded absently, his face closed. "What—what is it?"

He said harshly, "Reports of risings in Kent and Surrey. That damned strumpet's son. No, I should blame the mother. There's a plot to put Ned on the throne. A boy king who would bring chaos." He slipped his dagger in and out of its sheathe in his familiar nervous gesture.

She was soothing. "The plan will come to nothing. What can Lady Grey do from sanctuary? And you've told me the strongest army is worthless without a leader. Where is one who'd face you?"

His tension eased. "I was thinking of Tudor and that uncle of his. Nonsense, of course. Tudor wouldn't risk his precious body to fight for anyone but himself. Still, the rebels must be put down or mindless mobs will join them for the excitement of looting. When I ride south, take Eddie to Middleham."

Anne was pleased. The traveling and receptions tired her almost as much as Eddie, but she was concerned over Richard, too. "I wish you could come. You always go on and on no matter how exhausted you are."

He said simply, "It's my life. We must have peace so that I can carry on my policy of justice for every man, whether serf or lord. I had excellent order in Yorkshire, didn't I? And the citizens love me for it."

"Yes-s, because they're merchants and

farmers who are powerless alone. But the peers," she spoke slowly, "prefer their own justice. I'm not clever like you, but I heard how the nobles talked in my father's house. They resent interference."

His eyes flashed. "They'll abide by my laws. But," he smiled, "no need to make enemies. A king has enough gifts of estates and revenues to win allegiance."

She remembered her nurse's glum prediction on buying loyalty and Clarence's betrayal of her father at Barnet. She put out her hand to Richard. "Oh, my dear, be careful. Don't be too trusting."

His rare laugh rang out. "A protected little thing like you warns me who has been in too many battles and skirmishes to remember?"

"Perhaps you have too much faith in men and believe your good deeds are enough."

"Were all my deeds well done according to your standards? Still, even my mother never objected to necessary acts of justice. As you may know, she finally agreed to my brother Clarence's execution. She was wrong, saintly as she is, if her only reason was to silence him for the sake of a succession which wasn't legitimate."

Anne's lips parted in surprise. Never before had he criticized Proud Cis, in his eyes a paragon. Warm blood flooded her cheeks. "She's a pious woman, mass twice a day and religious readings at dinner, but she understood other things too. Or," she looked past him at a wall tapestry, at an inlaid table, "she would not have had thirteen children."

"But, but, my dear—" he turned half away, "my mistress, that was before our marriage. I would never be unfaithful to you, but she died in childbirth. You, too, are frail."

She said coolly, "Your passion, perhaps too much, is in your work. You're often in danger. I'm also willing to take risks."

"But how much more difficult! There are no trumpets or splendid banners to support a woman brought to bed with child."

"What is that to me? You are my world. Oh, Richard!"

He came to her that night hesitantly, held her gently until his need drove out all thought except desire. Then satiated, he felt instant concern. She laughed at him. "You wanted me. A woman wishes to be needed."

The night came to nothing as she had feared, but he left with too much on his mind. Wales and the western and southern shires had exploded into rebellion. So, she didn't write him when she had a flow of blood and another royal child was dead before it had a chance of life. But they had Eddie and next time they might be more fortunate, she thought with determined cheerfulness.

She was in the garden idly picking Michaelmas daisies flaunting their blossoms in the haphazard breeze, when Mistress Roxburgh bustled out. She sighed, wondering what disagreeable news she would be told when she saw the nurse's expression of morbid pleasure.

"I told you, didn't I, my lamb, that there's no gratitude for rewards? But there's worse stories than that, much worse, it'd make one weep."

Anne forced herself to say indifferently, "Stories? I've heard none."

"How glad I am. They're too horrible, they

can't be true, just wicked rumors, my poppet, you mustn't listen to them. Why they do be saying that no one sees them little princes no more, not for weeks."

Anne smiled faintly. "That's easily explained. My husband moved them from the Garden to the White Tower while we were in progress. He said the sentimental citizens were too easily stirred up at sight of them, but it's only while we're away."

The nurse said forebodingly, "Better in sight than out of sight, my lady. It's whispered, you shouldn't hear this, but 'tis whispered the boys were murdered. By the king's command."

Anne looked at her scornfully as she cut another daisy, bluish-red against her white tunic. "Go! And don't return with your vile tales. Ned and Dickon will soon be back in their old quarters." Her heart hammered angrily. Richard did so much for his subjects, how could they spread such a lie about him?

"Dismiss me!" Mistress Roxburgh held the hem of her skirt to her brimming eyes. "After these years of watching over you, tending you in sickness, comforting you. I will go, my little lady. Don't worry where I shall live, what I shall do. My heart is broken. I will not be in this world long. I thought it was—was my duty, that you'd want to know what's said, that—"

Anne said impatiently, "I didn't mean it, I spoke in haste. What would I do without you? But let's have no more on this matter of the princes."

The nurse wiped her damp cheeks with the back of her hand. "Not a word, my angel. Strangled, some say, and the boys begging for mercy while thick hairy hands pressed on them

313

thin little throats. But others say they were stabbed and died quite—"

She broke off at Anne's set face.

"But we won't speak of such dreadful things. Why, I almost forgot the important news. Them risings in the south, do you know who started them? I told you, didn't I tell you—hearts don't stay loyal." She paused, went on with gloomy satisfaction. "The Duke of Buckingham, he's raised an army, the ungrateful fiend, accusing our sweet liege of the princes' murder."

Anne started to shake her head. There were always envious tales about men in high positions. The duke was as faithful as a brother. But there were brothers like Clarence, with his dreams of grandeur. Only the rebellion didn't make sense if Buckingham believed the terrible story of the boys. Because while the revolt had the necessary leader, there was no one to place on the throne. Certainly the duke wouldn't risk everything for Henry Tudor— Then why?

The question was answered in a hastily scrawled message from Richard. He was marching against the untruest man who ever lived, one who had been so well paid that he came to think himself more than worthy of his great estates. And when Buckingham's shallow mind faltered under the difficulties, he was lured on by his prisoner. The smooth-tongued traitor, Bishop Morton, seduced him with a vision of absolute power. But Morton, believing the rebellion was for his master Tudor, had made an incredible error. He didn't realize even Buckingham had the wit to think—why jeopardize oneself for a shadowy prince across the water? The duke had a clearer Plantagenet claim than the Welshman, and he was here, better to seize the throne for himself.

She stared at the letter. It was quite true that the wars had so decimated the Plantagenet line that the duke's descent from Edward III's youngest son gave some validity to his insane pretense. She thought frantically, oh God, if he's victorious, what of our son? But he would never defeat Richard.

Her faith was answered. The rebellion was slowed by loyal guerrillas and then shattered by torrential rains, drowning rebels crossing the Severn and disheartening the rest. Within days their flamboyant leader, attempting to escape in a peasant's clothes, was sold by one of his servants for a thousand pounds and beheaded in Salisbury.

She was eager to see Richard, share his triumph. But when she joined him in London, his mood wasn't elated, but swept from gloom to white-hot fury. If his most loyal friend could turn on him, who now was there to trust?

And when she asked once of the young princes, he blazed, "Will you never be done with your questions about those brats, madam?" He added at her astounded expression, "You don't speak of them, but they're always in your mind. Why do you listen to the malicious rumors?"

She said quietly, "I can't help hearing the gossip. I beg you to answer the lies. Bring out your nephews or let your subjects know what happened to them."

She winced at his harsh laugh. "Have you thought—it isn't possible? I admit I wish they had died of plague, or better never have been born. They've disappeared, but I did not murder them. If I'd thought it necessary, I'd have acted

before our coronation. Why would I rid myself
of them months later?"

"You mean Buckingham—no one else had
the power—but he couldn't. No man could."

He said mockingly, "So then they're alive?"
His hand opened and closed. "But where in
God's name are their bodies?"

"Not buried in consecrated ground? Dear
heaven! But why wasn't the duke accused? At
least give out the truth now."

Richard looked at her as if she were witless.
"Who would believe me? Except those certain
Buckingham acted on my orders? I thought him
mad when once he hinted at their death. I
think—I think that then he meant it for my sake.
But later he saw himself as king. The boys were
a bloody nuisance to me, but his claim goes so
far back, they were an impossible obstacle to
him. So he strenghtened his cause first by
murder and then naming me the murderer. If I
were guilty, wouldn't I have said they died of
some disease and let every citizen gape at their
corpses? Now it'll be months, maybe years,
before some greater sensation will make people
forget."

He didn't usually say so much. The
thoughts must have been going over and over in
his mind in the days, haunting him at night. She
was about to repeat he should proclaim the
truth, then knew sickeningly he was right: Few
would believe him. Not after Lord Hastings was
executed without trial and the queen's—Lady
Grey's—brother and son beheaded because of
some unstated plot. Not many besides herself
would be convinced of his innocence.

He went on, speaking as if each syllable
were torn out of him. "I had to imprison them

or there'd have been conspiracy after conspiracy to put a bastard on the throne. Yet I know deposed princes don't live out their lives. Edward II, Richard II, Henry VI. Could I have guarded them better? But I was lenient with Margaret Beaufort who encouraged the rebellion, thinking like Morton, it was for her son. I reversed the attainder when she was stripped of her titles and lands."

Anne remembered that she had been skeptical of Margaret's loyalty as he stood up abruptly, crossed to the window to gaze toward Westminster Abbey. The tense lines were gone from his face as if by sharing his troubled thoughts, he had exorcised them. He said crisply, "We must persuade Lady Grey and her daughters to leave sanctuary. That will still some tongues. And speaking of our last Lancastrian king reminds me. I had Henry VI's body moved from Chertsey to the chapel at Windsor, a more fitting interment. Besides," he almost smiled, "he was so holy the credulous pray at his tomb expecting miracles. At Windsor my guards will prevent supernatural events which might cause disturbances."

Anne thought, as winter neared and frenzied preparations for Christmas began, that providence wasn't needed to create troubles. The story of the princes' murder swelled instead of diminishing. Richard said savagely, "Tudor and his spies," then added with determined hope, "the rumors will fade away."

To show his confidence, the holidays from Christmas to Twelfth Night were to be royally celebrated with banquets and dancing and even a tournament, though he despised the mock-heroics of a pretend battle. Anne was delighted with the festivities, rare in Richard's austere court, and with his gifts of jewelry—an emerald pendant, a dragon bracelet with ruby eyes and a sapphire ring circled with diamonds. She felt queenly as she presided in Westminster Hall though she could whirl and swoop through only two rondeaus on some evenings.

Nor was the gaiety dimmed at a report from France that in the Rennes Cathedral, Henry Tudor vowed to wed the late king's oldest daughter. Richard shrugged. So? The Welsh upstart must have guilty knowledge of the princes' fate from Bishop Morton who had escaped, or he'd have no desire to marry the boys' sister and be merely third in line for the crown. Let him dream. Better men than Tudor had also plotted. But where were Warwick, Marguerite's son, Clarence, and Buckingham now?

And soon he could laugh at Tudor's solemn oath to wed Bessie. Elizabeth Woodville agreed to come out of sanctuary, proof she held him guiltless of her sons' deaths. Or, the Woodville woman could believe that the boys were alive, though they hadn't been seen for months. No matter. Europe would no longer be scandalized by the plight of a widow forced to call on the Church's protection. Her decision acknowledged him rightful king and gave him authority to arrange her daughters' marriages.

CHAPTER 12

When Lady Grey was presented with her daughters, Anne looked admiringly at the oldest, Elizabeth Plantagenet. Bessie was tall and slim and golden, vibrant with health and eager to plunge into any activity after ten months of cloistered life. Richard smiled benignly at the laughing girl. She was eighteen, time to find her a husband. She retorted gaily she was in no haste and gave him an unconsciously seductive glance in her pleasure at being at court again.

Anne was sympathetic at Bessie's obvious liking for her uncle. The girl must miss her father. While Richard at thirty-one was too young for the role, he was a male relative who could give her security and share family memories. And Bessie was overwhelmingly grateful to Anne when she was asked diffidently if she would care to be lady-in-waiting. She had feared she would be married to an obscure gentleman living far from London.

Anne, relieved that the Tudor match wasn't mentioned, said the girl would have a voice in choosing her bridegroom, and then hoped, uneasily, that this would be possible. Even an illegitimate princess might make a valuable alliance for the state. Richard brushed aside her anxiety later in the Tower courtyard where he was inspecting a score of new Flemish serpentines. "You were quite right, my dear. Bessie has been through enough without a forced marriage."

She smiled a thank you, then frowned. "You've been working too hard. Is there trouble from abroad?"

"No, and this artillery should persuade the Scots and French to remain at peace." His eyes went to the shining guns. "Beautiful, aren't they? We're beginning to cast our own cannon too. A mistake to follow the commanders who think ordnance too dangerous to their own men and fight like their grandfathers."

She nodded absently, seeing nothing attractive in the unwieldy weapons created to tear men apart. "But you are worried."

He shook his head and folded her fur-lined cloak more closely about her against the chill spring wind. "You should go in. This weather isn't good for your cough."

A sudden gust made her shiver and she crossed the paved yard to the royal apartments. His silence was to protect her, she thought exasperatedly, when he should know she was aware of what troubled him. He was generous, but his gifts only helped the peers become more independent of the crown. And his refusal to collect benevolences brought him respect, but not the love his brother Edward had so easily commanded, in spite of exactions.

Richard couldn't lay aside his reserve to please his subjects. All his energies were thrown into striving for better government and building up the country's defenses. Few understood how intensely he labored for them, most preferring to listen avidly to the story of the murdered nephews rather than to the magnates who praised him for impartial justice. Just as they listened to that new couplet against his ministers, men unfortunately like him—appearing coldly aloof—Ratcliffe and Catesby and Lovell.

Thus people mindlessly chanted the doggerel pinned to St. Paul's door, "The Rat, the Cat and Lovell, the Dog, Rule all England under the Hog," and were horrified when the author was condemned to a traitor's death. They didn't bother to learn that the man was another Tudor spy. But surely it was more important that a king govern well than that he be loved by the mob?

As she entered her chamber, her depression lifted at sight of Bessie's laughing face and the lively chatter, as the girl helped her disrobe for a short sleep. Bessie had been out riding, had re-acquainted herself with her favorite hounds and horses and falcons, visited her dove-cote and been rowed down the Thames. Anne gasped, "Did you do all that today?"

Bessie whirled—her black skirt, still in mourning for her father, swinging wildly out. "And this lovely day isn't over yet, madam. Anne," she amended—they were cousins. "Later I'm practicing new steps with the dancing master. This freedom's like wine. I'm dizzy from it. We weren't unhappy in sanctuary, but the walls seemed to close in, and there was only the garden for exercise. I wonder if I'll ever have enough liberty."

Anne laughed. "You needn't have come back to attend me, so run along now."

She sighed, slightly envious of the girl's exuberance but sorry for her too. Bessie's eyes had darkened when she spoke of being free, probably thinking of her brothers, not knowing if they were dead, or if by some miracle, they had fled to the continent. Anne had begged Richard to tell the girl. He seldom refused her what she wished, but she could never reach him when the subject of the princes arose, and he forbade her to say a word to Bessie. Was he self-condemning because he hadn't protected them, or did he believe at times they might have escaped?

She pushed the question aside as she thought of his plans for another royal progress. In a few weeks they would be at Middleham, and perhaps Eddie was well enough to return with them. Her anticipation made her want to hurry the slow journey north. She would see him soon now, she reflected, when the cavalcade wound through the hills to Nottingham and stopped at the massive fortress. There were some angry shouts about the princes, but the voices were almost drowned in the cheering of the Townspeople.

Four days later the hateful cries could have been howled from every throat, and neither Richard nor Anne would have heard. The royal physician galloped to Nottingham Castle. He must see the king at once, repeating his demands loudly when he was told the king couldn't be disturbed.

He said, "Where? Where is he? My news won't—" He swallowed convulsively when Anne came into the hall. Yes, he'd just come from Middleham, but his message was for the king.

She said, "Of course, but how is our son? Your last report was hopeful. Is he better?"

"He is—the young prince is—he took a turn for the worse." He gasped with relief as Richard entered. "Your Grace, I came to—to—your son has been ill, he—quite ill—"

Richard said with terrible composure, "But you are not at his bedside. Does that mean he is—" He could not force the word through his stiff lips.

The physician turned toward Anne. "Her Grace—if she would retire—"

Anne screamed, "No, no! My son—what of him?" She swayed, steadied herself on Mistress Roxburgh's arm.

He said hoarsely, "Your son is—is no more. He died on April ninth in the early hours of the morning when the body is weakest." His voice broke.

"Oh God, no! Richard!"

The king gave no sign of hearing her. He said almost conversationally. "What day was it?"

"April ninth, sire."

"April—" Richard's hand closed on his dagger, pushing it up and down in its sheath. "What was the day? Tell me, what day? what day?"

Someone repeated, "The ninth of April, sire."

"You're wrong. That isn't possible."

Anne flung herself at him, clutching his sleeve. "Then it isn't true. I knew it couldn't be! But Richard, why did they say it?" Tears streamed down her cheeks. "I must go to Eddie now, now, and tell him—tell him—"

He caught her as she slumped to the floor, held her thin body against his chest. "What day? April—ninth? But that was the day my brother died—and left his sons to my care."

He was almost hidden behind the wave of flowing skirts and high headdresses as the women swarmed to Anne. The physician said, "I will tend the queen, a sleeping draught. And you, sire—"

Richard stared through him. "April—ninth?" And then, "My wife will never bear another child. I have no heir."

The physician, kneeling beside Anne, looked up. "You have a nephew, sire . . . John, Earl of Lincoln."

"A nephew! Jesu forgive you! What happens to a king's nephew? Go, go, all of you!"

They left, trying to be quiet, but the hall echoed with the clump of their feet and the women's sobs. His low voice was harsh in the empty room. "I must have an heir."

Anne, pale with staring eyes that saw nothing, went with him to Middleham and after the funeral to London where the physician ordered her to bed. Mistress Roxburgh fed her like a child, spooning up broth, creamed soup and milk custards.

"Eat, my little lady, grow strong. Dear Virgin, if you'd but weep! Then you wouldn't lie awake in the night moaning over your son, his poor frail arms stretched out for his mother as he cries for you—"

Anne put her hands over her ears, said shrilly, "Don't!" It was the first word she'd spoken since she fainted. "Would you kill me? I cannot bear—" She choked, then a storm of tears shook her.

The nurse dropped a bowl of gruel, rocked the fragile body in her old arms. "There, there, my angel, you will be better now. Your husband needs you. He comes every day, talks to you, but you didn't hear him. Now you will."

Anne nodded dumbly. Her wan face was streaked and her hair was a dull tangled mass on her shoulders where the bones pushed against the taut skin, but Mistress Roxburgh beamed. "You are beautiful. I will send word to the king you will see him. But first—" She sent a waiting woman for basin, soap, lotion and comb.

Bessie ran into the bedroom, the ladies on her heels. Anne was quiet as they groomed her except for occasional sobs that shuddered through her. She tried to suppress them when Richard arrived. He looked stricken though he managed a ghost of a smile at her freshened appearance. She hadn't thought beyond her own devastation, saw now their son's death had shattered him too. She put out her hand, whispering his name.

Mistress Roxburgh said, "Isn't my lady lovely again, sire? She will soon be well and there'll be other sons."

Bessie, glowing with health, her red-gold hair a light in the curtained room, adjusted a pillow at Anne's back. Her natural buoyancy broke through her subdued tones. "A baby in your arms again, madam, that will soften your grief."

Richard, who had been sitting near the bed, came to his feet, his abrupt movement sending his stool clattering across the floor. "How can you—" he paused to steady his voice that was ragged with fury—"speak so cruelly to a woman so ill she can't as much as feed herself?"

Anne said shakily, "They meant but to comfort me, Richard. They didn't think that in all these years, I had but one child, and now—" She was too unwell to feel anything. But even that numbness was briefly pierced when Richard looked at her ravaged body with pity and then at Bessie with what first was anger but changed to—to—She closed her eyes, not wanting to see his expression or put a name to the emotion that just touched his face and was gone.

He smoothed her hair gently back from her damp forehead. "We'll soon have you out in the sun, my dear, and don't fret over an heir. I will name my sister's son. Lincoln's twenty-one and already a veteran of the Scots' wars." He started to move away.

She whispered, "Don't leave yet. Tell me what you've been doing." She knew her mind would wander, she understood little of his work, but his voice flowing over her would drive away the half-formed picture that had leaped to her mind, one that only a sick woman would imagine. Bessie and Richard and the strong sons Bessie could give him. Dear God, how could she think such horror? Uncle and niece. But the Pope had granted dispensations for such relationships. She was feverish. She tried to listen to Richard but caught only random words.

He was saying something about commercial consuls in Europe to further trade and preparations for defense in coastal towns he'd visited. New ships were being built, soldiers and sailors recruited, artificers and gunners hired. Henry Tudor might never attempt an invasion, but it was folly not to be ready since there were reports the French showed some interest in backing the pretender. Tomorrow he'd ride to—to Nottingham to set up his military headquarters.

Her hand tightened when he said Nottingham, then went limp. She tried to say "Thank you" because the clipped voice detailing his whirlwind of activities had banished her mad fancy. And she wanted to urge him not to be away too long, but the effort to speak was too much. She could only resolve that when he returned she would be quite well again.

She was better, able to stay out of bed longer each day, and as Christmas neared she planned to have the festivities as gay as last year's. He agreed, smiling though they looked away from each other, as he said briskly that their own sorrow shouldn't darken the holidays. Also, he added the French ambassador's dispatches on their entertainments would show how firmly Richard sat on the throne in a country ringed with fortifications. Should France throw away men and money to aid a Welsh adventurer?

The winter air crackled with excitement when peers rode in from the farthest shires, each one appearing to outdo the next in jewelry and robes and personal attendants. Citizens were delighted with the splendid cavalcades, and the city was noisy with laughter and music and boisterous good humor.

Richard said wryly, "One would think I ruled a kingdom that's been at peace a hundred years, and that every duke and earl and baronet was my staunch friend."

Anne, looking from a length of white velvet to a shimmering sarcinet and to a pale rose brocade, said worriedly, "I can't decide which material to have made up for Twelfth Night." Then, "Some of the lords are arrogant, but aren't they all loyal?"

His mouth twisted. "Now, yes, while the country's quiet. But if there's trouble, men like Lord Stanley and his brother and the Northumberland Percies might weigh which side to support."

She said firmly, "You're the king. Can't they be fined or imprisoned?"

He laughed. "I'm apt to forget that you're the daughter of the Kingmaker." His laughter died. "I'm afraid I can't take your excellent advice to disarm a possible enemy. They may be as faithful as they claim they are." He studied the colorful array on the table. "I'll wear purple and gold, so perhaps the white velvet—" He shook his head, glanced up as Bessie entered with a chest of jewelry, opening it for Anne to see which gems to select. "Will the queen be too pale in white, Bessie?"

Bessie stroked the soft fabric. "It's beautiful, but the sarcinet would give you color." She draped the silk over Anne's shoulder, eyed the effect doubtfully and tossed it back on the table.

But Richard was enthusiastic. "That has warmth and life, my dear, and it'll give the lie to those clacking tongues forever gossiping about how ill you are."

Anne turned to Bessie who was frowning over the rose brocade. "Perhaps this more subdued shade—"

Richard waved it way. "Since Anne hasn't chosen, I will decide. The sarcinet will be exactly right for both of you." He answered Bessie's startled expression, "Whatever your parents' sins, you're a Plantagenet. I wish the court to remember that."

Anne agreed eagerly. "When our guests see we're dressed alike, they'll know how dear you are to us in spite of the unfort—how dear you are to us." Her voice trailed off.

Bessie would be lovely, a bright flame, but she herself a pallid wraith. She wondered if the similiar gowns, so cruelly emphasizing the contrast, would cause talk.

She wondered later how she could have been so blindly unprepared. When they entered the great hall, the courtiers froze. For a moment the only sounds were the faint clinking of a necklace, an indrawn breath, a nervous giggle, then there was as spate of whispers and sidelong glances were exchanged. But Richard, unaware, escorted her to the dais, sipped at a goblet of wine and signalled the musicians to play.

She had looked forward to this last festive night, but she shook her head at his suggestion to dance. With her heart slamming against her ribs, it was impossible to move lightly through the intricate steps, and it beat harder as he led Bessie out. Anne felt the buzz of talk rose and rose until the whole palace, the whole city, could hear the snickers, an ironic mention of two queens or a clipped remark that when the moon set, the sun would rise.

Even if such quips were tossed lightly back and forth, she didn't believe what she heard. She was just being fanciful so she wouldn't feed her imagination by watching the dancers. But she couldn't look away from Bessie with her overflowing vitality dipping gracefully into a curtsey opposite Richard, lean and wiry—every movement precise, or from the ritual exchange of kisses. Did Richard's lips linger on the girl's mouth a shade longer than when he greeted the next woman in the line?

But when he returned to the dais and his smile was only for her, she was ashamed of her suspicions. Until one of the Percies bent over Bessie. The girl hesitated, her eyes going involuntarily to Richard with an expression of—of disappointment that he wasn't asking her again? Anne stood up, wan in her brilliant gown. "I believe I will dance, Richard."

He was on his feet instantly, with a word to his chamberlain that the musicians change from the lively carol to the stately padovana. Anne was pleased at his consideration, knowing she looked her best in the slower dance that suited her quiet dignity. All the same she would speak to Bessie tomorrow. About what—she asked herself jeeringly. Wearing a robe the king himself suggested? Or an expression Anne might easily have misread? And how could she bring up such a delicate subject?

In the morning she found it unexpectedly easy. She had to rest and said casually she would like Bessie to read to her. She would enjoy hearing a romance, one of the Arthurian legends. Caxton was planning to print an English translation of *Morte d'Arthur*, but

Bessie could read the French copy, couldn't she?

Bessie laughed. "Indeed, yes. We all had to study French, especially me when I was betrothed to the Dauphin."

Anne caught at the opening. "The Dauphin—well, he's King Charles now—do you regret the broken alliance?"

Bessie said gaily, "He's not only unattractive and lacking intelligence, he's years younger than I am and not at all to my liking."

Anne unfolded her linen couverchef, folded it meticulously. "Still sometimes you think of marriage, don't you?" She added carefully. "The King arranged betrothals for your younger sisters. I wonder that he's found no bridegroom for you."

Bessie opened the book on her lap. "I suppose he remembers I said I was in no haste to wed."

"But that was months ago. Surely now with the Tudor pretender vowing again you'll be his wife, you must wish to be married."

"No-o. I can't believe he'll dare invade against a captain like Cousin Richard. I'd like to be fortunate like you and marry for love."

Anne said softly, "Richard has made me happy." Then she stiffened at the thought of another interpretation of Bessie's words. How much did the girl want to be like her? Richard's queen? Impossible. Unless for an heir? Neither she nor Richard ever admitted her health was failing, but they knew, and this girl was made for motherhood.

She forced herself to say indifferently, "I suppose Margaret Beaufort still has some hopes for her son, but she'll realize they're futile when you marry another man. Henry Tudor needs a Plantagenet wife to back his absurd claims. Shall I ask the king to find a score of young lords for you to choose one you can love among them?'' She lay back against her pillow breathless.

Bessie murmured, "That's kind of you but not yet." Her gaze went beyond Anne, and there was a tender expectant smile on the youthful lips.

Anne gestured tiredly toward the book, but she didn't listen to Bessie's clear light voice. She had learned nothing except Bessie might have a girl's infatuation for an older man, who was sophisticated and a brave soldier with the aura of kingship. A passing emotion, soon outgrown, but it might be wise to mention a betrothal to Richard when he came back. He had ridden north early this morning.

She waited eagerly each day for word of his return, feeling lost when he was away so frequently. In her preoccupation she scarcely noticed how the physicians' faces grew longer or how many sleeping draughts and potions they ordered. But she refused all medicine when Richard wrote he would be with her the next morning. Her eyes were bright as she was helped to a cushioned chair and cheeks faintly rouged before he entered.

He kissed her, asked quickly about her health, but his attention wandered when she asked about marriage for Bessie. He recalled that he had promised Lady Grey her daughters would have honorable marriages, only there were far more important affairs at the moment. There was talk that Tudor planned to invade this spring. She said, "Wouldn't it help—make him hesitate—if he knew Bessie were wed?"

Richard was incredulous. "Waste time on a chit of a girl now?" He stood up, walked to the window, impatiently pushed back the draperies that shut out the pale sun. "I have to see what I can manage with the taxes the Council grudgingly levied for a royal army. The blind ignorant fools refused to give me what's needed because—" he mimicked Lord Stanley's booming voice— "I have more than enough troops. Did I ask money to recruit twenty thousand men? Quite unnecessary, he assured me, I've almost that many ready to march immediately at my command."

He bit his lip savagely. "At *my* command. Stanley and his brother each have five thousand retainers and the Earl of Northumberland four thousand. What more could I wish? He conveniently overlooks the fact that they take orders from their own leaders, not from me." His voice lightened. "No matter perhaps. Few Englishmen want a Welsh adventurer wearing the crown, and my sister Margaret hates all Lancastrians. As Dowager Duchess of Burgundy she can send supplies and the trained Flemish gunners we must have."

He moved back to the bed. His brows drew together. The anxious frown wasn't over national defense, but for her. "The winter's been hard on you, my dear. You aren't recovering as swiftly as I'd hoped." He went on awkwardly, "I'm too much the soldier. I've no gift for you by—I sent for two Italian physicians. Perhaps they'll find a cure where our own could not."

Her lips parted. "Oh, Richard, and I—" She

broke off. He would be horrified if she mentioned her unforgivable suspicions. She wanted to make it up to him, but he was reaching for his cloak. She mustn't add to his burden by protesting that his presence was cheering. She knew he drove himself so hard that he slept little, and there were stories of his restless wandering through the palace at night. Her anger flared at the whispers that seeped through to her, that a guilty conscience kept the king awake.

She said furiously, "Who could relax with an enemy across the water and spies and malcontents at home?" All of them, she thought, trying to undo the frantic preparations to safeguard these very tattlers. Even Richard's wiry body could be strained too far, forcing him to live on his nervous energy.

He was fastening his cloak. "You look worried, my dear. No need, I have matters well in hand. Think only of being in good health again." He leaned over to kiss her, but his lips pressed against her hair, not her mouth. He explained wryly, "The physicians say your illness may be contagious. They didn't want me to visit you."

She whispered, "You must do exactly as they advise. All England depends on you." But when he had gone, she couldn't quite repress the forlorn thought—I depend on you, my love. Then she rated herself for her selfishness. Next time she'd refuse to let him near her.

Her resolve wasn't necessary. He didn't come to her room in the week before he rode back to Nottingham. Her thin fingers plucked at the silver monogram on her blanket. She must get better, she would. Soon. Or she might never again see Richard, be warmed by his smile, his gentle consideration. She blinked her eyes against a blur of tears as Mistress Roxburgh appeared with a tray of poultices and potions. She shuddered but gulped down the bitter concoctions and didn't complain at the hot poultice laid on her breast in spite of the odor of the herbs.

The nurse smiled approvingly and settled herself into a high-backed chair. "You drank them nasty medicines like a lamb, my poppet. Now you must rest, so close your pretty eyes." An unnecessary suggestion. Anne's eyes were already closed in the futile hope she'd be left alone.

"We'll have a wee talk, my angel, ease your mind about the king so that you can sleep. He'd have been here morning and evening but them physicians forbade him."

"I know." Anne stifled a yawn, but any hope of drowsiness fled when Mistress Roxburgh went on. "The stories about that hussy, lies, my darling, just wicked lies. Our good king wouldn't care for a whore. I shouldn't say that since she's your cousin, but what else can I call the Lady Elizabeth Plantagenet and her no better than her mother when a king walks by? Her big eyes all shining and her cheeks rosy—paints them I'll swear."

A picture of Bessie and Richard together leaped to Anne's mind, but she said, "Why so do I use color so I won't look too sickly. Perhaps Bessie wasn't well that day and wouldn't have others know."

"Huh! You're a saint, and that who—the Lady Elizabeth sparkling for our king morning, noon and evening, but he—"

Anne clenched her hands so she wouldn't shake the old woman. Go on, she begged silently, what, what, what does he think of Bessie? As mother to his heir?

Mistress Roxburgh sniffed virtuously. "I'm a God-fearing woman and not one to gossip like some spiteful creatures, but it's only right you should know what wickedness there is."

Anne swallowed an hysterical scream, said tightly, "You mean it's a lie that—that Bessie is—is too interested in Richard?"

"No, that's true as all them holy words we hear at church, my poppet. But the king, he don't encourage such silliness. He just smiles at her the way any uncle would at a flighty girl."

"Of course, and it's quite natural Bessie looks to her father's brother for kindness."

The nurse snorted. "Maybe, my angel, but should she ride with him like a hoyden when he inspects the latest recruits or—"

Anne said faintly, "She loves to be outdoors, and few can match her riding."

"Or," Mistress Roxburgh swept over the interruption, "play chess with him at night and only one attendant there, and asleep, most like while that—the Lady Elizabeth chatters and laughs and even sings sometimes because she says her dear cousin needs diversion. But there, my little lady, what are the antics of a foolish wench to a queen?"

"Nothing, nothing, but I mustn't k-keep you now that you've ch-cheered me with your news." She was seized by a fit of coughing after the nurse left, covered the sound with her couverchef pressed tightly against her mouth. She felt dampness and saw the spreading stain on the white linen. There had been red drops occasionally, but never blood soaking through the cloth. She thought, *I must hide it.* But the sleeping potion was too strong. The cloth fell from her nerveless hand, and her stricken senses were soothed by the healing dark.

She was awakened by the half-smothered cries of her ladies. Physicians were beside her too, going on and on about the best treatment for her. She glanced away from them all. She knew, she felt she'd known for months, that there was no cure. They were only mouthing words, hoping the Italian physicians would work some miracle, aware there was no miracle for her.

She started to speak, closed her lips firmly. She was about to ask for Richard. They'd send him word, and he would hurry back to Westminster, but he'd follow the physicians' orders and stay away from her room. She'd been dear to him, she was tiredly sure of that. She still was. But England, the crown, were more precious. He would risk his life in battle—how many times—for his country and the Yorkists. But not for a last sight of her, not to hold her while she fought off death for a few days, a few weeks.

Why should he? She was never robust enough to give him sons and daughters to establish a dynasty. And if he demanded to see her, she would refuse. But oh God, what in heaven if the queen's guards must be called to restrain him from entering.

He sent her exquisite delicacies twice, three times, a day. He left the palace only when new rumors drifted in about an invasion, returned quickly when the reports were unfounded. And there were scrawled notes of his concern for her and a few words occasionally of his meticulous plans. Bessie arrived with one letter. The girl's face was sympathetic, but was there another, deeper feeling in the tender young mouth, the shining eyes?

Anne whispered hoarsely, "You shouldn't be here. My sickness may be contagious, and the Holy Mother knows how few Plantagenets are left. I would not have you ill." At Bessie's careless shrug for possible danger, her radiant health that appeared to be youthful arrogance, Anne thought, *I do not wish you were ill, I wish you were in the*— Her father, her husband didn't scruple to imprison an enemy, but even to herself she couldn't wish anyone locked away from life.

Except, perhaps Mistress Roxburgh, who came in. The nurse said as sharply as she dared that she'd always tended the Lady Anne, she needed no help from an untrained girl. Bessie murmured gracefully she was sorry if she intruded, the next time she would wait until she was sent for.

Mistress Roxburgh said venomously as the door closed, " 'Twill be a long time you'll wait before you set foot in this room again. A viper, a snake." She wrung out a cold cloth to wipe Anne's damp face. "There, my angel, forget her and her devilish ways. God will strike her down, and may she burn forever for those greedy clutching hands that would steal what is yours."

Anne moved restlessly, wondering vaguely what the nurse meant, not really caring, when the nurse went on malevolently, "Brought you a letter from your husband, did she? Ask her what letter she sent the Duke of Norfolk." She didn't notice Anne's lack of interest. "You're too good to believe such evil, my lamb, but it's true. That letter was found, and there are whispers all the way from the Lord Chamberlain to the sluts in the stews. Sinful women them trollops are, but not as sinful as the Lady Elizabeth, and her writing the duke like a lovesick girl begging him to speak to a bashful swain."

Anne, as usual, doing what was expected of her, said, "Why not if the man's a friend of the duke's?"

The nurse's voice thickened with hate. "The hussy—can ye call her else—pleaded that the duke must be her mediator to—I can't tell you, my angel. It's too terrible. I will not say another word except she asks the duke to speak to the king himself, that them two have an understanding. Our sweet Richard and that whore's daughter! Dreadful, and she claiming so piteously that our king is her only joy and maker in the world, that she's his forever. But it's worse than that. No, no, I will say no more, not if my poppet should get on her poor knees."

Anne turned her head on the pillow, tired of the angry denunciations which only confirmed what Mistress Roxburgh had gossiped about a week, two weeks, was it—three weeks ago.

"But you'll soon be strong again for your loving husband, my little lady. He hardly knows that strumpet's alive."

He knows, he knows, Anne thought. Her heart raced and slowed and raced again as the nurse added "You'll get well and we'll laugh at that slut and her panting like a bitch for February to be past, and will the queen never die?"

But that could not have been written. Bessie knew the queen was Richard's beloved. Memories flowed through her. The day he had come to the cook-shop, his voice warm with passionate relief. His delight at their son's birth, and their wild shared grief when Eddie died. Richard's constant care for her. She sighed happily. He loved her.

And there were other recollections. The way his face changed when he looked at Bessie, vibrant and healthy. His need for a direct heir was never mentioned. But never forgotten. He must have seen Bessie's hero-worship, and he hadn't found a bridegroom for her. Did he leave his wife alone only because of contagion? Or to try to forget her? Was he, like Bessie, waiting for the queen to die? So he could have sons?

Not Richard, her tender considerate husband. She moaned through the night, brokenly calling for him, craving a last glimpse before she closed her eyes forever in this breathless ornate room with gold hangings and a seacoal fire never allowed to go out, and everywhere candles of the finest beeswax a fit setting for the Kingmaker's heiress and England's queen.

She moaned again, then whispered, "Richard!" and smiled. He was here. They were wrong to say he had gone to the west country. His face was blurred because of her weakness, but he was coming towards her, arms outstretched, to enfold her while she drifted from him, from them all, too weary for anything but rest.

PART VII

Elizabeth Plantagenet

CHAPTER 13

Proud Cis's lids lowered disapprovingly at my windblown appearance. I tucked a loose curl under my headdress and said laughing, "I'm sorry, Grandmother, but I was riding and didn't stop to tidy myself before I took the barge from Westminster. Your message sounded urgent."

A summons from Baynard Castle made us all nervous, but I wasn't so nervous this morning that I refused when Richard casually suggested I join him for a canter in the park.

"I sent for you because of an extremely serious matter, Bessie. This—this incredible scandal must not go on. I will not have it."

I was only vaguely aware of her frown. I was seeing another face, narrow, with thin lips and brown eyes with flecks of gold. I said meekly, "Yes, madam. I mean no, madam."

Her voice was sharp. "And I won't have that

insolent tone either, young woman. I am the Duchess of York and the first lady in the kingdom."

"Yes, m-madam." I swallowed a giggle. "I—I didn't intend to be impertinent."

No one, no one was ever allowed to forget Proud Cis's position. She looked formidable enough without the trappings of title—tall, unbending in spite of her seventy years, her wrinkled face stern under her widow's coif with its white barb beneath her chin. This great dull hall was a fit setting for her, with its oak chair carved to resemble a throne. A constant reminder that her husband should have been the first Yorkist king and she the queen dowager. Her silence now reminded me she expected me to speak.

"Is there something you wish me to do?"

I wondered why she wasn't bored with her pretensions, which didn't sort with the *Book of Hours* and the *priedieu* in the corner and the pearl rosary at her waist that gleamed against the black velvet skirt. Her grim answer jolted me back to the moment. "Stay away from my son."

She said—she couldn't have—but she had. Not be with Richard? I felt a spurt of anger. "We're all at the king's command, madam. It's for him to decide whether or not to see me."

Her hand moved up to the silver cross on her black bodice. Her mourning was for her long-dead husband, not for the queen whom she had held in contempt. Anne Neville had brought Richard land and revenues. So? What use was a woman who bore her husband one sickly boy, a child who hadn't even reached adolescence? Her lips moved soundlessly as if she were praying for patience or rehearsing her next words to me.

She hadn't been praying for patience. "We will not speak of the disgrace throughout Christendom that you've brought on His Grace's good name. Or that you, a mere Lady Elizabeth, should dare look so high when you should be grateful to be betrothed to a knight or baronet."

I stared, bewildered at the onslaught. "But I—I've done nothing wrong." An afternoon hawking when Richard, too much on edge, too taut, rode recklessly to forget the loss of a wife and a son; occasional hours of chess when I was one of the few who could make him smile. How could even Proud Cis condemn our innocent companionship?

"Nothing wrong to set all Europe gossiping? An appeal for decency is lost on a Woodville, though at least when your mother seduced my son Edward, there wasn't the added sin of intriguing to mate—I will not use the lawful word marry—within bounds forbidden by Church and State. I demand your promise to retire from—"

I choked past the fury in my throat, "I owe you reverence as my grandmother, but not when you insult my mother and me." I swept her the barest curtsey and turned to leave.

"You will stay, girl, until I've finished or the guards will bring you back." I hesitated, then swung half-about, unable to bear the humiliation of a sentry dragging me to her ornate chair of state. She continued as if there had been no interruption. "—retire from court or I shall tell the king you must marry at once or go to a nunnery."

Unexpectedly, I laughed, though I could as easily have cried. "He's not a child in leading strings. As you just said, he is the king."

For a moment she looked shaken. Richard would listen politely, but he made his own decisions. "*You* never forget who he is, do you? Another Woodville scheming to wear the crown."

A candle on the table flared dizzily before my eyes. This hag, this harridan, tearing at my dreams with those long buffed nails of hers. Tender dreams that gave me delight and hurt no one. Who knew better than I that all Richard's thoughts were on weapons and defense? On the daily reports of Tudor's preparations for the delayed invasion?

I flung at her, "*You* forget, madam, that my father was the Fourth Edward and my name is Elizabeth Plantagenet." I would have gone on, but I was afraid what dignity she left me would crumble.

"But not lawfully born. No legitimate princess would pathetically beg His Grace of Norfolk to forward an alliance between uncle and niece."

That wretched letter. That was why she was brutally trying to hammer me into submission. I had actually forgotten it and thought others had too. I held back my rage, somehow managed a shrug. "If that tale has just reached you, you should employ more competent spies, madam, men who won't take months to bring you such an interesting story."

Her pale face whitened. "How dare you treat your infamous conduct so lightly? You must send Norfolk another letter, say you were drunk, insane, anything, when you wrote earlier that there was an understanding between you and the king."

For this hour I would never forgive her. "My conduct, madam? What of your own?" Her stricken expression made me realize the old scandal she thought I referred to, and it steadied me.

"I'm not talking of those rumors about you and the archer in Calais, how he was the father of your oldest son. Such ugly tales should have made you kinder, yet you haven't the charity to ask if I am also a victim of gossip."

The shock of knowing the whispers were still being repeated showed in her pinched nostrils, the lines at her mouth.

"I've heard other things too about you and Richard, but the letter— Well, speak up! Do you deny it?"

"I do not know if there was one, or if someone merely said there was one, but I did not write the Duke of Norfolk." My voice wavered a little because part of the letter was true, that the king was my joy. Whoever and for whatever reason had started the story had found an easy task. Anyone could see plainly from my too-mobile face how I felt about Richard. But to put in that last sentence, "Will the queen never die—"

I shook with sudden anger and forgot that we were all afraid of Proud Cis and stepped forward. Her wrist was brittle under my hard grip. "Beg absolution of your confessor for your evil thoughts, madam. You believed I could wish anyone dead."

I dropped her arm and walked out. I did not know, I did not care, whether she didn't order me back because she feared I might storm on, or if she had said all she wanted to say. A score of guards couldn't have stopped me. I ran down the curved stairway with wall cressets in iron sockets flaring high at a draught and making a moving pattern of shadows on the stone steps. This part of the castle, the old Norman fortress, had a damp chill that cut through my wool cloak, though a fire blazed in the lower hall.

Two grooms in the York livery of blue and murrey escorted me under the raised portcullis to where my tiring woman waited in the royal barge that dipped and swayed in the gray river. The deliberate precision of the oarsmen was much too slow, as we passed the great houses with their gardens and trees reaching down to the Thames.

I must see Richard at once. Before his mother did. For all Proud Cis's gracelessness, she unintentionally had the grace to warn me. She was probably convinced I hadn't written that miserable letter, but she wasn't armored against the fact that others believed I had, just as some believed those vicious broadsides said to have been written by Bishop Morton. The worst was the accusation that Richard had been in such haste for his wife to die, that he bribed a physician to poison her so he could make an incestuous alliance with me. Though incest was never mentioned in either the Austrian or the Italian marriage when the Pope granted dispensation for equally close relations.

There were other spiteful tales, and Proud Cis would use every one to persuade Richard that for the good of the realm I be sent away, uncaring if it were to a disagreeable marriage bed or an isolated convent. She would point out that he couldn't afford a divided kingdom now.

The powerful Nevilles might turn against him, claiming marriage to me was an insult to his dead wife. Richard could deny and deny that he thought of taking any woman since Anne's death. The scandal mattered more to Proud Cis than the truth. He must prove to the world the rumors were lies.

She and the Duke of York were said to have been happily married— An unexpected situation among nobles when a wedding was usually an alliance between two families. The idea was to establish a new household with the wife taking charge of one manor while the husband managed another, meeting on occasion to carry on their line. But Proud Cis had refused to be separated often from her duke, so she must have known love. Had she forgotten tenderness in her bitter disappointment that the husband who should have made her queen was defeated by Marguerite of Anjou?

I wished her husband alive, I wished her back at her castle of Berkhamsted, anything to keep her attention from me. She couldn't understand that I had seen Richard so rarely I didn't think of him as an uncle. Or that while I knew I couldn't love a married man, it was quite all right to be fond of a close relative. Fond, dear God! I had to see him every day when he was in the city though it were only at a distance or in passing, hoping for one of his rare smiles that lighted up his too-serious face.

The barge was swinging toward the water steps. I hardly waited for the men on the stone ledge to coil the tossed lines around the iron stanchions. A rower leaped forward to steady me, and my tiring woman muttered at my haste as she clambered after me to shore. I could hear her heavy breathing behind me on the sanded path, but I didn't slow my steps. I hadn't asked her to attend me. She insisted because it wasn't decent for me to be alone on the river, even the short distance to my grandmother's. Perhaps Proud Cis was right—after all I was half a Woodville—that I didn't have a sense of decency.

I laughed at their old women's notions, my first feeling of gaiety since Proud Cis had torn it away with her monstrous demand. I felt vibrantly alive as I hurried through the great oak doors. I wanted so little. Richard would understand that. Only to be allowed my freedom, to stay here. But I was too late. Lord Stanley, the Lord Chamberlain, said, smiling, that the king would return in an hour or two. At a message from His Grace's mother, he had ridden into the city. Could he himself help me?

I think I shook my head. I remember turning away so he wouldn't glimpse my face. I felt like screaming or whimpering or striking someone, especially this blandly smug chamberlain who thought he could take the king's place and assist me. My mouth was dry from my sense of urgency, and my heart thudded but I had to wait while Proud Cis talked to Richard, persuading him that her advice was for his good, for mine, for the country's.

If he cared for me as I did for him, he would know how to answer her. But to him I was only a young kinswoman, pleasant enough to have around at times, but not important. Of no importance at all weighed against his mother's arguments. Later it would be different. When he recovered from Anne's death, when the invasion threat was over, he would turn to me and— A mad dream. His mother even now was making sure our companionship would have no chance to deepen into love.

I must have stood there frozen because Lord Stanley was still beside me, his pale eyes watching me as if trying to guess my thoughts. He smiled again, showing a broken tooth, and said his wife and my mother were in the great audience chamber, and he was sure they wished to see me. I nodded and walked numbly to the stairway. I would probably have agreed with equal indifference no matter what he'd suggested.

Half a dozen ladies were seated at an inlaid game table under the oriel window. Gauzy veils, black in mourning for the queen, floated darkly against the cool afternoon light as I crossed the room. Mother was speaking querulously to a page with a tray of fruit and sweetmeats. I wondered why she made her periodic visits to court, since at every turn she was unhappily reminded she wasn't the queen dowager but Lady Grey, widow of a man she had no doubt almost forgotten. Though she looked a queen. It was easy to see even now when she was forty-eight why a king had been enchanted by the beautiful Elizabeth Woodville.

Mother glanced up from the cards she was holding, smiled at me absently and returned to her hand. There was a flutter of voices as the other ladies saw me. They were so carefully groomed that I was reminded I was more wind-blown than when I was with Proud Cis, and I made ineffectual movements to tuck my frilled chemisette into my bodice and smooth my skirt as I sat down.

Stanley's wife, Lady Margaret Beaufort,

said, "You look lovely, my dear, so young and fresh."

"Thank you." I wished myself miles away. Stanley said that she was here, yet I had been too emotionally drained to think beyond the fact that he had given me a definite direction. No one could dislike Lady Margaret. Her oval face was intelligent; her eyes kind; her soberly elegant gown, belted below her breasts, was beautifully cut—never ornate like Mother's robes; her manner was charming, to me, in particular. It was impossible not to like her! I disliked her violently.

She showed her tact as we gathered up our cards. "My lead, I believe?" She put down the queen of Wands. "Doesn't that please you, Lady Grey? Whenever people play, they see your portrait and call it the queen of Hearts."

Mother smiled as she capped the play with her queen of Swords, the jewels on her ringed hand sparkling in the light. "It is more attractive than Marguerite as queen of Spades." She added bitterly, "A trifling memento of my nineteen years as Queen of England."

Lady Margaret half turned so that only my mother and I could see her face, and selected a marchpane from a page's tray. But before she nibbled daintily at the candied fruit, her lips formed the words, "Queen Mother!"

I threw down the unnumbered *fou*, losing a point. How dared she? My anger rose higher as she said in the horridly honeyed voice that her ladies praised, "You could have played the *chevalier* to stay in the game. Or better yet, my dear, the king who takes every trick."

Trick was the right word for that son of hers across the water with his ridiculous claim, but when I spoke my tone was as sweet as hers. "You put it so cleverly, dear Lady Margaret. Cousin Richard always wins, doesn't he? Barnet, Tewkesbury, forays on the Scottish border."

As I might have known, she ignored my implication that Henry Tudor had no matching victories. He had never been on a battlefield. She said approvingly, "You're so discreet, my dear. What an admirable wife you will make for—for some brave and gallant man. So young, yet you can teach me the ways of courtiers."

I swallowed an hysterical laugh. She'd been born knowing how to conspire. All the years her son had been in Brittany and now France, she plotted to make him king, yet escaped even a fine for her treachery while others were beheaded or imprisoned. A giggle escaped me as I thought of her description of him as a brave and gallant man.

She usually added, handsome and brilliant, doing even his wooing for him since he needed my name to give some legality to his cause. Her choice of words didn't fit the reports that I had heard—which were that Tudor was a young-old, balding man of twenty-eight who appeared closer to forty. That he was pedantic, with none of the careless Plantagenet charm, that he could be taken for a tradesman or an unimportant merchant at best. Someone said that he didn't look like a king, but under his uncle Jasper's training, he was beginning to look as if someday he *might* be a king. The sneering accounts were prejudiced, of course, but could hardly be more biased than Lady Margaret's. Or Lord Stanley's whose praises echoed hers, though he was Richard's man. For the moment. But for how long?

He changed loyalties easily, raising his standard on the side of the leader who could advance him. Was he tempted to hope that leader would be his stepson? The thought sobered me. I glanced at Mother. Where did her sympathies lie? Curiously, because it never used to be in doubt what faction she supported, I hadn't so much as a hint of her feelings about Henry Tudor. Rumor said she approved the match, but since the queen's death I noticed she no longer spoke of Richard as an ogre. She was practical, and Tudor, far away, was a mere claimant.

Did that mean—was it possible—but I couldn't ask her if she, like myself, thought of a dispensation for a marriage between the true king and his most loving subject. We were never affectionately close. Her Woodville family, and Ned as the heir, had come first. While Father used to say heartily it took a man to beget a girl, she wanted only sons. But now, now, perhaps she saw me as Richard's wife and herself royal again.

She was too absorbed in her cards and the pile of coins beside her to notice my questioning look. Lady Margaret was aware of my expression naturally. She missed nothing. "You're concerned about your mother, dear child. You mustn't be anxious. She also sees that only an alliance between the Lancastrian Tudors and the Yorkist Elizabeth will bring peace to our poor country. I understand Lady Grey very well."

The vellum squares cut into my skin as my hand tightened on my cards. I restrained myself from retorting bluntly, *You understand her*?

You're the first who ever did. Her mind is more on her winnings than on my future or even hers. She's never looked ahead or she'd have made friends with the peers and with Richard instead of enraging them by pushing her family into high positions too quickly. Or worse, I might have said, *If you want peace, then for the love of God let us have it and don't tear the people apart with your plotting to put a Welshman on the throne.*

I stood up abruptly. The room was airless, thick with the fog of treachery. I must get away, watch for Richard's return. I muttered I had a headache and was out of the room and on the stairs to the north gallery before Lady Margaret could offer to tend me and perhaps read me one of her books of philosophy. I wondered why she studied them. Her philosophy was to have her son crowned, a principle not found in the most scholarly work.

I stumbled as I ran to the window in the large gallery, but I couldn't see the street, only the gray bulk of the Abbey and the gabled rooftops of Westminster village. Still I could hear the cries of the vendors and the iron-rimmed wagon wheels clanging over the cobblestones so I would know by the cheering when Richard arrived. I smiled a little. The shouting would be soberly respectful. Richard was too remote and serious to evoke the wild response given my genial father.

In that, I could help Richard because the people greeted me enthusiastically when I rode among them, seeing me as King Edward's daughter, calling me their golden princess. I couldn't compare with Mother's silver-gilt loveliness, but somehow the crowds were

almost silent when she appeared. She said they
were envious of her beauty, her high station,
and ignored them. How could she be so coolly
indifferent? I was delighted to be one with the
London citizens who made me feel alive and
loved.

Would they be with me later, in six months,
a year, if I stood at St. Paul's Cross like the
itinerant preachers and said I wished with all
my heart to marry Richard, to be their queen?
After the first shock of the announcement,
surely they would be won over. If—if they could
forget the vicious rumors smearing us with the
accusations that the king and I had an understanding and the queen was taking too long to
die. Whispers spread by a tortuous schemer
who feared desperately that Richard would
marry me. Lady Margaret saving me for her
son?

Was that—? Yes, he was back. Trumpets
sounded below, dutiful shouts and hoofs
clattering in the paved yard. I would see
Richard before ministers and petitions
demanded his attention. The anteroom to his
private apartments were crowded when I
hurried in. Lord Stanley smiling, always
smiling, shook his head. He was deeply sorry,
but the king had so many appointments His
Grace couldn't possibly spare me a minute.

He bowed as if expecting me to retire
gracefully. He couldn't guess—that my whole
life might have been decided today. No
simpering officious Chamberlain should try to
stop me. Outside there were footsteps, then
Richard entered. I curtseyed and gasped, "Your
Grace, I must see you at once. Alone."

Even before Stanley's unpleasant laugh, I

realized I couldn't have thought of a worse
choice of words, underlining as they did our so-
called understanding. But I forgot him and my
own awkwardness as Richard's eyes gleamed
with amusement. The inner room was like him,
austere and soldierly. He motioned me to an oak
chair which might have been taken from a
monk's cell, but I couldn't have sat if it were
cushioned with goose feathers.

I stood stiffly before him, tried vainly to
speak. He poured two glasses of *malvoisie*. I
gulped down half of the sweet wine, choked and
managed to say, "Your Grace, I—I saw
Proud—saw your lady mother earlier and
she—she—"

"I know." His quick smile was kind. I
wished others could see him as I did, not only as
a king overburdened with ruling a country that
traitors attempted to disrupt, but as a young
man who cared about his subjects. He had a
hundred important affairs at hand yet wished
to put me at my ease.

"She explained. And to convince me, she'd
summoned Catesby and Ratcliffe to describe
the people's mood and to suggest—demand
rather—I make it known that I harbor no
unlawful passion for my niece."

His light tone said everything, said too
much. "You—you will marry me off or send me
to a nunnery? Richard!"

My wail was lost in his laugh. "My dear girl,
why should you be forced into a disagreeable
life because of a few lies?"

The king was standing, but I sank into the
hard chair limp with relief. "I may stay at
court?" Near him, I thought dizzy with
happiness. I froze at his next words.

"Certainly. Though they insist if you aren't sent away that I swear publicy that I've no intention of marrying you. Nonsense as we know—" He broke off as if unconsciously he responded to my rebellious thought. *It is not nonsense!*—went on simply, "I agreed of course. My answer will please Stanley or rather his wife. I believe, hope, that Stanley is loyal, but I can't expect so much from Henry Tudor's mother who would have you waiting for her son, neither a nun nor another man's wife."

I must have stood up because suddenly I was beside him. Our eyes met. I flung out, "You tell me what others wish, your mother, your ministers, the Tudor faction, but you—in the name of God, have you no wants of your own?"

"Bessie! But you're only a—" He started to say child, changed to, "You're young and sweet and beautiful and I am—"

I said solemnly to hide my joy at his praise, "Old, old, almost thirty-three, Your Grace."

He moved impatiently. "Years mean nothing. It's how one uses them, and I've done almost nothing."

He never rested from his painstaking work, his stern attention to detail, that made him too edgy, a quality so easily exploited. The Tudor broadsides insinuated that his labors were to forget his murdered nephews; he was sleepless because of a guilty conscience. His remark wasn't intended to be amusing so I tried to keep my mind on such serious matters, but in spite of the couverchef pressed against my mouth, he must have heard my giggle. His brows drew together.

I stuttered, "I—I'm just happy I may stay here." His intent eyes forced me to go on. "You said you have done n-nothing. Your friends claim you crowd into one day what would take another man a week, and y-your enemies state you c-commit some new evil every hour."

A smile touched his lips. "And what do you believe?"

I looked down. How did one say, that once I pitied his constant nervous drive. Until I realized sympathy from a sheltered girl was a mockery for one who since boyhood lashed back savagely. A soft-hearted man wouldn't have survived. He had to forge body and mind into steel and pay for his iron determination with raw nerves. My pity became—if every wicked rumor about him were true, I wouldn't care. There is space in my heart only for—this time I admitted the word—only for love. Yet he will deny me publicly.

His fingers were firmly on my chin, forcing me to look up. "I asked your opinion, but perhaps even a king hasn't the right to pry into a girl's thoughts."

I blurted, "I thank you for not sending me away. I do not th-thank you for swearing to the world that I'm so un-unimportant to you that you'll cast me aside like a n-nobody."

"Little Bessie!" I'm afraid I snorted. I was almost as tall as he. He laughed. "Young Bessie then! The oath isn't only to reassure the country. It's also to protect your reputation."

I said witheringly, "Let the world, let your mother, think what they will."

His voice was gentle. "Who knows what the next months will bring? Perhaps my mother was right and we should find you a bridegroom before—"

"If the Welsh pretender does invade, you'll

send him swimming back to France. If you foolishly let him live to plot again and—"

"You grow bloodthirsty, my dear—my dear child."

I went on recklessly, "And when you've put me out of the way, you'll marry some foreign princess who'll m-make you as miserable as I'll be with the h-husband you'll buy mè as if you were bringing me a toy from a f-fair." I swung toward the door without waiting for permission to leave. "I'm Elizabeth Plantagenet with as good lineage as any lady from any country."

He stepped in front of me and put his hands on my shoulders. His brown eyes flecked with gold were on me questioningly at first, then incredulously, and at last with the warmth of a summer's day. "You've always been dear to me." He corrected himself precisely. "Since you came out of sanctuary. You were a bright light in our staid court with your laughter and vitality, your rushing at life as if those dreary months in the Abbey had starved you. But I did not think—I did not dare to—except, except in my lonely dreams. Dear God, what would you know of the lost and limitless depths of aloneness? An empty arid country of the spirit that would make a desert appear teeming with life."

He was speaking to himself, he would never have confided those thoughts to another. I held myself rigidly as he went on, "One can love one's country, wear oneself out for it, but that doesn't fill one's life. I need—need someone to talk to, to be understanding, share my happiness, my unhappiness, to share hers."

He was thinking of Anne I was sure, perhaps of their sorrow for their son. But no one could mourn forever and stay sane. "Someone

to whom I can speak of uncertainties and cares
that I can't allow others even to guess. I need—"
He stopped abruptly as if he'd said far too
much.

He hadn't said enough. I whispered, "You
need a woman, a wife."

I don't know if I pulled his hands to my
breast or if they were already there, whether I
lifted my mouth to his or he sought mine. My
lips parted under his pressure, and his arms
were around me. I remembered Twelfth Night
when we'd danced and I had wanted to feel his
hard strength holding me to him. And like then,
only a hundred times more intense, my senses
leaped to life so that sight and sound and touch
and hearing and odor were close to pain. His
narrow face and glowing eyes, the warmth of
his body, the sensuous smell of roses striking
lightly against the window overwhelmed me.

He said, "My love," shakily. I wanted to
murmur, *And you are mine*, but I was past
words. His fingers slid under my bodice, and in
spite of hose and skirt our thighs were welded
together. His breath was hot on my cheek, and
the thud of his heart answered the wild hammering of mine.

There were sounds at the door. Richard
muttered, "God's blood!" and stepped back. I
could think only, *He cares for me, he cares, he
cares!* Yet a thread of sanity made me glad no
one could enter without his permission, and I
slid the frilled linen at my throat into place.

"Stanley grows anxious." His voice was
still husky. "He probably wants to be sure," his
smile was twisted, "that I haven't despoiled my
niece. Tudor expects a virgin. May Christ strike
the pretender down if I do not for daring to

think himself worthy of you." He added humbly, "Nor am I worthy. Or perhaps I am because you love me."

"Then you won't—you can't—swear that—" I couldn't go on.

His expression was remote, unreadable. "I'm no Henry the Sixth. He was too saintly to hold the throne. I will not chance losing even one supporter for a few scruples. I will take the oath not to marry you." I didn't realize I was crying, but my face was wet and there was a salty taste in my mouth. "Bessie, a forced promise—it isn't binding. Later my confessor will release me from it."

I blinked, patted my eyes so the tear stains wouldn't show and smiled dazzlingly, I think from the light on Richard's face. I would dream of the future, not of the endless plotting and turning, though I knew he was right. One had to live with maneuverings, untruths, if one wanted to live at all. I walked slowly out as he held the door for me. Stanley was in the anteroom I suppose, and the ministers and petitioners. I didn't see them, too intent on keeping my movements dignified so no one would guess I was fleeing to a new sanctuary, my room.

I prayed my sisters or a friend wouldn't be there for an hour of idle chatter, sighed thankfully at the silence that greeted me. I pulled off my headdress, ran my fingers through my hair, held out a strand critically. Yes, it was the reddish-gold of the Plantagenets.

"Bessie!"

I jerked around at the sound of my mother's voice. I hadn't noticed her in the shadowed corner near the bed.

"M-madam!" I wished angrily I didn't

always stutter when I was nervous. "I—I thought you were still at cards."

She said flatly, "I came up when I heard the news. Even you must have caught some whisper of it."

"You mean another report on the in-invasion?"

"In late summer, and this time it appears definite. But word of that came yesterday. If you'd get your head out of the clouds—" She broke off. I realized abruptly from her clipped speech that she was in one of her cold rages.

I was bewildered. Why was she furious now about a message that arrived a day ago? "R-Richard said nothing."

I shouldn't have admitted being with him I realized as her face sharpened. "I suspected that's where you were. Bessie, you didn't allow—? Of course not. My daughter wouldn't let a perjurer and murderer to so much as touch her. The rumor that's all over the palace is that the king will swear publicly he won't marry you."

I said faintly, "Yes," and then, "Of late you've spoken kindly of him, yet suddenly today—I don't understand."

"Dear Heaven! Need you be so thick-witted? I just told you he'll take an oath renouncing you."

I almost said "a forced oath," choked back the words, knowing she'd spread them around so they'd reach more ears than the story of the renunciation. She went on harshly. "Since he won't make you queen we must, as Lady Margaret said, look to Tudor to present you with that honor."

"Tudor! He wants me because I've a better

claim than he has."

She snapped, "But you don't have troops. He does."

We stared at each other as if we were antagonists. Incoherent, passionate words about Richard filled my throat. I didn't say them, knowing too well what I should say. Royalty dutifully married for political reasons, accepted the bridegroom the parents and ministers chose. I must agree that I deferred to her will. If she now wished to conspire with the Lancastrians so I might wear a crown, it was my wish too.

I spat out, "Should the pretender against all reason defeat Richard and offer me a crown, how could I accept it from his treacherous hands?"

Color crept into her pale face. I braced myself for a torrent of words on ingratitude, stupidity, a monstrous lack of feeling. None came. She said at last quietly, "Every girl ought to be able to marry for love as I did. But you can't, my dear. My husband was seated firmly on the throne. Richard may have traders, merchants, farmers supporting him, but as always, the lords will decide the battle, and you cannot guess how many have been bribed. Only the uniting of York and Lancaster will end the warfare and corruption." Her voice hardened. "I am doing what is best for my country and my family."

I was scornful. "So you have been corrupted by fine promises of the future."

"At least," she flashed, "I've been assured of a better title than Lady Grey, mother of bastards."

She went out before I could find an answer.

If there was one. The one retort was in my heart. Richard loved me. Which was no answer at all to scheming women like Mother and Lady Margaret. I wanted to rush to the king and tell him—In spite of my fury I almost laughed. Tell him what he knew far better than I, that he was surrounded by treason?

Had I decided to speak of the web of conspiracy, it would have been impossible. Richard was already off to London again to stay at his home, Crosby Place in Bishopsgate, with its roofs higher than all the other houses and set amidst flower beds and kitchen gardens. Unlike Proud Cis's castle, the house was restful with the wide windows and large private quarters in fashion of late with merchant builders.

But I doubted if he would rest. Since he hadn't been granted the taxes he needed, he was borrowing heavily for the upkeep of the fleet and his standing army. At least there were satisfying reports of loans subscribed by abbots and merchants and lords. Lady Margaret looked grim at this show of support. And more than grim, in a frenzied rage, when Richard finally published a broadside of his own.

He proclaimed that rebels and traitors had chosen as their captain a Henry Tudor, ambitious and insatiable, who would usurp the name of the royal estate of this realm of England. Tudor had no title or claim for he was descended of bastard blood both of his father's side and his mother's. Richard proclaimed that the pretender intended to commit murder and robbery and disinheritance on a scale never seen in any Christian country.

I wanted to sing because Richard had struck back with their own weapons though,

unlike their broadsides, Richard's was true. But
the next day I could have wept. Richard was
marching north to his headquarters at
Nottingham, and I dared not ask for an
audience before he left. That would have
damaged him after his oath in St. John's Priory,
that he had no plans to marry his niece. But I
might, might catch a glimpse of him.

No one was in charge, so I ordered out the
royal barge for a trip down the river and
casually invited any ladies who wished to
accompany me. Half a dozen came eagerly,
pleased with any diversion on this hot summer
afternoon. We had little entertainment with
most of the court in the city or traveling to their
estates. My companions' gay chatter and their
bright gowns gave our expedition an innocent
holiday air. I thought dully, So I, too, am
learning to hide my feelings, to scheme. But I
could not make myself care.

I couldn't quite conceal my interest when
we drew near the Tower, but my manner went
unnoticed as everyone leaned forward. Richard
must have moved from Crosby Place because
the royal Leopard fluttered from the pinnacled
White Tower. Yeomen of the Crown paced the
walls, and mounted men were riding out from
the gate toward Tower Hill under Richard's
White Boar. Behind them, clattered wagons
with bombards, fowlers, falcons and culverins,
the burnished weapons glittering in the sun as
the carts lumbered clumsily up the slope.
Trumpets blared as if already sounding the
inevitable victory while another company was
forming, Norfolk's, under his standard of the
White Lyon.

I wondered if the expert Flemish gunners

the king needed so urgently had arrived, and
then forgot them as a man galloped across the
drawbridge. Richard on his gelding, White
Surrey. He reined in briefly as if in answer to
my frantic prayers, and I could make out, or
thought I could, his long doeskin boots and
black doublet and the collar of York, gold
Sunnes-in-Splendor alternating with enamelled
white roses. Then, a dark figure among the
mailed cavalry, he was swallowed up in the
shifting mass of soldiers. I sank back wildly
grateful as if sight of him was an omen of
success like the brazen cry of the trumpets.

CHAPTER 14

I remembered my certainty of victory, clung to it when three days later, Richard ordered the Plantagenet heirs to retire to Sheriff Hutton. For our safety. That meant—could it be possible—that he wasn't sure of a swift triumph and wanted us where his army could throw a shield around us. I thought of Mother's remark about bribery and asked stammeringly of the lords.

The messenger, a leathery-skinned middle-aged man, said reassuringly that no one had deserted Richard. Lord Stanley was ill but expected to be well soon, and his son was with the king. The Percies of Northumberland hadn't rendezvoused yet either, but they promised to march south if—when—Tudor landed.

I said suddenly, "The Burgundians! How many Flemish gunners did Duchess Margaret send her brother?"

He shuffled his feet, looked down at his dusty boots, beyond the yew hedge to the river, said finally, "His Grace laughs at the pretender, my lady, and is out hawking or hunting every day, he is. Them orders you're to go to Yorkshire, why that's because he's a good general, Old Dick—I mean His Grace. Don't take no chances of abduction or something by a bloody Lancastrian. For a hostage you know."

I nodded. I'd never have thought of that possibility, but I couldn't find relief at the simple explanation. I repeated my question.

"Flemish?" He sounded as if it were a new word to him. He wiped his mouth on his torn sleeve, grunted at last, "Ain't no foreigners in Old Dick's—His Grace's—army, just good English fighting men, lady." He bowed and slid away before he had to think of more uncomfortable answers.

I stood rigid on the garden path above the Thames. Richard's own sister had failed him. How could she? The Dowager Duchess was probably the wealthiest princess in Europe. She could afford to send an army, but hadn't dispatched even a score of gunners, though she knew how few English were trained like the French and Flemish artillerymen. Tudor's spies must have persuaded her to believe every lie they had spread about Richard. So now, without spending a florin, she was supporting a nobody, a Welshman, who was bringing convicts from French prisons to war against the country where she had been born.

I was roused from my stunned fury by Lady Margaret Beaufort's voice saying pleasantly, "Shouldn't you see to your packing, my dear

child? When the king commands, one obeys.
While he's still the king." I looked after her as
she went up the path. Her amiable tone was
almost as chilling as the news of the Burgundians, underlining the fact that Tudor's army
was said to have French cannon and profes-
sional gunners.

I started to follow her slowly. The air was
oppressive, or was the heaviness the dull ache
of my spirit? Without warning lightning flashed
from a bank of clouds in the east, and thunder
roared like a dozen *bombards*. A rush of rain
drummed on the hard sand. I was wet through
in moments, but I stopped near a bench covered
with vines, a bright green pattern on the
glistening wooden boards. Lightning was a con-
tinuous streak now in the gray mass. I welcomed the forked splinters of light and the
crash after crash of thunder as if the swift
summer storm were crying out my new fears
and my desperate hopes.

A page darted from the hooded stone doorway above me, and suggested politely that I go
inside while he obviously restrained himself
from clutching my arm to drag me to the palace
before his plumed cap and murrey doublet were
as soaked as my dress.

The raging storms went on day after day,
and our carriages sank into muddy ruts on the
Great North road. Rain, slashing through the
canvas window flaps, dripped on whoever sat in
the outside seat. The fields were awash in the
torrents of water, and when we stopped at an
inn or an abbey for a night, we heard growling
among the farmers in common room or great
kitchen. A generation, longer, since there had
been such weather that destroyed most of the

crops. It was a judgment. They didn't say on whom, out of fear perhaps, not knowing whether their neighbors were for York or Lancaster.

The talk was upsetting, and I was relieved when we finally arrived at Sheriff Hutton though the castle loomed dark and uninviting through the downpour. I clambered stiffly from the carriage and stepped ankle-deep into a pool of water. But now the wide door was flung open, light streamed out and we were greeted by warm voices, a leaping fire on the hearth and a crowd of servants who carried in our chests. Two maids helped me change from my soaked clothes, then led the way to the great stone hall where ale, hot soup, bread, cold mutton and venison were being placed on a trestle table.

I thought myself too miserable to eat, but the aroma of food and the cheerful sputtering flames drew me forward, and I reached eagerly for a mug of steaming soup, which a smiling young girl handed me. She was too well-dressed to be a servant, and her unbound hair was reddish-gold like mine.

I said, "Why, you're Meg. It's so long since we met, I didnt' recognize you." Behind her a younger boy was staring at me, his mouth half open and face intent as if trying to place me.

During our journey north I had forgotten that all the Plantagenet heirs were to be here, realized now that naturally the Duke of Clarence's son and daughter would be among the group. Clarence had been attainted and his family barred from the succession, but if Tudor's questionable heritage was accepted by some, any of us could equally make a claim.

I glanced up as John, Earl of Lincoln,

strode in, his cloak plastered wetly to his body. A stocky, quick-moving young man, he was the true heir, the nephew Richard had named his successor after little Eddie died. Unexpectedly, in spite of my anxiety for the king, for the future, I felt happy and safe surrounded by my cousins in the fire-lit room with the storm howling outside. Lincoln didn't share my pleasure. He was scowling as he bowed to us and crossed to the table for a tankard of ale. I wondered at his lack of manners but hurried after him, introduced myself briefly and asked if there were bad news.

"No." He gulped down half his ale, then disparagingly eyed his cousins chattering over their bread and meat.

Ah, they—we all—were the reason for his sulky anger which I understood because I felt as he did. I too wanted to be with Richard. I smiled. "You think it an indignity to be penned up with women and children?" His dark eyes widening in surprise told me I'd guessed right. "You've been trained as heir and wish to be where the fighting is."

Some of his sullenness vanished. "Exactly! You're a girl so you can't know how degrading this is. I've led my own troops against the Scots, yet now I'm to wait behind walls as if I were a child." He added fiercely, "It's my right to be with the king. You'll never realize how hard it is to be denied even seeing him."

I held back an angry retort. What in God's name did he think I desired? But if I'd spoken aloud, he'd have brushed the remark aside. Waiting was a woman's duty. Perhaps it was, but waiting in a vast silence was intolerable.

I said tentatively, "I wonder—you can do us all a great service." One I'd gladly, gladly perform if I weren't hampered by skirts, by etiquette, by unbreakable tradition. "The king won't allow you to fight, but he didn't say you couldn't watch. Not in Nottingham, you would be noticed, but if you sent a messenger there, he could bring you word when Tudor lands. Then when Richard marches to meet him, you could follow."

I was afraid he'd sneer at the suggestion as a feminine ruse, but his face lit up. "Madame—Lady—Cousin Elizabeth, I'll post a man south at once." He started past me, stopped at my amused expression. Through the window there was complete darkness and the drumming of rain. He laughed, his scowl gone. "I'll give him instructions now so he can leave at the first light."

His contempt for the children because he'd been placed with them changed. They kept up our spirits with their games of hoodman's blind and hide and seek and *jeu de cartes* when otherwise Lincoln and I would have spent the dragging hours watching for a rider on the empty road. We worried that the messenger might have been recruited or that a battle had already been fought.

Then on a morning when the sun struggled palely through thinning clouds, Lincoln's man returned. He heard the news before he reached Nottingham. Tudor, he spat on the wet stones, had landed in Wales, at Milford Haven.

Lincoln barked, "King Richard! Where's he?" waited only to hear that supporters were to rally at Leicester and was calling his squire to ready his armor and to the grooms to saddle two horses. He was in the castle and out again while the messenger's mount was still being rubbed down. I shook my head when I saw that, he, like his squire, wore just a cuirass and carried an open-visored helmet.

He grinned. "I can move faster in light armor. And I'll have to be falcon-swift if the king discovers I followed him."

I gazed after them enviously as they clattered down the road and swung out of sight behind a stand of oaks and beeches. Abruptly I wanted to call Lincoln back. Now it was too late, I wondered what insanity had prompted me to suggest this action and him to welcome the idea. Richard's caution was right. The heir should be safeguarded. I tried to comfort myself with the thought that no one would respect Lincoln as the future king if he were willing to wait tamely until the fighting was over, and that besides, he wasn't in danger. He was too in awe of Richard to join the battle against the royal command.

Each day was endless as I watched the road again and with no Lincoln to share the unbearable suspense. Yet the nights were longer because there was little hope a messenger would arrive after sundown. Too many robber bands roamed the countryside for anyone to travel without a strong escort. I passed the time attempting to talk with the others but found myself stopping halfway through a question and too intent on listening for hoofbeats to hear an answer if anyone replied.

Lincoln himself returned late one afternoon. I was out riding with Meg and saw the muddied horses in the stableyard as we dismounted. I jerked up the hem of my skirt to run past the sentries, up the steps and into the hall. The light slanting through the narrow windows shone on Lincoln's fair hair, dusty unshaven face and stained half-armor. I gasped, "Are you hurt? What—what is the news?"

His squire unbuckled his cuirass, and he slumped into a chair. "I—don't know. No, I'm not hurt, but what if I were?"

I thought the same as I caught at his heavy shoulder. If he weren't injured, how dared he come back not knowing what had happened— how Richard was? He saw my expression, and the corner of his mouth twitched.

"I agree with you, Bessie. I'm as furious with my clumsiness as you are." His lips thinned. "I saw the beginning—our forces were on a hill and Tudor's below us—the king was all right then. Jesus! Jesus! The battle must be over now and I—I have so little to report."

I shrilled, "Tell us that much then, tell us!"

He said dully, "I wasn't noticed until after the first charge. The king ordered his gunners to fire. I thought the roar would shake the earth to pieces, and the chainshot tear their lines apart. But—but our gunners weren't well trained and most of the shot plowed into the ground."

At that my eyes went to young Meg and unreasonably I wanted to take out my rage on her because her father had named her after the Dowager Duchess Margaret of Burgundy. I said harshly to Lincoln, "Go on, go on, some of the fire must have struck the traitors."

"Yes, their advance wavered. Their officers had to whip the soldiers with the flat of their swords to prod them on. When they reached the slope, our bombards fired and the king signalled the Duke of Norfolk. They went in, the duke and his son and a mass of knights like a steel wedge. The rebels scrambled back to their own standards. We all cheered, yelled like madmen. We forgot, you know, the paper pinned to the duke's tent the night before.''

I said dazed, "Paper? *Paper*? What would—"

"A note that was found by a page, a sentry, someone. It read, 'Jockey of Norfolk, be not too bold, for Dickon your master is bought and sold.' And God's blood, the warning was true. Sir William Stanley, who had sworn to support King Richard, swung about and threw his whole force against Norfolk. The duke—the duke was unhelmeted and killed by an arrow.'' He wet his dry lips with his tongue, absently gulped the ale his squire brought.

I swallowed and swallowed at the bitter taste in my mouth, stuttered, "Lord St-stanley?"

"He didn't desert, and Norfolk's soldiers fought on even without a leader. The king spurred up and down our lines rallying the troops for the next charge. That was when he saw me, I had come too close. The way his eyes blazed, I'd rather have faced the turncoat Stanley's men. Placed me under arrest and to be sure I was safe—safe! Did that matter?—made me ride with his herald and pursuivants to see why the Earl of Northumberland hadn't come up with his moss-troopers, three or four thousand of them. Well, we met his army a mile out. While our herald and his bodyguard cursed each other, I slipped away.'' He stood up, kicked viciously at the bench and snarled, "So I'm here with not so much as a dagger prick while real men are—" He couldn't go on.

My fury that he had returned too early died at the misery in his face. I whispered, "Richard has never been defeated." Then because talking might dull his wretchedness, I said, "You've told us so little. Perhaps I won't understand the maneuvers, but can't you say more than that our army was on a hill?"

A growl behind me echoed my question. I'd been so intent on Lincoln that I hadn't realized the whole household, servants and stableboys and guards, had gathered to hear him. The sun was setting, casting fingers of purplish gold through the lancet windows, but no one moved to prepare supper or lay out trenchers and mugs and platters.

Lincoln crossed to the hearth, turned his figure dark as it blocked out the hissing flames. "Tudor landed at Milford Haven—you heard of that—and the Welsh joined those two thousand mangy men of his straight from the French jails. Some of the English came in with him too, lords from the West country like Shrewsbury, tearing off their badges of the Fanged Boar. Shrewsbury's screaming revenge on all Yorkists because King Edward promised to marry a daughter of his house, Lady Eleanor, then threw her aside and—but that's so long ago, everyone else has forgotten—" He broke off appalled.

It was a moment before I also realized with a shock that he was speaking of my father, of the precontract which had changed my queen mother's title to Lady Grey and made me and my family illegitimate. I said, "No matter. Go on."

His teeth gleamed as he smiled suddenly.

"But it wasn't all good fortune for Tudor. His convict mercenaries brought something besides weapons and supplies from France. The sweating sickness. No one offered them food now. The villagers and farmers gathered everything they had and ran from his army when they heard of the fever and delirium and death within hours."

He paused as someone handed him another tankard. "Unfortunately Tudor didn't have to live off the land. Still I couldn't worry that Tudor was well supplied and that Wales and the West Country were lost. Not when I saw the royal army leaving Leicester where the lords had rallied. The king rode his war-gelding across the River Soar and along the Kirkby Mallory Road in his white armor and with a gold crown on his helmet. No one could question he was the true king. The troops marched five abreast, three miles long I was told, knights and men-at-arms and foot soldiers under the standards of the Leopard and the Sunne-in-Splendour, th Lyon of March, the Falcon Unfettered, the White Boar. The world seemed filled with the glitter of steel and the scarlet and gold and white and blue of the banners." He stopped. In the dimness I saw color flood his face as he made an embarrassed gesture. "But everyone's seen an army on the move."

There were cries he should tell us everything. We were too far away to hear even the usual distorted rumors.

He cleared his throat and muttered, "Well, that afternoon we—I mean the king—camped twelve miles west of Leicester near the villages of Sutton Cheyney and Market Bosworth. It was sort of quiet around the campfires, but there was plenty to eat, the king saw to that. And bread and ale the next morning though he, King Richard, said he wouldn't break his fast until he destroyed the rebels. That was when the paper was found that Dickon had been bought and sold, and the king—''

Lincoln half-closed his eyes as if to recall the scene exactly. ''The king read the doggerel aloud, and even from a distance he looked— looked like death. Not moving, you know, and his cheekbones like ridges, and when he spoke his voice was iron. He said that he had been too kind, too forgiving to corrupt friends. After he dealt with the enemy on the field, the turncoats in his own camp would also drown in their own blood. Never again would he pardon secret treachery among those who pretended loyalty. He had tried to have peace at home, but from this day on there would be blood justice.''

Lincoln attempted a laugh, failed. ''I think every man there felt the king was speaking only to him. You could feel the terror as if he were accusing you. And yet, and yet, he made you want to go out and die for him. Then the trumpets sounded and we, the royal army, marched to Ambien Hill outside Bosworth before the pretender could seize it. It gave us the advantage of ground, the king's a master at that. The advance was on the south slope facing Tudor, and the bombards and serpentines on the hilltop. Lord Stanley was on our left and Sir William Stanley's dragons in the right wing.''

He darkened when he said Sir William's name, went on flatly. ''Tudor's cannons were dragged into position, but anyone could see they wouldn't be of much use with us above him even though he had French gunners. And the rebels had to cross the broken plain and maneuver about a swamp before they could charge."

He added in contempt, "Their standards looked brave, but the Dragon banner of Cadwallader was behind the others. The Tudor was staying well away from the field though he expects his followers to believe that he has the right to our Leopard as well as the Dragon."

He cleared his throat again. "They advanced—I told you that and how their officers had to prod them—but they finally came on in strength in their red jackets and half-armor. We waited and waited for the king to signal the bombardiers. He lifted his sword at last, and they put their matches to the touch-holes. The thunder was like the Last Judgment. Our archers and crossbowmen shot volley after volley into the enemy. Then Norfolk charged and—and was killed when Stanley threw his dragoons against his old comrade. And I was sent away."

His voice trailed off. I wanted to cry out that he must have more to tell us, to say what, what, what happened next. I thought of Richard riding up and down the lines, rallying his forces. A glittering, unmistakable target in his white armor and with the circle of gold on his helmet. Why wasn't he like the pretender, waiting behind his columns. He was my love, and what woman admired reckless courage at such a moment? The rash confidence that a will of iron would win the day? Oh Richard, my love!

I would have faith. The battlefield was his home, and Lord Stanley, in spite of his wife,

hadn't declared for his stepson. Perhaps he was
swayed by a deeper loyalty than his brother's,
Sir William. Or more likely he decided that
Tudor would fall, and he couldn't hope his
betrayal would be forgiven. My heart lightened
as I remembered that the Percies had been near
Bosworth. Thousands of mosstroopers, accustomed to the fury of Scottish raids in Northumberland, would be the hammer blow to drive
the rebels from the field.

Soon now, soon, the king's messenger
would arrive, and I'd return to Westminster. To
wait again but that waiting would be endurable.
In a few months, people would forget the frail
queen and wish the king to have a direct heir to
a throne no longer challenged.

I repeated the comforting words that a
messenger must come soon—soon. Yet I wondered how I would get through the minutes, the
hours, the days, until I heard trumpets and
hoofbeats and the jingle of metal and leather,
saw the horses clattering to the gate and men-
at-arms riding under the White Boar.

Each morning I woke thinking, *Today they
will be here*. And each night promised myself in
anguish, *Tomorrow*. This dreadful silence can't
go on. Richard must realize how I suffer, how
we all suffer in this desolate countryside, which
I once thought beautiful, without even a rumor
to feed our starving hopes.

That tomorrow came. At noon. Trumpets
blared, and I stood up from the table where we
were dining. A slice of veal slipped from my
fingers. I wiped my hands absently on my blue
skirt and looked feverishly at Lincoln. Had my
longing made me imagine— No, he was on his
feet too, striding to the narrow window, said,

"Christ! I can't see them yet. Wait, wait! There's the banner. It's—it's the Griffin Claw."

I ran to the door. My cousin's voice stopped me. "Bessie! It's more proper to receive our visitors in the hall."

I choked on an hysterical laugh. "P-proper? Proper?" Yet I turned at something in his tone, and his expression drew me back reluctantly. "Lord Stanley's Griffin Claw? That doesn't—it doesn't mean—"

He said gently, "No, it doesn't follow that Lord Stanley is a traitor just because his brother is. Still we are Plantagenets, and it is for him to come to us." I wondered how he could speak so kindly to me when he must fear his own world might be in ruins. When he thought of me only as the king's kinswoman, not knowing Richard was my life.

Stanley stood in the doorway, his pale protuberant eyes moving deliberately from the servants to Clarence's two children to Lincoln and me. He smiled, and the breath I'd been holding escaped me. Dear God, Richard was all right. He had sent Stanley. My throat was too tight to utter a word or I would have screamed, *Tell us quickly, what happened? What are the king's plans?* I recalled irrelevantly how I heard Stanley boast that he was the man who'd told Queen Marguerite—brutally I was sure—that her army was defeated and her son dead. But he would have no ill news for me, not when his smile was so friendly.

He came forward, a score of men at his back, as if, Lincoln said in low-voiced contempt, our small household might be an ambush. I think I guessed then. But that was impossible. I knew only that Lincoln believed the king was dead. But how wrong he was! Stanley was booming genially, "His Grace regrets he could not send word to you earlier. He's been too occupied with important affairs since his victory at Bosworth."

I nodded. The message didn't sound like Richard, but of course Stanley relayed it in his own words. Lincoln gestured to a squire to pour wine for the escort, said casually though I could feel how rigid his body was, "What are the king's commands? Do we return with you?"

One of the men-at-arms laughed, the sound harsh in the quiet. Stanley shook his head. "Not yet, my lord. You are to remain here until after the coronation—"

His voice went on, droning meaninglessly after that incredible word. Lincoln, better prepared, said tautly, "I asked about the true king. Would you have us believe a Welsh adventurer will be crowned at Westminster?"

"My lord, even the Earl of Lincoln isn't allowed to speak treason."

"*I* am not a traitor, Lord Stanley."

"Good! Then you will swear loyalty to our sovereign lord, Henry VII?"

Before Lincoln could answer, I caught at Stanley's slashed sleeve of purple velvet. "I d-don't understand. A T-Tudor the king? Why do you say something so terrible? Northumberland, all the Percies, they were near the field with over three thousand men. Lincoln told me. And you, you had thousands more. H-how can you pretend Tudor wasn't crushed?"

He patted my hand. "My dear Lady Elizabeth, when the order came to charge the Lancastrians, I thought of you stripped of your birthright, of your brother's crown which

384

Richard stole. Of both your brothers murdered by the man who should have been their shield. Could I aid a bloodthirsty usurper against the rightful king? I could not in," he hesitated, "conscience commit so shameful a deed."

Lincoln's laugh rang out, but I repeated stubbornly, "How can you pretend Tudor wasn't crushed? The Percies—"

Stanley flushed with irritation though his tone had a forced patience. "I had the courage to strike against the usurper Richard's flank, but Northumberland did nothing. He brought up his troops and then simply watched the battle."

"But you—the Percies—swore allegiance to R-Richard, you—you're playing some game with me. T-tell me the truth."

Lincoln said scornfully, "Bessie, he has. He blows with the prevailing wind. At a price. I hope it was high enough to help one forget broken oaths, betrayal of a trust, years of treachery. Does Tudor have that much money? Does anyone?"

I hardly noticed Stanley's scarlet face. I said proudly, "Richard, King Richard, always conquers. He is a soldier, not a man like the pretender cowering behind his lines while others fight. Richard won the day. Why will you not say it?"

He stared at me as if I were mad and said angrily, "The usurper Richard refused to listen to the supporters left him. They begged him to retreat. He shouted arrogantly he'd live or die as King of England. And he—you said he was a soldier—with only his bodyguard he spurred down the slope and up toward the Dragon standard."

Lincoln said drily, "A long ride?"

"Half a mile at the least." He gulped as though trying to recall the words. "No one expected a maniac without an army to charge victorious troops. King Henry was on a hillock waiting for his captains' reports on casualties. And then like a lightning bolt this madman and his mad guard strike toward the king through our men-at-arms, maiming and killing. The usurper's lance broke when he slew one knight, but he flashed out his battle-axe and cut through the helmet of the standard-bearer. It was murder. The battle was over."

I thought, *Ah, this part is true, Richard a whirlwind, scattering his enemies, not accepting defeat.*

Lincoln said tensely, "Murder? Because you hoped to God the battle *was* over so that your blood and brains wouldn't also be a pool on the earth greedy to suck them in."

Stanley looked shaken, recovered himself angrily. "When has Richard hesitated to murder? No one was safe from his vicious temper." His tongue touched his thick lips like one tasting a delicacy. "Much good his crimes did him. He caught up the royal banner of Cadwallader, tossing it away like a rag and turned on our king. King Henry," he paused to choose his words, "stepped back sensibly so his body-guards needn't worry over injuring him. They," he tasted the delicacy again, "were on the usurper like hounds fleshed on one of his white boars."

I waited politely for him to continue, to explain his story was a tasteless hoax, that the pretender had been killed or fled into the countryside. That Richard the king was—that

Richard—A sound forced its way through my throat.

The thick lips were smiling again. "The—shall we call it an execution—was over in minutes, and the white armor he was so vain about was hacked in a dozen places before it was torn from the unworthy body. Someone kinder than Richard threw the naked corpse over a mule and had it taken to the Grey Friars in Leicester. I suppose the burial was there, I didn't ask. More pressing affairs were at hand. The usurper's crown had fallen from his helmet, and my own brother found it and presented it to His Grace, King Henry."

I gazed past him, not seeing him, not hearing his escort's shuffling feet, a shout for more ale. Or did I? I do remember the solid strength of Lincoln's shoulder against mine, his fingers tight around my wrist, the stripes of gold the sun painted across the floor, and the sound of little Meg weeping. I would have gone to her, she must be terrified, but I couldn't move, could only envy her the relief of tears. Tears, the blessed comfort of crying out my anguish, but not here, not before Stanley.

They were still talking, Stanley and Lincoln. How could they attempt to fill this limitless silence with words? And why didn't the turncoat Stanley leave, give me privacy to face the truth, to try to believe the unbelievable? So that we all could? My loss had dulled me to my cousins' fears. What would become of them?

Stanley was speaking to me, repeating himself evidently from the sharp impatience of his voice, something about my returning to Westminster after Christmas. But Lincoln's answer was clear, like a knife. "Surely, Lord Stanley, if Bessie's to be your queen, shouldn't you practice a more courtierlike tone? And need you point out so often that the Tudor insists on an early coronation so he'll be acknowledged king in his own right, whatever that is, before he marries a princess who alone can make his claim secure?"

The pretender marry—me? I recalled vaguely he had sworn that long ago, but I was indifferent to the vows of a stranger living in exile. Now, now was I expected to forget Richard and become the Welshman's bride? My lips drew back. Proud Cis. She showed me the way. A nunnery.

Stanley said, "Our future queen smiles at your foolish remark, Lincoln. She's well aware His Grace needs no woman to help him hold onto the crown which he won on the field of battle."

"You don't understand our people. How could you? Your eyes and ears are used only for your own advancement. But I know our English. They believe the Plantagenets are the true heirs. If the pretender thinks otherwise, he'll find the chair of state rocking under his skinny buttocks."

"You speak rashly for one whose life and estates are dependent on His Grace. Your words won't be forgotten." He glanced at his escort as if longing for the power to do more than simply detain Lincoln at Sheriff Hutton.

Lincoln said cheerfully, "I hope you will remember, they are the truth." He turned to me. "I'm sure, Bessie, the Lord Stanley has your permission to retire?"

I nodded mutely, too numbed to have thought of the simple solution to be rid of our guests. Stanley jerked his head at his men, started to stamp out, then swung back and drew a rolled parchment from his doublet. He said ungraciously, "From His Highness to be delivered to the Lady—the Princess Elizabeth," and left.

The ribbons and seal on the scroll were a blur of scarlet and gold. What could the pretender possibly have to say to me? What did it matter? The document fell from my hand as I said urgently, "Lincoln, I'll never marry—"

I said shakily, "You were brave but so reckless, Lincoln. He'll never forgive your insults, and the castle will be well guarded. If you make the slighest move, Stanley will say you tried to escape and have you killed."

"I'll do better than try." My stunned senses stirred in surprise at his casual tone. "I've been in and out of Sheriff Hutton for years. I have ways to get past sentries, and my friends will help me reach the Continent. Bosworth wasn't the final battle, Bessie. No seedy adventurer will rob me of England. I'll raise men and money, and you'll be rescued long before your tardy suitor sends for you. You see, to back the support from abroad, I'll recruit loyal Yorkists here, and my army can live off the land."

I gasped in relief at his careless certainty of being safe, but couldn't make even that small sound as he finished. We weren't defeated. Lincoln would return and drive out the Lancastrians. We would—

I was only six our first time in sanctuary, but I still remembered the stories of Marguerite's troops plundering villages and farms,

remembered the slaughter of St. Albans and
Towton, the thousands of corpses buried
together in enormous graves. Was peace between Englishmen to be found only in death?

Lincoln was saying, "Sounds too glorious to
be true, doesn't it? A Yorkist on the throne and
the rebels scattered."

I wet my dry lips, wiped my hand across my
mouth, finally stuttered, "D-dear Christ,
no-no!" My voice rose. "L-Lincoln, no, no, no!
We must be done with war."

He laughed, said I was too shocked to think
now, but I would soon feel as he did. He kissed
me lightly and hurried away, to plan his escape,
I suppose.

His figure at the door was shadowy through
my mist of tears. I prayed God he would give up
his mad scheme, knew heavily he wouldn't, that
there would be more battlefields and plunder
and graves. I would at least try to prevent the
horror. So now for me there would be no retreat
to the haven of a nunnery, no mourning for
Richard. The future was not mine to spend. Let
the pretender, let our new—our new—king use
me as a sop to the people. Better than being
used to relight the flames of civil war. The
country had been washed in blood again and
again and again. I would have no more.

My head rose. The future *was* mine to
spend. I alone could draw Yorkists and Lancastrians together. I would go willingly to
Henry. Our marriage would be no worse than
that of most royal couples, and there'd be
peace, trade, laughter. I almost cried out, *But
there'll be no Richard!* I would not think of him,
of how one could ever, ever stir my senses,

awaken enchantment, arouse troubling desire as he had.

I glanced down startled as a small hand slipped into mine. Meg. I'd forgotten the child. Her reddened eyes were trustingly on mine. "Will—will everything be all right, Bessie?"

I smiled unsteadily and said as one always says, "Yes, darling, quite all right." Perhaps, perhaps it would be true. I would have children, and what greater victory than to create new life in a world I could make less brutal?

Her face lighted. "And you'll be our queen. Oh, Bessie! When will you be crowned? When?"

I said carefully, "The—the king will decide. The preparations take time and there's no reason for h-haste." The Plantagenet rulers—oh Richard, Richard—were more generous in giving immediate honor to their wives. My teeth cut into my lower lip at how quickly I forgot my resolve. My thoughts must be all for my husband. I tried to picture him, remembered my irritation with his mother's extravagant praises. But even then I'd been aware that Lady Margaret's description was no more biased than the Yorkist report which allowed Henry no pleasant qualities at all.

If I had ever seen him, spoken to him or at least—I turned abruptly, my eyes searching the floor for the message I'd dropped, indifferent to anything from him. The document had rolled behind a stool. I broke the gold wax seal, opened the crackling parchment and frowned as I tried to decipher the spidery writing.

His first sentence was a stiff inquiry about my health, then assured me with equal stiffness that he was well. He hoped I was looking forward to our wedding as eagerly as he

anticipated the event. Eagerly! It was early
September, and I was to go to London after
Christmas. As if in reply to my quick scorn, he
wrote that unlike his Plantagenet cousins, he
did not act precipitately.

I would have snorted agreement except that
he went on to say he trusted I wouldn't be too
disappointed that he also lacked his cousins'
dashing gallantry, but he would make a good
husband, faithful to me and to his country. I
would also find he was hard working in the
affairs of the kingdom and, his advisers told
him, almost excessively careful with money, not
a regal trait. The touch of humility was erased
as he added he wouldn't foolishly remit taxes
like Richard, but the levies he collected would
be spent on the realm, not in extravagant living
like Edward.

Did he expect me to be pleased with his dis-
paragement of my family? As to his coronation
before we even met—I wondered grimly what
soothing explanation he'd offer, then my lips
parted in surprise at a point I hadn't
considered—he begged me to understand that
he wasn't motivated by any ill feeling toward
me. It was for the security of the kingdom.

If he were not recognized as ruler by right
of birth—he had crossed out the next words,
but I think they were "and conquest"—the
country might again be divided, this time by
separate loyalties to husband or to wife. The
extremists would attempt to force the royal
couple to work against each other, and the
pressures would be difficult to resist. He was
sure I would see that we must do what we could
to discourage the war factions.

He ended as he began with concern for my

health, urging me to be careful so that we would have sturdy children. There must be no more uncertainty over the succession. And he sent his loving respect to his future wife the Princess Elizabeth.

I didn't know whether to laugh or cry at the passionless phrases. But of course he'd been in exile most of his life under watchful eyes, sometimes a guest, sometimes a prisoner, but always a prize that Brittany or France might sell at any time to the Yorkists. He must have learned years ago as a child to conceal any emotion.

I rolled the parchment thoughtfully, unrolled it, noticed there was writing on the other side, another assurance he was not a spendthrift. He wouldn't pour out money on his own coronation which was merely an official function to have his rightful title acknowledged. But when his beloved wife was crowned at what he considered the proper time, he'd give me the most splendid coronation the country had seen.

My spirits lifted. I believed at first that the letter said little, but now I realized some feeling seeped through the dry precise lines, holding out hope he wanted our marriage to be happy. Why else sacrifice what he valued most, lavishing money on me which he refused to spend on himself?

And I smiled almost tenderly at his striking out "conquest." While of necessity he proclaimed his triumph to the country, he was honest enough to say it to the woman he would marry, knowing himself only the figurehead of that victory. I shared Lincoln's disdain at his staying safely behind the Lancastrian troops. But now I thought that Henry, inexperienced in warfare, had a stubborn courage that I must admit for him to go into battle against a captain-general like Richard who had been born to military life.

Richard. I half-whispered the name before I put it aside forever. I knew, I must have, that my wild young dreams of him were a girl's first sweet love, that they could not come true. The headlong passion of youth must give way to a woman's love for her husband and her children, for the new world we would create together.

I had sons and daughters to dream of, to plan for, one of them the next king. Perhaps we would name him after his father and the last Lancastrian ruler, Marguerite d'Anjou's husband. And this boy, the Eighth Henry, would reign over a country united at last.

Glossary

artificer: *a skilled worker, a craftsman*

balk: *also "baulk," a plowed ridge of land*

billmen: *irregular soldiers*

bombard: *cannon that fired stone balls*

carol: *An old round dance, often accompanied by singing*

caltrop: *iron ball with four projecting spikes (crowfoot)*

cochineal: *a deep red dye obtained from pulverized insects*

comfits: *confection, sweetmeat*

compline: *time of day set aside for prayer (usually upon retiring)*

couverchef: *handkerchief*

cresset: *metal cup used as head of torch (when filled with oil)*

cuirass: *armor breastplate (also made of leather)*

culverins: *heavy cannon—also called serpentines*

dagge: *cloth cut in shreds, or pennants*

falconet: *small cannon*

fou: *in playing cards, the joker*

fowler: *nets*

frumenty: *wheat hulls soaked in sugar and spices*

gorget: *piece of armor that protects the throat*

gorse: *shrubs with fragrant yellow flowers*

greaves: *leg armor for below the knee*

hippocras: *spiced cordial (formerly used as medicine)*

jennet: *small, Spanish saddle horse*

jeu-de cartes: *game of cards*

malmsey: *sweet white wine (also malvasia, malvoisie)*

manchets: *small loaves of bread*

marchpane: *confection (marzipan)*

murrey: *mulberry color*
oriel: *a projecting bay window*
padovana: *a slow, stately court dance*
plover: *wading bird, also known as a rain-bird*
prie-dieu: *a low desk used for praying*
prickers: *men who carried rods to keep order in the ranks*
pursuivant: *a follower or attendant*
rondeau: *a 13-line song with two rhymes throughout, also a dance*
sarcinet: *fine silk*
serpentines: *see culverins*
tabard: *tunic worn over armor emblazoned with coat-of-arms*

Thrilling
Historical Romance
by
CATHERINE HART
Leisure's
LEADING LADY OF LOVE

BE SWEPT AWAY
ON A TIDE OF PASSION
BY LEISURE'S THRILLING
HISTORICAL ROMANCES!